The Prodigy

Also by Alton Gansky

J. D. STANTON MYSTERIES

A Ship Possessed
Vanished

The Prodigy | Alton Gansky

A NOVEL OF SUSPENSE

ZondervanPublishingHouse
Grand Rapids, Michigan

A Division of HarperCollinsPublishers

prologue

February 2, 1996
Lincolnsberg, North Carolina,
Blue Ridge Mountains

Mary Matthews clamped her eyes shut so tight tears trickled down her face and fused with the rivulets of sweat streaming from her forehead. She groaned. The pain was unbearable. Her belly cramped like a vise and her back ached as though she had been beaten.

"Make it stop," she pleaded through clinched teeth.

"Ain't nothin' gonna make it stop," came a calm reply. "You jus' do as I say and everythin' is gonna be fine. You hear?"

"But—"

"Ain't no buts about it," the woman said firmly. "Now jus' breathe slow and steady. You is almost ready."

"I wanna go to a hospital," Mary begged. She ran her fingers through her tangled black hair, then wiped away the streak of tears from her blue-green eyes.

"You know the hospital is a good hour away by car, and we ain't got no car."

"It's hard." Her face was hot, her hands cold.

"Course it is, dearie. What'd you expect?"

"I don't know, I just—" Mary stopped and her eyes widened. Her uterus began to contract again, feeling as if someone were tightening a broad steel band across her abdomen. "It's doin' it again." She moaned, then groaned, and then cried in pain. "Ain't there nothin' you can give me for the pain? It hurts awful."

"No, ma'am. I'm no doctor and you knows it," the woman said. She was a short, rotund, black woman with determined, intelligent dark eyes. No matter how terse her words, her eyes betrayed the compassion she felt. "You'll make it. I knows you feel like you're dying, but people out here been birthing babies without no doctor for many a year. You ain't no different. It hurts, then it's over. That's the way of it, missy. Been that way since creation. Ain't gonna change now."

Mary felt alone, afloat in an ocean of misery. She wanted someone, needed someone to stand by her. Tobias was too busy to be bothered with her pain, too drunk to care about anything but himself, but at that moment she would welcome even him. All she had was the midwife who stood at the foot of the bed, her assistant standing next to her. Mary lay on her back, the lumpy mattress offering no support. It was a mattress she was familiar with, having slept on it all her life.

She knew everything about the little house in which she lived. It wasn't much, just a white clapboard shack with one bedroom, a makeshift kitchen with a wood stove, and a tiny front porch that had never known a coat of paint. But Mary didn't need much, and small as the house was, it was much better than the tarpaper shacks in which some of her neighbors lived.

The view from the front window looked out on the green slopes of the Smokey Mountains. It was a familiar view that still impressed her. In the mornings, smoke from the chimneys of nearby cabins would twist into the air like silky columns holding up a cobalt blue sky. At night the stars shone so brightly and seemed so close that they looked as if they might snag on the tops of the trees.

Laying her head back, Mary let her eyes trace the dusty, rough beams of her ceiling, ornamented only by silver wisps of spider webs. Everything around her seemed more real, more actual than she had ever noticed. The dust of the cabin was pungent, the dirt of the floor deeper, the wind outside louder, the drafts that came through warped clapboard colder.

A deep shadow crossed the flat boards that formed the roof sheeting. It lasted only a second.

She lifted her head to look down her body, over her bowl-shaped belly, between her raised knees, and saw Miss Wynda frowning, her forehead wrinkled in concentration looking like the furrows of dark ground her daddy used to plow for their vegetable garden every spring. That was before the hunting accident.

"Okay," Miss Wynda said, "when I says push, you start pushin' and don't you quit. But don't you start until I tells you. You hear? You ain't ready yet. I'll let you know when. First babies, they's always hardest. They don't want to come out into this ol' world. Can't say I blames 'em much. World ain't got nuthin' but pain and heartache nowadays." She looked up from her work and stared into Mary's face. "But I imagine you knows all about that."

"I want Tobias," Mary said between contractions. Her words were breathy, as if she had just run up the mountain from the flat-land below. "My baby shouldn't be born alone."

"Your baby ain't alone," Wynda said. "You're here. I'm here. Besides, that man ain't comin'. He's no good, no way. I knows it and so does everybody hereabouts. You knows it, too."

"You don't know him like I do," Mary protested.

"Don't nobody understand that man, and I don't care if you tell him I says so." Her voice softened. "You're young, Mary. Just seventeen—"

"Eighteen," Mary corrected.

"I was there when you was born, young lady, so don't you go a lyin' to me. You're seventeen and a fistful of months, that's all."

Mary sighed loudly. She was only a teenager and about to deliver her first baby. In her world nestled in the recesses of the Appalachian Mountains, seventeen was an acceptable time to be pregnant. But those women had husbands. Mary didn't. All she had was a drunken, middle-aged man who stopped by her small home once or twice a week. The courting always ended up the same way, with her at his cabin and in his bed.

"Where's your mama?" Wynda asked.

"I . . . don't know," Mary answered honestly. She seldom knew where her mother was. "I haven't seen her in a week."

"Sure picked an odd time to disappear, you being so far along, I mean. She ain't been the same since your daddy up and killed hisself."

"Huntin' accident," Mary corrected. "It was a huntin' accident."

Wynda frowned but said nothing.

"How much longer?" asked Mary. "I can't take this."

Wynda chuckled. "I believe your mama said the same thing when you was born. Your mama took six hours to deliver you. At least best I can remember. It's been a long time since then, but I do remember it was a whole mess o' work for her. First babies usually are. You weren't no different and your baby ain't gonna be no different. Nuthin' changes hereabouts. Nuthin' at all."

Mary groaned again. She was tired of groaning, tired of the pain, tired of the people around her who talked behind her back. All she wanted was to be done with it all. She had been in labor for over four hours, and the thought of two more seemed impossible to endure. Surely she would die first.

"Your next baby will come a lot easier and a whole lot faster, hon."

Next baby! Mary thought. *I ain't never gonna do this again.*

Ninety minutes dripped by like a week. Contractions came more frequently and intensely. The urge to push was becoming overwhelming, but Wynda forbade her to give in. Mary complied, partly because of the midwife's reputation and partly because of fear.

"It's time now," Wynda said with authority. "Next big contraction you gonna start pushin'. Just like I said before. You push and don't stop until I tells you. But when I tells you to stop you stop fast. You hear?"

"I don't think I'll be able to stop."

"You just do as I say and things will work out fine. Now tell me when you get another pain."

It was less than a minute when the cramping resumed. Like a general, the midwife barked out orders, aided by a young woman no older than Mary. Mary grunted loudly as her body took control.

"Push, hon. Push." Wynda commanded. Other conversation went on between Wynda and her young assistant. "Don't pull the baby," she was saying. "You just let the mamma's body do the work. Most times, that's enough."

"What if it ain't enough?" the assistant asked, her eyes wide at the sight before her.

"That all depends. Breech babies is the worst—"

"My baby is breech?" Mary exclaimed between grunts.

"No, no, honey," Wynda said. "Your baby is just right. I was just talkin' about other times, other peoples."

The procedure continued. While Mary suffered, Wynda went about her work in routine fashion as though she were doing nothing more important than setting the table for supper.

"Here's the head," said Wynda. "Sunnyside up."

"What's that mean?" the assistant asked.

"The baby is comin' out faceup," Wynda explained. "Most times they comes facedown. This one's eager to see the world after all. Now get the towel," she ordered her assistant. "One more push ought to do it, hon. Then you can relax for a spell."

With the next contraction, Mary bore down with all her might. Suddenly, the pain was gone. Her back continued to ache, but the urge to push disappeared, evaporating like dew under a summer sun. The contractions ended, a sense of euphoria swept over her. She laughed lightly and then wept. The weeping was followed by more laughing.

"Outside plumbin'," Wynda said gleefully. "It's a boy and he's—"

"He's what?" Mary asked, concerned. "He's all right, ain't he?" There was no answer. "What's wrong? What's wrong with my baby? Why ain't he a-crying?"

Thoughts of stillbirth boiled in her mind. She had heard of it. It was Elizabeth Potter who gave birth to a dead baby just last year, and it wasn't even her first. New, hot tears flooded Mary's eyes.

"Tell me!" she demanded. "Why ain't my baby crying?"

"I don't know," Wynda said. "But he is alive. He looks fine, too. Mighty fine."

"He's got pretty blue eyes," the assistant said. "He's staring at me."

Did newborns stare? Mary wondered. A movement at the window caught her attention. "What's that?"

"What's what?" Wynda asked.

"I thought I saw something. A shadow maybe."

"Shadows can't hurt you none," Wynda replied.

The room chilled.

Wynda called for another towel, wrapping it around the newborn. Under her direction, the assistant began to clean the child with a soft piece of cloth moistened from a nearby pail. A few moments later, Wynda said, "Here's your baby. You hold him on your tummy while I deal with the cord and the afterbirth."

Aided by the assistant who stacked pillows and folded blankets behind her, Mary sat up a little and watched with anticipation as Wynda handed the child to her, setting him on her stomach. To Mary's surprise, the baby was looking right at her in an unblinking gaze. His eyes were the deepest blue she had ever seen, like the color of the summer sky just before sundown. The baby kicked twice and then smiled. Where once there had been great pain, there was now great pride in the bundle of life she held. "He's smilin' at me. Smilin' real big."

"Babies that young don't smile, hon. They make faces from time to time, but they don't smile. He will soon enough, though."

"This one does," Mary replied. "I'm going to call him Toby."

Mary looked up to see Wynda shake her head. "It's all up to you, hon, but personally, I wouldn't brand that boy with his daddy's name. Life is gonna be hard enough without that millstone around his neck."

"I don't care if my man ain't no good," Mary said. "He's the boy's father, and I think a boy should be named after his daddy. It's only right."

"If you say so, missy," Wynda said with another shake of her head.

Mary returned her attention to her son. "I'm your mama," she cooed softly. "Yes, I am. We're gonna have a good ol' time, me and you. Yes, sir. I ain't gonna let nothin' or nobody hurt you. You and me, little Toby, we is gonna take on the world. You can believe your mama."

The infant stared at Mary's lips as she spoke as if he were studying each movement. Then he began to move his own lips, pressing them together then allowing them to part. He emitted a small, breathy sound, no louder than that made by a spring breeze against a single oak leaf.

"Muh ... muh."

Mary's heart tripped.

Toby Matthews blinked at his mother and then began to look around the room. In a slow, jerky motion he turned toward the window. The sunlight dimmed.

Wynda walked to the window. "Looks like a storm is comin'," she said.

The shadow on the ceiling returned, darkened, then faded into the rafters.

BOOK I

the journey

*Does he not see my ways and
count my every step?*

JOB 31:4

chapter 1

I didn't know what to do," Mary Matthews said. "The wind jus' come up and closed the car door on his hand."

"Ouch," the doctor said, grimacing. He was a tall, thin man with gray hair cut near the scalp. Mary judged him to be in his late forties. She also noted that he had kind eyes. A plastic name tag on the breast pocket of his white smock read: ROBERT BAKER, M.D. "When did this happen?"

Mary looked at the clock on the wall. "About one o'clock. We waited in the lobby for two hours."

"I'm sorry you had to wait. Sometimes there are too many patients and too few doctors. Let's take a look at that hand."

Toby Matthews sat on the emergency room bed and let his feet dangle, banging his worn and dirty tennis shoes against the bed's metal side. The shoes embarrassed Mary. The soles were thin and each had a hole through which Toby's dirty socks could be seen. The Levis he wore were no better; faded and frayed at the cuffs, they were a size too small. Their clothes were billboards of poverty. She would soon have to find a way to buy him another pair of pants and sneakers. That meant finding another thrift shop and finding a few more dollars.

Toby was more interested in the medical equipment than the doctor. He was holding his left hand close to his chest. His blue eyes darted around the room. The doctor had to ask twice to see the boy's hand.

"It's all right," Dr. Baker said. "I'll try not to hurt you."

Toby held out his hand. It was red with an angry, puffy bruise along the back.

"How old are you, Toby?" the doctor asked.

"Six."

"Six a-goin' on forty," Mary added.

Dr. Baker smiled politely then asked, "Can you move your fingers for me?"

Toby looked at his hand and tilted his head to the side. It was as if he were seeing the injury for the first time. Slowly, he moved his index and middle finger, but only slightly. He grimaced as he did. "It hurts."

"I bet it does." Baker palpated the swollen tissue, gently pressing the skin with his thumbs. "I think we had better get an X ray. There may be a fracture of one or more of the metacarpi. I'm going to have a nurse take him down to radiology."

"Meta . . . carpi?" Toby said the syllables as if he were rolling them on his tongue.

"That's right, son." The doctor looked up at him. Toby gave him a questioning look. The doctor held up his own hand and pointed to the back of it. He ran a finger from his wrist to his knuckles. "These bones are called metacarpus. They connect the wrist to the fingers. They help you move your hand." The doctor made a fist.

"You said metacarpi," Toby said.

"That's right, I did. You're a sharp rascal, aren't you? Metacarpi is the plural of metacarpus. Do you know what the word *plural* means?"

"More than one," Toby answered without hesitation.

"Right again." Once more the doctor raised his own hand. "One metacarpus; five metacarpi."

Toby pressed his lips together and nodded.

The doctor patted Toby on the head, mussing his blond hair,

then turned to Mary. "He's a sharp lad. Brave too. I haven't seen a single tear."

"Oh," Mary said. "He never cries. Not even when he was a baby."

"Never?"

"No, sir, never."

Toby slipped from his place on the bed and started for the door.

"Whoa, buddy," Baker said. "Where are you going?"

With a shrug, Toby said, "Radiology."

Baker was taken aback. "You know where radiology is?"

"There are signs on the wall." Toby marched without hesitation to the door that connected the ER with the lobby. Mary rushed to follow.

Forty-five minutes later, Mary and Toby walked back into the emergency room. Mary was carrying a large brown envelope containing the X rays of her son's hand. Baker greeted them and led them into an empty cubicle.

"Radiology called to say you were on the way," Baker began. "They also said that Toby tried to talk their ears off. Is that true, Toby?"

"I guess so."

"He's very curious," Mary said defensively.

"That's okay," Baker said. "Curiosity is a good thing. You keep asking questions, Toby. There are a lot of great things worth knowing." Baker removed the X-ray films and slipped them under the clips of a lighted view box. A stark, bright light shone through the thick film, revealing the bones of Toby's hand.

Baker grunted.

"What?" Mary asked with concern. "What's wrong?"

Baker looked at the woman. "I expected to see at least one fracture, maybe several ..." He trailed off.

"But?" Mary prompted.

"I don't see any breaks at all. Odd." Baker scratched his chin. "I guess I shouldn't be too surprised. Children have very flexible bones. It looks like Toby was lucky."

Baker turned back to Toby and examined his hand again. The redness was gone, and the swelling had subsided noticeably.

"Will I get a cast?"

"You don't need one, buddy," Baker said softly. "I would have bet money when you came in that you would have walked out with a cast, but now ..."

"Now what?" Mary asked.

"Now it doesn't even look as if his hand is bruised." He turned back to Toby. "Does it still hurt?"

"A little," Toby admitted with a shrug. "But it's okay."

"I'm going to write a prescription for a pain reliever," Dr. Baker said. "The hand may hurt more than he's letting on."

Mary shuffled her feet and looked at the floor. "Is it ... expensive?"

Baker raised his eyes and stared at Mary as if seeing her for the first time. She knew she looked a mess. She wore her only dress, an old brown affair with a straight cut, and a pair of sneakers that were only slightly better than Toby's.

"You know," Baker said. "I have a better idea. Since we made you wait so long, why don't I just give you some to take with you." Mary started to object, but Baker cut her off. "Pharmaceutical companies are always sending us samples. I'll just let you have a few of those."

"Pharm ... a ... ceu ... ti ... cal?" Toby said. "What's that?"

Baker shifted his attention back to the boy. "They're companies that make medications."

"Pharmaceuticals," Toby repeated. "Medications. A medicine factory?"

"That's pretty much it," Baker said. He turned back to Mary. "He's a clever boy, all right."

"Too smart for his own good," Mary said, gently stroking her son's hair. "He's fixing my English. He loves to read and to ask questions. I guess you figured that last part out."

"Correcting your English," Toby said.

Mary shrugged. "See what I mean?"

"At least he's polite about it," Baker said. "I'll get those meds for you." He started to leave.

"Doctor?" Mary said before he had taken two steps. Baker stopped and turned. "I ... I don't know how to pay for this," she waved a hand indicating the ER room. "I told the nurse in the lobby that I would pay cash, but ... I can't. I just wanted to make sure Toby was seen."

Baker lowered his head for a moment then said, "Don't worry about it. I'll make sure everything is taken care of."

Ten minutes later, Mary and Toby, escorted by Dr. Baker, walked from the ER. "They won't stop you if I'm with you," he had said.

"Won't you get in trouble?" Mary asked.

Baker just shrugged. "I've done it before. They haven't fired me yet."

"You're a blessing, Doctor," Mary said. "God sent you our way."

"Perhaps," Baker replied with a polite smile. He led them to another corridor and pointed down the hall. "This will take you to the front of the hospital. You can exit there. If anyone gives you any trouble, you call for me. Okay?"

"Okay." Mary looked down the hall. She could see doors on each side of the corridor. Above each door was a small plastic sign with a number. *Patient rooms,* she decided.

Baker crouched down to face Toby. "You keep asking questions, buddy, and watch out for those car doors."

"I will," replied Toby.

"Say thank you, Toby."

"Thank you," Toby said to Dr. Baker.

Mary started down the corridor. She paused to look back at Baker, but he was gone.

"He was a nice man," Toby said perfunctorily.

"Real nice," Mary said. "Ain't many ... *not* many nice people in the world these days."

"What about these people?" Toby asked.

"What people?"

"In these rooms." Mary looked down and saw Toby glancing in the open doors of the corridor as they walked past. "When do they get to go home?" He stopped at one door and stared in.

"I don't know, Toby. Soon maybe," Mary said before she realized that Toby had stopped. She turned and reached for his hand. "Come on, son," she said. "It's best that we don't dawdle. We have to get back on the road."

"I didn't like the pain. It made me feel bad."

Mary smiled at her boy. At times he seemed like such an adult; other times he seemed younger, more innocent than his age. "The pills the doctor gave us will help."

"I don't need the pills now," he said. "The pain is gone. But their pain isn't."

"Life is filled with pain, son, just a mighty long stretch o' pain. Seems like there ain't no end to it. Jus' pain after pain."

"Why?"

"I don't know. But I do know it ain't fair. Not by any thinkin' I do."

A few minutes later, they exchanged the artificial light of the hospital with the late afternoon sun.

Bob Moss, age sixty-two, lay upon his hospital bed staring out the door and wondering if he had a future. More importantly, he wondered if there was a future for his family. The fact that he was thinking even these depressing thoughts was good news. The fog of the last week had finally begun to evaporate. He still struggled with words and names, but most of his thoughts flowed forward. It was an improvement, albeit a small one. His left arm was still limp and his left leg unresponsive. Both lifeless limbs were reminders of his body's betrayal. A blood vessel in the right side of his brain had given way like an old earthen dam. The stroke left his speech slurred and his body weak.

The doctors had said that therapy would help but that the road back would be long and arduous. He knew he would never be the same again.

Bob needed to be the same. His family needed him to be the same. He was the sole provider for a family of four: his wife, himself, and two grandchildren that had come under his roof when their daughter had entered a drug rehabilitation center. Where would the money come from now? His meager savings could support them for maybe one or even two months, then they would be destitute. The trucking company for which he worked had been gracious and supportive during the first two weeks of his illness, but no matter how accommodating they were now, a time would come when they would have to let him go. He could not drive a big rig with only one working arm and leg.

His life was changed forever, altered by a tiny weakness in a small conduit of blood in his brain. The doctors called him lucky. He lived. Bob didn't feel lucky. He felt despondent, angry, depressed, and fearful, but not lucky. What good was life if a man couldn't live, couldn't do that for which he was trained?

What was he good for? He had asked that question a hundred times that day alone. *All I can do is stare out the door and watch people walk by,* he thought. It was their walking that bothered him. Nurses, doctors, janitors, orderlies, and visitors all walking by, easily putting one foot in front of the other. That was something he had done for sixty years without giving it a thought—millions of steps through the decades of life. Now there was nothing else he longed for more.

The image of his grandchildren came to mind and with it an onslaught of emotion. He had been told to expect this. Stroke victims often experience mood swings, they said. Great kids. Kind and courteous, despite their mother's problems. At least she was getting help. Maybe this time next year things would be back to normal. The kids would be with their mother and he ... He couldn't think about where he would be next year.

A tear trickled down his cheek; his vision blurred. He closed his eyes hard and then opened them again. In the doorway stood a little boy. A lad with blond hair, blue eyes, and dirty jeans gazed back. Bob watched as the boy cocked his head to the right, to the left, and then smiled.

A thin, hollow-cheeked woman with black hair stepped into view and took the lad by the hand. The two disappeared down the corridor.

Cute kid, Bob thought. *Someone is lucky to have him.* "Bet he ... likes ... to play ball," he said aloud. He froze, his heart tripping in his chest. "I bet he likes to play ball," he repeated. Something was wrong. No, something was *right*. His speech sounded normal. No slurring. No struggling to form words. An electric thrill surged through him. He sat up and said it again. Halfway through the sentence, he realized what he had done. He had risen to a sitting position without aid from anyone.

Slowly, as a man fearful of what he might see, Bob raised his hands to his face. Both hands responded. He laughed. He wiggled his toes; all ten complied.

"I'm dreaming," he said to himself. "I know I am. I'll wake up in a minute and everything will be the same."

Bob did not wait to wake up. He threw the covers back, reached over the stainless steel, tubular guardrail and released its latch. It fell to the side of the bed with a crisp clatter. Swinging his legs over the side, Bob hesitated only a moment, then slipped from the mattress and let his bare feet touch the cool linoleum-clad floor.

His legs held him. Despite the nagging voice of caution and disbelief in his mind, Bob danced a little jig, laughed, and clapped his hands. Then he bolted for the door. Someone had to see this. Someone had to share this miraculous event with him. It took only four strides—Bob counted each one—to make it to the door where he had seen the blond boy.

The corridor was bedlam—joyful madness. Others, dressed in the same style of hospital gown as he, were milling around. Some were weeping while others laughed loudly. In their midst stood a half dozen awestruck nurses and doctors.

A doctor—his doctor—stopped next to Bob, frozen by the sight of him. His face was pale and clouded with confusion.

Dr. Aaron Pratt stood behind the worn oak lectern silently counting. *One. Two. Three. Four. Five.* Before him was a tiny sea of students, all gazing down at the notepaper in front of them. *Six. Seven. Eight.* He said nothing, choosing to wait for a response. One would come soon, it always did. Unlike many of his colleagues, he knew how to wait in silence. *Nine. Ten. Eleven.*

A face looked up. A moment later a hand was raised.

"Yes?" Pratt said, nodding at a young man with wavy brown hair and hauntingly sad eyes.

"Hermeneutics," the student said.

"That's right," Pratt replied. This was the part of his class that students complained about most—the opening quiz. The reading schedule for his Bibliology class was taxing and tiresome. This was especially true during the summer quarter, which was three weeks shorter. One student likened reading theology texts to watching paint dry—dull, dull, dull. The quiz was meant to keep his graduate students immersed in the reading and to open the class to questions. "Now define the term."

The student sighed loudly and squirmed in his seat. This was just the third day of classes and most of the students had yet to adjust to the rigors of graduate study. "It has something to do with interpretation."

"Right again," Pratt said, "but that's hardly a definition." He looked around the class. Twenty-five students, most of them recent graduates from various colleges and universities, avoided eye contact. He turned to an olive-skinned man who sat in the last row of chairs. Even from the front of the class, Pratt could see the man was doodling in his notebook. Bored. Unlike the other students, this was Thomas York's second year at Riverside Graduate School of Theology. A part-time student, it would take him five years to earn his Master of Divinity degree. The degree was a three-year program for a full-time student, but Thomas was working his way through school. Pratt admired that. He had done the same. "How about you, Mr. York? Any ideas?"

Thomas looked up from his paper. Pratt knew him to be an able student with a keen and insightful mind. Another professor had gone so far as to use the term "genius" to describe him. He was the faculty's darling, someone certain to advance through his degree work and take a teaching post at some seminary or graduate school. No one used the term genius in his presence, however, because Thomas had made clear his resentment of the term. A child prodigy, gifted in math and languages, he had heard the appellation so often that he protested each time it was uttered.

Thomas looked at Pratt for a moment, blinked in confusion, and then said, "I'm sorry, Dr. Pratt, what was the question?"

"I'm looking for a definition of hermeneutics."

Thomas York was thickly built, with broad shoulders and a tapered waist. He looked every bit the football player and varsity wrestler he had been in college. His greatest strength, however, was not his twenty-three-year-old body, but his mind. In college he played well enough to make the team, but not well enough to be noticed by scouts from the NFL. That had been of no concern to Thomas. He had a ravenous curiosity that professional sports could not feed. He wanted more school. Pratt knew this because he had been Thomas's academic advisor during his first year.

"Hermeneutics is the science and methodology of interpretation as it pertains to ancient documents," Thomas said fluidly. "In our case, it is the set of rules by which we interpret Scripture."

"Bravo, Mr. York," Pratt said with a broad smile. "But why do we need a set of rules for interpretation?"

"To avoid doctrinal error and to glean God's meaning from his inspired Word."

"Right again," Pratt said. "Without reasonable guidelines we can fall into heresy very quickly. History shows just how often that has happened." Pratt stepped away from the lectern. "This is why we study as we do. Theology is the greatest of the academic disciplines. Science is a wonderful study, but when you examine theology, you are learning about the God who authored science."

"So hermeneutics is to the Bible what science is to nature," a female student offered.

Pratt shook his head. "No, not really. While science follows a prescribed set of rules for observing nature, it also involves experimentation. Biblical interpretation does not. What we do is look at the text from a grammatical, historical, and objective point of view. We examine, and analyze, but not experiment."

"Excuse me, Professor," Thomas York interjected. "Is there no room for experimentation in theology?"

"None that I can see. What do you have in mind?"

A silence flowed through the class. Pratt waited patiently while Thomas pulled his thoughts together. "How do we know that the information we have in the Bible is all the information we can have?"

"All the information we *can* have?" Pratt prompted, hoping Thomas would venture a little more of his opinion.

"Yes," Thomas said, taking the bait. "In our first class you taught us about general revelation, about those things that can be learned of God from nature and the universe. I think you even called the universe the sixty-seventh book of the Bible. Then you taught us about special revelation, which is a much more detailed unveiling of God."

"That's correct," Pratt agreed. "General revelation tells us many things about God, but we need special revelation to understand salvation."

"I understand those two points, but how do we know there isn't a third or fourth type of revelation?"

"Such as?" Pratt prompted.

"Personal insight," Thomas responded.

"You mean like the mystic who has a vision?"

"Perhaps. Couldn't God write on our hearts and minds the things he wants us to know?"

Pratt nodded. "That's the wrong question, Mr. York. The question isn't what God *can* do. He can do whatever he wishes. The question is, What *has* God done? We could spend a lifetime guessing what God might do. The number of hypothetical suppositions is enormous. What should interest us is what he has done and is doing. It's not a question of divine capability."

"So," Thomas said, "you rule out any present-day revelation?"

"Yes," Pratt answered. "But don't misunderstand my statement. I'm not saying that God is inactive in our world or in our lives. I believe just the opposite. I'm saying that there is no *new* revelation. That is to say, that God is not adding to what we already have. He might direct you to do something. He might place a call on your life as he has with many people here, but he is not revealing himself more than he has in the past.

"There have been many," Pratt continued, "who have said that they speak for God and that God has spoken directly to them. An examination of their teaching will show a sharp contrast with the teaching of the Bible. In that case, whom do you believe?"

"The Bible," several students intoned in unison.

"That's right," Pratt said. "And why do we put so much emphasis on the Bible? Because it has proven itself the inspired Word of God. It also provides an objective authority. The keyword is *objective*. Without an objective authority we are left to the opinion of anyone who comes along, and their opinions would carry as much weight as anyone else's."

"I see," Thomas said, leaning back in his chair.

Pratt wasn't sure he did. "We all long for the miraculous in our lives. We hunger for the dramatic. Like the Pharisees of Jesus' day, we want to see a sign. But remember what Jesus said to them, 'A wicked and adulterous generation asks for a miraculous sign! But none will be given it except the sign of the prophet Jonah.'"

Thomas smiled slightly then said, "The author of Hebrews said in the second chapter, 'God also testified to it by signs, wonders and various miracles, and gifts of the Holy Spirit distributed according to his will.'"

"And when you see the signs and wonders, Mr. York, how will you know they're authentic?"

"I'll know, Dr. Pratt. I'll know."

chapter 2

The wind whistled by the white Ford van with an ear-piercing shriek, its invisible fingers clawing at every edge and seam of the boxy vehicle. Jerry Barnwell wrestled with the steering wheel, struggling to keep the automobile on the road. His arms and shoulders ached from the effort, and his palms were wet with fear.

"We chose the wrong car for this," Jerry shouted.

"It's all we have," Bill Packard yelled. He was sitting in the back, a video camera resting on his broad shoulder. The lens of the camera was pointed out the side window.

"How are we doing?" Jerry called out.

"We're okay, but it's a big one."

"As big as the Oklahoma F5?" Jerry said, referring to the May 3, 1999, tornado that plowed a devastating swath of destruction through Oklahoma City.

"Could be," Bill admitted. "The footage is great. The cone just dropped."

"What direction is it moving?"

"Right at us, buddy. Right at us."

Jerry pressed the accelerator down. Outside, the sky was capped with angry, swollen, black clouds that reminded him of an enormous bruise. Silver sheets of rain were falling in a torrent.

"I want to know everything it does, Bill, and I mean everything. I don't want someone telling my wife they found my body in the next county."

"You love this and you know it," Bill said.

Jerry didn't love it. As a freelance videographer, he had taped many unpleasant things. He had even been the only cameraman on the scene of a bank robbery gone wrong. Flying bullets were only mildly frightening compared to the monster bearing down on them. An F5 tornado had wind speeds over 300 miles an hour, enough to peel the flesh from a man as easily as a child might remove the skin of a banana. Jerry wanted nothing to do with it.

"How far away is it?"

"A couple of miles maybe."

"Too close. Much too close."

"I'm getting great shots."

Jerry pressed the accelerator closer to the floor. As he did, a gust of wind hit them broadside, forcing the van into the oncoming lane. Fortunately the road was deserted. No one with any sense would be out here.

"Whoa, easy Jerry," Bill complained. "It's hard enough keeping the camera steady without you changing lanes."

"It wasn't my choice," Jerry snapped. "Is it still coming our way?"

"Absolutely and—" Bill stopped suddenly. Something hit the van, the impact sounding like a gunshot. It happened again. Then again.

"Hail," Jerry shouted. "Hail the size of my fist!"

Bill set the camera down and looked at the road. Tennis-ball-size hunks of ice were falling from the sky, bouncing off the asphalt road ahead of them and off the metal skin of the van. "Wow," Bill said. He hoisted the camera back on his shoulder and started taping out the windshield.

A resounding crack echoed through the Ford, and Bill let loose a long stream of curses.

"It broke the windshield," Jerry said. A spiderweb of white cracks spread across two-thirds of the window. He let off the accelerator as he tried to peer through the fractured safety glass. More hail pounded the van. It sounded to Jerry as if he were in a metal trash can and someone was throwing fistfuls of rocks at him.

"Don't slow down," Bill said, his bravado evaporating.

"I'm having trouble seeing." Jerry had to lean against the driver's door and lower his head to see enough of the road to stay in his lane.

The hail stopped as suddenly as it had begun. Jerry had lived in Oklahoma long enough and seen enough tornadoes to know that sporadic hail was associated with the storms. The icy onslaught could cause as much damage as the tornado itself.

"That was fun," Bill deadpanned. The sarcasm was not wasted on Jerry.

The rain resumed, the road deliquescing into a long, flat, black river. The wind gusted. Jerry wrestled with the steering wheel. Bits of debris flew past, missiles propelled by a malevolent force. Mud splattered on the broken windshield and the side windows. "The funnel. Where's the funnel?"

"Still behind us but closing fast. Real fast." Bill said. He started taping again. "I wouldn't object if you wanted to call it a day."

"Consider it called," Jerry said. "I quit ten minutes ago." He sped up again, fearing the vicious storm more than any road hazard he might face. Suddenly he hit the brakes. Bill almost slid off the backseat.

"What are you doing? Don't stop. Stopping is not good."

"There's someone in the road," Jerry said.

"What?"

"There's someone in the road waving her arms."

Bill swore. "Great. Someone crazier than us."

"It's a woman," Jerry said. "She needs help."

"You think?"

The van came to a screeching halt. The wind rocked the vehicle on its axles and rain pounded the body in a loud, steady rataplan.

A woman stood in the middle of the lane, frantically waving her arms above her head. Through the shattered glass, Jerry could see an old station wagon bouncing in the wind. Its hood was up, bending and twisting in the wind like a dry leaf. It looked as if the hood might fly off at any moment.

The woman fought her way forward until she stood next to the driver's window. Jerry rolled down the glass and was instantly awash in warm, humid air. Rainwater dripped on his head and arms. Fortunately the wind was striking the other side of the van.

"Help me!" the woman cried. She struck Jerry as being in her middle twenties, but the lines around her eyes made her look older. Her coal-black hair was soaked and clung to the sides of her head as tightly as her saturated dress clung to her rail-thin body.

"Are you nuts, lady?" Jerry shouted back. "You're going to get killed standing out there."

"We're going to get killed if we don't get moving," Bill said from the backseat. "That monster is closing in on us. Get her in here and let's go."

"Stand back, lady," Jerry demanded as he opened his door. He knew the pressure from the wind would never let him open the passenger side door. He dropped down on to the wet pavement. "Get in. Crawl over the seat. We don't have much time."

"I can't," she protested.

"You have to," Jerry countered. He raised his head against the driving rain and caught a glimpse of the twister. It was hideous, evil. A dark, twisting band bridged the distance between the flat ground of fecund farm land and the swelling black sky. A skirt of dirt and debris danced around the serpentine column of wind. To Jerry it looked ten miles wide and a thousand miles high. His heart pounded against his chest like a trip hammer.

Jerry took the woman by the arm and began to pull her toward the door.

"No," she cried out. "My son!"

Son? He turned to her. Her blue eyes were awash in dark terror. Mud streaked her face. "Where's your son?"

"In the car. I have to get my son and my things."

"Forget your things. I'll get your boy."

"It's all that we have. It's everything we own."

"I don't care, lady." Jerry pointed across the field at the giant tornado that was closing in on them. "That's all I care about now. Get inside, I'll get your son."

Hail began to fall again. A hailstone grazed Jerry's shoulder, sending scorching pain through his body. He grabbed his shoulder, spun around once, then reached for the woman. He wasn't going to wait to be hit again. Grabbing the woman by her left arm, he gave a firm tug. She tried to resist, but Jerry's muscles were fueled by abject panic and the adrenaline of pain. He lifted her then pushed her through the door and onto the driver's seat. He saw Bill's hands grab her and pull. She disappeared into the van, her feet kicking wildly.

"Tooobyyy!" she cried.

"Let's go," Bill shouted. "Now, now, let's go."

Jerry ignored him. Despite the pain in his shoulder and the blinding terror he felt, he ran to the disabled car, leaning into the wind that was pressing against him with unbelievable force. The work would be no harder if he were attempting to run a marathon at the bottom of the ocean. Bits of dirt, grit, and grass flew through the air at speeds that turned them into tiny razor blades. He felt as if his face and arms were being stung by an angry swarm of bees.

Part of his mind drove him on; the rest of his mind told him he was a fool. Fool or not, he was going to make it to the car. It was a ten-step trip that felt like ten miles. Several times he came close to being knocked off his feet. Once down, he knew he would never get back up. Forcing himself to ignore the skin-shredding wind and the behemoth of terror bearing down on him, Jerry forced one foot in front of the other until he reached the side of the car. He ducked behind the vehicle to shield himself from the onslaught. Two deep breaths later, he swung open the rear door and looked inside.

Empty.

"Hey, kid," he called. "Where are you?" His voice sounded tiny in the gale. Slipping into the back, he peered over the front seat, checking for the boy. Maybe he was hiding on the floorboards. Who could blame him if he was?

Nothing.

Was the woman insane? he wondered. *Was she playing some demented trick on him?* He searched everywhere he could see, but found no child. The wind poured in the rear passenger window, making Jerry's eyes tear . . . It struck him. Why would the rear passenger window be open? His heart seized. "Oh no," he said aloud. Forcing himself to face the biting wind again, Jerry looked out toward the storm. He saw what he feared. A small blond child was crawling on his hands and knees through the bare dirt field next to the road—and he was crawling straight toward the tornado. Hailstones fell around the boy like ice bombs.

Jerry put his mind in neutral. He could not allow himself to think, to reason. Reason demanded that he run back to the van and drive off. Saving one was better than saving none. Every second he waited made escape all the more impossible. But he knew what he had to do. He had to get the boy.

With Herculean valor, Jerry exited the car and ran head-on into the storm, pulled forward by the wind as it rushed toward the swirling column of destruction. A hailstone clipped his knee and he stumbled to the ground. Ignoring the excruciating pain, he forced himself forward until he was ten yards from the lad. Ten yards seemed so very far away, so distant.

The maelstrom was closing in. He no longer thought of the storm as a natural thing, a normal thing, but something intelligently evil and ravenous for any life it could consume.

"Come here, boy!" Jerry shouted against the shrieking wind. "Come back!"

If the boy heard, he gave no indication of it. Instead, he crawled three more paces, then slowly stood. The wind pushed him forward several steps, but the lad continued to stand, leaning back against the unyielding force. To Jerry it appeared the storm was attempting to suck the boy into its churning, twisting maw. The hailstones continued to fall.

Jerry turned around and could see the woman's terrified face pressed against the window of the van. She was pounding at the glass with her fists. He turned back to the boy who, against impossible odds, remained on his feet, staring into the oncoming tornado. Jerry pushed himself up, struggling to his feet, and started forward.

It was hopeless, he realized. The twister had closed the distance between them by half. In a few minutes the wind speed would double, maybe triple. The debris in the tornado's skirt would fly by at deadly speed, cutting down anything it touched. They would never make it back to the van in time to get away.

It was over, but he had to try. If he was going to die, he would do so on his feet doing what needed to be done. As if he had read Jerry's mind, the boy turned and faced him. He smiled.

Jerry watched as the boy returned his gaze to the spiraling death that stalked them. The child raised one hand, then the other, and held them out in front of him as if he were about to push the tornado back to the dark womb where it had been conceived.

The silence was almost painful. It came with an inexplicable suddenness. So fast was its arrival that Jerry's ears hurt. The hail was gone. The rain had ceased. With shaky trepidation, Jerry directed his gaze to the tornado. It too was gone. Vanished. Bits of debris—the spindly remains of barns, trees, and more—plummeted to earth. All that remained of the twister were the dark clouds overhead and a small wisp of dark circulating air, no larger than a man.

The boy's eyes were fixed on the now tiny, tumbling, twisting wind. He seemed hypnotized by the sight of it. The boy took a tentative step backward, retreating. Jerry thought it odd that the boy would walk fearlessly toward the twister only to back away from what was now nothing more than a dust devil.

Jerry heard a voice behind him. "Toby. Toby." He turned and saw the woman running toward them. He turned back to the boy, who was now crouched on the ground, looking at something. The woman ran to him and then dropped to her knees. She wept loudly as she took him in her arms.

"Mom, stop it," the boy said. "You're squishing me."

"I was so afraid," the woman said. "So afraid I'd never see you again."

"I'm okay, Mom. Look," he said, wiggling out of her grasp. "I found this pretty rock for you. You can have it."

Jerry tried to understand what he had just seen, but his brain simply would not work.

"That was the bravest thing I've ever seen, buddy." Bill was standing next to him, and he was holding the video camera. "And the weirdest thing I've ever seen."

Jerry nodded at the camera. "Did you . . . ?"

"Oh yeah," Bill said. "Every second of it. It's a good thing too, because no one is going to believe this."

"I don't believe it myself," Jerry whispered.

"You're a brave man, Jerry. I'm proud to be your partner."

Jerry leaned forward and threw up.

Toby, still in the loving clutch of his mother, could see where the tornado had been and gazed unblinkingly at the remaining swirl of wind. Slowly the image changed, condensing into a vague form—a dark form that stared back at Toby.

Icy fear chilled him.

Richard Wellman sat down in his leather office chair, pulled the headset over his ears, positioned the microphone just below his lower lip, and took a deep breath. "Is he on the line yet?" He glanced through the glass wall that separated his studio from that of his producer. A young man of twenty-four with basset-hound brown eyes, a narrow nose, and wide lips was looking back.

"Not yet, Rich," the producer said. "I have tried his house twice and his office once."

"Stay on it, Rudy. The last thing I want is three hours of call-in."

"The people like it," Rudy Horner said. "We get positive letters all the time."

"*I* don't like it," Wellman said. "It's getting old. We need something fresh, something new and dynamic."

"Like what?" Rudy's voice came over the headphones.

"Something other than UFOs, ghosts, and government conspiracies. We've been doing those for six years."

"It's made you the most-listened-to radio personality in the country," Rudy said.

"I know that. I just need something unique." Wellman leaned back in the chair. "Take tonight's guest. Terrance Lemmon, an expert on secret underground bases. We've had him on the show three times this year. Four, if we can get hold of him. Besides, the competition is picking up."

"The Harry Goodwin show is in a different time slot and not on a third of the stations you are. I don't think you have any competition."

"That's dangerous thinking, Rudy. That's when they get you."

Rudy laughed. "You sound like some of the paranoids who call in."

"Even paranoids can be pursued."

"One minute," Rudy said.

"Usual stuff?"

"Opening bumper music, greeting, then we'll go to three minutes of commercials."

"Still no word from our guest?" Wellman asked. He drummed his fingers on the console.

"Nothing."

Wellman swore and shook his head. "Okay, we'll start with open calls, but let me know when you have Lemmon on the line."

"Will do."

Wellman watched through the glass partition as Rudy popped two tape cassettes called carts into a player. They looked like old eight-track music cartridges. Rudy raised a hand with five fingers spread. He retracted one leaving four up and began his countdown. Wellman heard music swell in his headphones. Rudy punched a button and an announcer's voice, a deep baritone made eerie with artificial reverberation, said:

"Pushing back the darkness with courage and reason; exploring the unseen and hard to believe; discussing in the open what others speak of only in whispers is ... Richard ... Wellman."

The music continued on for a few seconds. Wellman took a sip of water, then spoke into the microphone of his headset as the music faded. "Good evening to all our listeners from coast to coast and border to border. This is Rich Wellman back for another night of intrigue, speculation, and the ongoing search for truth, no matter how eerie it might be. It's 10:05 P.M. here in the beautiful desert of Arizona, the heart and soul of our country. Tonight we have as our guest an old friend, Terrance Lemmon, the premier civilian authority on secret and underground bases. His new book, *Your Secret Neighbor,* was released a few months ago. He'll be here to tell us all he knows about the secret military installations that may be in *your* backyard. Has he found a new Area 51? We'll have to see.

"First, however," Wellman continued, "it will be open lines. So run, don't walk to your phone, and start dialing. I want to hear from you. What strangeness has been happening in your corner of the world? This is Rich Wellman, and I'll be back after this."

Music swelled in his earphones followed by his own voice promoting the benefits of an in-home water filter that was guaranteed to remove all impurities and additives. He leaned back in his chair, drew a cigarette from a pack that rested on the console before him, and lit it. He inhaled a lungful of smoke, then blew it into the air. In the still environs of the studio, the smoke formed a stagnate blue cloud around his head.

A glance at the phone on the console revealed a string of blinking lights. Ten callers were waiting for their few minutes of fame. Wellman then looked at the nearby computer monitor. Names and locations of the callers were spelled out on the screen. Rudy, who screened every call, would type the caller's name and city into the computer, and that information was relayed to Wellman's monitor.

"Good start as usual," Rudy said. "The phones came alive immediately. The world is at your doorstep."

Another spot played in Wellman's ears. In this one, he was promoting a new Internet service provider. Wellman voiced eighty percent of the radio spots that played over his airwaves. He possessed an interesting, believable, "everyman" voice. Every sponsor wanted a Wellman voice-over.

"What's caller eight about?" Wellman asked Rudy. Wellman read the line again: *Brian from Duluth, The Second Coming.*

"A religious nut, I think."

"These guys never give up," Wellman said. "Their concern for my lost soul is getting on my nerves. Leave him on hold for a while, then bounce him. I don't want to deal with his kind tonight."

"Will do," Rudy said. "He's eighth in line. Lemmon may call in by then."

"He had better, if he ever wants to be on our show again."

"You're coming up in ten," Rudy said.

Wellman set his cigarette in an ashtray and repositioned himself in the chair. The bumper music cued up, played for ten seconds, then faded into the background.

"Strangeness is everywhere, folks," Wellman said into the microphone, "maybe even in your town. I want to hear it. America wants to hear it.

"Tomorrow's program is one you certainly don't want to miss. Albert Genni, the president of Americans Against UFO Secrecy, will be with us to discuss the latest flying triangles seen right here in my own Arizona. It promises to be very interesting. Now to the phones." Wellman studied the computer monitor for a second, his practiced eye taking in the information. "Mark from Jefferson City, Missouri, you're on the Richard Wellman show." Wellman punched a button on the multilined phone.

A voice came over the headset. "Um, Rich? How ya' doing?"

"Outstanding, thanks. You're on the air. The world wants to know, what's going on in Jefferson City?"

"Well, I probably shouldn't be talking about this on the air, but I need to tell someone."

"I'm the man to tell, Mark."

"Mark isn't my real name."

"I guessed that, but that's all right. I understand the need for secrecy. What's on your mind?"

"I don't think you're going to believe this," Mark said in a wavering voice. "I wouldn't believe it if I didn't see it myself."

"We've heard it all here, Mark. You can't surprise us."

"I'm not so sure," Mark said. "But I can prove it."

"Really? Tell us, Mark, and don't spare the details."

"I work in a local hospital, Rich, and something really weird happened a few days ago."

"A few days?" Wellman asked.

"I've been trying to work up the courage to call."

Wellman looked at Rudy and raised an eyebrow. He had been hosting this radio program for years and had learned to distinguish between the practical joker, the mentally disturbed, and a sincere caller. Mark was showing every sign of being genuine. He was nervous, as revealed by the tremor in his voice. Wellman could hear the man lick his lips.

"You're among friends, Mark. Let it fly."

"Okay." Wellman heard the man take a deep breath. "As I said, I work for a local hospital and something weird happened."

"Are you on staff there?"

"No. I'm not a doctor or anything. I do ... other things."

"Other things?"

"I don't want to say what I do," Mark said. "That would give me away."

"Of course, go ahead."

"A few days ago, some people were healed."

Wellman shook his head. Had he misjudged this caller? Maybe he was a nut case, after all. "Isn't that why people go to the hospital?"

"No, you don't understand. I mean healed outright. Sick one moment, well the next."

"Miraculous healings, you mean," Wellman prompted.

"Yeah, that's what it was. A miracle. A real miracle. People were just laying in their beds sick with all kinds of stuff. A minute later a dozen of them were suddenly well."

"That's certainly out of the ordinary," Wellman said. "I have to admit. It's a little hard to believe—even for me."

"Like I said, I have proof."

"What kind of proof?" Wellman was enjoying the call. The night was picking up.

"Video," Mark blurted. "I saw it on video."

"You have tape of someone being suddenly and miraculously healed?"

"Yeah. The hospital has a closed-circuit video system. They use it for security. Things get stolen in hospitals all the time. This particular hospital has a security system that records what goes on in the halls, the waiting rooms, and lobbies."

"What about patient rooms?" Wellman inquired.

"No, not in the patient rooms. That would be a violation of the patient's privacy."

"I imagine it's been done before."

"Not at this hospital," Mark said.

He's defensive, Wellman reasoned. *He does work for the hospital. That makes him credible.*

"Okay, go on. This is fascinating."

"Well, like I said, these cameras monitor certain areas of the hospital. I have the tape, and one minute everything is the same; the next, patients are dancing in the hall. It's weird."

"It sure is . . . Wait a minute," Wellman said. "You said you *have* the tape. You didn't just see it?"

"Well, I have a copy of the tape. I wouldn't take the original."

I hope your boss isn't listening, Wellman thought. *You're giving yourself away. How many people could have access to security tapes?*

"You have the tape in your possession right now?"

"Yes, but I can't show it on the radio."

"You might be surprised," Wellman said, casting a glance at Rudy. "Do you have a computer?"

"Yes."

"Do you ever go on the Internet, Mark?"

"Yeah, lots."

"Okay, one more question. Can you convert the video to a computer file?"

"I don't know how to do that."

Wellman's heart sank. Now he would have to convince the man to send him a copy of the tape. Even if the man agreed, and there was no certainty of that, it could take days.

"My neighbor can," Mark interjected. "He's always doing stuff with his video camera and computer. He's a nut about those things."

Hope. "Do you think he's home?"

"Yeah, I know he is."

"Okay, here's what I want you to do," Wellman said in his best I'm-your-buddy-trust-me voice. "Have your friend convert the video into a computer file and email it to me. My producer will give you the email address. When all that's done, I'll call you back. That way I can see what you're seeing. I can even put it up on our Web site."

"I don't know, Rich. I'm not sure I should even be talking about this—"

"But you already have, Mark. This is good stuff . . . assuming it's true."

"It's true, all right." Mark was defensive again. It was just the response Wellman wanted.

"Okay, I'm going to turn you over to my producer. He's a genius at these things. Then we'll make you our special guest in the next hour. How's that sound?"

"Okay, I guess."

"Great, Mark. You're a super guest. We'll talk soon. Now stay on the line. Rudy will be with you in a moment." Wellman put Mark on hold and then said, "Interesting. Very interesting. Okay, America, we'll be back after we hear from our sponsors." He motioned to Rudy. Again music rose in his headphones and was soon replaced by the sound of a commercial spot. Wellman activated the switch that let him speak to Rudy. "This is good stuff, Rudy. Make it happen."

"And if Lemmon calls in?"

"He's late. Reschedule him."

"What if Mark and his friend don't come through?"

"They will," Wellman said. "This guy needs to get this off his chest. He also likes to be the center of attention."

"How do you know that?"

"Years of experience. Just make it work. I'll take a few more calls."

The phones remained hot, and Wellman deftly moved from UFOs to haunted houses, from stories about ubiquitous men in black to out-of-body experiences and remote viewing. Normally, each show had a theme and at least one guest, but with Lemmon being a no-show, Wellman was forced to hear whatever topics his callers wanted to discuss. Through each call his mind drifted back to Mark and his tale of healing. During commercial breaks, Rudy gave him updates. With each update, Wellman became more impatient.

"Will he pull it off?" Wellman asked.

"We're close," Rudy answered. "His neighbor is pretty savvy about computers. Works with some Internet company. He's got the conversion completed and is sending it to our Web master."

"You got Peter out of bed?" Wellman asked with a laugh.

"We're his biggest client, he won't complain."

"So how long before we switch back to Mark and his miracle hospital?" Wellman asked.

"Ten minutes," Rudy said. "Peter is uploading the page now. When you go back to Mark, you can tell the listeners how to access the site. There will be a hot link on the home page called 'Hospital Healings.' Once they click on that, they should be able to see the video."

"Great. You're the best, Rudy."

"That's what I keep telling you. You're on in five."

Wellman took one more call, which took him to the top of the hour. He broke for the network news, which gave him five minutes to use the rest room, light another cigarette, and view the video clip.

The clip was two minutes and thirty-two seconds long and showed a woman taking a small boy by the hand and walking him away from a doorway which, Wellman assumed, led to a patient's room. A little over a minute later, patients dressed in hospital gowns appeared in the corridor. Even though the image was grainy, Wellman could see their broad grins. Seconds later the small crowd was hopping and dancing.

"What do you think?" Rudy asked.

"Gold, Rudy. Pure gold. Is Mark on the line?"

"Line five."

"Good. I've got questions. Lots and lots of questions."

Hey, Thomas," Roger called across the house. "You've got to see this."

"I'm studying," Thomas shouted back. He was in the living room, propped up on the sofa, a book on his lap and several more scattered on the floor.

"You're always studying," Roger complained. "Be a good roomie and come look at this."

Thomas looked up from his Greek New Testament and toward Roger Leland's bedroom. Roger was one of two roommates with which Thomas shared a three-bedroom home. Kurt, his other roommate, was out on a date. "I have to have this passage translated for tomorrow's class. Leave me alone."

"Don't make me come out there," Roger threatened good-naturedly.

"It's not about some movie starlet, is it?"

"Give me some credit, will you? I'm not that shallow. A man can use the Internet for scholarly pursuits, too."

Thomas laughed. Roger was a good student, but not an academician. He attended the Riverside Graduate School of Theology with Thomas and Kurt. Roger had set his sights on a counseling ministry.

With a sigh, Thomas laid his book facedown and open to mark his place, stepped over the textbooks on the floor, and walked into Roger's bedroom. "This had better be good. You pulled me away from my Greek."

Roger shuddered. "I don't know what you find so enjoyable about Koine Greek. I barely made it through the first-year class."

"It's food for my intellectual soul," Thomas replied. "What's so important that I had to leave the couch?"

"I'm listening to the Richard Wellman show over the Internet," Roger said.

Thomas groaned. "What is it tonight, suburban witches? Yuppie meditation? Alien conspiracies? Atlantis in a pyramid?"

"You're a cynic."

"Guilty as charged."

"This is different," Roger said with a serious tone. "This is about miracles. Videotaped miracles. You're fascinated by miracles, aren't you?"

Thomas had to admit that was true. He had bored his roommates to tears with his views of the supernatural. "Real ones. Not the stuff you hear about on late-night radio."

"Watch this." Roger moved the mouse of his computer and clicked on a link that activated a streaming video file. The picture of a hospital corridor appeared and showed a woman leading a small boy by the hand. "This is the Richard Wellman Web site. One of his callers provided this video. It's from a security camera in a hospital where the guy works. Isn't technology wonderful? He's talking to the guy now—well, after the commercial break."

Thomas could hear the radio announcer touting the benefits of an herbal memory aide. "You mean some guy called tonight, talked about this video, and we're looking at it right now?"

"Exactly. Wellman's never done that before. This must be real."

"I wouldn't bet on it. It could be a setup. Something to boost ratings."

The video played across the computer screen in a choppy, jerky fashion.

"Not very smooth, is it?" Thomas commented.

"That may be the security camera. They don't tape continually, but snap a frame every few seconds."

"How do you know that?" Thomas asked.

"Haven't you ever seen those security tapes of robberies? They show them on television all the time."

"How often do you see me watching television?"

"Not much," Roger admitted. "Your face is always in a book or journal."

"Who is that?" Thomas pointed to a man coming out of the doorway.

"A patient. The caller said the guy was sick and suddenly he was well. And not just him. Watch."

Thomas took in the scene as patients from different rooms emptied into the corridor. They were hugging and jumping up and down.

"Let's see that again," Thomas said. Roger worked the mouse and replayed the video stream.

"Pretty amazing, isn't it. If it's a fake, it's a good one."

Thomas left the room and returned with a chair from the dining room. He sat down just as the Richard Wellman program resumed.

Lemmon is on the line," Rudy said. "And you're on in thirty seconds."

Wellman shook his head and chuffed with disgust. "I told you to reschedule him. He's forty minutes late."

"He said he had a flat tire on the freeway," Rudy explained. "He sounds a little rattled and winded."

"Okay, but I can't take him now. Tell him we'll call back during the third hour. I want to stretch this video thing out some more. The phones are hot." Wellman looked at his monitor. Rudy had posted the names of a dozen callers waiting to talk on the radio.

"You're telling me," Rudy said. "They're stacking up like cordwood." He paused for a moment, then said, "You've got five seconds."

Wellman adjusted his headset and let his finger hover over the button that would activate his mike. Five seconds later the intro music began; five seconds after that Wellman spoke. "We're back with what has to be one of the most interesting videos I've seen, and you know I've seen a lot of videos in this business. Still, there are questions. With us tonight is Mark of Jefferson City, Missouri. He has been kind enough to let us upload a video file from a hospital near where he lives. Something remarkable has happened there, and you don't want to miss seeing it. So, if you can get on the Internet, then do it. Go to my Web site and click on the link that says 'Hospital Healings.'" Wellman gave the site address again.

"You still with us, Mark?" Wellman asked.

"I'm here, Rich."

"Tremendous. Your friend did a great job getting us that video file so quickly. Pass on our thanks, will you?"

"Yes, but he's listening now, so he knows."

"Well, I am appreciative, as are our listeners." Wellman's voice lowered a half octave. "This is amazing, Mark. Did you see the patients yourself or just the video?"

"I arrived a couple of minutes later."

"Tell us what you saw."

"Not much more than what appears on the tape." Mark's voice quavered. Wellman recognized the sound of nervousness. The more he could get Mark to talk, the more relaxed the man would become.

"So the patients were walking around when you got there?"

"Yes. Sort of milling around."

"Like in a trance?"

"No, not at all. They were happy, talking, but it was like they didn't know what to do next. Some went back in their rooms to call their families. But they disconnected the phones."

"Who disconnected whose phones?" Wellman pressed.

"The hospital brass. The doctors and nurses were pretty shaken up."

"I imagine," Wellman said with a sympathy he didn't feel. "But who cut off the phones and why would they do that?"

"I don't know why, but I know a couple of patients ... you know, healed patients ... were pretty upset. They wanted to call home."

"Odd," Wellman said, "very odd, indeed. Then what happened?"

"The hospital administrator came down."

"What's his name?"

"I'd rather not say," Mark admitted.

Wellman smiled to himself. Mark was being coy. Perhaps he feared for his job. That was understandable, but he was missing the point. Even if Mark wasn't his real name, he had already identified himself as an employee ... an employee with access to security tapes. There couldn't be too many people who fit that description. He also spoke like a man with a limited education. Wellman doubted that Mark was a male nurse or a physician's assistant, and he certainly was not a doctor. Those positions required rigorous training and good communication skills. Most likely the caller was an orderly or a security guard.

"I understand," Wellman said. "What else can you tell us?"

"Not much. I know that they want to keep a lid on things, but I just can't keep quiet. I mean, this is weird, really weird. It has me spooked."

"Why spooked, Mark? It's a good thing, isn't it? People were healed."

"Yeah, but ... but ... it's not normal, that's all. It's just not normal."

"Well, Mark," Wellman said, "my listeners will be the first to tell you that there are a lot of things going on that are not normal. We just think this is the way things are. In truth, none of us has a clue."

"I suppose."

"Any idea who the woman with the boy is?" Wellman asked as he studied the video again. "The boy seems fascinated with the doors that lead to the patients' rooms."

"No. I saw him and the lady on the video, but people walk down that hall all the time. They probably had an appointment or were visiting someone."

"I don't know, Mark. The kid seems pretty intent, and they're in the hall just minutes before the first healed patient steps out and does his little jig of joy."

"Maybe. I don't know."

"Okay, thanks, Mark, and hang on the line. We're going to take some calls and see what our listeners think."

"I really should go," Mark said nervously.

"You don't want to stay around a little longer?" Wellman wasn't surprised. He could hear Mark's anxiety rising. He was having second thoughts. It was too late now; he had pulled the trigger. There was no turning back.

"No, not really."

"Okay, Mark," Wellman said softly. "You've done a good thing. I appreciate your bringing this to our attention." Wellman changed tones as easily as flipping a light switch. He spoke to his audience. "Let's hear from you out there. What do you think? Are people being miraculously healed in Missouri? This is the Richard Wellman Show, the place where truth is paramount. Let's take our next caller."

chapter 3

The dawn pushed past a filigree of flimsy clouds, through the warm summer air, and into Aaron Pratt's living room, caressing his face with alabaster fingers. His neck hurt and a dull pain roared in the middle of his back. A pungent film coated his tongue and mouth. He smacked his lips and twisted in his recliner. A moment later, he blinked open his eyes and stared at the textured ceiling above him. The sunlight that eased in through the small decorative windows in his front door stung his eyes. He raised his hands and rubbed his face, his fingers making a scratching sound as they ran across the black and gray stubble on his chin. He took a deep breath and forced his mind to focus.

"Not again," he said to the empty room. He studied his watch. He had seventy-five minutes before his first class. That was plenty of time to get ready and make the twenty-minute drive to the campus—assuming he ate no breakfast. He was used to that. During a good week, he would be able to stop by his favorite Denny's three times. But that only happened when he actually went to bed and set the alarm. More and more he was sleeping in his padded lounger.

Pratt took another deep breath, then lowered the footrest. A book, an Adam Bridger novel, tumbled from his lap to the floor. The book had been his companion last night, as it had the night

before and the one before that. Aside from the occasional solo
excursion to the movie theater, Pratt spent most of his nights home
reading. He was a solitary man with few friends. This was not
because he lacked any of the social graces. In point of fact, he was
good humored, sociable, and inoffensive in every way. Despite this,
the ill-defined bonding that makes for friends never seemed to take
hold. All of his fellow instructors were married with families. Most
of his students were too young to form a comradeship with a middle-aged man, and even if that weren't the case, professional ethics
required that he remain detached from them. He could not be their
professor and their best friend simultaneously.

Rising, Pratt made his way into the bathroom to prepare for
the day. The image in the mirror made him recoil. His dark hair
was rumpled, his shirt twisted and wrinkled. His pale blue eyes
looked dull and were set in a nest of crow's-feet. A small patch of
white was stuck in the corner of his mouth, the remains of last
night's dinner of two Jack-in-the-Box tacos and a vanilla shake. He
shook his head and laughed. "You don't look like a man with two
master's degrees and a doctorate."

As he brushed his teeth and shaved, he thought about the hours
ahead of him. He would arrive in class one minute before it was
scheduled to begin. He always did. It was a game he played. He
would march through the door, set his notebook on the lectern, turn
to the appropriate page, link his hands behind his back, and watch
the sweep hand on the clock mounted at the rear of class complete
its orbit to the top. As it swept the twelve he began his lecture. It
never paid to be late to one of his classes.

He allowed himself only ten minutes in the shower. The hot
water poured over his neck and down his trim body. Many of his
male colleagues had congratulated him on his successful avoidance
of the middle-age bulge that plagues most men. They asked about
his exercise routine and dietary habits. He had none. What he did
have was a genetic mix that allowed his trim figure to remain while
the other men around him struggled to fend off the impending
descent into chubbiness.

Pratt had been a man consumed with a hunger for knowledge, especially spiritual knowledge. From high school, he had entered California Baptist University, where he distinguished himself as a quick study. Graduate school followed, and he spent the next three years earning a Master of Divinity degree at Golden Gate Theological Seminary. It was there he developed a real taste for the deeper study of theology. During his second year, he surrendered his dream of ministering in a small church and embraced what he felt was God's higher calling on his life—teaching.

Armed with his professional degree, he began a track of study more academic and specialized. Returning to Southern California, he enrolled in the Riverside Graduate School of Theology, earning an additional master's degree in biblical languages and a Ph.D. in theology. His skill and intellect were quickly recognized by the staff. Upon his graduation, he was offered a teaching post. That was twenty years ago. Now, at the age of forty-eight, he was a tenured professor of biblical studies. He loved the post; he loved the teaching. On campus, before the upturned faces of students as they sat in their class chairs, he felt most alive.

Twenty-five minutes later, Pratt examined himself in the mirror. He was wearing a light gray shirt with a maroon silk tie and a charcoal gray suit. The dress code for professors was lax at the school, but he always wore a suit. For him it was a uniform.

"For a dusty old professor, you clean up pretty good," he said to the image in the mirror. He often referred to himself as old. Not yet fifty, he knew that "old" was an exaggeration, but he often felt more aged than his years. At first he thought it was his workload, but later had come to face the truth of the matter: loneliness weighed on him more than work.

After a short stop at his in-home office to pick up his briefcase, Pratt exited his small middle-class home and started his day.

I'm hungry, Mom," Toby said softly.

The 1972 Pontiac station wagon bounced on shock absorbers that had long ago given up the battle. Two hundred thousand miles had worn the car to the breaking point. A subtle but distinct knock came from under the hood. Mary felt her stomach tighten into a fist. She knew nothing about cars, but understood new sounds couldn't be good. "I know, honey," she replied. She also knew that she had five dollars left to her name and not a penny more. The gas tank indicated three-quarters full because Mary had put in ten dollars worth of gas at their last stop. If she couldn't come up with more cash, they would end up stranded by the roadside.

"Can we get something to eat?"

Mary glanced at Toby, who sat in the front seat with her. He was looking out the window at the Oklahoma farmland. The morning sun was still behind them as they drove west toward California. Mary had no idea why she wanted to go to California other than it was as far away from Lincolnsberg as she could get, and far away from Tobias.

"Sure, son," Mary said. "We'll stop in the next town." *Maybe there was a fast food place,* she thought. Dollars went farther at a McDonald's than a sit-down restaurant. She would buy him a breakfast sandwich and an orange juice. She would also tell him that she was not hungry. Maybe she could save a dollar or two. Then she would see if she could work a day for some cash. She could wash dishes and wait tables. She had done it before, she would do it again. If that failed, then she would make the circuit of churches. Mary hated doing that. Begging was beneath her, but she would do it for her son. Then there were the churches. There was something about them, something she could not define. Whatever it was, it made her uneasy. Her family had never gone to church. They seldom left the small community of Lincolnsberg. Such an outing was costly in time and money, and her father couldn't see the need of coming off the mountain, especially for church. "What has God ever done us for us?" he used to ask. "Did he weed our garden or milk our cow? Did he ever patch our roof so the rain don't pour in? You ever see him pick up a hammer and nail a board to the side of this ol' house? I never did, and you ain't gonna see it neither."

Jacob Matthews was a good man, as far as Mary had been able to see. He loved his family, he worked hard, and he remained faithful. Then he died, the victim of his own gun. A hunting accident, her mother said. The neighbors said different. The hole he left had remained unfilled until Toby was born. It was then that Mary began to see that life might have some purpose, that some reason for living might actually exist. As it turned out, the churches were seldom any help. None would give money. Some would offer canned food and clothing. Mary made use of such gifts, but she preferred to work for anything she received. There was a great deal of her father in her.

As they passed from Oklahoma into the Panhandle of Texas, Mary noticed a sign.

"Glennary, five miles," Toby read.

"Five miles," Mary repeated. "Well get some breakfast there. Okay?"

"Okay," Toby said.

Mary stole a glance at her son. He sat in silence studying the terrain as it streaked by. He was looking for something to occupy his mind. She had never known anyone, man or boy, who was so interested in everything. He had learned to speak at a very young age, much younger than the other children in Lincolnsberg. Toby could speak before he could walk and while this made Mary proud, it troubled her neighbors. They never said anything to her face, but when they thought she couldn't hear they would call him "witch boy." "It ain't normal," she had overheard one neighbor say. "No boy that young can do what he does exceptin' the devil be involved. That's the truth, plain and simple. I take no joy in sayin' it, but it's gotta be said."

It was then that Mary knew she'd have to leave. Lincolnsberg could never be her home. They feared Toby, and they would make his life miserable. She had to get away. Away was better. It had to be better. "It can't be no worse," she said aloud.

"What, Mom?"

"Nothing, son," Mary answered. "Jus' thinkin' out loud."

Toby nodded.

It took six years for Mary to save enough money to buy the rickety car she now drove. Six years of doing the most degrading labor, but she did it with purpose. She took in sewing, weeded gardens, and did whatever would bring her a dollar. Six years of slave work. Six years dreaming of escape.

Tobias helped after a fashion. Not with the money. Not with encouragement. He did, however, provide motivation. As a rule, he avoided Mary and Toby, until he had a physical need to come by. Then he only stayed the night. He never offered to marry her and make her an honest woman. Never once called Toby "son." He just came every week or two, then left to tend a still he kept tucked away three miles into the thick forest. Every time he showed up on the porch he was drunker than the time before. And he was turning mean, vicious. It began with accusations of unfaithfulness, then came the name-calling. It wasn't long before the hitting began. The night he hit Toby was Mary's last night in Lincolnsberg.

Glennary, Texas, was little more than a wide spot in the road, just like the scores of other places she had passed since leaving North Carolina. Mary slowed the Pontiac down as she entered the town limits. "Look for a McDonald's or a Burger King or something."

"Okay."

They were two miles out of town before they realized that they had seen all of Glennary there was to see. Mary pulled to the side of the road and then made a wide U-turn.

"I didn't see a McDonald's," Toby said.

"Me neither," Mary replied, "but I did see a café. Maybe we can get you some pancakes."

Toby turned to his mother and smiled. Pancakes were one of his favorite foods.

The restaurant was a small white building with a pitched roof covered with faded green asphalt shingles. Near the road was a weathered wood sign that read BEAU'S COFFEE SHOP. Several eighteen-wheelers were parked out front, kept company by four pickup trucks. Mary pulled the car to a stop on the gravel lot. She and Toby exited, careful to lock the car. They didn't have much, but Mary was determined not to lose what little they did have.

Inside they were greeted with the smell of coffee, fried bacon, hotcakes, and eggs. Mary's stomach quivered in anticipation. She looked around the building. Booths of red Naugahyde that had been new twenty years ago lined the side walls. Formica-covered tables filled up the open space of the dining area. A woman holding a globular pot of coffee worked her way through the maze of tables with machine precision.

Mary saw an empty booth near a window that overlooked the parking lot. She led Toby there and sat down. The morning sun had climbed higher and flooded the booth with warmth. The day was already warm but Mary didn't mind. She was prone to feel cold. Sitting in the sun was preferable because of the warmth it brought, but also because it allowed her to keep an eye on the car.

"Be right with you," the waitress said. Mary looked up and saw the thin woman walk past them. She filled the coffee cups of two men who sat in the next booth and took their order. Mary heard words that made her stomach ache with hunger: hash browns, eggs over easy, and orange juice. Mary closed her eyes and willed her stomach to settle. It remained disobedient.

The waitress disappeared.

"What are you going to have, Mom?"

"I'm not hungry. I think I'll just have coffee."

Toby looked at her suspiciously. "You didn't eat last night either."

"Travelin' steals the appetite, son." Mary hated lying to Toby. Partly because it wasn't right, but also because he was so smart. Every time she told this lie, he would look at her like he could read her mind. He never said anything, but he always looked so sad it broke her heart.

"What will you folks have?" The waitress had returned. She wore a yellow and brown pantsuit uniform. Her name tag read RUBY.

Mary looked up. The woman's face was taut, lined, and her mouth was pressed into a permanent frown. Her voice was coarse like that of Mary's mother, whom Mary could not remember ever seeing without a hand-rolled cigarette dangling from her lips. Her eyes revealed a deep weariness. Mary recognized the look; she had seen it on the faces of many women who had hoped for more in life, only to be beaten down by reality.

"Pancakes for my son and just coffee for me."

"Anything else?" The woman asked brusque.

"Jus' a question," Mary said, then leaned forward and spoke softly. "Any work to be had 'round here?"

The waitress studied Mary as if she were trying to determine if a carton of milk had gone bad. She shook her head. "Nothing around here." She paused then asked, "You got money for this?"

"Of course," Mary said indignantly.

"Good," the waitress said. "The owner's got a real short temper."

Mary shook her head as the waitress walked away. It was nothing new. Everyone looked down on her. Dressed in a dirty brown gingham dress, hair unwashed for days, and wearied from days of travel, she wore her poverty like a billboard. Most she met treated her as though poverty were contagious. "What a grouch," Mary said to Toby.

"She's scared," Toby said. "Can I have a pencil?"

"What do you mean, Toby?" Mary asked as she reached into her small purse, pulling out a yellow pencil that had been ground to half its original length. She handed it to Toby.

"She's scared and unhappy," Toby explained. "I think it's because she's sick."

"How do you know she's sick?" Mary watched her son. He began drawing on the paper place mat before him, leaning over the table and placing his face so close to the paper that his nose hovered just inches above it.

"She has lumps and bumps."

"What?" Irritation percolated in Mary. Sometimes it was a chore to understand her son. "Sit up for a minute, Toby. I can't hear ya' when you talk into the table like that."

"Sorry, Mom," Toby said, raising his head. He repeated his words. "She has lumps and bumps."

"Lumps and bumps?"

"Yeah, right here." Toby pointed at his chest.

"Her heart?"

Toby shook his head. He seemed embarrassed. Mary thought for a moment, trying to make sense of lumps and bumps and Toby's discomfort. She leaned forward and spoke softly. "Her breast? She has a lump in her breast?"

"Yeah," Toby said, redirecting his attention to the paper. "Lumps and bumps. It scares her a lot."

Breast cancer. It was a frightening thought. She had known several women who had battled the disease. They had to leave Lincolnsberg to be treated at the county hospital. Judy Miller had lumps in her breasts but refused to leave the mountain. Mary had watched her waste away.

"Here's your coffee." Mary jumped. She had not seen the waitress return. "Hot cakes will be up in a minute."

"Um, thank you," Mary said.

She turned her attention back to Toby. Once again, his head was just above the table. "How do you know these things?" Mary asked. It was not a new question. She had known that Toby was special from the day he was born. Every week he surprised her. Every month, he became more impressive. Most of the time Mary was proud of him, but there were times when she felt uneasy, uncertain. He was not like other children. He never cried. He was smart, smarter than anyone she had ever known. He never showed any rebellion, never back talked her.

Toby shrugged. "I don't know. I just do."

Ten minutes passed before the waitress brought the pancakes and set them on the table between Mary and Toby. She refilled Mary's cup. Toby continued drawing. The aroma of the food made Mary's stomach leap to life, quivering with anticipation. Three large, round, brown hotcakes lay on the plate, a scoop of yellow butter moved slowly from the center of the stack toward the edge of the plate, leaving a buttery river behind.

"Your boy needs glasses," the waitress said.

The woman's statement caught Mary off guard. "Excuse me?"

"Your boy. It looks like he needs glasses. Look at how close his face is to that paper."

Mary wondered if the waitress was right. Whenever Toby would draw or write he would drop his head close to the paper. "He's always done that," Mary admitted.

"That's what I mean. His eyes are bad. I have three kids of my own. I know a little bit about child rearing."

"I'm sure you do," Mary said kindly, remembering what Toby had said. "How old are they?"

"All grown now," she answered. Mary could hear a sadness in her voice. "All moved away. Nobody wants to stay around Glennary. If they can get out, they do."

"You should call them," Toby said, putting the pencil down and pulling the plate of food to himself. He picked up a knife and began meticulously spreading the butter. He did so in an orderly fashion, starting in the center and pushing out until an even layer of butter had covered the entire surface of the top pancake.

"What?" the waitress replied. Mary saw her eyes narrow.

"Don't be rude," Mary said to Toby.

"They should know," Toby said.

"Toby, hush," Mary commanded.

"Know what, young man?"

"About the lumps and bumps. If you tell them, you won't feel so alone."

"Lumps and bumps?" She turned to Mary. "What's he talking about?"

"He's jus' a boy," Mary said quickly, avoiding the woman's eyes. "You know boys and their imaginations."

"It's not my imagination, Mom," Toby said, reaching for the maple syrup. "I'm not making it up."

"I don't understand," the waitress said. "What's he mean, lumps and bumps?"

Toby put the syrup down and looked at the woman. He said

nothing. Instead he pointed at his chest as he had done before. Mary saw the color drain from the woman's face, and for a moment she thought the waitress would fall over in a faint.

"How dare you? How could you possibly know?" She stammered. "I . . . I haven't told anyone."

"You should call them," Toby stated. "They'd want to know."

Mary's heart fluttered with apprehension, certain that the waitress was about to cause a scene. The woman raised a finger, but Toby continued to calmly stare at her. Instead of the blast of rage Mary expected, the woman lowered her hand, turned, and walked slowly away. A patron at one of the tables called out to her, and held up his empty coffee cup. She ignored him. Mary watched as the woman disappeared into the kitchen area.

"Why do ya' do that?" Mary demanded. "You've gone and embarrassed that woman."

"No, I didn't, Mom. She knows I'm right. You want some of my pancakes? They're good."

Mary picked up her fork, reached across the table, and cut off a small wedge of food. It was dripping with syrup. Toby had drowned the meal in the sticky brown fluid. It tasted wonderful. For a moment, Mary felt like crying. She took another bite, then set her fork down. She wanted Toby to eat his fill before she had anymore. "Toby, you can't go round sayin' things like that. It makes folks mad."

"But it's true," Toby replied.

"That doesn't matter. It still riles them."

"The truth makes them angry?" Toby seemed confused. "I was just being nice."

Mary sighed. "I know, son. No one in the whole world is nicer than you." She reached across the table and gave his arm a squeeze. "We jus' have to be careful what we say."

"Okay," Toby conceded. "Want more pancake?"

"Not just yet," Mary said. She watched her son eat for a few moments, taking in each moment and unconsciously committing it to memory as only mothers could do. His blond hair shone in the sunlight, and his eyes danced with delight at each bite he took. She smiled at the three freckles that dotted his right cheek. "You're a mess, you know that, don't you. A real mess."

"I didn't spill," he said, looking down at the white T-shirt he wore.

"That ain't what I mean and you know it."

Toby laughed. His laughter was contagious. Every time Mary heard it, her spirits were lifted. No matter how depressed she might become, his giggle could raise her mood and lighten her load. If it hadn't been for Toby, Mary would have descended into an abyss of despair from which no one could rescue her.

"Is it true, Toby?" Mary asked. "Do you need glasses? Do you have trouble seeing?"

"No."

"Then why do you put your face so close to the paper when you draw?"

Toby shrugged. "It's fun, I guess. I like to watch the pencil make its mark. If you look close enough, you can see the mark go right on the paper. It's neat."

The waitress reappeared. In her hand was a plate of eggs, bacon, and hash browns. She set the plate in front of Mary. Mary stiffened. "I . . . I didn't order this."

"I know," the woman said.

"But I can't pay—"

"The cook made a mistake. This isn't what the customer wanted, and I can't see throwing it away."

A wave of embarrassment rolled over Mary. "Thank you."

"I hope you like your eggs over hard."

"They're fine, real fine." Mary said, fighting back the tears that threatened to betray her emotions.

"How's them pancakes, boy?"

"Good. I love 'em. Thanks."

"I should be thanking you, son," the woman said. Mary saw her tear up. "I'm going to make that call." She turned to Mary. "I spoke to the owner. He said you can work for a few hours. I have six hours left on my shift. You can work with me. You have waited tables before, right?"

Mary nodded. "Many times."

"Okay," the waitress said. "Eat your breakfast, then I'll take you to the back. We have a uniform that should fit you. Your boy can wait back there. I'll see if I can't find some more paper for him to draw on."

"Thank you," Mary said. "This . . . this means a lot to us."

"You have a special boy there."

"I know," Mary said with pride.

"I don't know how he knew what he did, but . . . well, I'm glad he did."

Harrison Donald Burdick III sat in his overstuffed leather chair and gazed out his office window. Before him stretched a wide expanse of rich vineyard. Green leaves glistened in the late morning sun, dancing like a million ballerinas on a warm breeze that blew through the Sonoma Valley. The temperature was mild for the season, but Burdick knew that would soon change. In another day or two the temperature would rise to the mid-nineties again. That was fine with him. He no longer worked the vineyards. Not the one that was before him or any of the forty he owned. Those properties, and the thirty central California farms his company operated, had made him a wealthy man.

It had not been all his doing. His father, Harrison Jr., had built the business on the solid foundation of his father. Grandpa Harrison had started with a small farm near Fresno, California, and worked it into a prosperous concern. Burdick's father took over the farm at just twenty-three when the elder Harrison had died of colon cancer. One patch of ground was not enough for him. He added an almond ranch to his soybean farm two years after control had been passed to him. He added another farm or ranch or vineyard every three years until he presided over an agricultural empire worth nearly a half-billion dollars. He ruled powerfully and confidently until stricken with lung cancer. His death laid the multimillion dollar operation at the feet of twenty-five-year-old Harrison Burdick III. He continued the policies of his family acquiring more and more farmland. He also diversified by buying up several farm equipment businesses. Today, he was worth five billion. "Not bad for an old farm boy," he was fond of saying. Except Burdick was far from being just a farm boy. His family's wealth had allowed him to attend the best schools and to study abroad. There wasn't anything he didn't know about the agricultural business or the politics that affected it. At least three congressmen, five state assemblymen, four state senators, and the sitting governor were indebted to him. That was the way he liked it.

Control was important to Burdick. He preferred being addressed as "sir" and required full and complete information of all business concerns. He would allow nothing to sneak up on him—at least nothing he could prevent.

He had known of his family's history with cancer and had taken every precaution available. He didn't smoke, avoided red meat, had frequent checkups, and exercised daily. But genetics were stacked against him. When he took over the business, he was robust and gregarious. That was thirty-seven years ago. Now, at the age of sixty-two, rising from bed was work enough to weary him to exhaustion. Burdick had always been a fighter. He had faced hostile takeover attempts, lawsuits that lasted years, a wife who divorced him and sued for hundreds of millions of dollars, and a son who was somewhere in Europe enjoying himself and adroitly avoiding the family business. Burdick had already cut him out of the will, knowing that he would sell everything the first month he was in charge.

Burdick was determined to fight on. Twice each week he would be driven to the spacious office where he had spent so many hours. The trip alone was so taxing that he could do little work for the better part of an hour. His appearance at the office was show. He wanted it known to his executives and employees that he was still alive, and very much in charge. The day would come when the cancer that had spread from his spleen to his liver would make such appearances impossible, but that day was not today. And it would not be tomorrow. Until that time, he would cling to Burdick Enterprises like a drowning man clings to a life preserver.

There were decisions to be made, assets to be dispensed, and lawyers to be instructed. He had to do those things now. Cancer was an impatient disease; liver cancer was pure evil. Despite chemotherapy that assaulted every cell in his body leaving him a shell, forty pounds lighter than his healthy one hundred ninety, he was still a man possessed by an invasive, malevolent disease.

At first he had prayed to be spared, but prayer required faith, something he had never experienced. His supplications were shams, simple words of desperation directed to a God he didn't believe existed. In business dealings, Burdick might be cunning, elusive, and slippery, coloring the truth to suit his goals, but with himself he had always been brutally honest. When he and Colleen married, he knew that she had walked the aisle not because she loved him, but because he was rich. It was a business deal from which both benefited. She had even provided him with the son he longed for— although he had turned on the family to pursue . . . *art*. While Burdick's work filled the bellies of hundreds of thousands of Americans, his son spent his days looking at pretty paintings created by equally useless people. Burdick had no time for art, and no stomach for laziness.

How things had changed. When he was healthy, he could look to the distant future and plan the perfect itinerary to take him there. Now, looking just a month in advance seemed like optimistic, foolish hubris.

Burdick closed his eyes and leaned his head back. Nausea roiled within him. His breath tasted sour and his eyelids felt heavy as stone. Every part of him ached.

Burdick was a man in need of a miracle, but miracles were in short supply. That left him pain medication, a twenty-four hour nurse, and a determination to live out every last second of his life. If he was going to die, then death was going to have to stalk him down like an animal and seize him. Burdick would not walk easily to the grave. He was determined to make the Grim Reaper earn his wages. It was a lost cause, but he didn't care. Surrender was not part of his world view. Hang what the doctors said. They were right, he knew that. His impending death was chiseled in implacable stone, but that didn't mean he couldn't shake a fist in the hooded face of Death.

Turning his chair away from the window, Burdick addressed the papers on his desk. It was time to get to work. If he was lucky, he could expect to get two hours of effort in before having to lie down and rest.

But that was two hours of productive life.

chapter 4

The video suite was silent. The room was lit by the soft glow of several color monitors. A dark, eerie image played across the screens. A voice, broken and distant, wormed its way through the screeching, swirling sound of demonic wind. "Come back, boy! Come back."

Bill Packard slowly shook his head. "No matter how many times I see this, I still can't make myself believe it."

"You were there," Jerry Barnwell said.

"My presence there doesn't mean my brain believes what I see."

Jerry sighed. He knew Bill was right. He too could not believe his own eyes or his own recollection. Unconsciously he touched one of the many cuts on his face where debris, propelled by nature's fury, had cut him.

"I thought you were a dead man, Jerry," Bill said. "I just knew that twister was going to pick you up and drop you in the next county." Bill paused. "Actually, I thought we were all dead."

"What do you make of the boy?" Jerry's eyes were fixed on the monitor. He had watched the scene twenty times as he and Bill edited the video footage. The raw footage had been turned over to a local network station for a good price. It would appear on the evening news. Soon what only a few had witnessed would be seen across the country.

Bill shook his head. "I don't know what to think. I'm a rational man; I don't believe that the kid stopped the tornado. That's impossible."

"So then, what happened?"

Leaning his head back over the chair, Bill rubbed his eyes. "I have no idea. You explain it to me."

The conversation was not new. They had traveled this ground before, but the implausible nature of their experience demanded that it be revisited time and time again. Jerry was tired. In the last twenty-four hours, he had chased a tornado and nearly been killed by it. The skin of his face was raw and covered with small cuts and red abrasions. He could feel the evidence of the event every time he moved his lips. It had happened. He bore the proof in his body, and the images that played in his brain were more vivid than those on the video monitor. Another thought haunted the corridors of his mind—the boy was unscathed. Not a single cut, not a single bruise on his skin, and he had been twenty feet closer than Jerry. How was it that Jerry felt he had been pressed through a meat grinder, and yet the boy looked as if he had just walked off the school yard?

"Maybe we shouldn't try to explain it," Bill said. "It is what it is and as journalists we recorded the truth of it. Let the scientists bust their brains on this. The good news is, our little operation just got an infusion of cash. Maintaining the copyright was a good idea."

The money was good. For freelance videographers, work was feast or famine, and lately it had been more famine than feast. It was their diminishing bank balance that had pushed them into actions beyond what more reasonable men would undertake. They had known that there would be scores of videos of the tornado. Theirs had to be special.

Jerry gave a grunt of agreement. "We have no other choice. Let's get some copies made. We should be ready when the phone begins to ring."

"I can do that. You look beat. Why don't you catch forty winks."

"Yeah, I could use it." Jerry left the video suite and made his way into the office he shared with Bill. The office was spartan, with two metal desks and two worn executive chairs. Taking a seat in his chair, he put his feet on his desk, leaned back, and closed his eyes, willing himself to relax.

The image of the tiny boy in the maelstrom of wind flashed on the screen of his mind as it had every time he closed his eyes. *It's impossible,* he reminded himself. *It was all just a freak occurrence of nature, and we happened to be there to see it.* Jerry knew he was lying to himself. *Sometimes,* he thought, *a lie is preferable to the truth.*

The note in Aaron Pratt's hand was written in a flowing, feminine cursive. Heather McCall, Pratt reasoned. Heather was the personal assistant to Morris Edison, president of the Riverside Graduate School of Theology. The note was short and to the point: "President Edison would like to see you after your last class." The small pink piece of paper had been set on his desk. Slipping the note into his pocket, Pratt walked the carpeted corridors to Edison's office. He was greeted by Heather. She was a pleasant-looking woman in her early thirties, with a keen mind, a quick smile, and a genius for organization.

"Dr. Pratt," Heather said with a toothy smile. "You must have found my note."

"I did indeed," Pratt said. "I'm reporting for duty as ordered." He snapped a little salute.

"Dr. Edison is waiting for you." She stood and walked to a large but plain wood door. It was a door Pratt had passed through many times. As the chairman of the theology department, he had frequent meetings with the president of the school. Pratt walked across the small lobby, past Heather's desk, and into the office.

The room was twice the size of the small eight-by-eight office Pratt had. The walls were a white plaster that matched the exterior stucco of the school. Designed in California mission style, RGST was quaint and functional. Large date palms stood outside like sixty-foot sentinels, overseeing spacious, grass-covered grounds lined with the black macadam of parking lots. A pair of French doors separated Edison's office from an enclosed garden area decorated with blue and white patio furniture. The whole area was sheltered by a large oak tree that provided shade from the summer sun. One of the doors was open, and a breeze made sweet by a freshly mowed lawn rolled in through the opening. Edison was seated at a table in the garden area.

"Dr. Pratt is here," Heather announced as she led him through the office. On the walls were the framed diplomas of Edison's exceptional education. He had studied at no less than five schools and had earned two doctorates. His mind was as sharp as any Pratt had ever encountered, and his knowledge was not limited to matters of theology. He could converse intelligently in world events and topics of science as easily as he might discuss the weather.

"Thank you, Heather." Edison stood.

Pratt stepped across the threshold and into the warm southern California air and shook hands with his boss. Birds in the large oak chirped in unison like a feathered choir, giving the patio an Eden-like ambiance.

"Can Heather bring you some iced tea?" Edison asked. His voice was smooth and full of kindness.

"I'd love some," Pratt said. Heather disappeared without a word and returned a few moments later with a large plastic tumbler of brown tea.

The men sat around the glass patio table. Pratt could see several thick folders and one thin one.

"You look like you've been busy." Pratt nodded at the file folders.

Edison sighed. "Our accreditation is up for review again. The review team will be here next week. I'm trying to make certain our ducks are in order."

"You need me to help with that?" Pratt asked.

"No, your department is right where it should be. The library has a few things they need to do. They'll be burning the midnight oil for a few days. I wanted to talk to you about something else—or maybe I should say, someone else."

Pratt raised an eyebrow. "Really? Who?"

"Before we get to who, let me tell you why." Edison took a long sip of tea and then set the glass down. "We have a benefactor who wants to create a new scholarship. The G. P. Youngblood Scholarship would be given to the student most likely to advance the study of theology."

"Who is G. P. Youngblood?" Pratt asked.

"The father of Donald Youngblood, a corporate tax attorney here in town," Edison explained. "He was a history professor in the University of California system. He died last spring."

"I'm sorry to hear that." It was an odd truth that the grad school benefited when its patrons died. Money left in wills and trusts provided a large share of the needed money to keep the doors open. Every administrator felt the contradictory emotions of sadness at a death and expectation of what the estate might leave them.

"G. P. was a scholar of the highest caliber and a fine Christian man. He believed in education and devoted his life to it. I had dinner with him about three months before his heart attack. That's when he first mentioned his desire to set up the scholarship. In true humility, he wanted to call it the Excellence in Theology Scholarship, but his son Donald wants us to name it after his father."

"Hence the G. P. Youngblood Scholarship."

"Of course, I agreed to it. The man is worthy of the honor the scholarship will bring his memory."

"Did he have something special in mind?" Pratt knew that those who endowed higher institutions of learning often had pet causes they wanted to champion. Some gifted the sciences, others one of the arts.

"Yes," Edison admitted. "He felt that the academic pursuit of theology has fallen on hard times. Liberalism, German rationalism, and all the rest have left conservative, Bible-believing scholars in the minority. What he wants . . . wanted is to pay the entire tuition and living cost for one student throughout their entire education. A new student will be added to the list each year. The money will be provided as long as the student remains a theology major throughout their graduate studies."

Pratt blinked hard. "Throughout the student's entire education?"

"Yes," Edison acknowledged with a twinkle in his eye. "From first year through a Ph.D. or Th.D. program."

"That could be better than five years of full-time study. That's a generous grant."

"It is, and that's why I want us to be careful in the choices we make. We need to choose a promising student right away."

"You have someone in mind?" Pratt prompted. He knew that Edison did. He was a thorough man in all matters. This meeting wouldn't be happening if most of the work hadn't already been done.

"I do," Edison admitted. "He's in your systematic theology class."

"Thomas York," Pratt said.

"Exactly."

"He's a good student," Pratt said, "and he possesses a keen mind. The kind of student every professor longs for . . ."

"You have reservations?"

"Not really, but I don't think he's planning the academic path. He's an M.Div. student. That wouldn't keep him from pursuing a doctorate, but he's gone on record as wanting to enter the ministry."

"That's why I wanted to talk to you," Edison said, leaning forward over the table. A leaf from the tree dropped on one of the folders. "This is an awkward situation in many respects. I would never suggest to a student that they need to change their career goals for the sake of a scholarship. But the endowment is very specific. It is meant for students who will advance the *academics* of theology. G. P. wanted to elevate the world's view of our discipline. He's not opposed to people entering the ministry. I know from my previous conversations with him that he respects the clergy. He just had a different goal in mind."

Pratt nodded and drank his tea. He could appreciate Edison's quandary. The school had many fine students, but exceptional scholars were rare. Thomas York was one of those rare individuals. "So, for Thomas to get the scholarship, he would have to . . . what?"

"Declare his intent to teach and do research."

"He couldn't be a pastor?"

"Technically, his profession would be that of an academician. If he wanted to pastor on the side . . . well, who could fault him for that?"

"I see," Pratt said. He had felt that Thomas could best serve the kingdom of God by teaching, but that was up to Thomas, not his professors. If he felt the call of God on his life to be a preacher, then he should follow that call. What he as a professor and Thomas's academic advisor thought meant nothing.

"How well do you know young Mr. York?" Edison asked.

"As well as I do any of my students. I did his initial academic workup. He's sharp and inquisitive, a genuine child prodigy— math, I think." Pratt paused as he weighed his next few words. "He once told me that he chose to study theology because it was the only thing that didn't come easy to him. He's seeking something. Searching."

"What do you mean?"

Again Pratt chose his words carefully. "He seems unsatisfied with the orthodox position. I don't mean to say that he holds heretical views, just that he seems to be looking for something the rest of the world doesn't know exists."

"Such as?" Edison prompted.

Pratt shook his head. "I don't know how to explain it."

"Well," Edison said, "curiosity is a good thing in a student. I have another question for you. I reviewed Mr. York's files and noticed that he has no church affiliation, and by that I mean, he doesn't attend church anywhere. I thought that was odd so I took it a step further. He rooms with two or three other young men in a house a few miles from here. One of his roommates works as an aide with our janitorial staff. It helps pay his tuition. I asked if he knew where Mr. York went to church. He said that he had never seen him go to church. In fact, he said that he's refused the invitation of his fellow students to attend. It strikes me as odd that a young man who wants to be a preacher avoids church."

"Perhaps avoid is too strong a term," Pratt suggested. "Maybe he hasn't found one that ministers to him." Despite his words, Pratt found the revelation unusual.

"I bring it up because I can't help but wonder if he hasn't had a change of heart. Maybe he's decided that being a pastor in some church isn't for him. It's not for everyone."

Pratt knew that all too well. He had once thought that the pulpit ministry was his calling. He soon learned otherwise. "You want me to talk to him?"

"Please. I believe him to be the most promising student on campus right now. He deserves this scholarship. With it he can quit his part-time job and study full-time. There are few such opportunities in life."

Pratt rose. "I'll have a chat with him, Dr. Edison. I'll let you know what he says."

"Do more than chat with him, Aaron. Convince him that this is a wonderful opportunity."

The ringing of the phone awakened Wellman from a light, fitful sleep. It was the fourth time the ringing had echoed through the rooms of his spacious home in the suburbs of Phoenix. It was a shrill ring, a piercing, annoying, unrelenting ring. Wellman could take it no longer. He rose from his bed and looked at the clock, 3:15 in the afternoon. A normal time to be awake for most people, but then most people didn't have a daily radio show that began at ten in the evening and ran until two the next morning. He was seldom home before four. His routine was chipped in stone. Home, breakfast, bed for five hours, rise to make phone calls and conduct the day-to-day business of his program. The next few hours were spent doing the odds and ends of life. At 3:00 he would return to bed for a few more hours of sleep before heading into the station to prepare for his program.

The phone was upsetting that balance. He had forgotten to turn off the ringer and now it was hounding him, refusing to be quiet and go away. Wellman snapped up the phone. "What?"

"Is this Richard Wellman?"

"Who wants to know?" Wellman concealed none of his anger at having been disturbed.

"Mr. Wellman, you don't know me, but we must talk."

"You're right, I don't know you." Wellman hung up and started back for the bedroom. The phone rang again. He turned and reached for the switch that would shut off the ringer. He hesitated, then picked up. He said nothing.

"This is serious, Wellman," the voice said in dark tones. "Don't hang up again."

"Or what? You gonna come over here and work me over or something? Bust a kneecap or two? As you can tell, I'm real scared. How did you get my number? I'm unlisted."

"That doesn't matter," the voice said.

"It does to me."

"What matters is who gave you the hospital video."

"Who are you?" Wellman demanded.

"That doesn't matter, either."

"It does if you want to talk to me." Wellman swore and slammed the phone down. It was ringing before he could reach the switch. He reached for the button marked "Ringer Off," but hesitated. The ringing continued. Four rings, five rings, six, seven. He could feel the muscles in his jaws tighten like constricting steel springs. Eight rings, nine. He glanced down at his caller ID. It read "Private Caller." No help there.

He picked up the phone and started speaking before the receiver was near his mouth. His words were hot and sharp. "You have precisely ten seconds to tell me who you are and why you feel it is necessary to hound me."

"My name is Anthony, and I want to know who gave you the video of the hospital situation."

"Why is that any of your business, Tony?"

"It's Anthony."

"As if I care, Tony. Answer my question."

"That video," the caller said tightly, "is private property and it belongs to the hospital."

"And which hospital is that, Tony?"

"You know very well which hospital." Wellman could hear the anger boiling in the man's voice.

"Hang on a second," Wellman said as he lowered the hand piece of the phone. A few seconds later, he pressed one of the keypad buttons. Even with the phone away from his ear, he could hear the beep. He raised the hand piece again. "Just so that we're clear on things Tony, I'm recording this phone conversation. I'm required to tell you that, so now you know. Okay, Tony, so the hospital has hired you to harass me. Why?"

There was a long pause. Wellman knew that Anthony had bought the lie.

"The video is private property, Mr. Wellman," the man said in softer tones.

"I don't possess the video," Wellman said. "A short clip was sent to me over the Internet. You'll have to badger someone else."

"I'm not talking about the original tape," Anthony snapped. "I'm talking about what's on your Web page. I need to know who sent it to you and when you're going to take it off your Internet site."

"I don't know and I'm not taking it off. Does that finish our conversation?"

"You must know who sent it to you."

"Not really. People call my show with all kinds of craziness. They seldom tell me their real name. The tape was uploaded to my site. That's it. That's the whole story."

"Who uploaded it?"

"Look, Tony, I don't know if you're smart enough to understand this, but you have no right to expect answers. Do you honestly think you can call me up and demand my attention? Do you really think I'll ask 'How high?' simply because you say 'Jump'? You're a moron."

"Take the video off your site," Anthony demanded.

"Or what, Tony? Come on, Tony, speak up for the recorder. Are you threatening me?"

Anthony fell silent.

"You there, buddy? Cat got your tongue?"

"I would consider it a favor."

Wellman guffawed. His laughter rebounded throughout the house. "A favor? A favor? A few seconds ago you were threatening me, now you're asking for a favor. All you've told me about yourself is that your name is Anthony. That's probably a lie. You still with me, Tony?"

"I'm here."

"Let me tell you what I think," Wellman said. "I think you work for the hospital, probably in security, and someone has put you in the pressure cooker because the video got out. Am I close?"

No answer.

"Okay," Wellman continued. "Now that you're in hot water, you want me to bail you out by giving you the name of the person who sent the video. Well, I don't have a name, so you're flat out of luck, buddy."

"If the video clip was uploaded to you, then you must have the email address of the sender," Anthony said. "I would settle for that."

"You're going to settle for nothing, Tony. I don't handle those things, and even if I did I wouldn't give you the name. It would be unprofessional to reveal my sources."

"You're not a journalist, Wellman," Anthony's words were bitter. "You're a radio jockey who talks about flying saucers, out-of-body experiences, and little green men."

"Oh, please. I've been criticized by intelligent people, Tony," Wellman snapped. "You're out of your league."

"I want that information." Wellman could hear desperation in the caller's voice. He enjoyed that.

"And I want a mansion in the Caribbean, and I'm a lot closer to seeing my wish come true than you will ever be."

Wellman set the receiver down and pressed the "Ringer Off" button.

chapter 5

The car's worn cloth seat felt good beneath Mary. Her legs ached from seven hours of waiting tables with only two short breaks. Yet the pain was a positive reminder that she had once again found a way to make a few more dollars to see them along their journey. In her hand was a small wad of cash, the combined result of tips and the pay the owner had given her. The pay had been six dollars an hour plus meals for Toby and herself. By most standards, it was paltry, but she had made another thirty dollars in gratuities. All told she held seventy-two dollars. It would take over twenty dollars of that to fill the gas tank of the station wagon. She could afford to do that twice and still have money left for several meals, if she were careful.

Mary had learned to be careful, making the most of each dime. Tomorrow she would make a stop at a grocery store and stock up on dry cereal, canned milk, bread, and cheese. It wasn't much, but it kept the hunger away. Bananas were good too. They filled Toby up. She glanced at her son. What a wonder he was. He never complained. While she worked, he split his time sitting in the small storage room amidst the cardboard boxes of condiments and paper supplies, and sitting in one of the booths when business was slow.

The owner, a big-bellied man with a harsh face, proved to be as gentle as a drugged bear. His hard exterior was a thin veneer covering a much softer man. Without mentioning Mary and Toby's obvious need, he had allowed her to work for the cash she now held. He also insisted that they take some food with them. "I can't use it. I'll just end up throwing it out, so you might as well have it. You might get hungry tonight." He made several roast beef sandwiches, poured a large coffee for Mary and a soft drink for Toby. "You wanna work tomorrow?" he had asked.

"No," Mary had said. "I gotta get back to the road."

"I could use the help," Ruby added.

"I'm sorry, Ruby," Mary answered. "I should keep going."

"What are you running from?" Ruby asked.

"Nothin', I jus' got a ways to go."

"But where will you sleep?" Ruby asked. "I got some room at my place."

"Thank you, but I want to put a few more miles under us before we call it a night." Mary saw Ruby's face slip into sadness.

"I want to thank you again," said Ruby. "I don't know how ... well, I plan to make that call. That boy of yours, he's a blessing of God. A real mercy, all right."

"I hope it all works out for you."

"It will," Toby said.

Mary looked at Toby as he sat in the passenger seat, lit only by the dim lights at the front of the diner. She turned to see Ruby raise a tremulous hand to her mouth. Her eyes brimmed with tears.

"I got the feeling that I'm missing something here," the owner said, his forehead furrowed in confusion.

"It ain't none of your business, you big oaf," Ruby said. Her words carried no animosity. It was a statement made between people who had grown to respect one another. The big man said nothing more, and Mary thought that was to his credit.

She started the car, and with a brief wave, pulled from the shallow pools of light that dotted the parking lot and onto the dark street.

Thirty minutes later and twenty-five miles west of Glennary, she breathed a small sigh of weariness. The flat Texas terrain scrolled by, and Mary had to force herself to stay awake. She was weary, so very weary. The days of driving, compounded by a full day's work, sat heavy on her. Her neck ached, and she could feel a fist of tension knotting in her back. California was her destination, and she was only halfway there.

"Will that woman really be all right?" Mary asked.

Toby was staring out the window, gazing at the distant sparkle of stars. His gaze remained fixed, as if the tiny flicker of lights had lulled him into a trance. Mary had watched him do this each of the three nights they had been on the road. He would gawk at the dark sky until he fell asleep, his little head laid against the metal car door.

"Toby? Did you hear me?"

"She will be okay," Toby said without moving his head an inch.

Mary wondered about her amazing boy. She loved Toby as much as any woman ever loved a child, but at times he frightened her. It wasn't right, a six-year-old boy knowing all he did and seeing right into people's lives. If they lived at an earlier time, Mary mused, he would be called evil names: witch, sorcerer, even possessed. People would be frightened of him, maybe even try to hurt him. Most days, Mary feared for Toby. He was an unusual boy, and horrible things happened to unusual folk. She knew this, not from experience, or even from stories she had heard. Instead, she knew it intuitively. The truth of the matter stuck in her stomach like a large wad of unbaked bread dough.

"You're tired," Toby said softly. "You should sleep."

"I'm just fine, Toby," Mary said. "You don't need to worry about me."

Toby turned his gaze from the dark heavens and stared gently at her. She knew he had caught her in another lie. He never said so, never contradicted her, but she could never fool him. "I have my coffee and it will help me stay awake," Mary added.

Toby turned back to the stars.

"I tell you what," Mary offered. "I'll just drive to the next town, and if it's big enough, we'll do what we always do." What they always did, each night since leaving Lincolnsberg, was to pull from the highway and find a residential community. Mary would then search for a safe-looking street, well lit if possible, and park in front of one of the dark houses. There, she and Toby would sleep until awakened by the rising sun. She never slept in the rest areas, having heard stories of robbery and rape. During the daylight hours, she might use their rest rooms, but they never stayed long. "How's about that?"

"Okay," Toby said.

What Mary wanted to do was drive all night. A person could cross the whole country in about three days if they didn't sleep. Three days without sleep was more than Mary could imagine. Already her eyes burned from weariness and her stomach seethed from the acidic coffee. Every part of her was tired, as tired as she could ever remember being. Sleep beckoned her. The sweet sensation of closing her eyes was becoming impossible to resist. She would stop in the next town. She had to. Another hour or two and she would be a danger to herself and Toby. What sense did that make, to run away from one danger only to become a threat to herself and her son? She rolled down the window and let the warm summer air blow across her face. *A few more miles,* she told herself. *Just a few more miles.*

I gotta tell ya, folks," the voice of Richard Wellman said over the radio, "it was weird. This guy calls me and demands—and I mean *demands*—to know how I got that video of the hospital. I knew the hospital would be upset about the news getting out. Who can blame them? But to call me at my home, on an unlisted number, well, that's just too bizarre. But we've talked about these things on the air before. There are people who do not want you to have the truth about anything. And it's not just the government, folks, oh no, not by a long shot. Big business is serious about secrecy, too. Well, let it be known here and now, I will not be intimidated. This radio show is about the truth. It always has been, and it always will be. So, it's open lines for our first hour. Let's talk about what's on your minds. What do you think about this?" Wellman gave the phone number to call. "Should I take the video clip off my Web site, or shall freedom of speech continue to prevail?"

"He'd better be careful," Roger Leland said to Thomas. They were in Roger's bedroom listening to the Richard Wellman show again. "He might be playing with fire."

Thomas looked at his roommate. "How so?"

"Can you imagine what that hospital must be like?" Roger said. He was seated in an old leather chair in front of his computer terminal. Thomas was seated on Roger's bed. "It must be a mad house. Nothing like a miraculous healing to bring folks out of the woodwork."

"If that was what it was."

"Come on, Thomas. You're Mr. Miracle. You're the one who says that there should be more miracles in churches."

"I said there should be more of the miraculous in the Christian community."

"Same thing," Roger replied.

It wasn't, but Thomas didn't argue the point. Roger was right about his desire to see the miraculous. All his life he had read of God's supernatural intervention and longed to see such works for himself. He had always been disappointed. Every modern miracle described in church had been too speculative, too subjective. Empirical evidence was missing. He attended a community church all through high school and during the first two years of college. There he heard of healings, miraculous rescues from auto accidents, and more. Never had he seen actual evidence. Thomas spent the next two years of his college visiting churches in his hometown of Stockton, California.

"I need to study," Thomas said, standing.

"Don't you want to hear this? It's right up your alley."

"We don't even know that it's true. It could all be a publicity stunt."

"Maybe," Roger conceded, "but maybe not. Stick around for a while. I'll call up the video again so you can see it."

"The clip is inconclusive," Thomas said. "Two people, a woman and a boy, walk down a corridor, then people step out of their rooms and mill around."

"Mill around? They were dancing in the aisles," Roger exclaimed. "What are you afraid of, Thomas?"

"I'm not afraid of anything."

"I think you are and you're just not admitting it."

"Excuse me," Thomas quipped. "I didn't know you were a psychiatrist. I thought you were a graduate student."

"I am," Roger admitted. "I'm a graduate student in biblical counseling."

"I don't need counseling."

"No, but you do need to relax. Sit down and kick back. The books will still be waiting for you."

Thomas acquiesced with a disgruntled sigh.

Wellman was listening to a caller rant about how the government was covering up the real cause of airline crashes when he looked at his monitor. He saw what he was hoping to see. Someone from Jefferson City, Missouri. The name on the monitor was different from last night's caller. Next to the name was the description inputted by Rudy: "Wants to talk about the hospital thing." Motioning to the monitor, Wellman held up three fingers to let Rudy know that he was taking line three next.

With some adroit verbal jujitsu, Wellman segued from the current caller to the one from Jefferson City. "And the story continues, folks," Wellman said into his mike. "We have Harold from Jefferson City, and he wants to talk about our mysterious hospital in Missouri. You're on the air, Harold. Regale us."

"Hi, Rich. How ya doin'?"

"Just great." A young voice, Wellman noted. Early to mid-twenties. "You have some word on healings in Jefferson City?"

"I wasn't there when that happened, but I was there today," Harold began. "Rich, the place is a zoo."

"Okay, now wait a minute. Why were you at the hospital?"

"My wife had a baby the night before, and I was there to pick her up."

"And the baby too, I hope," Wellman laughed at his own joke. He was trying to put Harold at ease.

Harold joined the laughter. "Yeah, the baby too. It's a boy."

"Congratulations, Harold. Is it your first?"

"Yes."

Wellman nodded. Definitely a younger caller. "Well, I along with all our listeners wish you the best. So the hospital was a zoo, you say."

"You wouldn't believe it. The place was mobbed. The lobby was packed. Camera crews. Security guards everywhere. It was nuts."

"How did word get out?" Wellman asked.

"A lot of people listen to your show down here, Rich. Everybody loves you. Besides, one of the patients is related to someone who works at the local television station."

"So this went out on local news." Wellman wondered if his name had been mentioned. Any publicity was good publicity.

"Yes."

"So what's the hospital brass saying about all this?"

"They're playing it down, saying that facts have been blown out of proportion," Harold said with a chuckle. "They don't like you much."

"The hospital execs? I'm getting that idea. We've been trying to get them to come on the air, and they're not having anything to do with us. Any word about the boy?"

"Not that I know of, but I've been kind of busy with the new baby and all."

Wellman chuckled. "I imagine. Well, thanks for the call, Harold, and good luck with that new son. Don't spoil him too rotten." Wellman disconnected the line, then said into the mike, "We'll be right back after this." A crescendo of music, then the voice of a newsman filled his headset.

"Lines are hot, Rich," Rudy said with a wide grin. "And they're about to get hotter."

"What do you mean?"

"Caller six has another video for you. If I understand him correctly, the hospital clip is nothing."

"This I need to hear. How much time?"

"You have about four minutes of news left, followed by two sixty-second spots."

Wellman nodded and punched line six. "Mr. Packard? Bill Packard?"

"Yes. Are we on the air?" The voice was smooth and calm.

"No," Wellman said. "We have to get through the top of the hour news and a few ads, then we'll be ready to go."

"Ah," Packard said. "I was wondering why I couldn't hear myself on the radio."

"You'll have to turn your radio off. We broadcast with a ten-second delay. It'll drive both of us nuts if you don't."

"Okay," Packard said.

"So what have you got for me?"

"You're not going to believe this, but I have footage—footage I took myself. Me and my partner are freelance videographers in Oklahoma. We took this footage and tried to sell it to the media. We had a deal, but they pulled out at the last moment. They don't believe us. They think we made the whole thing up, that it's all special effects wizardry."

"Is it?"

"No. On my honor, Rich, it's the truth. I swear it. You can take it to any video specialist you want and have them test it."

"Okay, fill me in quickly. If the story is as good as my producer thinks it is, then we'll put you on the air and let you share it with the world."

Packard told the tale of the tornado, the boy, the mother, and the miracle he taped. Wellman listened intently, interrupting occasionally to ask questions. The hands of the clock moved through the minutes quickly. "Okay," Wellman said. "How do I see this video?"

"That's the good news," Packard said. "Like many small businesses, we have a Web page. I created a special page that I can give you and your listeners. If you want, I can send you a copy of the actual video."

"I'd like that. Give me the Web site address." Packard did, and Wellman typed it into his computer. As he waited for the site to load, he said, "Okay, here's what we're going to do. We're coming out of the break, and I'm going to put you on. I want you to tell your story, just like you told me. I'll ask some of the same questions so our listeners can hear your answers. Just pretend like it's the first time you've heard them. Okay?"

"Okay."

"After a few minutes, I'll give the Web address. Do you have time to be our guest tonight? You might be on for thirty minutes or more."

"Yeah, I can do that." Packard sounded enthusiastic.

"Great," Wellman replied with genuine excitement. "Now when you hear the music coming up, that means we're coming up on a break. You need to wind up whatever you're saying at the time. After the break we'll pick up where we left off. Okay?"

"Got it."

"Great. It's show time."

Harrison Donald Burdick III lay in his bed with his eyes wide open. The darkness of the room was as deep and thick as that of an Egyptian tomb. The sarcophagus-like blackness prevented him from seeing anything more than the blue letters of the DVD player that was part of the massive entertainment center that stood opposite his bed. The center, an expensive conglomeration of high-tech electronic devices, was designed to take the mind from the slums of reality and transport it to worlds of intrigue, entertainment, and adventure. The center had it all: digital television and radio, expensive speakers to carry every nuance of music to each corner of the room.

Burdick seldom made use of any of it. Instead, he preferred the simple pleasures of radio. Classical music was his favorite, second only to the all-news and finance stations. Tonight, as he reclined in his bed covered in abysmal darkness, he pressed a button on the remote control he held in a tremulous hand and scanned the channels.

The day had been grueling. He felt as if he had put in twelve hours when, in truth, he had spent less than three at the office. Three hours. Three measly hours. Six months ago, he routinely put in twelve or more. Now he couldn't stay awake twelve hours.

Part of that was his disease, but it was made worse by the pain medication he took. While it alleviated some of the agony, it made him drowsy and sick to his stomach.

He twisted in the bed in an endless struggle to find comfort, but comfort was elusive and lasted no more than ten minutes. The problem lay not with the bed. It was top of the line and fully adjustable, but his body continued to search for a relief that did not exist.

Burdick hated the bed. It was a token, an icon of the illness that was sucking his life from him. His bedroom was richly appointed, the walls adorned with mahogany paneling, the floor dressed in a deep cobalt blue carpet. The furnishings were French imports and gave the room a regal quality, the kind an eighteenth-century king might admire. But the institutional bed, with its shiny metal rails, stood in stark contrast to it all. The furniture, the décor, and the very spaciousness of the room itself testified to his wealth and power—but the bed belied the image. It said he was weak and dying. It said that some things were beyond the control of his iron will and out of reach of his vast fortune. Gone was the majestic four-poster, replaced by a symbol of decrepitude. In retaliation, Burdick kept the room dark whenever possible. It was a useless, childish response, but it was the only one he could make.

Dr. Townsend had stopped by as he did every week. Burdick was one of the few, if not the only man on whom doctors were willing to make house calls. His advice this week had been the same as last week. "You should take it easy. Strain makes it harder on the body."

"Will I get well if I rest?" Burdick had asked. He knew the answer to the question, but he had a point to make. His situation was hopeless. He was standing on a very slippery slope and sooner or later, certainly sooner, he would fall and begin the slide to the open maw of a grave that awaited him.

"No," the doctor had said. "We've discussed this."

"So I'm left with a choice between working myself to death or resting myself to death," Burdick snapped. "Death is part of both formulae. What difference does it make whether I die in my office chair or in my bed?"

"I was just thinking of your comfort."

"I haven't been comfortable in months, Doctor, and I'm not likely to be comfortable in the future."

Townsend had finished his exam and left. Burdick was alone in his dark room. Just outside his door, however, was one of the many nurses he had hired. Each worked an eight-hour shift, and each made twice the money they could anywhere else in the world. The press of a button attached to the side rail of the hospital bed would bring the nurse running.

He didn't want the nurse, didn't want to watch television, and didn't want to listen to music. What he desired was distraction, something to take his mind away from his illness and loneliness. So he pressed the button on the remote again and the radio scanned the frequencies until it found another signal. Burdick listened for a moment, then, dissatisfied with what he was hearing, pressed the button again.

He was just about to change the station again when he caught the phrase, "miracle boy," followed by, "mysterious healing." Burdick paused and listened. "We'll be right back after this. You're listening to the Richard Wellman show. Stay with us. It appears that miracles really do happen." The voice disappeared, replaced by an advertisement for herbal vitamins.

Miracles? *Rubbish and lies,* he told himself. *There are no such things as miracles. Stupid people believing nonsense about the impossible.*

Still, Burdick hesitated. *A discussion of miracles might prove interesting,* he thought.

Shifting his weight in the bed, Burdick waited for the program to resume.

chapter 6

Mary gasped and bolted upright. Her heart fluttered rapidly in her chest and perspiration dotted her face. She raised a trembling hand to her forehead and forced herself to calm down. She was safe, still seated behind the wheel of the car, still parked in a residential neighborhood of a town whose name she could not remember.

It was dark outside, the blackness swallowing the small houses and the street. She rolled the window down and drew in several deep breaths. The air was scented with the smell of lawns, trees, and flower beds. The place she had parked after leaving the freeway was quiet and pleasant. She had, at Toby's insistence, parked so that she could sleep for a few hours. Those few hours had been as tumultuous as any she had spent.

The dreams. They came often and refused to let her rest. She had left Tobias back in North Carolina but he still haunted her, still plagued her like an awful illness that would not go away. It was unfair. Tobias had abused her mentally and physically. Now that hundreds of miles separated them, he still tortured her in her dreams and recollections. The thought of him made her ill. How could she have deceived herself for so long? Loneliness had turned her into a fool.

Mary had only two desires in life: to live peaceably and to watch Toby grow into a man. They were simple hopes, reasonable wishes.

Yet how could she achieve any peace if Tobias still lived in her mind? Time would have to settle it. Only time could diminish the evil that Tobias had become. Only time could erase the pain he had caused.

The dreams were the same. She and Toby were back in Lincolnsberg sitting in the car, ready to drive off for California. As she reached for the key, she would hear the guttural swearing of Tobias. Turning her head, she would see his beefy hand grab the handle of the car door and pull. No matter how hard she tried, Mary could never get the car to start. The keys would be suddenly and mysteriously gone. Tobias would snatch the driver's door open, grab Mary by the hair, and pull her out of the station wagon and onto the ground. He would then crawl halfway in the car, seize Toby, and brutally pull him from the front seat, dangling him in the air as if he were a rag doll. Mary would then watch helplessly as Tobias would sneer, swear, and then pull back his big fist ready to unleash his fury on Toby.

"It's this momma boy's fault," Tobias would scream. "You were plenty happy with me until he come along."

Mary would see the fist start toward Toby's small face, then she would wake up. It was a dream she had had countless times, and it always terrified her.

Reaching forward, Mary started the car and then, not wanting to wake Toby, who was curled up in the backseat, she gently pulled away from the curb. She knew that she had slept only three or four hours, but it would have to be enough. It was time to be back on the road.

An hour had passed when Mary heard stirrings from the backseat. Toby was waking.

"You go on back to sleep," she murmured. "No reason for you to be up."

"I can't," Toby said. Deftly, he climbed over the seat and took his spot by the passenger door.

"Is the driving keepin' you awake?" Mary asked. "You ain't sick, are you?"

"Naw, I'm okay. I just woke up and don't want to sleep anymore." He resumed staring out the window as he had done before. His face was again turned skyward.

"What do you see up there, Toby?"

"Stars."

"You have always been taken by the stars."

"I want to study them," Toby answered, his face still turned skyward.

"Do you have a favorite star?"

"No. I like them all."

Mary wished she knew more about the stars and the planets. If she did, she would teach Toby all about them. But she knew nothing of the sky. There was so much she didn't know, and Toby was so hungry to learn. He used to ask questions, so many that Mary thought she would go mad. He asked adult questions, and she knew none of the answers. One day, Toby stopped asking. He had never said so, but she was sure he had come to understand how little his mother knew. The thought caused her heart to ache.

"I'm hungry," Toby said. "I wish we had some doughnuts."

"There's the sandwiches from the diner," Mary responded.

"I know," Toby answered without enthusiasm.

"Maybe we can find a store or doughnut shop in the next town. Doughnuts don't cost much. I could use some coffee."

"Me too."

Mary laughed. "You want coffee? You're a little young to be drinkin' coffee. How's about orange juice instead?"

"Okay," Toby said. He turned from the window and gave Mary a small smile. He was trying to cheer her up. "I'm sorry about the dreams."

"What do you mean?"

"You have bad dreams. I wish you didn't. It's my fault."

"No, it's not. Don't you say such things. Ain't nothin' your fault," Mary replied quickly. After a moment she asked, "How do you know I've been having bad dreams?"

"You talk when you're asleep. It's about Pa, isn't it?"

"Yes," Mary said weakly, uncertain what else to say.

Toby returned his gaze to the stars. "The stars are really far away. Lots farther than California."

"Yes, they are, Toby."

"I wish we could go to the stars."

So did Mary.

On the eastern outskirts of Amarillo, Mary pulled from the highway and directed the car through the edge of town. Less than a mile from the freeway, she found a small market. Its parking lot was nearly empty and awash in yellow light from street lamps. The store looked old, its concrete block exterior walls covered in paint built up layer by layer through the years. A small planter of anemic juniper bushes separated the oil-stained parking area from the windowed wall of the storefront. Only three cars were in the lot. Parking near the front, Mary peered through the market's windows. She saw a woman moving inside.

"Can I go with you?" Toby asked.

"Course you can. No need for you to sit in the car, unless you want to try to go back to sleep."

"I'm not sleepy anymore."

Once outside the station wagon, Mary took Toby by the hand and walked through the self-opening doors and into the store. The bright lights of the store's interior hurt Mary's eyes, and the air-conditioning made the place ten degrees colder than the outside air. She shivered.

A woman, the one Mary saw through the window, looked up and gave a friendly wave. Mary smiled back. A row of four cash registers ran along the front of the store. Only one was open. A wide aisle separated the register area from the rows of shelves laden with grocery products. A young man, barely out of his teens, was polishing the floor with a large and loud buffer.

"Over here, Mom," Toby said, tugging at her hand. "I see them."

Mary followed his lead until they stood next to a rack filled with prepackaged cupcakes and other sweets. Toby lifted a box of chocolate-iced doughnuts and turned a smiling face toward her.

"You don't mind boxed doughnuts? They're not fresh," Mary asked.

"They look good."

"Okay," Mary said with a small laugh. "Let's get a small orange juice—"

"Milk," Toby interjected.

Mary shook her head. "We still got a long way to go and milk won't keep in the car."

"We could get a little milk. Like they have at McDonald's and Burger King. You know, those little cartons."

"All right, you win."

A few minutes later they stood at the cash register. Mary had also picked up dry cereal to snack on throughout the day as well as a small bunch of bananas. The cashier behind the register was a plump, middle-aged woman with graying hair and a face that was used to smiling. She beamed when Mary and Toby approached. Mary wondered how anyone could be so chipper just an hour before dawn.

"Don't recall seeing you folks before."

"We're just traveling through," Mary offered. She was uncomfortable explaining herself to strangers.

"We get a lot of that, being located so close to Highway 60 the way we are." She directed her gaze at Toby. "You're up awful early, son. When my boys were your age, I couldn't get them out of bed before eight. It only got worse when they became teenagers. So which way are you headed?" the woman asked as she rang up the purchase.

"West," was all Mary said.

"California I bet," the woman said. It struck Mary that the cashier must be lonely. Working late nights when business was so slow had to be boring. "Seems everybody is going to California these days."

Mary smiled without comment and looked down at Toby. Her heart skipped a beat. Toby was no longer looking at the cashier. Instead, he was looking out the large windows of the front wall. His eyes were wide and his body stiff.

"Toby?" Mary said as she turned to follow his gaze. A man was entering the store. He was tall and painfully thin. Black stubble sprouted along his chin and a ragged, untrimmed mustache hung on his lip. He wore army khakis and a Houston Astros ball cap. His strides were long and purposeful, his mouth taut and his eyes narrow.

Mary was immediately afraid.

She started to say something, but the man was upon them before she could form the first word. He drew a large gun and pointed it at the cashier who, at first, didn't see him. The gun shook wildly in the man's hand.

"Open the register." His voice was ferocious and loud. Drops of spittle flew through the air, borne by the force of his words.

The cashier turned and then screamed.

"Shut up. Shut up. Shut up." The man was ranting. Mary could see his rheumy eyes were rimmed in red. His pupils were so wide his eyes appeared black. He pulled his lips back in a sneer, revealing yellow and brown teeth. "Don't make me shoot you."

"Okay, okay," the cashier whimpered.

The man swung the gun around and pointed it at the young man buffing the floor. "You. Get over here. Now, now. Get over here."

The young man hesitated.

A shot erupted and the air was filled with the miasmal, acrid smell of gunpowder. Mary's ears rang from the explosive report.

It missed the employee by a yard. Mary couldn't tell if the gunman had planned to miss or was just too agitated to shoot straight. The employee switched the machine off and dropped the handle. He raised his hands above his head and slowly walked toward the attacker. He stopped near one of the empty registers.

"On the ground! Get on the ground. Do it now! On the ground." His words were hot and erratic, and his eyes flared wide when he spoke.

Drugs, Mary reasoned. *Drugs or insanity.* Either way there would be no reasoning with him. Mary reached for Toby. He wasn't there. She turned and looked down at the spot where he had been standing only a moment before. He was gone. Her already pounding heart thundered. Where was her boy? Frantically she scanned the store, but there were too many things in the way, too many racks and registers and displays. Toby could be anywhere. She prayed that he was hiding somewhere safe.

"Open the register," the man commanded loudly. "Open the register, open the register."

The cashier turned to do just that when the sound of the automatic door opening caught her attention. Mary heard it too and turned to see who was unlucky enough to walk into the store in the middle of a robbery. She saw two men in their early twenties stroll into the market. They each wore jumpsuit uniforms and were talking loudly.

The gunman spun and leveled the pistol at the two men, who caught sight of him just in time to duck. The glass door behind them erupted into a million shards of glass and rained down on the two. One man swore, the other screamed; both ran back out the opening.

A hot stream of curses poured from the robber's lips. He was angry and frightened when he entered the building; now he was furious.

"The register. Open it now."

A small bell chimed as the cash register door opened.

"Take out the money and put it in a bag. Hurry up. In a bag. Put the money in a bag."

The cashier complied. Mary could see her hands shaking as she took a plastic grocery bag and began filling it with money.

"That's not enough," the man shouted. "Open the other registers."

"They're all empty," the cashier whispered. "We only use this register at night."

"Open the other registers . . . *now.*"

"I can't," she shouted back in fear. "I don't have a key."

"I said—" He stopped abruptly. His eyes narrowed, then he charged forward, grabbed the woman by the hair, and pressed the gun in her neck. "I'll kill you, lady. I really will. Open the other registers." Mary could see the barrel of the gun dig into the woman's flesh.

The woman broke into tears. "No, please don't. Only the manager can open the registers."

"What about a safe? You got a safe?"

"Yes. In the manager's office. Don't hurt me. Please . . . please don't hurt me."

"Where's the office? Where's the office?"

A small voice was heard. "Hey, mister?"

Mary's heart plummeted at the words. It was a voice she knew better than her own. Acid poured into her stomach. She felt ill and faint; her legs wobbled. It was Toby's voice she was hearing. She snapped her head around to see him slowly walking toward the gunman. Somehow he had left her side and walked around the adjoining register and counter to make his way to the expanse that separated the checkout area from the front windows.

"Toby, come here," Mary cried.

Toby ignored her. He took another step. "Hey, mister?" His voice was calm and even, not reflecting the thick atmosphere of terror that saturated the store.

The attacker turned, stared at Toby for a moment, then cocked his head to one side. He seemed confused. His eyes darted from Mary to Toby to the clerk on the floor then back to Toby. "Shut up, kid. I'll hurt you—hurt you real bad. Do you hear me? I'll hurt you like you ain't never been hurt before. You got that?"

Toby still showed no fear. He held out his hand, palm up, as if waiting for a piece of candy or gum. "Can I have the gun?" Then, as if an afterthought, he added, "Please?"

Mary watched her son for a long moment, then started for him.

"Don't be stupid, lady," the gunman spat. "I'll kill you where you stand . . . or I'll kill that boy . . . or I'll kill this woman. I'm gonna kill somebody tonight."

Mary stopped midstep, paralyzed by the threat.

Toby took another step forward, his hand still before him.

The gunman redirected his pistol, pointing it at Toby's head. "I'll blow them blond curls right off your head, boy. You best stay put."

"Toby," Mary pleaded, "don't move." Tears streamed down her face.

Toby didn't look at his mother. He didn't look at the cashier. Instead, he stared deeply into the gunman's eyes, as if seeing into the criminal's brain.

"What you looking at, boy?"

"You're scared," Toby uttered.

"No such thing. I'm not scared of anything. Not scared. Hear? Not scared."

A distant, tenuous wailing rang in the air—a pitch that rose and fell rhythmically. Police sirens. The two young men who had narrowly escaped a bullet a few minutes before must have called for help. Would the police make it on time? Mary wondered. *Oh, God, please let them get here in time*.

"You don't need to be afraid," Toby said. "It's gonna be all right. You'll see. Can I have the gun, mister?"

"I ain't givin' my gun to nobody," he answered. "I certainly ain't givin' it to no stupid little kid."

"Please, don't hurt him," Mary pleaded. "He's just a boy. If you let me, I can just pick him up and go away. We won't be no bother."

"Stay where you are," he shouted. "Nobody moves. I gotta think." He tapped the pistol on his head.

The sirens sang louder as they approached. This time the gunman heard them. Mary could see him tense, looking as much like a trapped animal as a madman. He was like a guitar string strung too tight. She knew he could break at any moment, and if he did—

"It will all be better if you give me the gun." Toby took another step forward.

"No, it ain't. Nothing can make it better. You don't know what you're talking about."

Toby advanced another step. Mary saw the hammer of the gun pull back as the man slowly squeezed the trigger. Toby was looking down the barrel standing no more than six feet from the crazed robber.

"Toby, *stop!*" Mary ordered.

Red and blue lights splashed on the front windows. The man snapped his head around at the sight. Mary started forward. The man returned his attention to Toby, saw Mary's movement, and squeezed off a shot. The bullet ricocheted off the aging linoleum floor, gouging a deep crease in the material and the concrete beneath it. Mary screamed, the cashier wailed. The ululation of police sirens pierced the air.

"No, no, no," the man screamed uncontrollably. "It ain't supposed to go this way." He returned the barrel of the gun to the cashier's neck. Mary saw her wince and knew the barrel was hot.

"Don't be scared, mister," Toby said firmly. "It's gonna be all right."

"No, it's not. The police are here. They're gonna kill me first chance they get. They've been after me for years."

"No, they won't," Toby said. "They will help you."

"I don't need no help."

"Yes, you do," Toby insisted.

"Toby, hush," Mary pleaded. "Please hush up."

"It's okay, Mom. He's just mixed up. The police will help him. They will take him someplace to make him feel better."

"I feel fine, boy."

"You're worried. You're sick, mister. But you're gonna get better soon."

The man fell silent. Mary could hear his coarse breathing.

"You have a daughter who wants to help you, too."

"How . . . how do you know about my daughter?"

Toby shrugged. "I just know."

The automatic doors to Mary's right slid open and several policemen entered slowly, their weapons extended before them. One officer carried a shotgun. The store had two sets of doors at the front. The police entered through the right side, sandwiching Toby between them and the gunman. One officer must have realized the problem and sent the patrolman with the shotgun back outside. Mary could see him move across the front of the building, his eyes fixed on the attacker.

"Let's not do anything stupid, buddy," one of the officers said loudly. He stood in the lead, his gun held steady on the man. The cashier was still in the clutches of the attacker, who used her as a shield.

"Back off," the gunman responded with a growl. "I'll waste her. I'll waste her. I'll kill her good." He was repeating himself again.

"Can I have the gun, mister? Please."

"Step aside, son," the policeman firmly.

"If he moves, I'll do the woman."

Mary saw the officer with the shotgun enter through the other pair of doors. He leveled the weapon at the man's back, but Mary knew that he could not shoot as long as the cashier was held captive and Toby was in the line of sight.

"They won't hurt you, mister. They'll help you."

"Fat chance—"

Toby started forward. Mary pleaded, the police shouted, but Toby strolled forward as easily as if he were walking through the doors of a school, his gaze fixed on the dirty, frightened man before him. When he was close enough to touch the cashier, Toby extended his hand again. This time he said nothing; he just continued to gaze into the man's wide manic eyes.

A fresh silence descended. The air was charged. Mary's heart seemed to seize in her chest. Fear burned in her mind, and Mary started forward, but then froze. The man was moving the gun. He pulled it away from the cashier's neck, then lowered it toward Toby. The gun continued its slow descent in the man's hand until it was level with Toby's head.

"Don't do it!" one of the officer's demanded.

But the gun continued down. A half second later, the gunman released his grip and the gun swung on his finger, held only by the trigger guard.

"Here kid," he said as he released the cashier. She scrambled away.

Toby took the gun in his hand, and the man fell to his knees, his face buried in his palms. He began to weep, his shoulders shuddering with each sob. "I'm sorry. I really am. I'm sorry. I'm sorry. I'm sorry."

Mary raced forward but an officer beat her to Toby. He lifted the boy off the floor while simultaneously snatching the weapon from his hand. Two other officers charged forward, knocking the attacker to the ground. The man offered no resistance as he was handcuffed.

Mary was by the officer's side a step later and pulled Toby from his arms. The officer said, "That's one brave kid you have there."

Tears prevented Mary from replying.

"His brain is sick," Toby said.

"What?" the officer asked

"His brain is sick. Right here." He pointed to the right side of his head.

"He has a drug problem," the officer replied. "I've arrested him before."

"His brain is real sick," Toby insisted. "He needs to go to the hospital. Will you take him to the hospital?"

The officer studied Toby for a moment.

"I told him that you would help him," Toby pressed. "You're a police officer. You're supposed to help people. That's what my mom told me."

The officer smiled. "How old are you, son?"

"Six."

"I have a boy who's six years old. He kinda looks like you."

"He would want you to help the man."

"I suppose you're right," the officer admitted. "I'll make sure a doctor looks at him, son. It's the least I can do for you." He paused, then added, "That was very brave, son, but not very smart. You could have been hurt."

"He didn't want to hurt anyone. His brain is just sick."

Mary held Toby tight, convinced that she could never let him go again.

Toby clung to his mother's neck as she stepped away from the sobbing man on the floor. He watched as the policemen roughly adjusted handcuffs on his wrists. Toby felt sad for the man. He was so scared, so confused. He needed help. The policeman said he would get help and Toby believed him.

Everyone had been so afraid, but Toby knew that it would be all right. He always knew things that others didn't, and he often wondered why.

Suddenly he tensed. He did so with such intensity that his mother stopped and turned. "What is it, Toby?" When his mother turned, Toby had to jerk his head around to see that which had captured his attention.

An icy chill of fear crawled through Toby. He shuddered.

"What is it, Toby? You're shivering."

Toby didn't answer. He couldn't. It was back. The same thing he had seen before. It was back and it was staring at him, despite its lack of eyes. Toby squeezed his mother's neck.

"It's okay, Toby. The bad man can't hurt us now. You're safe."

But Toby wasn't looking at the handcuffed man on the floor. He was looking at a dark, blurry, faceless thing standing over the man. The policeman that was searching the gunman's pockets took no notice of the figure, nor did the other officers. It was as if it wasn't there, but Toby could see it. Why couldn't they?

The figure was dark and lacked any substance. To Toby it was like a shadow of a man without the man. Although it had no face and where the eyes should have been there were only holes, Toby knew it was looking at him, and that it was angry—very, very angry.

"What is it, Toby? You're choking me."

Toby looked at his mother and saw the concern on her face. It saddened him to see it. He turned his attention back to the thing.

It was gone. Toby looked around the store. No thing. No it. No smart shadow. It had disappeared as quickly as it had arrived.

"Don't run off, ma'am," one of the officers called. "I have to get your statement."

Toby shuddered again and laid his head on his mother's shoulder, but was too afraid to close his eyes.

chapter 7

When Wellman strolled into his studio one hour before the next broadcast, he immediately knew something was wrong. The expression on Rudy's face was the giveaway. He looked irritated, several steps past annoyed.

"What's up, Rudy? You look like you just got an audit notice from the IRS," Wellman said, closing the door to the producer's studio behind him. He held a blue file folder in his hand.

"Him," Rudy answered, nodding at Wellman's studio. Wellman looked through the glass partition that separated the two work areas. A man sat in his studio chair reading a magazine.

"Who's that and what's he doing in my chair?" Wellman snapped.

"He wouldn't give me a name. He said he had a message for you and that it was none of my concern. I felt like popping him one."

"Why didn't you?" Wellman said.

"I didn't want to spend the night in jail."

"I would be happy to serve as a character witness at the trial."

"Thanks," Rudy said, "but I think I'll just skip all that. I told him you didn't have time for visitors or fans. I don't think he's either one."

"Really? What do you think he is?"

Rudy shrugged.

"You don't suppose he's from that hospital in Missouri?"

"Could be," Rudy replied. "He didn't seem too happy with me, and he wouldn't leave."

"How long has he been here?"

"About ten minutes. You want me to call the police?"

"Not yet," Wellman said. "Let's see if I can't get rid of him." He removed three sheets of paper from the file and handed the folder to Rudy. "We have three new spots to lay down and put in the rotation before we air tonight. These are your copies. Go ahead and set up the carts. I want to get on them as soon as I evict our friend."

"Do you want me to go in with you? Maybe you shouldn't be in there alone with him."

"No. Just keep an eye on things. He might be a nut case."

"Turn your mike on when you get in there," Rudy said. "That way I can listen in. You never know when you might need a witness."

"Good idea."

Wellman snapped open the door between the two studios faster and harder than was needed, but he wanted to set the tone. The man in the chair rose and straightened his suit coat. He was wearing a dark blue suit and a bright yellow power tie. To Wellman, he looked like a banker or a senator. He extended his hand. Wellman ignored it, choosing to walk past the man. He laid the papers on the console, his back turned to the unwanted guest. Subtly, he activated the studio mike switch.

"Mr. Wellman," the man said. "My name is Melvin Torr, and I need a few moments of your time." His voice was smooth and his words carried an aristocratic English accent.

"I believe my producer told you that I was busy."

"He did, indeed, sir. Nonetheless, I must speak to you."

"Mr. . . . ."

"Torr."

"Mr. Torr," Wellman said brusquely, "I am a man of limited time. I go on the air in less than an hour, and I have several important matters to deal with before I do. I'm afraid I don't have time to visit with you."

"And I'm afraid you don't understand."

"No, I'm afraid *you* don't understand," Wellman interjected. "My show is heard by millions of listeners. Each of them would like a few moments of my time. A few moments multiplied by a few million listeners . . . you do the math."

"I'm not a listener."

"All the more reason I shouldn't be talking to you."

"We're going to talk, Mr. Wellman," Torr stated.

"Is that a threat, Torr? I can have the police here in a matter of moments."

Torr stepped to the console and picked up the handset to the multiline phone. "Shall I dial for you?"

Wellman turned and faced the man, not believing his audacity. He was tall, at least three or four inches above Wellman's six feet. "What?"

"I can call them for you, if you like. The police, I mean."

"Look, if this is about the hospital video, then I can't help you. I don't have it. I just put it out on the net."

"I don't care about that," Torr said, replacing the hand piece. "I know about it, but I'm here on other business."

"Business? Business has to do with money."

"Indeed it does. I have ten thousand dollars with me. It is yours for thirty minutes of your time."

"Ten grand. Why am I having trouble believing that?"

Torr reached inside his front coat pocket. Wellman took a step back. For all he knew, the man was reaching for a weapon. Torr smiled, showing perfectly aligned white teeth, and removed a banded bundle of money. He held it out to Wellman. "Thirty minutes."

Wellman extended a hand, but Torr pulled the cash back. "Privately." He nodded at the console. Wellman knew what he meant.

"It's okay, Rudy. I need to talk to this gentleman." Wellman flipped the mike switch to off. To Torr he said, "Okay, you have my attention."

Torr set the cash on the console, then placed his hands in his pockets. *He is cool,* Wellman thought. That realization made him uncomfortable. What kind of man can waltz into someone else's place of business, demand an audience, and then lay down ten grand?

"I represent a California businessman who is in need of your services."

"What's his name?"

Torr shook his head. "Not so fast, Mr. Wellman. I can tell you that he is legitimate and well thought of. He is also quite wealthy."

"If he can pay ten grand for a half-hour's conversation, he must be rich."

"Money is not a concern of his, as you will see."

"What does he want with me?"

Torr gave the kind of smile that men in the know give to those outside the loop. "He wants to hire you. He needs your help."

"Your employer needs the help of a radio host? Can't tune in my show? Need help with his radio?"

The smile evaporated, and Wellman knew he was crossing the line of Torr's patience. There was something about the man in the suit that unsettled him. Wellman had played poker since high school and had quickly learned that the quiet players were the ones to fear. He had also learned to judge a man quickly. There was an ill-defined danger about Torr.

"The task is a little more serious," Torr said, his voice barely above a growl. "My employer believes that you can help him find someone."

"Who?" The comment surprised Wellman. He didn't know what to expect, but this certainly wasn't it.

"The boy."

"The boy? The boy in the hospital? The tornado boy?"

"Precisely."

Wellman's show had been dominated the last two nights with discussions of the blond boy. The "hospital miracle," as it was now being called, had generated tremendous interest, but last night's discussion of the vanishing tornado had sent things through the roof. Every line had been busy for every minute of the program. Callers were left holding for hours and into the wee hours of the morning. His Web page had received so many hits that his Web host had threatened to cut access unless Wellman paid for the additional work.

"You understand what I'm asking, Mr. Wellman?"

"Yes, of course. I just don't understand why you're asking me for help. I'm not a private detective. I'm a radio host."

"Exactly. That makes you the best man for the job."

"I don't see how."

"Think about it, Mr. Wellman. If my employer hired a private detective, then he would have one man looking for one boy. A boy, I might add, that appears to be on the move. Missouri one day, Oklahoma the next. Even if he were to hire an entire firm of investigators, he would have a dozen or so people searching the country. But you, Mr. Wellman, you have resources like few others."

"My radio program."

"Exactly. A well-worded request by you could bring great results."

"And speedy results."

"I think you understand."

"Let's see if I do. You want me to go on the air and ask my listening audience to help track down the boy?"

"Track down is a phrase I would avoid. It sounds too much like a manhunt."

"Isn't that what we're talking about?" Wellman asked. "What does he want with the boy?"

"I'm not free to discuss that."

"I expected that answer." Wellman sat in his chair, the only one in the room, leaving Torr standing just three feet away. "So I go on the radio, say that we need to find this kid—"

"No," Torr interrupted. "It's very important that your words carry no terms that could be perceived as conspiratorial. It is best that terms like 'we' and phrases such as 'must find' be avoided."

"What approach do you have in mind?"

"Simple and direct. Put the conspiracy on others. Your listeners like conspiracies."

"My listeners are not stupid, Torr . . . at least not most of them." Wellman paused, leaned back in his chair, and thought. "It could be done," he said. "It's all in the presentation. The boy is in danger. We—and by that I mean everyone associated with my show—need to help him. He must be found before the 'others' get him. Is that what you had in mind?"

"In essence, yes."

"I don't know, Torr. It's a little underhanded and it means a whole lot of work for Rudy and me."

"The pay is good."

"How good? More than ten thousand dollars good?"

"My employer pays well. If you find the boy in a month, he will deposit to any bank you choose, one million dollars. If you find him in three weeks, then you can expect two million. Find him in seven days and you'll be ten million dollars richer than you are now. You can pay your producer whatever you wish."

"Ten million dollars?" Wellman whistled.

"If you need staff to help, to answer phones or whatever, I'll make sure that you get them. So what do you think, Mr. Wellman?"

Wellman grinned. "I think you've come to the right place."

Mary stepped reluctantly from the tub of warm water and bubbles and dried herself off. She had already showered once that day, but she still felt dirty. Three days and nights in the car without a bath had made her feel as grimy as if she had been working in the garden back home. Her house back in Lincolnsberg had no indoor plumbing, but it did have a large clawfoot tub in which she would spend as much time as possible. It was hard work hauling water in from the well, filling the tub, and boiling water to warm it, but it was worth every minute of effort. Here she had sat in a modern tub, with hot and cold running water. Mary considered spending the rest of her life there.

When the police had finished asking their questions, Darla Deerborne, the cashier, had approached Mary with an invitation to return home with her. "After all, this little boy saved my life." She reached down and patted Toby on the head.

At first, Mary had refused, insisting that she needed to get back on the road, but Darla was insistent and could not be dissuaded. "You're in no shape to drive, honey," Darla had said. "You're shaking like a leaf in a storm."

Mary had been. Her stomach was churning and she had felt like she would throw up. Her hands trembled and she couldn't stop crying. "You come home with me and I'll fix us some breakfast and then you can sleep as long as you want. It's just me now, ever since my Harry passed on. I could use the company. Truth be told, I'm still shaken up myself." The temptation of food and a bed had proved too much for Mary. Her resolve crumbled, and she accepted Darla's invitation.

True to her word, Darla had scrambled eggs, made toast, and cooked sausage patties. Toby had eaten hungrily. Mary had to force herself to eat, commanding her stomach to settle. After breakfast Mary had accepted Darla's offer of a shower, but only after she had seen that Toby was clean first. She had drawn a bath for him. He took little time in the tub, having noticed that Darla had several shelves of books. When Mary took her turn in the shower she had left Toby on the floor of the living room surrounded by several books.

Afterwards, Mary and Darla visited for a few minutes. Darla sat in a thickly cushioned loveseat while Mary reclined on the sofa. Mary learned that Darla was a widow with two children, both grown and gone. She worked at the store to pass the time and spent her free moments doing volunteer work at her church and the local community hospital. The conversation had been short. Mary fell into a fitful sleep midsentence.

She awoke four hours later, groggy, and with an unsettling sense of dislocation. It took a moment for her to remember where she was. Glancing about the living room, she found Toby still on the floor, still surrounded by books and fast asleep. Next to him was a small plate with a half-eaten peanut butter and jelly sandwich on it.

With Toby asleep, Darla had suggested a bubble bath. Mary had put up only mild resistance. Now she crossed the house and found Darla in the kitchen washing the breakfast dishes. Toby was still snoozing on the floor.

"He's still asleep," Mary said.

Startled, Darla jumped. "Mercy," she said. "You scared me."

"I'm sorry."

"I guess I'm still jumpy." She turned off the water and wiped her hands on a pink hand towel. "How was your bath?"

"Real fine," Mary replied. "I coulda' stayed there all night."

"We've been through a lot in the last few hours."

"Did you sleep?" Mary asked.

Darla shook her head. "I usually sleep in the late afternoon. It's a habit I got into when I started working the graveyard shift. Can I get you something to drink?"

"No. How long was I in the tub?" Mary asked.

"About half an hour or so. For such a young boy, he sure likes to read."

"He's smart," Mary said with pride. "He'd read all day if he could get away with it."

"I'm going to fix myself an ice tea. Sure you don't want one?"

Mary declined again. "You've been very kind to us."

Darla laughed. "I'd probably be dead if it wasn't for Toby. I thank God for him. When I think of what might have happened ..." Mary watched as Darla fought back the urge to cry. "I keep seeing him walk up and ask for that man's gun. Just like he knew everything that was going to happen. It's unbelievable."

Mary followed Darla back into the living room. Once seated Darla said, "I hope you'll stay the night. You need the rest. I can tell that just looking at you."

"I should go," Mary answered.

"California will still be there," Darla said. "Unless someone is expecting you. A husband maybe."

Mary cut her gaze away. "No, no husband. No one a waitin'." Mary was suddenly awash in loneliness. There was no one in her future, and only one person in her past—a person she hoped never to see again.

"Then one more day won't matter. I'm not working tonight. That cowardly manager gave me the night off. It's the least he could do."

A smile crossed Mary's lips. Darla had had some sharp words for her manager, a young man not yet through his twenties who had hid in his office during the attack. "It was fortunate that those two men called the police."

"Something my manager could have done if he weren't such a—" Darla cut herself off. "I suppose he was as frightened as I was."

"Don't let him off the hook so fast." Mary studied Toby as he slept on the floor. A small pillow lay under his head, put there, Mary assumed, by Darla.

Darla studied Mary for a moment. Mary could tell that she wanted to ask another question, probe a little deeper, but was holding back. "Where did Toby learn to read so well?"

"He comes by it naturally, I think," Mary said. "I taught him some, but mostly he learned in school back home."

"He can't be much past the first grade," Darla said.

"He started talkin' real young. I sent him off to first grade, but he already knew how to read and write. He was way ahead of the other kids. He got bored, so I let him stay home and help me. He reads everything."

"Do you have a place to go in California?"

Mary shook her head. "But I got plans." Actually she had no plans but to put miles between her and Toby's father.

"I see," Darla said, but Mary was sure she didn't.

Toby stirred and then sat up. He looked around the room and saw his mother on the sofa. "You woke up," he said, rubbing his eyes.

She smiled. "And so did you."

He got up and crawled onto the sofa by his mother. "Can we stay here tonight?"

"I don't know, hon," Mary said.

"I really would love to have you, Mary," Darla said. "You could use the rest, and I could use the company. I don't much feel like staying alone tonight. I'd consider it a favor if you stayed."

"I don't want to sleep in the car again, and besides, she has books." Toby pushed out his lower lip. It was a fake pout he used when he wanted to get his way. Artificial as it was, it always worked.

She pulled him close to her and hugged him. "All right. We'll stay the night—but just this one night. Okay?"

A wide smile crossed Toby's face. "Okay. Just one night." He wiggled from her grasp and sat back down on the floor surrounded by the books he had gathered from Darla's shelves.

"That's a hard book, Toby," Darla said. "That was written for adults. I may have some children's books from when my kids were your age."

"That's okay," Toby said. "I like this one."

"But that's a history book," Darla said. She turned to Mary. "My husband was nuts about history books. Read them all the time."

"This book is fine," Toby said. He then lowered his head and began to read.

Darla looked at Mary with surprise. Mary shrugged.

chapter 8

L et me see if I understand," Thomas said, leaning back in the old oak secretary's chair that Pratt used for guests who visited his office. The chair matched the rest of the furnishings, making the small room seem more like a museum of 1950s office furniture than the workplace of a twenty-first century theology professor. "This new grant would allow me to study full-time without my having to hold down a part-time job."

"That's correct," Pratt said. "No more mopping floors." Thomas worked part-time for a custodial company that serviced banks and office buildings. The work allowed him to attend classes and study during the day, work a few hours at night, then return home to study more and rest.

"Tempting," Thomas said. "And the only string is that I have to declare my intent to pursue an academic course rather than prepare for church ministry."

"Yes," Pratt said. "There's no restriction on church work. You can still be a pastor if you want, but it would be ancillary to your research and teaching."

"That would be hard to do," Thomas replied. "Can they really make that kind of stipulation? What if I change my mind? Why would they care?"

"The man who set up the grant wanted to help train scholars, those who can add to the theological body of knowledge as well as train others. He wasn't opposed to students entering the ministry; he just felt that the Christian community needed more scholars who could do solid research. There are not many who fit the bill. As far as changing your mind, I suppose you could do that at any time. There's no contract to be signed. It's on the honor system."

"What would keep someone like me from signing up just to get the free ride?"

"Nothing," Pratt answered quickly. "The candidate is selected by the president of the school and chairman of the theology department."

"You and Dr. Edison."

"Correct. Do you feel a call to the pulpit ministry?"

Thomas rocked the old chair, which squeaked with each movement. His large frame taxed the seat. Sitting next to Thomas made Pratt feel small. He was thin and trim, while Thomas's body still showed the results of his football and wrestling days in college. "No," Thomas said abruptly. "I'm not sure what a call would feel like. I've heard other students talk about God's call on their lives, but I've never understood it."

"Then why choose the ministry?" Pratt asked, confused.

Thomas shrugged. "I like the study of theology; I'm drawn to it."

"But there is much more to being a minister in a church than understanding theology."

"I know," Thomas said. "But I needed to put something down on my application."

"So you're not drawn to the ministry?"

Thomas shook his head. "Not really. I don't even attend church all that much. It seems a little shallow. Not like what I get here. In some ways, your class and the others are my church."

"I see," Pratt commented softly, mulling over what Thomas had said.

"Is there a problem?"

"No. Not really. I just thought you had your heart set on the pulpit."

"I don't know what my heart is set on," Thomas admitted. "I'm still searching."

"But—"

"Don't misunderstand me, Dr. Pratt. I'm not saying I'm an agnostic or an unbeliever. The issue of belief was settled in my heart years ago. I'm searching for a deeper meaning to my faith. I want to know more, to dig deeper than others. I'm not content to paddle around in the shallows when there is a whole ocean of faith to explore."

Pratt understood. Many Christians were happy to believe everything they were taught. Unbelievers often refused to believe anything no matter how persuasive the evidence. Some, like Thomas, were people of faith and intellectual hunger. No matter how much they knew, no matter how intricate the information they mastered, they still needed more. Pratt not only understood, he empathized. There was so much more to faith than Sunday school lessons and sermons.

"I understand," Pratt said. He too had thought the ministry was his calling, only to learn a few years later that he had no talent for it. He had been the pastor of a small Baptist congregation of one hundred people in Corona, California. The church members were supportive and encouraging, but Pratt had never felt comfortable. For two years he had taught them, preached to them, visited in their homes, performed funerals and weddings, and conducted all the church business, but he did so always feeling like a fish out of water. The pulpit always seemed alien. Each Sunday he would awake with a knot in his stomach and a chilly fear in his heart. He knew he didn't belong. Pratt had admired his colleagues who moved so smoothly through the day-to-day challenges of ministry. Some seemed born to the work, but no matter how hard Pratt had tried to fit in, to make things work, he never could. Two years after his ministry began, he resigned in front of a shocked and tearful congregation. Thirty days later, he was back in school, pursuing a Ph.D. It was there that he found his genuine love and what he believed to be his real calling: teaching. Twenty-two years later, he had not looked back.

"My goal," Thomas said, as if revealing a long-held secret, "is to see God working."

"We can see that every day," Pratt began. "All we have to do is look around—"

"That's not what I mean," Thomas interjected. "I'm not talking about seeing God in nature. I'm looking for the undeniable evidence of the Creator's existence. I want to see his hand reach out and do something that can't be rationalized away."

"You're talking about miracles."

"In some ways, yes." Thomas leaned forward in his chair. "I hunger to see the power of God."

"You can't see that in nature?" Pratt inquired. His professorial tone had risen. "That's the very essence of natural revelation. We've talked about this in class."

Again Thomas shook his head. "You taught about it in class, but we didn't discuss it. I believe in natural revelation. I believe that God has revealed himself through creation in general and specifically through the Scriptures, but it's all *a posteriori*—after the fact. I'm looking for something more immediate."

"A before-your-eyes miracle."

"That would work."

"You're looking for authentication of your belief," Pratt suggested.

"No. Not authentication. Experience."

"The religious leaders of Jesus' day saw miracles, and it had no impact on them."

"True," Thomas said, "but those same miracles changed the lives of others. Don't you ever hunger for something a little more concrete in your faith, something a little more dynamic?"

"I think we all would like to see an overt expression of God's power," Pratt conceded. "I—" The phone on Pratt's desk rang. He answered it before it could ring a second time. A moment later, he said, "Dr. Edison wants to see me. Shall I tell him you'll take the grant?"

"Yes," Thomas said. "I'd be insane to turn it down."

"Great." Pratt stood. "I think you've made the right decision. Maybe we can carry on this conversation later."

"Maybe." Thomas rose and shook Pratt's hand.

Burdick ached from the inside out. The pain was not localized—
he hurt everywhere equally. Breathing was difficult, every breath
coming as if it first had to travel through a wet towel. Pain shot
through his body with every gasp. A small tired voice spoke from
the back of his mind, urging him to give in, to let the cancer have
its way, but Burdick silenced it with the steely determination of a
man who refused to surrender anything in his life. If death wanted
him, then it would have to come and drag him off. But death
wouldn't visit today. Despite his discomfort, he knew he had several more months to live. Nothing was going to deprive him of that.
Nothing.

"Perhaps I should go," Melvin Torr said. He was standing next
to the bed upon which Burdick lay.

Burdick had returned home from two hours at the office. He
did so because he could remain no longer. He had to lie down. Sitting was too exhausting today. Once home, his nurses had helped
him to bed and given him morphine. He slept. Three hours later,
he summoned Torr.

"I can see this is one of the bad days," Torr said.

"They're all bad days," Burdick said. "And they're only going
to get worse."

"Maybe with some more rest—"

Burdick cut him off with a feeble wave of a hand. "I've been
resting."

"Perhaps some more pain medication, then."

"No. It fogs my mind. I want to be as sharp as possible now.
Any word from Wellman?"

"No, sir, not yet."

"You made our point clear to him?"

Torr nodded and clasped his hands behind his back. "I did. He
took the money. He mentioned the . . . need last night."

Burdick nodded. He had tried to listen to the program, but the
pain medication made it impossible to stay awake. Some days the
cancer seemed to take a break and Burdick could function normally. Those times were becoming rare, being replaced by greater,

unrelenting pain which required stronger meds. Burdick wondered when he would reach the point that his mind would be so clouded that he would no longer be able to control his own destiny.

He still considered suicide—euthanasia, they called it. For enough money someone would certainly aid him in taking his own life. He pushed that thought aside. If the kid was for real, if he could actually heal people, then Burdick had to meet him. What did he have to lose? Some might think it a desperate act of a dying man, but so what? If he was wrong, if the kid was a fake, Burdick would soon be dead, and a man couldn't hear the sneers and mocking laughter of others from the grave.

"Do you think it will work?" Burdick asked. He so desperately wanted assurance.

"There's a very good chance, sir. Your idea is sound, and Wellman has the means of reaching tens of thousands of listeners. He can do more in one night than a hundred private detectives could do in a month."

"But will it be enough?" Burdick wondered aloud.

"It may take some time, sir," Burdick offered. "It's a big country."

"We don't have to search the whole country. We know two places the boy and his mother have been and when they were there. They're definitely moving west. Besides, I don't have time. That's a luxury for the healthy."

"Yes, sir."

"What else have you done?" Burdick shifted weakly in the bed.

"I have hired a string of private detectives, one from each town we know the boy to have been in and one from each major town along the path we assume them to be traveling. Unfortunately, we don't know if they're traveling by freeway, or taking lesser traveled roads. Nor do we know their destination. They may have stopped moving already. If so, our work is going to be all the more difficult."

"We know they're traveling by car," Burdick said.

"True. One of our private detectives asked some questions around the hospital in Jefferson City. He found the ER doctor who treated the boy. He said a car door had closed on the boy's hand."

"Hence the car," Burdick said.

"Correct. We also can see the car in the Oklahoma tornado video. Unfortunately, we can't make out the license plate number, but we do know that it is a 1974 Pontiac Catalina Safari station wagon. That's what the private eyes are looking for."

"A car that old should be easy to spot."

"We think so."

"What else?"

"I'm afraid that's it so far, sir."

Burdick closed his eyes and took several shallow breaths. All his money, all his power, all his influence, and the one thing he needed remained out of his reach. It was a cruel joke for life to play on him. He was a man of talent, insight, and purpose. Not like the average people who surrounded him. He produced something worthwhile. His company fed thousands of Americans each day from the produce of his corporate farms. And here he lay on an expensive bed in an expensive house watching his life slowly ebb away like water leaking from a pail.

"Stay on Wellman, Melvin. I want you on him like white on rice. Pay him more money if you have to, but don't let him ease up. Not for a minute. I want that boy found as soon as possible. Do you understand?"

"Yes, sir, I do."

"Good," Burdick said. "Now please send in one of my nurses."

Torr walked from the room. He knew Torr to be a good man, competent in everything he had been asked to do. Always loyal, always astute, and always successful. He could even be dangerous if need be. Burdick trusted him more than he trusted any other man. But he wondered if that would be enough.

chapter 9

Well, it's just after the witching hour," Wellman said into the microphone, "eight minutes past midnight here in the beautiful desert of Arizona, making it a brand new day. You folks on the East Coast have a few hours head start on us out here. Wherever you are in this great land, you're listening to the Richard Wellman show. Speaking of the witching hour"—Wellman nodded to Rudy in the control booth—"we have something special for you tomorrow night. Judithe—that's spelled with an *e* on the end—is going to be with us during the second hour. Now get this, Judithe is a self-professed witch. Big deal, you say? It's true, we have had witches on this show before, but this is different. Judithe says that she is a consultant to major businesses around the world. They hire her to predict the future and even put spells on the competition. So I suggest you join us," Wellman lowered his voice as Rudy turned up the reverb and cued some eerie music, "or she may put a curse on you."

Wellman released a hearty laugh. "The key to talk-show business, at least our kind of talk-show business," he had said to Rudy many times, "is not to take yourself too seriously. Be serious when you have to, but don't forget to have some fun."

"Okay, folks," Wellman said, "we have Joel from Amarillo on the line with us. How are things in the great state of Texas?"

"Um, hi, Rich. Things are weird."

"Really? How so?" Wellman took another look at the monitor upon which Rudy had placed the caller's name. He had also written "strange robbery."

"Well, I'm one of the night managers of an all-night grocery store and I listen to your show when I'm doing paperwork. Well, I heard you say earlier that you were looking for that little blond kid."

"That's right, Joel." Wellman leaned over the console before him and listened intently, his attention riveted on Joel's every word. "You think you may have seen him?"

"Yeah, I'm sure of it. He was in my store last night."

"Really. How do you know it's the same boy?"

"After I heard you talk about it, I put two and two together. I had been to your Web site before and saw the video from the hospital and the one from those video guys who taped the tornado. Well, I saw the boy after the robbery, but things were so weird and hectic because of all that happened . . . well, I just didn't make the connection."

"Are you saying the boy was involved in a robbery?"

"Yes . . . I mean, no. He wasn't with the robber, but he disarmed him."

"The boy?" Wellman was confused. Often, people would become nervous on the radio and he would have to guide them through their story. They either talked too fast and skipped important details, or offered too little for Wellman and his listeners to understand. Over the years he had learned how to draw out the particulars. "The boy disarmed a gunman who had come into your store?"

"Yeah, that's what I mean. The guy, the gunman, was nuts. I mean he was truly out of his gourd, or hopped up on some drug. He was screaming and giving orders. He put his gun to the head of one of my cashiers and threatened to blow her brains out."

"And you were there through all of this?" Wellman asked.

"Yes."

"Face-to-face with the gunman?"

"No, not face-to-face. I ... I was in my office. My office has a window that looks out over the store. It's got a mirrored window so that I can see out, but people can't see in. Most grocery stores have them."

"I've seen them," Wellman said. "Part of the store has two floors and the upper floor has offices. It allows employees to see what's going on in the store, right? Watch for shoplifters—that kind of thing."

"Exactly."

"Okay, so you see this robbery occur. What happens next?"

"Well, that's the weird part. I watch as I'm calling the police, and the guy with the gun is going ballistic ... I mean he was nuts, screaming and shouting. I knew he was going to kill someone. I just knew it. All of a sudden, this little blond kid walks up to him and holds out his hand, like he's asking for candy. At first, the guy starts screaming again, but then a few minutes later, he gives the gun to the boy, falls to his knees, and starts weeping like a baby."

Wellman turned to face Rudy, who stared back at him through the thick glass that separated their studios. Standing next to the producer was the aristocratic Melvin Torr. Internally, Wellman objected to the man being in his studio, but he couldn't argue with the money. Wellman supposed the man had a right to see that he was getting his money's worth. As long as he stayed on the producer's side and out of his area, he could live with it—for a while. Torr had his head cocked to the side listening to the program as it poured out of the speakers above Rudy's head.

"So everyone is all right?" Wellman asked.

"Yeah, thanks to the kid."

"That's great. Glad to hear it." Wellman paused for less than a second as he gathered his thoughts. That was all the time he was allowed. Dead air was the ghost that haunted all radio professionals. It simply was not to be allowed. "Let me ask a couple of questions. Does your store have a video surveillance system?"

There was a pause. "Um ... yes."

"You don't sound very sure."

"It wasn't working that night," the caller said. Wellman shook his head. Most likely it hadn't been working for some time. "The tape machine had broken down and it was being repaired. The police wanted the tape, too."

"No problem," Wellman consoled. He already had two decent videos. A third would be useful, but there was nothing that he could do about that. "So the police did arrive?"

"Yeah, a few minutes after I called. Someone else called, too. I think it was the customers the guy shot at."

"He fired his gun?"

"Yeah, didn't I mention that? Two guys walked in and the robber squeezed off a shot. Broke the glass in the entrance door. They took off real quick."

"Who can blame them? Did the police talk to the boy?"

"Yes, and his mother."

Wellman had a hundred questions, but most he wanted to ask off the air. "So the boy just talks the gunman into surrendering his weapon?"

"I guess so. I couldn't hear what they were saying."

"That's right, you were in your office." *Cowering in fear, no doubt,* Wellman said to himself.

"Did you get to talk to the boy?"

"Yes. He was a quiet kid, and his mother seemed a little over-protective."

"What mother wouldn't be in that situation? What was your impression of him? Did they say where they were going or staying?" Wellman cringed. He was letting his excitement get the best of him, and he was compounding questions. *Slow down,* he chastised himself. *One step at a time.*

"No. I didn't ask."

Again Wellman turned to Rudy. Torr was pacing behind the producer, a cell phone pressed to his ear.

"Fascinating story, Joel. Hang on the line, we've got to take a break." Actually, he had eleven minutes before the next break, but he wanted to ask some questions off the air. "We'll be right back

with Joel from Amarillo after we hear from some of our sponsors."
Wellman punched a glowing red button that indicated he was on
the air and the button went dark. "Hang on just a sec, Joel," he said,
putting the caller on hold. Next he spoke into his mike knowing
that he could be heard only in Rudy's studio. "Give me five minutes with this guy."

"That will leave you only six minutes until station break."

Station breaks were "hard breaks," and couldn't be pushed to
different times. Every hour the local stations that carried the show
were allowed time to air local advertising spots. Since that had to
be done from their respective locations, Wellman had to break right
on time.

"Can't help it," Wellman said. "I need five minutes with this
guy."

Torr leaned over Rudy's shoulder and spoke into his microphone, "I want to hear this, too."

Wellman nodded. "Make it happen, Rudy. The man's paid for
it." Turning back to the phone, he released the hold button and said,
"Thanks for the call, Joel. You're making this a great show tonight.
I wanted to ask you a few more questions, but some I didn't want
to ask on the air."

"Why not?"

"A lot of people listen to this show, and I don't want them
swarming your store looking for things that aren't there. The store
owners might not like that, and it could make both our lives miserable. My lawyers are always warning me about that kind of thing."

"I hadn't thought about that."

"I'll put you back on the air for a few minutes before I have to
move on to another caller. Okay?"

"I guess."

"Good." Wellman began a string of questions, all of which Joel
dutifully answered. Where was the store located? Did the police
file a report? What condition was the boy in? What was his mother
like? Did he or the police get a license number from her car? Did
he see them drive off? What could he tell them about the car they

were driving? Why were they in the store? What kind of goods had they bought? The five minutes passed quickly, too quickly. "Okay, Joel, we're about to go back on the air. We'll talk for a couple of minutes, then I'll let you go. You've been a super guest." *And a most useful one, too,* Wellman thought.

Mary felt ill and considered pulling the car off the road, but she pressed on. Toby was in the backseat asleep. He had spent the day reading some of the books that Darla the cashier had given him, but when the sun had set and he could read no longer, he once again began to stare at the sky. One day, she would buy him a book about the stars, she told herself. Maybe, if her luck changed and she could find a decent job, she might be able to save up and buy him a small telescope. That dream, however, seemed far away and impossible to reach. Still, she drove toward that dream, toward California where, for no reason she could determine, she believed her and Toby's future lay.

For the last two hours, Mary had fought sleepiness. Since leaving Darla's house that morning, she had put several hundred miles behind her. Now she felt weary and wished she had stayed one more night with Darla. One day's rest had been insufficient to wash away the profound weariness and stress she had experienced over the last week. She so wanted to find a place to rest, to shut her eyes even if for a few minutes, but she pressed on. They had been losing time each day, and she was eager to get to the West Coast. Reaching forward she turned on the radio. It poured out loud static like water from a faucet. Turning the dial, she tried to find a station. The radio was old and worked only intermittently. Mary had learned that if it cut out, she could slam her fist on the dashboard and it would come back to life. She figured a wire was loose somewhere. A voice, smooth and resonant, came out of the speaker. Mary sat back, gazed into the coal-black night, and steered the old Pontiac along the freeway.

"Well, you've got to admit," the voice was saying, "that there were some strange things happening in Amarillo."

The words seized Mary's attention and her stomach roiled. *He can't be talking about the store,* she told herself, knowing that she was wrong.

"Joel gave us a lot to think about," the man on the radio said. "Strange, maybe even supernatural, but that's what we deal with here on the Richard Wellman show. All of this brings me to a point: Out there, somewhere, in the gloom of the night, is a young boy and his mother. They seem alone, maybe even lost. As I said last night, we can help. If you know how to contact these two mysterious travelers, let me know. I want to help. That's my sole motivation, folks, to help. In fact, I want to send a message out to the two wayward travelers: Call me. I can help you. I want to help you. My listeners want to help. I know the world can be a pretty scary place. We talk about that six nights a week here on the Rich Wellman show. Call me. I mean this with as much sincerity and concern as a man can feel, let us help you." He gave a number to call, one of those easy-to-remember 800 numbers: 1-800-HELPBOY.

He was talking about them. Mary couldn't believe it. How could he know? How many others knew about them? The realization came like a punch—thousands knew. It was on the radio for everyone to hear.

"I know it's hard to trust strangers," the man was saying, "but sometimes the best help comes from those you don't kn—" The radio went dead. Mary swore and slapped her hand down on the dash twice before the radio came back to life. ". . . and I mean that from the bottom of my heart. This is the Richard Wellman show and it's open lines tonight, folks. Give me a call and tell me what's on your mind."

"What are you listening to, Mom?" Toby asked from the backseat.

Quickly, Mary turned off the radio. "What are you doing up? It's late."

"I heard a loud noise."

Mary frowned. "That was me. You know how the radio is. You have to show it who's boss. Go back to sleep."

Toby climbed into the front seat. "I'm not sleepy anymore."

"You need your sleep."

"I'm okay. I want to look at the stars."

She shook her head. "You and your stars." Mary fell silent as she thought about what Richard Wellman had said. His appeal sounded sincere, but Mary was slow to trust anyone. She had plenty of reason not to.

"Where are we?" Toby asked.

"New Mexico. I saw a sign that said 'Santa Fe' a few miles back."

"It's different than Texas."

"We're higher now. Up in the mountains."

Toby nodded. "I like the trees. It reminds me of home."

Home, Mary thought. *That place hadn't been home since Daddy died.* Where they had lived would never be home again. She could never go back, even if she wanted to, which, she assured herself, she didn't. "You ain't gettin' homesick, are you?"

Toby shrugged in the pale light. "Just a little, maybe."

A new sadness swallowed Mary. It had been her decision to leave, to run away. She hadn't discussed it with Toby, never given him a reason for their sudden departure. He never asked for one. He simply did as his mother told him. His obedience, his unquestioning support convicted her. Sure he was young, but he was smart, smarter than most adults she had met. He could understand, maybe he already did. But to talk about it, to mention the drunkenness of his father, the cruelty of the man who had so often promised to marry her but only gave harsh words and physical abuse, hurt far too much to remember and to discuss. To speak of it gave it life, transforming it from unpleasant memories into present-tense terror. The stubble-covered face of Tobias Kinkade appeared to her every night, haunted every dream. It was as though his grizzled features had been engraved on the inside of her eyelids. In the late-night hours of the past few days she imagined she could see him in the rearview mirror, sitting in the backseat with a short, hand-rolled cigarette tucked into the corner of his mouth. His eyes were red and narrow as if holding back an ocean full of fury, ready to be released the moment Mary spoke. The thought made her shiver. Fear crawled up her spine.

"That place ain't home anymore, Toby." Mary spoke softly. There was sadness in her words.

"I know," he said, his face directed out the side window. "I knew that when we left."

"I'm sorry, Toby. Real sorry. I know these past few days—"

"Don't be sorry, Mom. There's nothing to be sorry about. What is, is. That's all there is to it."

Mary felt burning tears lace her eyes. She took a deep breath and tried to calm herself. All she wanted was to get away, to have a new start, but it was all going wrong. They had little money, and now they were talking about her and Toby on the radio. "It's going to be all right, Toby. Everything is going to work out just fine."

"Maybe," Toby said.

The New Mexico terrain glowed under the light of a half-moon, and Toby watched it gallop by in a continuous procession. He tried to focus on the trees or the dark buildings as they appeared out his window only to disappear again. He wondered who lived in those lightless structures. What did they do? Why did they live here? He stared at the stars again. They were there, always there. Over the last few days things had changed. They had traveled from city to town, from state to state. The landscape changed, the people were different, but the stars remained the same. He could depend on that. At night, when the sun had finished its work, the stars would take their places in the sky and move slowly across the black background; he could gaze skyward and find them in the same place they were the night before. There was a sense of peace and certainty in that, a sureness that brought him comfort.

Lowering his eyes, Toby studied the road in front of them. It was four lanes wide, and his mother was driving in the far right lane. The dashed line that separated the lanes flickered past. Toby counted them for a while until his eyes became heavy. Leaning against the door, he rested his head on the window. He could feel the vibration of the engine and the road work its way through his body. Sleep was hovering just above him. He closed his eyes, and then willed them open again.

It was there in the road. In the middle of the lane. Standing there. Staring through absent eyes. Unmoving. Defiant.

Toby sat bolt upright. "Mom!" He raised a hand and pointed at the road before them.

His mother jerked her head around. "What? What is it?"

Toby felt the car slow.

"I don't see nothin'," his mother said.

The car charged forward, its speed only slightly reduced by the sudden release of the accelerator.

Still it stood. Still it stared. Empty eyes, unblinking. Shadow body, unmoving.

One second followed another and they motored forward. The distance between the Shadow Man and the car reduced to nothing. Toby raised his hands to shield himself from the impact.

Nothing.

"Toby, what is wrong?" his mother demanded.

Toby opened wide eyes. The man-thing was gone. Toby scrambled to his knees on the bench seat and looked behind him. In the pastel moonlight, he saw the shadow-thing-man still standing in the road, staring back at them as they drove off.

"What's the matter with you, boy? What'd ya' see? An animal?"

"No, not an animal," Toby said.

"What then? I didn't see nothin'. Maybe you had a bad dream."

"Maybe," Toby said shallowly. Toby felt very, very cold.

chapter 10

When the sun began its daily climb into the summer sky, Pratt was awake to greet it. He had, in fact, been awake for several hours. Sleep had come to him late the night before and departed long before he was ready. In the darkness of his bedroom, he had lain on his side, gazing at the dim moonlight that fought its way past the tree outside his window and through the narrow slits of the blinds. Occasionally he would hear the muted passing of a car, driven by someone whose job required a very early start. In those still, near-silent hours, Pratt let his mind churn, ruminating on the events of the past few days. Only one thought seemed important; only one haunted him: Thomas York.

Every few minutes, Pratt replayed in his mind the meeting he had had with Thomas, and each time he replayed the scene he became more uncomfortable. What was there to feel uncomfortable about? Thomas had said nothing that should raise red flags in Pratt's mind. Indeed, he had been eager to receive the grant. Still, there was something in his manner, something hidden not in the words, but behind them, like a forest that conceals the creatures within it. Perhaps it was Thomas's keen intellect that was troubling him, but Pratt dismissed the idea.

Thomas was different than the other students and not just in his intelligence or talent. There was a spiritual dynamic that was too nebulous to identify. Thomas spoke easily of biblical matters. He understood the terms, was well acquainted with the Bible, and knew more theology than most college graduates, but that indefinable something was still missing. *Was that what was troubling him?* Pratt wondered.

Perhaps it was something else. Thomas was seeking the miraculous in his life. What was it he had said? "My goal is to see God working." *Not a bad goal,* Pratt reasoned. Any believer would want to see the power of God in any fashion, but Thomas seemed intent on discovering that for himself. Pratt had met others with the same desire, many of whom became frustrated with their faith and chased after strange doctrine. Could such a thing happen to Thomas?

What else had Thomas said? "I'm not content to paddle around in the shallows when there is a whole ocean of faith to explore." At first Pratt had thought the statement a finely tuned phrase, something a preacher might say, but he soon realized that there was much meaning stacked behind those words.

As the dark of the predawn surrendered to the pressing light of daybreak, a new and troubling realization surfaced in Pratt's mind. What troubled him was not Thomas but a nerve that the student had struck. Was he, Dr. Aaron Pratt, professor of theology, paddling around in the shallows? Did he still have the youthful zeal to know and experience God that Thomas York possessed? A disturbing thought began to ache in his soul. He could recite scores of Bible passages, converse intelligently about church history, and shed light on every nuance of theological debate. So what? Did that make him a good Christian? Because he understood the deep arguments of theology, did that make him a true servant of Christ?

Pratt sat up and pulled the chain on the small lamp by his bed. The light evicted the darkness of his room. *When was the last time I had an encounter with Christ?* he wondered. No answer came. *I lead a good Christian life,* he told himself. *I educate young minds so that they can take the gospel to the world.* True. All true, but it brought him no comfort. His prayer life was limited to short expressions before each class he taught. All of his Bible study revolved around his teaching. Church life was secondary to him, he had to admit. *How ironic,* he thought, *that I should wonder why Thomas is not involved in church, when I do little more than he.* Pratt was a member of a large nearby Baptist church. He enjoyed the preaching and the singing, but his involvement was limited to one hour on Sunday morning. Was he any different than Thomas in that respect?

It occurred to him that what had troubled his sleep had not been his concern over Thomas's spiritual well-being, but his own. Thomas had struck home without trying, and Pratt had just now realized it. The question was serious. Each school day he stood before a gathering of men and women who had come to learn all they could about God and then go into the world to serve him. Some would become teachers, others ministers, and still others missionaries on foreign and sometimes dangerous fields. He taught them earnestly year after year, filling their heads with knowledge that he had hoped would blossom into wisdom. Yet what of his own spiritual journey? Was he the teacher standing in the shadows of his students? Their zeal was fresh, fed by godly ambition and a belief that they could make a difference; his zeal had been replaced by the comfort of monotony. He taught the same lesson plans, assigned the same books, and remained the same person he had been a decade before.

Pratt did not challenge his faith or salvation. Those he knew to be alive and well. The working out of his faith was another matter. That was what had become stale and insipid. Faith was a muscle, and underused it was doomed to flaccidity.

Slipping from the bed, Pratt entered the master bath and started the shower. He had some thinking to do, and he did that best under a cascade of hot water.

Mom!"

Mary snapped her head around. A loud, blaring sound erupted somewhere to the left. "What?" Another horn. Mary yanked the wheel hard to the right, then to the left, narrowly missing a pickup truck that crossed a few feet in front of her. The screaming of tires filled the air. Mary saw that they were in an intersection, cars bearing down on them from both sides. She didn't remember entering the crossing.

The squeal of tires was replaced with loud curses. A man in a white sedan angrily shook his fist. "You nuts, lady?"

"I'm ... I'm sorry," Mary said, but the words were confined to the car, where only she and Toby could hear them. The traffic around them ground to a stop, and Mary pressed the accelerator and steered the car through the crowded juncture. Her heart tumbled erratically and she gasped for breath. "What happened?"

"You fell asleep," Toby said. "I told you, you were tired."

It came back to her. She had driven all night, not wanting to stop, not even for sleep. Toby had kept her company for several hours. Although he seemed agitated and fearful, he had fallen back to sleep about three that morning. It had been her plan to stop in the next town or city for coffee. The next town turned out to be Albuquerque, a city much larger than she had expected. She had left the freeway and found herself surrounded by tall buildings, lost in a maze of structures and confusing streets. If she weren't so sleepy, she might have been impressed by the city. As it was, she struggled to keep the car in the lane.

A new sound caught her attention: a whoop of a siren. Mary saw the blue and red lights of a police car behind her. In embarrassment, she looked around. The downtown streets were packed with cars; the sidewalks bustled with people starting a new day's work. Each person she saw was staring back, some with confusion, some with annoyance.

The siren whooped again and Mary's pulse quickened all the more. Frantically, she searched for a place to pull the car over. She found one a half block away. The space was in the shadow of a midrise office building. Tears were welling in her eyes. "What do I do? What do I do?"

A loud tap exploded near her ear. A policeman dressed in a dark blue uniform was tapping the glass with a large ring on his right hand. "Roll the window down," he said. Then, as if an afterthought, he added, "Please."

Mary complied, slowly turning the handle on the door until the window was all the way down. Her mouth was dry. She could think of nothing to say.

"I assume you know why I stopped you," the officer said.

Looking up, Mary saw a tall man with a young face, who looked to be in his mid-twenties. "Because I almost hit that car." Mary's words were weak.

"You ran a red light," the officer said perfunctorily. "Not only that, but you did so at the height of morning traffic. You're lucky someone didn't plow right into you."

"I'm sorry," Mary said. "I didn't mean to."

"May I see your driver's license, registration, and proof of insurance?"

It was the question Mary feared. "I . . . I don't got a license."

"You don't have a driver's license?"

Mary shook her head.

"Is this your car?"

"Yes, sir. I didn't steal it. I bought it with my own money."

The officer looked over the car and grimaced as if he had seen something unpleasant lying in the road. "Where did you buy it?"

"Back home in North Carolina. Lincolnsberg, North Carolina."

"I'm pretty sure they require a driver's license in North Carolina, ma'am. May I see the registration form, please."

"I don't have one of them, neither."

The officer sighed. "I need you to step from the car, please."

"Why?"

The officer opened the door. "Step out of the car, ma'am, and stand on the sidewalk."

Mary did as she was told. Pedestrians walked by and stared. She felt conspicuous and awkward. She smoothed her old dress. The officer joined her on the walk. Pulling a microphone that was attached to the lapel of his uniform to his mouth, he spoke, combining words and numbers into a sentence that Mary barely understood. She did hear the phrase "female officer." "Is that your son in the car?" he asked.

"Yes, sir. We're traveling to California."

"Why California?"

"It's far away from Lincolnsberg," she wanted to say. Instead she offered, "I think I can get a good job there."

"You have relatives there?"

"No."

"California is a big place, lady. It is no easier there than anywhere else. Have you ever been arrested?"

The question caught Mary off guard. "No. Of course not."

"Are you aware of any warrants concerning you?"

Mary had no idea what a warrant was. "No."

"Are you using?"

"What?"

"Your eyes are red and you seem disorientated. Are you using drugs?"

"No," Mary snapped. "I don't use no drugs. I was jus' sleepy 'cause I've been driving all night, and I'm not used to driving in the big city."

"Do you have any identification at all?"

Mary shook her head.

"Nothing at all? No checkbook, credit cards, pay stub, nothing?"

"Nothin'."

"What's your name?"

"Mary Matthews."

The policeman's radio that he wore on his belt came to life. He listened, then responded with "10–4."

"We have another problem, ma'am. The car comes back as registered to a John Links."

"Johnny Links," Mary said. "That's the man I bought the car from. He lives about two miles from my place in Lincolnsberg."

"Well, it's not reported as stolen, but you're still driving without a license, in a car that is registered to someone else, and you have no identification."

"Can't I just go, Officer? I'm real sorry for running that red light. Nobody got hurt."

The officer looked back to the station wagon. "What is your son's name?"

"His name is Toby."

"What else do you have in the car?" the officer asked. Mary felt that he was stalling.

"Just a few of our things. Some clothes for Toby, a few pots and pans and things like that. It's all we have."

Another white police car pulled up and parked just in front of Mary's station wagon. A woman officer got out and approached them. Mary felt even more apprehensive. Everything had slipped from her control. All because she nodded off for a moment. If she hadn't done that, they would be on their way out of Albuquerque. "This officer is going to pat you down. It's just for your safety and ours."

"Pat me down?"

"Turn around, ma'am," the female officer said. Her voice was firm but not unkind. "Raise your arms to the side, please. This will only take a moment."

Passersby stared. A few shook their heads. The search took less than ten seconds, but it felt like half an hour.

"Do you mind if I search your car, ma'am?" the male officer asked.

"Why do you want to search my car?"

"Do you have anything you're hiding from me?"

"No, but ..."

"May I have permission to search your car?" the officer asked again.

The sound of the car door opening caused both officers to turn. Mary watched as Toby pushed the heavy door open. "Stay in the car, son," the first officer said.

Toby ignored him and exited the vehicle. He was looking skyward.

"Toby, do as the policeman tells you," Mary said with a quaver in her voice.

Toby ignored her as well. Instead, he stepped onto the concrete walk and pointed upward. "Look."

The officer did, and swore loudly. Mary turned and looked up the tall building and saw what had captured Toby's attention. Twelve stories up was the silhouetted image of a man standing on the parapet of the building. The man wavered from side to side and occasionally forward and back—too much forward and he would fall. Mary raised a hand to her mouth. Behind her, she heard the officer speak into his radio. He spoke quickly, excitedly. Mary heard the term "jumper."

The sun was behind Cliff Blackwell, its rays warming his back. An already hot wind circulated around him as if caressing him in an embrace of air. His senses were in overdrive. He could smell the dust and tar of the roofing material behind him and hear the steady roar of traffic from the streets below.

Below.

Twelve stories below his feet. One hundred and twenty feet, give or take. It was enough to do the job. One step, and it would all end in the passing of a second. There would be no pain. A moment's terror followed by the bliss of nonexistence. He had thought it all out. This was the easiest way for him. He didn't have the courage to use a gun, and he feared poison might do something less than kill him. Jumping was the best, most logical course of action. And he was nothing if not logical.

The parapet upon which he stood was six inches wide and rose two feet above the roof. The heels of his brown wingtips hung over the edge on the roof side while his toes hovered over empty air. Cliff took a deep breath and closed his eyes. Death was near, just seconds away. There was no need to rush, no need to hurry, he had an eternity to spend in a grave.

A brief moment of satisfaction filled him. It was something he had not felt in six months. Six miserable, lonely, depression-filled months. Half a year without his wife Donna; half a year without his eight-year-old, fawn-haired daughter, Jenny. Half a year of hell and anguish and sorrow and doubt. Ten years of marriage had been carried away in the cab of a Dodge Ram pickup truck, driven by a man Donna found more exciting, more alluring than Cliff. The divorce had been wicked, dripping with animosity and accusation. His lawyer had told him that he had won. He had kept the house, the money, the stocks, everything but his eight-year-old daughter. Cliff had not won. He would gladly have swapped everything he owned to see his daughter's smile daily. He had not seen it in the last half year.

He had tried to keep things together, tried to live a normal life. He showed up at his job each day, did his civil engineering work, even put in overtime, but when the day was done, he had to return to a house empty of life and joy.

Women found him attractive, and he had dated twice since the divorce, but he could talk of nothing but Jenny. Words flowed about her dimples, her contagious laughter, and her desire to be a dancer. The women had been patient, kind, and understanding, but he found no allure in them. His depression grew, taking him in, swallowing all that was precious to him, like a black hole absorbing all matter and light around it.

Cliff's employer had suggested seeing a counselor and mentioned that the health plan covered such things. Cliff told him he would make the appointment. He never did and knew he never would. The engineering firm that Cliff worked for employed close to fifty people. Several had been divorced. Two of the men had taken him to lunch to cheer him up, to remind him that life goes on and that there was a great big future ahead of him. "More starfish in the sea," they said. "True," he acknowledged, "but there is only one Jenny."

They drank their lunches from beer glasses, and what had started as an effort of "experienced" divorced men to cheer the newest initiate had ended with all three deep in despair. The men never asked Cliff to lunch again.

He had been told that things would improve with time, that he would soon feel like his old self, but each day grew longer, each minute weightier. No matter how often he resolved to be strong and to make a new start of things, he found himself weeping— sometimes in public. That mortified him.

Cliff's legs were becoming tired. Standing on the narrow ledge put an unusual strain on his thighs. He chuckled to himself. What difference did that make? Pain was inconsequential now. In a few moments, he would feel nothing.

The time was drawing close. He would have to make his departure soon. They would be there any minute, the police, the firemen, all intent on talking him out of his foolish act. *Foolish act,* he thought. *What did they know?* Could they fathom the depth of his despair? They couldn't feel the scorching pain he felt each time he looked at a picture of his daughter.

Cliff opened his eyes and looked down. When he first pondered his suicide, he doubted he had the courage to make that last and very final step. He had convinced himself that the last stride could only be made if he didn't look down. It was strange to learn how wrong he was. The distant ground below frightened him not at all. Instead it invited him to make the step. There was peace to be found down there on the concrete, and it was all one step away.

Something caught his eye: lights. Red and blue lights of police cars. Two officers stood on the sidewalk. Someone, a lady, stood between them. It didn't matter. They could never talk him out of his decision. Below him people were now looking up. Some pointed. He could hear distant voices, but the words were pressed out of shape by distance and wind. They carried no meaning.

As Cliff watched, one of the officers disappeared into the building, no doubt making his way to the elevators, calling for the building manager or whoever could help him get to the roof. It wasn't that difficult. Cliff had just taken the elevator to the twelfth floor, found the stairway, and walked up one level to the roof. He expected the door to be locked, but it opened easily.

He continued to watch the scene below. The other officer was pushing the growing crowd back. "Afraid I'll take someone with me?" Cliff asked the empty air. He had no desire to hurt anyone else. He would allow the officer another moment or two to get the crowd safely out of impact range, then he would lean forward. He wouldn't have to lean far. Once started, there would be no return.

The woman that had been standing between the two officers took a boy by the hand and started backing away. The boy looked young, but Cliff couldn't guess his age from that distance and angle. Too young to be a teenager, he reasoned. He wondered if the boy was the same age as his Jenny.

The sadness returned in a flood, deluging his mind in a wave that no dam of reason could hold. It was time to end the pain. Cliff started to lean forward when the boy pulled away from the woman and raced to the spot directly under him. Cliff had to jerk back. What was the lad doing? He could have gotten himself killed. Where was the boy's mother? She should take him as far away as possible. He didn't need to see this.

Cliff hesitated.

The boy looked up as if trying to make eye contact. The woman appeared again and grabbed her son, but he wiggled free. Snatches of her concerned cry made their way to Cliff's ears. The lone officer was still pushing bystanders back. She had her hands full.

Sirens filled the warm air. To his left, Cliff could see a fire truck arrive, followed by an ambulance. To his left, two more police cars made their way through the crowded streets.

"Show time," Cliff said feeling no humor in the comment. The boy was still struggling with his mother. "Come on, come on, kid, get out of the way." The woman gathered the lad up in her arms like she was lifting laundry. Before she could turn, the boy looked up again and waved. It was a small wave, simple and unassuming, the kind of wave a child gives to a friend.

Cliff felt something new inside him, near his stomach. A warmth, not hot pain, but a golden effulgence. He watched as the boy's mother carried him away. The lad continued to wave. With each wave, Cliff felt warmer inside. More importantly, he felt less pain, less sorrow.

"What ... what is happening?" He said to himself. The warmth tingled and spread from his abdomen through his chest, arms, and legs.

Then it touched his mind.

Cliff giggled. Then he laughed. He looked up and the sky was so blue he felt he could touch it. The air was different, too. It had been redolent with acidic smells of car exhaust and diesel fumes. Now it smelled sweet, like an orange grove in blossom. *Odd,* Cliff thought.

He looked down again. The boy was gone, lost in the gathering crowd with his mother. The drop no longer looked inviting. The desire to step out into nothing was gone. But where had it gone? Cliff had no idea, and to his surprise, he didn't care.

"Whoa, whoa, now wait a minute, buddy," a voice said behind him. "Let's talk about this first."

Cliff looked over his shoulder to see a policeman, his face drawn with tension.

With a shrug, Cliff said, "No need." He took a step backward, lowering himself from the parapet and planting both feet on the solid roof. "I suppose you want to arrest me."

The policeman stood silent for a moment. "Let's step away from the edge, and we can talk about it."

Perched in his mother's arms, Toby kept his eyes trained on the man who stood at the edge of the roof. His mother pushed through the crowd until she stood next to the driver's side door of their car. Toby could feel her shaking. He put an arm around her neck and squeezed, and she returned the embrace. As Toby watched, the man on the roof took a step backward. Some in the crowd gave groans of disappointment, but most applauded.

Toby felt good. The man would not jump. The good feeling evaporated as a new but familiar figure emerged on the parapet. No one seemed to notice it, but Toby saw it and felt it. The dark, faceless Shadow Man stared down at him from the rooftop.

His mother was crying, screaming. A woman police officer held his mother's hands behind her back and was pushing something like shiny bracelets around her wrists. Toby struggled to free himself from the grasp of the policeman that held him in his arms. Something sharp stuck Toby in the side. The policeman's badge was digging into his flesh.

"Easy, buddy. Take it easy," the officer said in soothing tones. "It's going to be all right."

"Let me go," Toby demanded and reached over the officer's shoulder, toward his mother. "Mom, Mom!"

"Toby!" his mother cried.

Toby watched with fear as the woman officer struggled to hold his mother back as she pulled and wriggled, trying desperately to break free.

"Don't let them take me away, Mom!" Toby tried to wrestle free from the policeman's strong arms. "Let me go. I want my mother. Let me go."

"It's going to be all right, son," the officer repeated. "No one is going to hurt you or your mother."

Mary broke free, but the woman officer caught her before she could take two steps. Both tumbled to the ground. Mary landed hard on the sidewalk.

"Don't take my boy," Mary pleaded. "Don't take my baby! No, no, no. Please bring him back."

Toby watched as crowds gathered around. He could see them; worse, he could feel them. Their emotions were dark, filled with disgust, pity, and even pleasure at the sight of the arrest.

"Here we go, buddy," the officer said to Toby as he set him in the back of a patrol car. "Just have a seat here and I promise that we'll get all this straightened out. Maybe we can find some ice cream for you."

Ice cream? Why would he offer ice cream? "Let my mother go. You're hurting her."

"No, we're not, son. The other officer is just helping her calm down."

Toby looked at the man and saw more than anyone could. The policeman hated his job; his wife always yelled at him; his teenage son sniffed white powder up his nose. The man hated his life and his family. "I want my mom, she loves me."

"I'm sure she does, son."

"She loves me more than you love your son."

The officer stopped. "What?"

"My mom loves me more than you love your son. I want my mother. Let her go."

The officer clenched his jaw. He then slammed the door shut. The sound of it hurt Toby's ears. Immediately Toby tried to open the door, but the handle didn't work. He tried the other door, but it too refused to operate. *Locked in,* Toby reasoned. He looked forward and saw a metal cage that separated the backseat from the front. He could not climb over the seat the way he had done so often in their car. Toby realized he was trapped.

Kneeling on the back seat, he watched through the rear window as the female officer helped his mother to her feet. "TOOOOBYYYY!"

Toby's fear turned to horror. The Shadow Man stood next to his mother and the officer. The faceless entity circled the two as his mother fought with the policewoman. Circling, circling, as if he were trying to see all sides of the confrontation. The officer who had locked him in the car jogged over to where Toby's mother struggled.

Shadow Man stopped next to the policewoman, and then was gone. For a second Toby felt a mild relief, then he realized what he had seen. Shadow Man had disappeared *into* the female officer.

In a fluid motion, the policewoman pulled a long black stick from her gun belt and raised it over her head. Even in the locked confines of the patrol car, Toby could hear her shout, "I have had enough of you." The club started down.

Toby screamed. "Noooo!"

The club never found its mark. The officer who had carried Toby to the police car had caught the woman midswing. He said something that Toby could not hear, and the woman lowered her arm. He then watched as his mother was escorted to another police vehicle.

The policewoman stood on the sidewalk looking at the nightstick in her hand. Toby thought he saw her start to shake.

The Shadow Man was suddenly beside her, except he was no longer looking at the woman officer. Instead, he directed his faceless gaze at Toby.

Mary sat on a fiberglass chair in the police station and wiped another tear from her face. Things had deteriorated quickly. She had hoped that the police officer would just write her a ticket, but they were far beyond that. "Child endangerment" was the phrase they used. "Resisting arrest" was another term she heard. She didn't resist anything. All she wanted was to reach her son. They shouldn't take a boy from his mother. Of course she tried to get away. They would have done the same.

Toby had been taken from her and placed in foster care, and she had no idea where he was. The thought of another woman caring for Toby ate at Mary. Geysers of anger and despair erupted within her. She was helpless. The more she pleaded, the less the police responded. They looked at her like she was an evil being. She wasn't a bad mother, she told herself. No woman cared more for her child than she. She had endured beatings, been ostracized, and forced to live in poverty. Now she had made it out on her own, and they took away her son. It was more than unfair—it was criminal, evil.

Where was Toby? she wondered. Who was watching him, feeding him, listening to him? Would they understand how special he was? How unique? Were they kind? Back home she had heard stories of such places, and the stories were not good. People were paid to take in kids. They didn't want them; it was a job. The children were just a means to a paycheck. Mary had no idea if such things were true, but at the moment, they seemed right.

For the tenth time she reminded herself that she needed help. The police told her she would need an attorney and if she couldn't afford one, then one would be appointed for her. What kind of attorney would that be? Would he be any less judgmental? And how long would it take? They were processing her now—whatever that meant. She did know that she would spend the night in jail, separated from Toby, all because she had been too stubborn and impatient to rest for the night.

"What have I done?" she whispered to herself. "I have to get Toby back. No matter what. I have to get him back."

A thought struck her. At first she dismissed it out of hand, but it kept orbiting her mind. Each time she thought of it, it seemed a better and workable idea. *It can't be no worse,* she reasoned.

"I need to make a phone call," she told a woman officer who sat at a desk nearby. The woman frowned, rose, and led Mary to a pay phone in the hall. A man in dirty clothes and smelling of wine passed in front of them, led by a sour-looking policeman. Mary grimaced, as did the female officer with her.

"Keep it short and to the point," the officer said. "I almost have your paperwork done."

"Then what?"

"Then we put you in a holding room and wait for bail to be assigned. If you can pay the bail, then you can go."

"What about my son?" Mary asked. She knew she didn't have enough money for bail. She had less than twenty dollars left from what she had earned waiting tables at Beau's Coffee Shop in Glennary.

"That's not my department, ma'am. Your lawyer can fill you in." The officer stood next to the phone and waited.

"I need some privacy," Mary said.

"There's no such thing around here. I can't have you wandering off now, can I?"

Mary sighed and removed a quarter from her small purse. They had searched the purse and her car, and being assured that she held no drugs or weapons, they had allowed her to keep the handbag for a while longer. She had been told that it would be held for her once she had been processed.

Mary picked up the phone and tried to remember the number she had heard on the radio: 1-800-HELPBOY. She was uncertain if she needed the quarter for a toll-free number, but she dropped the coin in the slot anyway and dialed. Four rings later Mary heard the voice of the man on the radio. "This is Richard Wellman and you've reached the Help Boy hot line. If you have information on the mystery boy, then please leave a message including your phone number. Someone will get back to you." There was a sharp beep.

"Please," Mary began. "I ... This is Mary Matthews, and I'm the one you're looking for. I ... I need your help."

When the phone rang, a sleepy Richard Wellman swore. It wasn't even noon yet and he had been up all night. He grabbed the receiver. "This had better be important," he said sourly.

"It's Rudy," another sleepy voice said. "We got the call."

Wellman bolted upright in bed. "A listener found the boy?"

"Not a listener, Rich. It's better than that."

"Stop toying with me, Rudy. I'm in no mood."

"The mother called."

"When?"

"Less than an hour ago. Jill snagged it off the service." Jill was Wellman's research assistant and aide. She spent the daylight hours pulling news stories, trivia, and guest information together for Wellman to use in the evening program.

"Outstanding. We owe her dinner." Wellman was jubilant. "Fill me in?"

"Her name is Mary Matthews and she's in jail in Albuquerque. She wants our help."

"Jail?"

"She's a little hard to understand," Rudy explained. "She kept breaking down, but it seems that they've taken her son from her."

"That's not good," Wellman said. "Not good for her, not good for us."

"What do we do next?"

"Give me a sec." Wellman's mind raced, analyzing the possibilities. "Who else knows about this? Not Torr. Tell me Torr doesn't know."

"I'm the only one Jill has called. I swore her to secrecy."

"Good. I don't want Torr to know yet. We need to verify this." He fell silent as he churned the situation over in his mind. "Meet me at the studio."

"When? Now? I've only had a few hours of sleep."

"You can sleep—" Wellman stopped short. Something had caught his eye.

"What? I can sleep next month?" Rudy said wearily.

Wellman didn't respond. Instead, he looked around the dim room, a room lit only by the light that managed to push past the heavy drapes of his bedroom window.

"You still there, Rich?"

"Yeah, I'm still here," he said slowly. Reaching for the lamp on the nightstand by his bed, he switched on the light. He saw nothing unusual, nothing out of place. Still, he felt anxious. "I thought I saw something."

"In your house?"

"Yeah, in my bedroom. A shadow or something. I thought it was a man at first."

"Probably someone you owe money. Maybe you should sleep a few more hours."

"Nice try, Rudy. I'll see you at the office in one hour. Better get someone to cover for me tonight. Chuck Michaels will do it. He owes me." He hung up before Rudy could finish groaning.

There was a smell that Mary found unsettling. The jail was full and reeked of too many people in too small a place. The only good news of the evening was that she had not been placed in a holding cell—yet. Instead, she had to sit on a long wood bench. Behind it, a metal pole ran along the wall. Three other people shared the bench with her, each handcuffed to the metal bar. At least Mary was no longer handcuffed. Someone had taken that much pity on her.

Mary wanted to see Toby. She wanted to hold him, comfort him, and then get back on the road. But she had no idea where he was, or even where they had taken the car. She was alone, lost, and intimidated by everything she saw. Uniformed officers joked across the room, and Mary felt they were laughing at her.

She felt dirty. Not just from the days spent on the road, but also from the way the police treated her. They didn't look her in the eye, they wouldn't answer her questions, they just led her from place to place, to be questioned and fingerprinted. Now she waited, waited and hoped.

The man who answered the phone when she called the 800 number said that someone would get hold of her to let her know what to do. That had been four hours ago. No home. No money. No lawyer. No way out. The new life Mary had hoped for seemed impossible now. She had no reason to live without Toby. Mary shook her head in an effort to dislodge the despair that crawled through her mind. She would get Toby back, she vowed. Some-how, someway, she would get him. She'd travel any distance, pay any price, and if need be, break any law, to get her son.

They were brave thoughts fueled by a mother's desperation, but they were just thoughts and she knew it. Toby remained as far out of reach as possible. She needed a miracle.

Why had they taken him? She was a good mother. She didn't have fancy clothes and she got confused in big-city traffic, but that didn't mean she didn't love her son. He always had food. Maybe not the best food, but he never went hungry. She made sure of that. He always came first in her life. Couldn't they see that? So what if they lived in their car?

"Ms. Matthews?"

Mary looked up. A man with a slight smile and bright eyes stood next her. "Yes?"

"Ms. Mary Matthews? Correct?"

His voice sounded familiar, yet different. "Yes, sir, that's me." He wore a brown polo shirt, white pants, and expensive-looking sneakers.

His smile broadened. "I'm Richard Wellman. You talked to one of my staff on the phone."

"The radio man?" Mary said with excitement. "You drove over here to help me?"

Wellman laughed. "Yes. I'm the man from the radio, and I'm here to get you out of here, but I didn't drive. I live in Phoenix so I chartered a private plane. I didn't want to waste time on the road."

"What about my son?" A small flicker of hope began to burn within her.

"I wouldn't forget him, Ms. Matthews. Not for a moment. You can trust me on that. I'll get you two back together."

"They said I attacked that policewoman, but I didn't. I was jus' tryin' to reach my boy. They stole him from me, said I was a danger to my child, my own flesh and blood, but I ain't, Mr. Wellman, I ain't at all. We may be poor, but we love each other. I'd sooner give my own life than let one hair of my boy be hurt."

"I know that, Mary. May I call you Mary?"

"Yes, sir."

"You don't have to call me sir. Just call me Rich or Richard. I don't care which."

"Yes, sir. Can you really get my boy back?" Mary asked. "Are you a lawyer, too?"

"No, Mary, I'm something far worse than a lawyer. I'm an angry radio host. Let's just see how much of this the mayor and chief of police want me to air on my radio program. I think we can strike a deal."

"Surely?"

"I think so," Wellman said. "Come with me."

"They told me to stay here."

"It will be all right."

Five minutes later, Mary and Wellman were sitting across a desk from an officer with white hair. He was a man with sad eyes and a face full of wrinkles. He seemed weary from a life of too much stress and too little joy.

"How can I help you, Mr. Wellman?" the officer asked.

"You're the watch commander, is that correct?" Wellman asked. He seemed so smooth, so sure of himself that Mary allowed herself a little more hope.

"That's me. What's this all about? Why does a radio talk-show host want to see me?"

"I'm here to predict your future, Officer," Wellman replied.

"My future?"

"Oh, yes," Wellman said. "Do you know what Tarot cards are?"

"They're like playing cards except people use them to forecast the future," the commander answered. "It's all nonsense, of course."

"Of course. That's why I brought a different set of cards." He reached into the pocket of the shirt he wore. Mary could see that they were small white cards. "Instead of Tarot cards, I'm going to predict your future with business cards. Take this one, for example." He set one card down on the table. "This card belongs to James L. Burke, attorney at law. He practices in Los Angeles. He's going to represent Ms. Matthews in her lawsuit against the city of Albuquerque."

"Are you trying to intimidate me, Wellman?" the officer said. "Because if you are, it isn't going to work."

Mary shot a glance at Wellman. The officer was now angry, and Mary was afraid that things were about to get worse. Wellman just smiled and put down another card.

"This card belongs to Frank Lawrence, also an attorney. He will be representing the boy. This card belongs to Bill Jenkins; he will be representing me in my lawsuit against the city and against you."

"You have no valid grievance against us," the officer objected. "On what grounds would you sue?"

"We're dealing with lawyers here, Officer. I'm sure they can find some grounds for a suit. You know how litigious attorneys are. Why, some would sue Mother Nature if it rained on their golf day."

He laid down two more cards. "These will be bringing suit also. I know that once all this gets in court that the judge will combine all the cases into one, but that's okay. By that time, your office and the offices of the mayor, city attorney, and the chief-of-police will be filled floor to ceiling with paperwork. Have you ever been sued, Officer?"

"No," he snapped in response.

"I have," Wellman said. "It was a real estate deal that went bad. But here's the kicker. I wasn't involved. Some other guy with my name failed to honor an agreement. You know what? It cost me forty thousand dollars just to prove I wasn't the guy on the contract—forty big ones, Officer. Fortunately, I pulled a card out of my hat." He leaned forward and pushed the card across the desk. "It was Mr. Jenkins's card, to be precise. I got my forty thousand back, and some to ease my troubled soul. Now let me ask you: What crime—I mean *real* crime—has Ms. Matthews committed?"

"You're not her attorney so I don't have to answer that."

"Here's what I propose," Wellman said, ignoring the officer's comments. "I propose that you release Ms. Matthews and her son into my custody. I will see that both are well taken care of."

The officer looked at the cards then back at Wellman. Mary could tell he was thinking.

Wellman broke the silence. "Officer, I'm not here to make your life more difficult. I'm not here to make threats. I just want you to know what the future holds. Let her go and you can go home tonight with one less problem on your mind."

The phone on the watch commander's desk rang. He answered it, listened, and then hung up. "The mayor," he mumbled.

"That's right," Wellman remarked, slapping his forehead. "I forgot to mention that my producer was calling him to set up an interview. We wanted our national audience to hear why the city of Albuquerque is forcibly separating a child from his mother."

Mary watched as the tired police officer closed his eyes. When he opened them, he said, "It will take thirty minutes to tidy up the paperwork, then you can go."

Mary squealed with joy.

Wellman looked at her and smiled.

"Thank you, Mr. Wellman," Mary cried. "Thank you so much. If I can do you a courtesy sometime, you jus' tell me."

"I'll keep that in mind," Wellman said. "I will certainly keep it in mind."

BOOK II

fame

I saw the tears of the oppressed—
and they have no comforter; power
was on the side of their oppressors—
and they have no comforter.

ECCLESIASTES 4:1

chapter 11

He doesn't look very happy," Rudy said.

Wellman cut a quick glance at Toby, who sat at the head of a large table, a two-tiered birthday cake towering in front of him. Stacked next to his chair was a pile of gaily wrapped gifts. Children ran around the expansive banquet room squealing in delight at the antics of a white-faced clown who was adroitly making animals from balloons. "The clown should pay more attention to Toby."

"He tried, Rich. I watched him. Toby wouldn't have anything to do with him."

"Maybe he's tired," Wellman suggested.

"He has a right to be," Rudy replied. "You've kept him busy for the last year. Busier than most corporate executives."

"He's a special child. He's changing the world."

"He's still a child, Rich. A child should enjoy his birthday party."

"I know that," Wellman snapped. "He may be a little sober now, but he'll come out of it. Look how much we've changed his life. Less than a year and a half ago his mother was in an Albuquerque holding cell and Toby was on his way to a foster home. I rescued them from that. Now look at him. He's clean, well fed, loved, and doesn't have a care in the world. He can have anything he wants. And his mother . . ." Wellman nodded at the woman who stood next to Toby. She was well dressed, wearing a blue vest and pleated pants. Her hair was shiny and full, unlike the dirty, oily mane with which he had first seen her. Her rail-thin body had lost its anorexic appearance but still remained fashion-model thin. Her face and arms were tan from the California sun. Gone was the poor backwoods mountain look. Now she looked like a native of the island community. "Let's just say, she's blossomed."

"No argument there," Rudy said. Blossomed seemed such an inadequate word. Mary had metamorphosed into a beauty, and not a single male head on the island had not been turned by her. "I just worry about Toby. This isn't a normal lifestyle for a boy."

"There's no such thing as a normal lifestyle anymore, Rudy. Our lives aren't close to being normal, but that doesn't mean they're bad. In eighteen months we've built a thriving enterprise that not only helps people, but makes money . . . a lot of money. Toby is the key to all of it. Without him, we would still be doing late-night radio. That was a good gig, but it's nothing like this."

"I suppose."

"Just look around you, Rudy. How many children's birthday parties have you seen like this? We've rented the biggest banquet hall on the island, filled it with forty of our key employees and their kids, and hired a band, a clown, and a magician. Toby is sitting next to hundreds of dollars worth of gifts. We're certainly not abusing him." Wellman raised a glass of punch to his lips. "He lives in a great house on the compound, has a view of the ocean, all the books he could ever want—"

"But he has no friends," Rudy interjected. "A boy should have friends."

"We're his friends. Burdick is his friend."

"We're adults, Rich. Burdick is way beyond middle-age. Toby needs children his age. It's part of his social adjustment."

Wellman shook his head. "Look at him, Rudy. He's surrounded by kids his age and takes no interest. Toby is no ordinary boy; he's extraordinary. He has an intelligence that dwarfs anyone we are likely to meet. And he has a power to change lives. Just ask Burdick. He broke into tears at first sight of him. Burdick was frail, his skin was yellow, and his body eaten with cancer. He didn't have one foot in the grave—he was buried up to his neck. Then I brought him Toby. You should have seen it, Rudy. It was amazing. No, beyond amazing. He just stood in Burdick's bedroom, the old man lying on the bed gasping for breath, drugged half out of his mind with morphine. Three minutes later, the old boy is sitting up weeping like a baby."

"I've heard the story before," Rudy said.

"What is with you?" Wellman barked just loud enough for Rudy to hear. "You are part of all of this. We're a team. Together, with Burdick's money, we have built an institution: The Church of New Jerusalem. Ten thousand dues-paying members strong and more being added every day. Twice a week, masses of people come to see Toby and pay handsomely to do so. In return they get faith and some get help. Our book is selling like hotcakes; audiocassettes and CDs are doing even better."

"I want to show you something," Rudy said and started toward the balcony of the second-floor banquet hall.

"Where are you going?"

"Let's step outside for a minute," Rudy answered. Wellman followed and a dozen steps later found himself standing on a covered balcony that ran the length of the large Hotel Pacifica. The deck was covered in terra cotta tile which contrasted with the rich white stucco of the walls. A cool, salty breeze driven by the warm California sun blew in off Avalon Bay. The Pacific Ocean was a crystalline blue and shimmered in the direct sunlight that fell on it from a cloudless sky. A wrought iron, glass-topped patio table was situated near the painted wood railing. Two matching chairs were next to the table and facing seaward. They sat and Rudy pulled a folded set of papers from his pocket. *"Time* magazine," he said handing the little bundle to Wellman.

"Small issue this week," Wellman quipped, taking Rudy's offering.

"It's just the cover and the related article," Rudy explained. "This is supposed to be a party and not a business meeting, but I thought you should see this."

Unfolding the neat bundle, Wellman saw the familiar front cover of *Time*. On the cover was a picture of Toby with the one-word question: "Messiah?" Wellman chuckled, then said, "I haven't seen this. I gave the interview, but haven't seen what they did with it!"

"I didn't think you had. It arrived today, and frankly, I don't think it's all that humorous."

"It's just a come-on," Wellman said. "Newsmagazines always use some emotionally evocative tagline. It's how they sell magazines."

"The article is no better. It's loaded with words like *miracles, healings, supernatural powers,* all spoken of in neutral journalistic fashion, but the idea is there. It causes me some concern."

"Why?"

"Because we can barely handle the number of people calling, showing up on our doorsteps, and filling our meeting room."

"Sanctuary," Wellman corrected. "We're a church, remember? At least that's what it says on our IRS 501–3(c). We are officially a nonprofit, religious organization."

"One that has more people than it can handle. We're growing too fast. The stress on the staff is growing, and the drain on Toby is becoming more and more obvious. This article is only going to make matters worse." Rudy rubbed his forehead. "I've got calls on my desk from *U.S. News & World Report, USA Today,* and *People* magazine. They all want to talk to you and especially Toby."

"No one from the press talks to Toby. Set up the meetings and I'll chat with them."

"They insist on seeing Toby."

"Let them insist, but it's not going to happen. They pass through me or not at all."

Rudy just nodded.

"Look, buddy," Wellman began softly. "We've been through a lot together. You've been by my side for years. Don't let the pressure screw that up. Stay the course and everything will be just fine.

I've treated you well, haven't I? You have a great home on the island, and you make more than most CEOs. Come on, partner. Life is good. Enjoy it."

"I know, I know." Rudy sighed. "I'm just tired and a little confused. And I worry about Toby."

"Toby is fine, and he's going to stay fine. I'll see to that." A loud cheer erupted from the banquet hall. "Come on, let's see what all the noise is about."

The men walked back into the cavernous room. A crowd had gathered around Toby. Wellman could see a tall man standing next to the area where Toby had been seated. It was Torr. "If Torr is here, Burdick can't be far away," Wellman said.

"He was invited," Rudy said.

"I know. I approved all the invitations. I wonder what extravagance he is bestowing on the boy this time."

Wellman and Rudy worked their way through the crowd and found a healthy-looking Burdick on one knee next to the chair in which Toby sat. A broad smile was pasted on his face. Toby was grinning, too, for the first time that day. Mary stood behind her son. Burdick was speaking: "...with your love of the stars and all, well, I thought you might like this." He reached out a hand and touched the shiny black body of a Celestron telescope. "With this you can gaze at the moon and the stars all you want. Oh, and I got you something else. Mr. Torr?"

Melvin Torr stepped forward and set a thin rectangular object on the table, next to the cake. It was wrapped in blue and gold wrapping paper. Torr took a step back, saw Wellman, and nodded.

"Go ahead," Burdick prompted. "Open it up. It's yours."

The children, excited by a new present, pressed in closer hoping for a good view. Toby reached out and slowly tore the paper back. "What is it?" he asked.

"You have to open it to see," Burdick encouraged. He was clearly enjoying himself.

Toby tore at the paper with a new enthusiasm. Seconds later, with wrapping paper crumpled around his feet, Toby shouted,

"Cool! Way cool!" Before him was an IBM Notebook computer. He ran his fingers along the smooth plastic case as if he needed confirmation that the gift was real. "Thanks, Mr. Burdick."

Burdick smiled broadly, and Wellman felt a stab of jealousy. Burdick and he had been partners, but it had become an uneasy alliance. In the early days, Wellman needed Burdick's money and influence, but now the Church of New Jerusalem was fully functional and self-supporting. Burdick was no longer needed, but he was a better businessman than Wellman and had secured a place on the board of trustees. His name also appeared on every significant legal document that concerned CNJ. Burdick was so entrenched that nothing short of death could remove him, and Wellman was sure that Burdick had made contingencies for even that occurrence.

"The computer comes with everything you need," Burdick said. "It has an astronomy program that helps you find all the stars, planets, and constellations. I bet you can fill up a few hours with that."

Several of the children said, "Wow!"

Burdick beamed and stood up. "Well, Toby, what do you think?"

"It's great. It's amazing. Thank you. I'll be real careful with it."

"There are books that come with it. If you have trouble understanding them, I'll get someone to help you."

"That's all right, Mr. Burdick. I think I can figure it out."

"I have no doubt about that, buddy," Burdick said. "You're the smartest person I know." He turned his attention to Mary. "I hope it's all right with you, Ms. Matthews. He's done so much for me that I want to do something in return."

"You've done a lot for us already, Mr. Burdick," Mary said smoothly. "In some ways, you and Richard saved our lives."

A year and a half in California had not removed her Appalachian accent, but it had taken the edge off. Wellman had watched Mary change over the months. She worked hard on her speech, trying to sound more refined and to expurgate those speech patterns that revealed her lack of education. He hadn't heard the word "ain't" in six months. He also knew that she sat in on each of Toby's tutoring sessions that were conducted by hired teachers. Although the lessons were meant to aide Toby and meet state law, she attended to glean what knowledge she could. Wellman had given instructions to the teachers to answer whatever questions Mary might have. It couldn't hurt, and it might even help. What surprised him was with what fervor she struggled to make herself better both mentally and in appearance. Something was driving her, and Wellman had yet to put his finger on it.

"It's been my pleasure," Burdick replied. "How does one pay back a life?"

"One would think you're trying to spoil our Toby," Wellman said, no longer able to stay quiet.

"Guilty as charged," Burdick said. "And I take pride in my crime. What did you get the boy for his birthday?"

Wellman gave a reserved smile. "You mean besides the birthday party? Well, let's see." Wellman raised a finger to his chin as if contemplating some memory. "I can't seem to remember what it was. Can you, Toby?"

Toby stiffened slightly and pursed his lips before speaking. "A video arcade."

"A video arcade?" Burdick said. "You bought him a whole video arcade?"

"Not quite," Wellman answered. "I had four or five of the new games set up in a recreation room near Toby's bedroom. It looks pretty good, I think. Don't you, Toby?"

"It . . . looks nice," he murmured.

"And you said I was trying to spoil him," Burdick said. "It appears you have outdone me."

"It's not a contest," Wellman said. "Toby is special and deserves special things. We want him happy. What about it, buddy. You happy?"

"Yes, sir," Toby answered without a smile. "Very happy."

chapter 12

Aaron Pratt had ceased listening to the sermon. It wasn't the preacher's voice or delivery that made his mind wander. In fact, the pastor's words had struck a chord, a chord that continued to resonate in Pratt's racing mind. He wished it was a good feeling, the kind that he had often received while worshiping in the large Baptist church off Magnolia Avenue in Riverside. He had been a member of the church for the last ten years, ever since moving to the city to take his teaching post. The large white colonial buildings were always a welcome sight to him.

Pastor Lawrence had moved into his third point of the morning's sermon, but Pratt was barely aware of what he was saying; his mind was stuck on an earlier comment in the message. The sermon text was taken from the gospel of Luke the fifteenth chapter: "Or suppose a woman has ten silver coins and loses one. Does she not light a lamp, sweep the house and search carefully until she finds it?" The parable was familiar to Pratt. He enjoyed its simplicity and the way Jesus combined great truth into just a handful of words. It was that truth that bothered him today.

The story was the simple account of a woman who owned ten coins, Greek drachmas, each roughly worth a day's wages. After discovering that one was missing, she began a thorough search, "sweeping" the house. The pastor, a detail-oriented preacher, had brought to mind something Pratt had long forgotten. The word *sweep* was significant. How many times had he read those words without seeing the glint of truth contained within them? The woman in the parable had to sweep the house to look for the coin because, unlike modern homes with wood, or carpeted floors, ancient Middle Eastern homes had dirt floors. If the coin were lost, it would most likely be lost in the soil beneath her feet. To find the coin, she would have to light an oil lamp and systematically work her way through the home, moving from one corner to another.

When was the last time I extended that kind of effort? Pratt wondered. The coin was small but of great value. It was just one of many, but still worth the searching. Were not people more important than coins? He knew the answer.

He felt sadness and even remorse. Conviction was the church term for it, but regardless of what it was called, it was still weighty and uncomfortable—and he knew why he felt it. Thomas York had been gone for nine months, abruptly dropping out of school with just a little more than a year of his studies left. It had not been an unexpected move on Thomas's part. Pratt had sensed his ever-increasing dissatisfaction. After receiving the G. P. Youngblood Scholarship, Thomas had quit his job and poured himself into his studies. He excelled with each passing week, but he never seemed happy. Contentment eluded him. Pratt had made several attempts to counsel his prize student, but no progress had been made.

"It's hard to describe," Thomas had said as he sat in Pratt's office. "I love my studies, but I'm still dissatisfied."

"With the school?" Pratt had prompted.

"No, not at all. I think I'm unhappy with myself. I'm still looking for something I can't define."

Pratt had been unable to guide him to any sense of peace. The more they spoke, the more disenchanted Thomas seemed to become. He struck Pratt as a man who knew he should be somewhere, at some meeting, but didn't know where. *Adrift* was the only word Pratt could come up with to describe what he saw in the young scholar.

Nine months after accepting the grant, Thomas York dropped out of grad school. It was not uncommon for students to leave school. Every graduate school lost a small percentage of students who could not keep up the grueling study schedule, or who had to leave for pressing financial or family problems. Thomas was different. He left when he had everything. Tuition was no longer a concern; even his housing was covered in the generous grant. Nonetheless he walked away, and Pratt had not heard from him since. Pratt was beginning to feel that he had not done enough to help the young man stay in school, nor had he made any effort since to check on his well-being.

Not one of your shining moments, he said to himself.

What could be done now? Three quarters of a year had passed since his "coin" had disappeared. That was a lot of time. That knowledge only elevated his sense of guilt. He felt the need to repent and did so, but while his penitence changed him, the situation remained the same: Thomas was still out there searching for something he couldn't even describe.

The preacher's voice rammed its way into Pratt's meditations. "We as a church, we as families, we as individuals need to pick up our broom and sweep through the dirt around us, finding what we should never have lost."

Pratt nodded to himself, then closed his eyes in prayer, asking God to give him the right broom and a bright enough lamp.

Thank you for coming," Wellman said, rising from his place at the antique cherry table that rested in a large bay window overlooking the ocean. The sun had begun its early afternoon descent toward the Pacific horizon. The blue of the sky had darkened several shades, and not a single cloud had dared to mar the perfect canvas. Wellman was dressed in the same casual dress he had worn earlier at Toby's birthday party. "Can I get you something to drink? Tea? Soda? Iced latte?" He smiled and held up a glass of golden liquid. "Beer?"

"No, thank you," Mary answered. She had changed from her earlier outfit into a pair of tan slacks and an ivory shell top. Even in February the weather was warm and comfortable, something Mary still found amazing.

"Have a seat, please," Wellman said, motioning to the empty chair opposite his. "It's been a beautiful day."

"Yes." She picked up a small cocktail napkin and began to fold it, then unfolded it again. Despite his kindness, and for reasons she could not explain, Wellman made her self-conscious. She felt inferior in his presence—she also felt attracted to him, and that made her nervous. "Thank you for the birthday party for Toby. I'm sure he appreciates it very much."

Wellman pursed his lips and leaned over the table, pushing aside his tall glass of beer. "That's what I wanted to talk to you about. At the party Toby seemed . . . out of sorts."

Mary knew exactly what he meant. Toby had been somber throughout the entire celebration, lighting up only after seeing the telescope and Notebook computer that Burdick had bought for him. Not long after, however, he descended into his private gloom. No amount of children's laughter, no matter the number of gifts, Toby refused to enter into the spirit of the party. She had tried to encourage him to participate in the games or to respond to the hired magician that wandered the ballroom where the party was held, but he silently refused.

"Is he ill?" Wellman pressed. "I can have a doctor come over and look at him."

The napkin in Mary's hand was becoming frayed on the edges. She twisted the delicate paper repeatedly. How could she tell him that Toby was afraid of him? If it weren't for Wellman's speedy intervention, she and Toby might have remained separated by the social service bureaucrats of New Mexico. It had been Wellman who chartered a plane and rushed to her side, bailing her out of jail. It took two days, but somehow he had been able to cut away the red tape that tied Toby to a foster home and an administratively heavy child protection agency. How he did it, Mary still did not know, nor did she care. She did know that he had pulled them from poverty and given them a home, money, food, and dignity.

No longer did she wear frayed dresses and soiled shoes. No longer was Toby forced to wear jeans that were a size too small or sneakers with holes in the soles. It was true that Wellman had pressed Toby and his special gifts into service, but was that too high a price to pay? Her son was not abused or pressured. Toby did all that he was asked to do without complaint. Never had he said, "I don't want to."

At first he had enjoyed meeting people and helping them. Mary could still remember the shock on Toby's face when he was flown to Fresno and there met Burdick in his home. It was in Burdick's well-appointed bedroom that she and Toby first met the multimillionaire. The man was so ill that Mary was sure her face reflected the same astonishment that she saw on Toby's. However, it had taken only a moment before Toby's expression had changed, replacing shock with childlike concern and wonder.

"You're dying," Toby had said innocently.

"We've been looking for you, boy," Burdick had said, a weak smile on his face. "I hear that you are ... special."

Walking to the wealthy man's bedside, Toby stared at the emaciated figure on the bed. "Bad body," Toby said.

"Yes," Burdick had replied. "My body is bad. I'm very sick."

"Your skin is yellow," Toby said. "I've never seen a yellow person before."

"Toby!" Mary was aghast. "That ain't polite—"

Burdick cut her off with an upraised hand. "It's all right. The boy is correct." Making eye contact with Toby he added, "It's my disease. It's the cancer."

Toby cast a questioning glance at Mary. "It's a bad sickness, Toby. It's like that waitress in Texas."

"Lumps and bumps." Toby nodded, and Mary could tell that he was absorbing the information. Turning back to Burdick, Toby said, "This is different lumps and bumps. Your body is eating itself."

"What?" Burdick asked.

"Your body doesn't like itself. It's making itself sick."

Burdick had looked confused, then said, "Some of my cells are multiplying too fast. It has affected my liver and pancreas."

Tilting his head to the side, Toby considered what he had heard. Mary had wondered how to explain the difficult concept to him. Before she could try, Toby shrugged and said, "Okay." He then walked casually from the bedroom.

"What's that mean?" Burdick asked Mary harshly.

"I don't know," Mary said. "He's jus' a boy, he don't understand."

Burdick had turned to Wellman. "Do something. Don't just stand there. Make him come back in here."

Wellman walked from the room, Mary close behind. Mary sat next to Toby, who was sitting on a wide black leather sofa. He had found a magazine and was flipping the pages looking at the pictures. Mary sat next to him and put her arm around his tiny shoulders.

"Listen, kid," Wellman started. "That man in the bedroom is important. He made it possible for me to find and help you and your mother. You'd still be in the foster home if it weren't for him and his money. Now he needs your help."

Toby looked up at Wellman. "What does he want?"

"To be well, what else?" Wellman shot back.

Toby shrugged and looked at the magazine.

"Can't you do anything, Ms. Matthews?"

"I don't know what you want him to do." Mary pulled Toby close. "He ain't no doctor."

"Of course you know. You're his mother. How can you not know?" Wellman ran a hand through his hair.

"It's okay," Toby said. "You don't need to be angry."

"Angry?" Wellman said with surprise. "I'm not angry."

Toby pulled his mouth tight. It was what he did when he caught Mary in a lie.

Wellman crouched down to be at eye level with Toby. His eyes narrowed slightly, belying the smile on his face. "Listen, kid, I've gone through a great deal of trouble to find you. I know you have a gift, a very special gift. You can help people the way no one else can. That's true, isn't it?"

Toby shrugged. "I dunno."

"He knows things sometimes," Mary said, "but that's all."

"That's not all," Wellman said firmly. "There's more. I don't know why you're keeping it secret from me. I already know about it. I know about the hospital and the tornado. Why won't you help Burdick?"

"Leave him alone" came a solid voice from the bedroom door. Mary looked up and saw Burdick standing in the doorway. He looked different. His skin was smooth and the yellow tint was gone. Mary blinked with disbelief at what she saw. Burdick looked heavier, his silk pajamas hanging evenly from his frame. "No need to pressure the lad. Look at me! I'm whole." Burdick crossed the room and scooped up Toby in his arms. Tears were rolling down his face. "I don't know how to thank you, son. I owe you everything ... everything." He began to weep.

Still in Burdick's arms, Toby twisted until he could see his mother, then shrugged.

"Mary?" The voice brought Mary back to the present.

"Are you still with me?" Wellman asked sternly.

"I'm sorry. I was just thinking." She shifted in her chair.

"If Toby isn't ill, then what's bothering him?"

"I don't know for sure," she replied softly. "A lot has happened in the last year. I think he may be having trouble with all the changes."

"That's understandable," Wellman said. "But will he be okay for tonight and the future?"

Tonight, Mary thought. Sunday night, the night when the rallies were held. She looked out the bay window that not only overlooked Avalon Bay with the California coastline in the distance, but also allowed her a line of sight to the converted theater that now served as the Center of Praise Sanctuary. At 7:00 tonight, nearly two thousand people would fill the expanded auditorium, each having paid for the privilege of attending. Each one coming to see Toby. Each one hoping to gain his attention for a few moments.

"He'll be all right," Mary said. "He just needs a little rest."

"Rest is all he needs?" Wellman leaned back his chair and folded his hands across his trim stomach. "Is that all that is bothering him?"

Mary wanted to say yes, but Wellman had always been able to see through her. She looked up from what was now just a wad of napkin and saw Wellman studying her. "I think he's lonely."

"Lonely?" Wellman's eyes widened with surprise. "I don't understand. He has everything any boy could ever want: books, satellite television, video games, a beach just a few yards from his front door. He lacks for nothing."

"He doesn't have any friends," Mary explained.

"He has lots of friends. I'm his friend. We bring in children to play with him. He can't see that?"

"You don't understand," Mary objected, tossing the napkin aside. "He's not like the other children. He's so much smarter that they can't relate to him. They don't meet his needs. They like his toys and games, but no one really likes him. Everyone else he knows is an adult, and he's smarter than they are."

"You're saying that he's lacking sufficient mental stimulation." Wellman leaned back over the table again.

"I guess. He's still a little boy, but his brain is not."

Wellman stood and walked to a window, hands clasped behind him. "I can understand that," he said, as if speaking to himself. "I should have expected it. A boy like that has different needs."

"He needs a friend he can talk to," Mary said. "Someone he can trust. I'm his mother, but he's getting older now. When he was six, I was all he needed. Now . . ." She paused. "Now, I'm not sure." She cleared her throat and tried to press down the rising sadness.

Wellman turned. His voice was soft, but his eyes remained hard and cold. "I'll take care of it, Mary. Don't worry, no one can ever replace a mother." He stepped to her side and ran a cool hand across her face, pushing back a strand of dark hair. Without thought she moved closer to the caress. "We must keep him happy, Mary. What we do here is important. We can't let anything derail our work.

Do you understand?" He cupped her chin in his hand and turned her face toward him. "Tell me you understand."

She nodded, feeling as if she could fall into the depths of his brown eyes.

"Say it."

"I understand."

With an actor's smile, Wellman said, "I knew you did."

chapter 13

"Another great crowd," Rudy said as he stood just off stage right. "We've had capacity crowds for a solid six months."

Wellman peeked past the heavy stage curtains at the milling crowd taking their seats. They were a mixed lot. Some arrived laughing and joking with family and friends. Others came bound to wheelchairs or supporting themselves on crutches. Mothers held ill toddlers in their arms, hopeful anticipation on each woman's face. Husbands helped enfeebled wives walk down the sloping center aisle. Music, piped in through the public address system, filtered down softly from overhead speakers like a fog descending from heaven.

The auditorium was enormous and had once been the pride of Catalina. Built in 1935 to compete with the popular Casino ballroom, the Gull House had been the most popular attraction on the island. Barry Gull had been an automotive inventor who made good in the 1920s. A competitive man by nature, he undertook the building of the Gull House to provide a new stream of income and to build a public name for himself. Barry Gull succeeded. He made barrels of money and passed his legacy down to his children. The next generation kept the dream alive, and the business flourished. It was under the leadership of Gull's grandson that the Gull House fell out of favor with the crowds. While the Casino remained a popular attraction, Gull House was driven into bankruptcy by young

Peter Gull's hunger for cocaine. Bills went unpaid, as did property and business taxes. Liens were laid against the establishment like cordwood, and the property went on the auction block—an auction that did not escape the notice of Wellman and Burdick.

The purchase, back taxes, and renovation dug deep into the financial pockets of Burdick's empire, but it had been worth it. Four months later, the Church of New Jerusalem was born.

Wellman guided the organization; Burdick funded it. They started slowly at first, letting word of mouth be their advertisement. The crowds came. Slowly at first—fifty the first month, a hundred the next. Six months later, the 1800-seat auditorium was filled every other Sunday night. And unlike traditional churches, there was no offering; there was, however, a price to be paid at the front door. Admission was charged, but it was never called such. "Donation" was the preferred term, keeping the organization credible and the IRS away. The suggested donation was eighty dollars per person. Additional money came from their "faith supporters," who received a newsletter each month and seats closest to the stage. They had no doubt that the IRS would someday challenge their tax-exempt status, but they could tie up such an investigation in the courts for years. Burdick had that kind of money.

Wellman looked at his watch. "Twenty minutes." He turned to Rudy. "Toby needs a friend. Someone we can trust."

"A friend?" Rudy said. "That's the point I was making at the birthday—"

"He's withdrawing, and Mary thinks he's lonely. I agree. The problem is that no one can keep up with the kid's brain. He can outdistance any one of us, but he's still a kid."

"So he needs an adult who can relate to him on an intellectual level?"

Wellman nodded. "Apparently I don't cut the mustard with the kid. Sometimes I think he doesn't like me ... no matter how nice I am to him."

"He is perceptive," Rudy said.

"What's that supposed to mean?" Wellman snapped.

"Nothing," Rudy replied. "I'm just saying that the kid sees things we can't. He knows things. That's what all this is about."

"You're saying that he doesn't like what he sees in me?" Wellman's words were terse.

"Don't get me wrong, but yeah, that's what I'm saying."

"I'm not here to be his friend," Wellman admitted. "I'm here to make all this work. Look out there. The people keep coming. They're here because of *my* dream, *my* vision. If it weren't for me, Mary and Toby would be living in a tarpaper shack somewhere. I've given them a home. I've given them purpose, and hundreds of people have been helped. So what if we make money off this? Every preacher in every church makes money for what he does. Why should we be any different?"

"I'm not saying we shouldn't or that we're doing anything wrong," Rudy said, raising his hands in surrender. "I've been with you from the start. Remember? I'm here now. And you don't hear me complaining."

"All right," Wellman said, taking a deep breath. "I'm a little on edge. Any ideas how to cheer Toby up?"

"Maybe," Rudy answered. "There's a young man that's been working in our marketing department. He's pretty sharp. A former seminary student who first came to us to research a paper. He saw Toby at one of the rallies and has never left."

"You think he can keep up with Toby? Mentally, I mean."

"I did the background check on him myself. The guy is a genius in his own right. Maybe he and Toby can hit it off."

"What's his name?"

"Thomas York," Rudy replied.

"Has he ever met Toby?"

"No, but he has put in a petition to do so."

Wellman rubbed his chin. He had kept Toby isolated from all but a few people. Thousands had requested to see him, which was a physical impossibility. "Okay, set it up. In fact, find him now and bring him backstage. Fill him in on what he needs to know. The sooner we get started on this, the better."

"He's probably in the crowd."

"Get security to help you locate him. I don't want to lose any time on this. Make it quick."

Pratt had just picked up his car keys when the phone rang. He looked at it for a moment, casting a frown in the direction of the noisy device. "What now?"

"Mr. Pratt?" A woman's voice.

A grumbling sound erupted from Pratt's stomach. He was headed out the door, his mind set on a fish dinner at a nearby restaurant. He was in no mood for a sales call. "This is Dr. Pratt," he said solemnly.

"I'm sorry. I should have said Dr. Pratt."

"I don't mean to be rude," Pratt said, "but I'm not looking to buy anything."

There was a pause which Pratt found odd. Phone solicitors tended to be pushy, seizing every gap in a conversation and using it to pour more enticing information through the phone.

"I'm not selling anything, Dr. Pratt." Something was wrong with the woman's voice. It faltered, hesitating between words, and was breathy. Pratt realized that the caller had been crying. "I'm Joyce York ... Thomas York's mother. Thomas was a student of yours."

"Yes, Mrs. York," Pratt said quickly, hiding his embarrassment. "I'm sorry. I thought you were a telephone solicitor."

"I need your help," she said without preamble. "I'm trying to find my son."

"I don't understand." Pratt set his keys down next to the phone. "You don't have his number?"

"I haven't seen him since he left school. He moved and didn't leave a number or address for us."

"That's strange," Pratt said. "He always seemed so responsible."

"I need to find him. It's ... it's his father. He's had a heart attack."

"I'm so sorry," Pratt said. "If you don't mind me asking, how serious is it?"

A soft weeping came over the phone. "I'm sorry ... I shouldn't bother you with all this, but you were Thomas's favorite teacher."

"It's no bother, Mrs. York. I'll do whatever I can to help."

"Jim is bad. He's on a ventilator. He was just sitting at the table having lunch when he groaned, grabbed his chest and ..." The weeping increased, and a deep sadness welled up in Pratt.

"How can I help, Mrs. York?"

"I need to find Thomas."

"I'm afraid I don't know where he is. I haven't seen or spoken to him since he dropped out of school almost a year ago."

"I was afraid of that." She sounded despondent.

"He's been on my mind of late. Did he say where he was going? Didn't he give you some indication of his plans?"

"No, not really. He did mention that he had applied for a job with a church."

"What kind of church?"

"I don't know. We haven't gone to church much—Jim and I, I mean. Thomas was the religious one in the family. I guess we should have been more faithful. Maybe this wouldn't have happened."

"Church people have heart attacks, too, Mrs. York," Pratt offered. "However, I do encourage you to speak to a minister, or maybe the hospital chaplain. I'm sure you could use the spiritual support."

"I don't, Dr. Pratt. I mean, it's religion that has separated us in the first place."

Pratt was puzzled. "You mean when Thomas came to the graduate school? That shouldn't separate a family."

"Well, it took him from his home here in Richmond, but that's not what I mean. I'm talking about that new church group he's gone to work for."

"And you don't remember the name of the church?"

"No, I'm not thinking all that well."

"That's understandable, Mrs. York."

"It had something to do with Jerusalem."

Pratt's stomach turned. "The Church of New Jerusalem?"

"Yes, that's it. I don't know what he's doing for them, or how to contact him. Do you know where the church is?"

"I've read about them," Pratt admitted. "They're located on Catalina Island. They're not a real church ... not as we would think of a church, anyway."

"What do you mean?"

Pratt wanted to be delicate. "I had a conversation with one of the other professors who specializes in comparative religions and cult groups. He has been following the Church of New Jerusalem. They're not an orthodox faith, but they're not really a cult either."

"Then what are they?"

"They're hard to describe. Usually, cult groups have a strong central leader and some source of authority beyond the Bible. This group has a strong leader, but they hold no real doctrine. According to my colleague they blend New Age thinking, self-help chatter, and whatever else strikes their fancy. The sad thing is that at the center of it all is a young boy."

There was silence on the phone, then, "I must get hold of Thomas. He needs to know about his father." She began to weep again. "I feel so lost. Do you know how I can get in touch with this church?"

Her words brought that morning's sermon rushing back. *Another lost coin,* Pratt thought. "No, I don't, Mrs. York, but I'll find out. Better yet, I'll try to find Thomas myself."

"I'm sure you're a busy man, Dr. Pratt. I don't want to be a bother."

"It's no bother. Actually, it's something I should have done a long time ago."

Mary stood just off stage, her hands on Toby's shoulders, gently massaging his tiny muscles.

The music was loud, reverberating off the art deco walls of the former Gull House theater. A small band of mixed instruments, guitars, drums, and several horns were situated to stage left. On stage right was a string quartet and harpist. The program was always the same. Rousing music started the service, the band playing tunes familiar and new. The crowd would enthusiastically clap their hands to the beat of the music. Soloists, and at times, well-known entertainers would sing for the gathering, resulting in uproarious applause.

Then the "witnesses" would come. Three or four congregants would stand on the stage and each, in the ten minutes allotted them, would tell of the wonderful and miraculous things that had happened to them since joining the Church of New Jerusalem. Each was young, good-looking, well kept, and financially well-off. Tonight there were three witnesses, two pretty women, one a mother, the other a lawyer, and a young male stockbroker. The mother, a tall blond with a slender figure, had come to CNJ suffering with systemic lupus, a disease that affected her skin and joints. She testified that a smile from Toby had cured her. The attorney stood and, fighting back tears, related how a single touch from Toby had freed her from a life that doctors told her would be childless. She proudly announced that she was barren no longer. A standing ovation followed. The third witness had to wait five minutes for the crowd to settle enough for him to speak. Once silence had settled again, the stockbroker, who reminded Mary of a movie star, told of his addiction to cocaine and alcohol. His family had one foot out the front door and he was on the verge of losing his job when he came to CNJ. Toby "saw right through him," he said, but he passed no judgments. Instead, Toby had just touched his face and said, "No more." Mary, who seldom left Toby's side, didn't remember the man or the woman lawyer. But that had happened before. Once she had asked Wellman about these people, and he had been quick to say that she had forgotten or that some were healed while sitting in the audience. His words lacked the firmness of truth.

The band struck up again, and another two songs were sung, led by a handsome, gray-haired man, but this time the music was more sedate. The first song, a gentle chorus in which the same words were sung over and over, flowed into an even calmer piece led by the stringed instruments.

"Feel the music," the leader said in a full but gentle voice. "More than hear it, more than sense it, feel it. It's like the warm water of a beautiful ocean slowly ebbing and flowing through your soul. It cleanses you, makes you whole. Feel it wash away your concerns and fears. Let it do its work. Let it do its work. Let it do its work."

From her place at the side of the stage, Mary could see the people standing, arms raised high, swaying to the soft music. Their eyes were closed. She could see tears in the eyes of those closest to the stage. Mary felt sorry for them. Despite their fine clothes and their positions in society, they were hurting, anguished people, folks whose souls had been burned and scarred by the uncontrollable things in life like disease, depression, sorrow, and doubt. They had come for help, and that help was to be found in her son, Toby. It all fell upon his shoulders, the small, delicate shoulders she was now massaging. Wellman and his people could orchestrate everything, but in the end, everyone looked to Toby.

From the opposite wing of the stage, Mary saw Wellman walk slowly on stage. He was wearing a collarless ivory shirt and a pair of blue jeans and white Reeboks. He carried himself with confidence and with the air of a man who loved to be center stage in every aspect of life. He reminded Mary of a rooster walking through a yard filled with hens. Still, he looked awfully good.

He raised his hands like a priest offering a blessing on his church and spoke softly, the lapel microphone he wore picking up every syllable. "You are you, and I am me. Just as the Great and Universal Spirit has made us. You are blessed, as we all are blessed." He motioned for them to be seated. "For those of you who have never been to the New Church of Jerusalem, I am Richard Wellman, your host."

Polite applause rolled forward from the crowd.

"Some consider me the preacher of the church," he laughed. "I deny it. The world has enough preachers. What we need are fewer messages and more miracles." The crowd erupted with laughter, applause, and cheers. He raised his hand to quiet them. "We need fewer preachers and more producers, fewer ministers and more people who make things happen." Again the audience applauded. "That's why we're here. That's why this church has been raised up. That's why you're here. You've gone out of your way to make it to this place at this time. You've made the effort, you've seen the value. We exist because many of you have made it your business to see that we continue this important work, to make sure that everyone who wants to can receive a blessing from Toby."

The words were similar to all the other services, and Mary had heard them many times, yet they still gnawed at her. They seemed somehow wrong, somehow untrue. Toby was special. Toby was indeed unique, and people had been helped by him, but Wellman made him sound like a god instead of a little boy.

"Your support keeps us going," Wellman said. "Your financial gifts keep the doors open and the lights on." He then chuckled and slowly waved a hand at the audience. "No, I'm not going to take an offering. No one is going to pass a plate here. You might be used to doing that in the old churches, but we do things differently here at the Church of New Jerusalem. I know you paid money to be in the beautiful theater tonight, so I'm not asking you to reach for your wallets. Instead, I'm asking that you reach for your hearts. I'm asking that you become part of the partners that keep this ministry going. Toby will be out here with us in just a few moments, but before he does step on the stage tonight, won't you consider becoming a CNJ supporter? Your gift of fifty, one hundred, five hundred dollars— whatever you feel this place, this ministry is worth—will make a big difference. Many of you have signed up to provide monthly support ... well, in fact, let's have a show of hands. How many of you here tonight support this ministry with a monthly financial gift?"

Hands shot into the air, with most of them centered down front. Anyone could see that those who gave got to sit closer than the others. Mary even recognized some of the faces. She had seen them in the off hours, working around the building and in the offices. They were employees. She couldn't help but wonder if they really gave money or if this was just part of their jobs. Did they get overtime for coming to a Sunday service?

Mary shut out Wellman's words. She had heard it all before. The delivery was different each time, but the conclusion was always the same: be a supporter, send money, and send it regularly. The money he raised supported her and Toby in a manner she would never have dared dream. But was that all there was to life? Perhaps it was. At least she was secure and surrounded by luxury. She could not overlook Wellman's generosity.

"Mary," a voice whispered behind her. She turned to see Rudy and a strong-looking young man. "I want you and Toby to meet someone. This is Thomas York."

The young man held out his hand for Mary to shake. "It's a pleasure to meet you," he said in hushed tones. Everyone backstage spoke in muted words once the program began. Thomas's hand felt huge in Mary's delicate grasp, yet his grip was gentle and his skin smooth. His lips parted to reveal large, even, white teeth.

"Hello," Mary said, nodding her head slightly.

The man crouched down and looked Toby straight in the eyes. "Hi Toby, I'm very glad to meet you."

Toby returned a half-hearted smile and obediently shook Thomas's outstretched hand. Toby tilted his head to one side. "You're not sick."

Thomas seemed puzzled. "No, I'm not. I don't understand—" Thomas began, then stopped. "Of course. Everyone you meet wants something from you. Is that it?"

Toby shrugged and cut his eyes away.

"Well, Toby," Thomas said softly. "I don't want anything from you. I'm just happy to meet you. Honest." There was a pause as Thomas and Toby stared at each other. "You're lonely," Thomas said.

Toby's eyes widened. "You know me? I mean, you can see inside me, like I see inside other people?"

Thomas shook his head. "No, Toby, not like you. You're unique in the whole world, but I can see that you're lonely. I can sense it, because I was lonely at your age, too. I didn't fit in anywhere. Didn't have many friends either."

"How come?" Toby asked.

"I was smarter than all the kids in my neighborhood, and I wasn't interested in the same things. When I got older, I learned to like football and wrestling—mostly to please my dad. I was pretty good actually, but most of the time I would rather read."

"Did you read a lot?" Mary saw Toby's eyes brighten, something she hadn't seen in weeks—too many weeks.

"Yes," Thomas said with a laugh. "I still do. I especially like languages."

"What kind of languages?"

"Ancient Greek and Hebrew. Have you ever studied those?"

"No," Toby said.

"I could teach you, if you want."

"Really?" Toby turned to his mother. "Would that be all right, Mom?" Mary nodded. "When? When can we start?"

"As soon as you want," Thomas replied. "Maybe after the service we can get some ice cream and I can teach you the Greek alphabet."

Again Toby turned to Mary. "Do you think Mr. Wellman will let us?"

"No problem, Toby," Rudy interjected. "I'll make all the arrangements. Now you better get ready. It looks like Mr. Wellman is winding up. You're on in just a few moments."

"It's good meeting you, Toby," Thomas said, remaining in his crouched position. "I look forward to our ice cream."

"Me, too," Toby said. The boy turned and walked confidently to the area of the wing nearest the stage. Wellman announced his name, and Toby strolled out into public view.

The applause was deafening.

"He's a wonderful boy, Ms. Matthews," Thomas said. "I bet you're very proud of him."

"I am," she said. "More than you or anyone in the world can know."

chapter 14

Toby took in a deep breath and released it in a slow sigh. He waited for the words he knew would come.

"Ladies and gentlemen ... Toby ... Matthews!"

Richard Wellman took two steps back, clapping his hands in loud applause. The crowd, eighteen hundred strong, stood to its feet like a tsunami rising from the deep ocean. The sound of the applause reverberated like thunder, bouncing around the cavernous room until every inch was filled with the noise of it.

The band played loudly, the electric guitars and drums pounding out a rock beat. What had started as spontaneous applause grew into a rhythmic, pulsating beat that rolled through the room in a unified, cacophonous din. The sound of it made Toby's ears hurt and his heart skip. They were all there for him. They all wanted him.

"Toby, Toby," someone called. Others joined the chant. "Toby ... Toby ... Toby."

Minutes dripped by as Toby stared past the glare of stage lights and into the faces of the people. Toby saw them. He saw them as a group, he saw them as families, he saw them as individuals, but he saw them in other ways. He saw them with a vision that had nothing to do with his eyes. Their feelings were as clear to him as their physical appearance. There was so much pain. So much sorrow. So much doubt and fear. And they wanted him to take it away.

The emotion was strong and Toby felt it as he knew others could not. It was like standing in front of an open oven, its heat pouring out in a steady blast. Except this heat came from the fear and anxiety that the people felt. It burned Toby, and he took a step back as if he had actually placed his face in a scorching furnace.

There was a man there whose lungs had spots on them. A woman, a mother, whose brain hurt because of a ball of something in her head. A girl younger than Toby had bad blood. He didn't know the right terms, although he had heard others speak of cancer, tumors, and leukemia. Over the months he had seen many illnesses and could have learned more about them if he chose. He could learn the names, read books, and understand the diseases more, but he refused. Every disease reminded him that he was different from everyone else.

Toby wanted to be the same as others. There was nothing so lonely, so isolating, as being different.

The loud music and applause continued, and Toby could feel the vibration of it rise from the wood stage and up his legs. His every sense was once again on fire. The lights seemed brighter, the noise louder, the heat hotter.

A man, a businessman, was thinking of killing himself. His bank account was empty and he had been lying to his wife. But he sat in the back and no one in the back ever got to come forward. This was his last hope, Toby intuited. He had a gun in the car and he planned to use it this very night. Mr. Wellman would never pick him, and because of it the man would die.

Sadness washed over Toby, saturating him with the heaviest sorrow. It came in waves, like mountains of water pounding the sandy shore. So much pain. So much fear. So much desperation. And there was just him, just Toby. He was alone. So very alone. He wished for the days in the car, when it was just he and his mother, alone and on the road. He didn't mind sleeping in the car; he had the stars to keep him company. His clothes were dirty then, and he had no books to read, but he was happier. Now he would trade every book, every toy, every game, every minute spent in the fancy house built for him and his mother, for just another night or two on the road.

The emotional fire of the crowd glowed hotter, fanned by a wind of desperation. But there was a coldness, too. A frigid, icy, heavy air blew across the back of Toby's neck. He knew what it was. It was there every time he stepped upon the stage.

Slowly, reluctantly, Toby turned to face Wellman, who stood four steps away and to the side. Just behind him, so close that certainly they were touching, was the Shadow Man with his insubstantial appearance and absent eyes. No matter how many times Toby had seen the figure, it frightened him, but he refused to react. Instead, he pressed down his fear, pressed it down in his belly, keeping it secret. Maybe if he didn't seem afraid, then the Shadow Man would leave. He hadn't left yet.

The chill of its presence surrounded Toby with its icy fingers. The Shadow Man had no face, but Toby could sense that it was perversely pleased. Toby swallowed hard and turned back to the audience.

To the front right of the stage was a short set of stairs that allowed people from the audience to walk up on the platform. Two men, each dressed in a cobalt blue T-shirt with the words *Church of New Jerusalem* embroidered over the breast, stood at the foot of the stairway with a line of ten people behind them. The men held wireless microphones in their hands. One of them nodded to Wellman.

"What a warm welcome," Wellman shouted over the clamor. He raised his hands and motioned for quiet. Two minutes passed before the crowd settled enough for Wellman to speak with any hope of being heard. "I'm sure Toby appreciates your expression of love. Isn't that right, Toby?"

Toby looked up at Wellman, who towered above him. A chill spiraled through him, but he smiled and nodded.

"Without further ado, then, let's seek the blessing." Wellman turned to the side of the stage where the small line of people stood. "Who do we have first?"

One of the men with a blue shirt raised his microphone to his lips and said, "Toby, this is Jamie, and she needs your help." That was all he said as he took her arm and walked her up the steps and onto the stage. Toby knew that no other information would be given. It was done this way every time. Ten people would be selected from the audience, almost always from those seated in the front rows, the seats reserved for the major financial supporters. One by one a staff member would bring a "seeker" to Toby, who would tell the nature of the problem, take the person by the hand, and then utter firmly, "Receive the blessing." Toby wasn't sure why Wellman insisted that he say the words. If the person was going to be helped, then they were helped. He understood that he could see the problems of people and that somehow they were made better by being near him, but that was all he knew. Toby felt no sense of control over his gift. He was just what he was.

The woman was shaking, her hands trembling, and her steps uncertain. Toby looked at her. It took no special skill to see her fear. Toby understood that. It had taken him several months to finally put away the pulse-racing, stomach-churning feelings he had each time he stepped on stage. Now he gave it no other thought than to remind himself how much he hated the whole thing.

Tears began to roll down the woman's face, and Toby felt sorry for her. Wellman stepped behind them with Toby to his left and the shaking Jamie to his right.

"You've come for a blessing," Wellman said. "You have a problem and you want Toby to bless you, is that right?"

"Yes." Her voice wavered as much as her hands shook. "I'm so nervous and so excited. I don't know what to say."

"You needn't say anything," Wellman offered. "This is not the act of a charlatan. Toby is the real thing. He can see your problem. Isn't that right, Toby?"

Toby ignored Wellman, keeping his eyes on the woman. Her tremors had nothing to do with illness; she was just terrified. Looking into her eyes, Toby held out his hand. Wellman had taught him to do so. "Touching is a good thing, son," he had said. "It makes the people think that you care." He hated being called son by anyone other than his mother, and he didn't need someone to tell him how to care. He didn't have to pretend.

"Take his hand, Jamie."

Her quavering hand took his. It was hot and damp and Toby didn't like it, but he liked her. "Your children love you," Toby said. Like Wellman, he wore a lapel mike clipped to his white polo shirt. He also wore white pants and white shoes. All of it Wellman's doing. Toby had told his mother that he thought that he looked like a glass of milk. "You don't think they do, but they love you lots." The woman raised her other hand to her mouth and began to weep softly. "Your son is in jail because of drugs."

"Yes," she admitted.

"He's thinking about you. He's like you. He thinks that nobody loves him."

"But I do love him," she protested.

"I know," Toby said, "but he doesn't. Tell him. He will be released in two days. He needs to see a doctor."

"Because of his addiction?" the woman asked.

Toby shook his head and then touched his abdomen. "His stomach is bad from worry and drinking too much. The doctor will make him better."

"Is that her blessing, Toby?" Wellman asked. The once boisterous crowd was silent, the expansive room as quiet as a tomb.

"No," Toby answered. "That's his blessing." He continued his gaze into the woman's eyes. "Your muscles don't work right. You think that it's going to get worse and worse."

"That's what the doctors say," Jamie said. "It's called myotonic dystrophy. My muscles get weaker, and it can affect my heart."

"They're wrong."

"Oh, thank you, thank you." She began to weep loudly. "I was praying for this."

A whispered voice said, "Toby."

Toby looked up to see Wellman giving him "the look." It was an expression he shot at Toby anytime he forgot something. Wellman motioned toward the woman with his head and mouthed the words, "Say it."

With a slight sigh, Toby said, "Receive your blessing."

"Oh, thank you, Toby." She leaned over and hugged him. Toby hated being hugged. Another staff member came from the wings, a woman in a blue pantsuit, and ushered Jamie off the stage.

"Who else do we have in need of a blessing?" asked Wellman, turning back to the stage stairs.

"This is Robert," the man at the foot of the stairs said into his microphone. He then walked a round, balding man in a black suit onto the dais.

"Robert, you've come for a blessing from Toby, is that right?" Wellman asked, a broad grin on his face. Toby sensed his insincerity. Why couldn't his mother see Wellman for what he was? "Toby, please tell us about Robert."

Toby stared up at the man. He had dark brown eyes over which hovered wild, thick eyebrows. His skin was smooth and his head was nearly completely bald. When he smiled, Toby could see a straight row of white teeth. Toby studied the man for a moment, then frowned.

"What is it, Toby?" Wellman asked. "You look sad." It was the setup. Wellman had told him repeatedly to draw out each moment and each emotion. He was to work slowly, like he was reading a book, struggling to pull out the details of a person's need.

"He has no need," Toby said.

"I don't understand," the man countered.

"Yes, you do," Toby corrected. "You're not sick or troubled. You're a reporter, and you don't believe any of this is true."

The man fidgeted and glanced at Wellman. Toby looked at Wellman too and could see his face darken with anger. "Um . . . that's not true."

"Yes, it is," Toby insisted. "You work for a newspaper in San Diego, but you haven't been there very long. You were fired from your last job, and now you're trying to get your new boss to like you. You want to prove to everybody that I'm a fake. I'm not a fake.

You are." Toby felt a hand touch him on a shoulder. Instantly he fell silent and looked up at Wellman.

"How could you do this, sir?" Wellman said with disgust. "This is a special place, a holy place, and you have defiled it with your cynicism."

"You can't believe him over me," the man said. "He's just a kid. I'm a grown man."

"Toby has never been wrong," Wellman said. "I bet we can verify your employment quickly. Does your paper have a Web page? Maybe we could find something you've written there."

"Okay, okay," the man said. "But just because I work for a newspaper doesn't mean that I don't have needs. I can't help it if the boy can't see what they are. I came here to be helped."

"Why did you bring the tape recorder?" Toby asked.

The man stiffened. "I'm a reporter. Reporters often carry tape recorders."

"Why is it on?" Toby pointed to the man's front suit coat pocket.

"May I?" Wellman said and, without waiting for permission, turned the man to face him, reached in the front of the coat, and removed a minicassette recorder. With a flourish, he held it over his head.

"Hey!" the man shouted. "You can't do that."

The crowd began to boo.

"I'll sue," the reporter said. "You can't treat me like this."

Toby watched as Wellman reached down to his side where the transmitter for the lapel mike was clipped to his belt. He switched it off. With a hand on the man's shoulder he said just loud enough for Toby to hear, "Listen buddy, you can sue all you like, but every moment of this service is video recorded by four different cameras. If you want that video shown to your boss and office mates, then sue away. I'll be happy to show this little fiasco in court. Am I clear?"

The man nodded. Wellman gave the recorder back to him. "Here, keep this. This is proof that Toby is real. Now get off my stage."

Red crept up the reporter's face and bald head, and perspiration speckled his brow. Without another word, he marched from the stage awash in boos and hisses.

With a flick of a finger, Wellman's mike was back on. "It's always been that way," he announced. "There are always the detractors, those bent on taking something good, wholesome, and beneficial to humankind, and sullying it with the dirt of innuendo and rumor. I know Toby is real. I know his gifts are real. What about you?"

Instantly, the crowd was on its feet, offering first its applause, then a chant: "We believe. We believe. We believe."

Toby watched the reporter race from the stage and start up the side aisle that led to the lobby. Before he reached the door, two thick-armed men in blue staff shirts met him and escorted him from the theater.

"Nice job, Toby," Wellman said. "You never cease to surprise me."

Toby looked up into the broad, knowing smile of his mentor. Peering over his shoulder was the faceless Shadow.

Mary watched the events closely as she did every service, but this time she also watched the young man standing in the wings with her. From the moment Toby had walked on to the stage, Thomas York had kept a steady gaze upon him, a smile so consistent that Mary wondered if it had been tattooed in place. He applauded loudly with the congregation and seemed enraptured by the events that played before his eyes.

"You're worried," he said to Mary as he watched the reporter hastily exit the stage.

Mary looked at him. "I am?"

"You seem to be," Thomas answered. "I don't mean to pry, but I imagine that this must be hard on you. Mothers are prone to worry."

"Does your mother worry about you?" Mary turned back to the stage. She was uncertain what to think of Thomas. There was nothing about him that alarmed her. The reverse was true. He seemed genuine, bright, and concerned.

"I'm sure she does." He chuckled. "She always has."

"Yes, I worry about him."

"He's worth worrying about. There's no one like him."

"Yes, that's true."

Thomas turned to Mary and said, "I hope he likes me. I would like to be his friend."

Mary started to ask why a man in his twenties would want to be friends with an eight-year-old, but she didn't. "He needs friends—real friends. What he doesn't need are more people to use him."

At first, Thomas seemed shocked. Mary was surprised at her own words. She never spoke up for herself. Instead, she always acquiesced to the will of others. That's why she had run away at night. Had she tried to leave Toby's father with him present, he would have made a scene, and she would have quietly shrunk back into the shadows. When her father was alive, he would tell her, "You're too timid for your own good, girl. You need to straighten up that backbone and show the world you got courage, real courage." She had never known a moment of courage.

"Ms. Matthews," Thomas stated, "I would never use Toby, I would never hurt him, nor would I ever allow anyone else to do so. I was asked to meet him and was glad to do so. I think we may have a few things in common. Maybe I can lift his spirits a little."

Staring at her son, Mary reminded herself how somber Toby had become over the last few weeks. He could use cheering up. "I hope you can, Mr. York."

"Just Thomas. I'm not much on formalities."

She studied him again. Maybe he was what Toby needed. Still, that remained to be seen.

chapter 15

I don't mind saying that this is a little creepy," Morrison Edison said, his back pressed against the starboard railing of the ferry.

"Not getting seasick, are you?" asked Pratt with a small smile. "We have another ninety minutes to go. Wish we had taken one of the faster ferries?"

"Not hardly. I love boats, just as long as they stay afloat."

"I feel guilty that you've interrupted your routine for this." Pratt turned his attention from the passing sea and, like Edison, leaned his back against the white enamel painted rail. A brisk breeze, made heavy with salt air, blew along the upper deck of the Direct Express Ferry.

"Ah, guilt, the gift that keeps on giving," Edison said with a laugh. "Stop beating yourself up, Aaron. I'm here because I choose to be. When you told me about Thomas's father, I felt that I should help you find him. I spend too much time in my office pushing paper and asking for donations. Somewhere along the line, I lost track of my real calling. I'm an educator, not just an administrator."

"Well, I'm glad for the company," Pratt said.

"Jesus sent out his disciples two by two. That's a pretty good precedent. I'm glad you told me how the Lord had laid all this on your heart. We do let people slip through our fingers far too easily. I'm as guilty as anyone on that. Students drop out all the time, and occasionally I try to talk them into staying. I should be doing more. As you said, looking for 'lost coins' is important."

Overhead white and gray gulls called loudly. A small, dark tern plummeted from the sky, striking the water headfirst only to emerge a moment later with a wriggling anchovy in its beak. Pratt marveled at the sight. "You never did say what you found creepy."

"Look around you, Aaron. Anything strike you as odd?"

Redirecting his attention to the exposed deck, Pratt saw a handful of people milling around in the warm sun. Most of the passengers were in the ferry's enclosed cabin. As Pratt had walked through the seating area, he had noticed several individuals in wheelchairs. A woman whom he judged to be in her early thirties leaned heavily on a pair of aluminum crutches. An elderly man wore dark glasses and held a thin, red-tipped white cane. Another man who appeared to be in his forties walked across the deck with a limp, his left arm hanging useless at his side.

"I see what you mean," Pratt finally said. "Tugs at the heart, doesn't it? These poor people are investing their hope in a cult that can never meet their expectations."

"Are you sure?"

"What do you mean? Surely you don't mean to say that the Church of New Jerusalem is in any way authentic."

"I don't know enough about it."

"Dr. Tucker said that two of his students researched the group and found its doctrine little more than New Age pabulum."

"Tucker is a good man. One of the best in my opinion, but I'm not talking about the Church of New Jerusalem in particular. I'm talking about the boy."

"The boy?"

"After you left my office Monday, I did a little research. I pulled down the *Time* article from the Web and did an Internet search. I found several other articles. At first I assumed, as you do, that this was just another fly-by-night group out to make money off gullible people, and for the most part I still believe that to be the case. It's the boy that makes me wonder."

"Children have been used in such things before," Pratt interjected. "Marjoe Gortner comes to mind."

"You're talking about the child evangelist of the sixties who went on to produce a movie showing how he worked the innocent congregants of the churches he spoke in."

"Exactly. The youngest ordained minister in history. He was the center of quite a movement before giving it all up as an adult to pursue an acting career."

"I see the point, but I still wonder about the lad. What if he is genuine?"

Pratt frowned. He was surprised to hear the president of the school talk this way. "Is there any historical precedent for such a thing? I don't know of any."

"Nor do I, but that's a dangerous way to think," Edison counseled. "Can we say that God works today only the way he's worked in the past? Can he do nothing unique or extraordinary?"

"I would not presume to put limitations on God," Pratt agreed. "Still, using a boy like this is too much to believe—"

"David," Edison interjected.

"What?"

"A shepherd boy by the name of David."

"That's different," Pratt objected. "David wasn't a miracle worker."

"God has always been the one who works miracles, Aaron. He has chosen people through whom to work those miracles, but they always begin and end with him."

Pratt knew Edison was right. He had assumed from the beginning that the whole Church of New Jerusalem was a cult. He still believed that, but he saw where Edison was headed. The boy did not start the organization; he was, after all, just a lad. It was adults who had created the entity that had grown into a highly publicized business. "You're saying that the boy may be real while the organization may be false."

"Exactly. Of course, I have no way of knowing, but the idea occurred to me when I read the articles I found on him. One reporter,

I think she wrote for the *Los Angeles Times,* described their meetings. It appears the boy never speaks to the group. A man by the name of Richard Wellman does that for him. The boy comes out on stage later, and they bring him, one by one, a dozen or so people from the congregation."

"Wellman? I know that name."

"He used to be a well-known radio host. He's the one who discovered the boy and brought him to the public eye. Unless I miss my guess, he's the brain behind all this. The boy is the draw."

"And you think the boy might be for real—a real miracle worker?"

"I don't know what to think," Edison admitted, "but I don't want to dismiss the idea prematurely. Most likely your assessment is correct, but I'm withholding judgment for a little longer."

"If the boy is special, then it would explain a few things."

"You're thinking of Thomas?"

"Yes. Without a doubt, he's the smartest student I've ever had. Maybe he sees something in the boy I can't."

"I hope so. I can't imagine him buying into the tripe that they're passing off as doctrine. I read on the Web their statement of faith, and I wouldn't give you a dime for it. It's nothing but a blend of New Age thinking and positive self-help psychology. Thomas could never swallow all that."

"I pray that's true."

An odd, uneasy feeling percolated in Pratt. Edison had hit on some important points. Could the boy be a tool in the hands of greedy men? It wasn't without precedent. If so, then they might be facing a problem much broader in scope than finding Thomas.

Mary lay on the thick emerald green carpet of Toby's recreation room. Toby sat cross-legged on the floor. Between them was a chessboard with handcrafted wood pieces. The sun's effulgence streamed through tall windows that overlooked a seamless blue tapestry of ocean and sky. "What's this piece again?" Mary asked.

"That's the castle," Toby said, looking up from a thick book he held on his lap. "Sometimes it's called a rook."

"Are you sure you wouldn't rather play on the beach? It's a beautiful day."

"Maybe later," Toby said.

Mary knew there would be no later. When they had first moved into the spacious house overlooking Lover's Cove on the east side of the island, Toby had begged to go to the beach daily. The last few weeks, he had barely left the house.

"It's a beautiful day," Mary repeated.

"You said that already."

How much he had changed in the last year and a half. Day by day, he seemed to become more formal, even referring to her as "Mother" in front of others. He had changed in other ways too. His once syrupy thick Southern accent was all but gone. While she had worked hard to soften hers so as to blend in with the others around her, he had successfully eradicated the twang. He had grown three inches, put on weight, and lost some of his childlike qualities. None of that bothered Mary. What did concern her was his newfound somberness. When they were dirt poor, living in a car, and uncertain where the next meal would come from, he had smiled frequently, joked with her, and talked openly and freely. Now he spoke less, read more, and seldom smiled.

"This game is too hard for me, Toby," Mary said. "There are so many pieces, and they all move in different ways."

"It is complex."

"Complex, huh? Well, maybe I'll just come over there and tickle the stew out of you. We'll see how complex that is."

"I'd rather you didn't," Toby said solemnly.

"You used to like it when your old mother tickled you."

"You're twenty-five, Mom. You're not old."

Mary rolled over on her back and looked at the white ceiling above her. Like everything in the house, it was detailed with various moldings. The room was large and contained a sixty-inch television, DVD player, several commercial video games, and hundreds of books lined up in neat rows in a cherry wood bookshelf that covered one entire wall. "Sometimes I feel old, Toby."

"You're not happy," he said, his face still buried in the book. He turned the page. One minute later he turned another. His reading speed continued to accelerate each week.

"Neither are you," she shot back. "And I don't need no special power to know it, neither."

"Did you know that you use double negatives when you're upset?" Toby asked. His voice was soft and carried no tone of accusation.

"Yes, I know that," Mary said, rolling on her side to face Toby. "Old habits are hard to break."

Toby just nodded.

"So why are we unhappy, Toby? We have more than I ever dreamed we could. We have everything we could ever want. We'll never be hungry again. No more scratching for a living."

"It's Mr. Wellman," Toby said.

"Yes. He has made all this possible. We owe him an awful lot."

"That's not what I mean," Toby corrected. "We're unhappy because of Mr. Wellman."

"What do you mean?"

"You're attracted to him, but you're not sure you can trust him."

"That's not true, Toby." Mary sat up, crossing her legs on the floor. He just looked at her with those eyes that seemed to read her mind. "I know you're lonely, Toby. I'm lonely, too. Mr. Wellman has been such a help."

"And you find him attractive."

"Is that so wrong, son? A woman needs a man. Being lonely ain't . . . isn't good for anyone, but it's hardest on a woman."

Toby shook his head. "A woman *wants* a man, not *needs* a man."

"What do you know about such things?" Mary said a little harsher than she meant.

"I don't know how I know anything, Mom. I just know." A sadness crept across his face that broke Mary's heart. She moved the chessboard and scooted over to her son, taking him in her arms.

She began to rock. Minutes passed in silence, the only communication being that which a mother can transmit to a child through a gentle embrace.

"I'm sorry, Mom."

"Don't be. You're right. I am attracted to Mr. Wellman, but I don't think he's attracted to me. He's so different from your father. Your father was cruel. He frightened me. I was always afraid that he'd hurt you. Now we don't have to worry about that."

"Mr. Wellman likes you," Toby admitted. "He likes you a lot."

A strange emotion ran through Mary. She was at once thrilled and uneasy; warmed by the knowledge that she was desirable to someone, yet chilled by the uncertainties she felt for the man. "You know that like you know other things?"

"Yes."

Mary hugged Toby closer and tighter. "There's something you're not telling me, Toby, isn't there?"

He lowered his head in silence.

"Toby, we've been through an awful lot together. We've made it because we trust and share with each other. You can tell me anything. You understand that, don't you?"

"Yes."

"Say it, son."

Toby shuddered in her arms. "Mr. Wellman has a dark heart. He has the Shadow Man; the Shadow Man has him."

Years of motherhood had taught Mary to be patient with Toby's cryptic statements. "Dark heart? Shadow Man?"

"Mr. Wellman acts nice, but he doesn't care about the people who come to the meetings. He cares about the money and the power, but not about the people."

Mary suspected as much, but had convinced herself that none of that mattered. People were being helped. So what if the church made money? It helped her and Toby. All churches took money from the people who came to the services. At least they were up front about it all. People paid at the door and through voluntary contributions. Nothing wrong in that.

"I don't understand about the Shadow Man. Who is the Shadow Man?" A shiver caused Toby to quiver, then tense. Mary could sense his fear. "Toby?"

"The Shadow Man, he's with Mr. Wellman now."

"You're not making sense, son. Who is the Shadow Man, and what does he have to do with Mr. Wellman?"

"I've seen him, Mom." Toby sounded as he did when he was six: more vulnerable, less knowledgeable. "I saw him last night at the meeting. He was on the stage with Mr. Wellman."

"I didn't see him," Mary said, confused. "I was watching you the whole time."

"I'm the only one who sees him. He was there. I saw him just like I saw him before."

"Before? What do you mean before?"

"I saw him before. I saw him at the tornado place and the robbery place and just before the police took you away from me, and I saw him last night on the stage. He was on the stage and he was by Mr. Wellman and I saw him and he has no face, no mouth, but he does have places for eyes, but no eyes and no ears or anything and he looks like a man but he doesn't look like a man and he's black all over and—"

"Toby, Toby, settle down." Toby began rocking, and Mary tried to hold him still.

"But I saw him. I really did. But no one else can see him. Just me and I don't know why it's just me but it is just me that sees him and he's always on stage."

"It's all right, Toby. It's all right. No one is going to hurt you." A loud ring echoed through the house, and Toby jumped with fright. "Doorbell," Mary said. "I'll see who it is. Then you can tell me more about this. Whatever it is, we'll face it together."

The recreation room adjoined the foyer. Mary stepped to the door and looked at a small four-inch square video display that played an image fed to it from a tiny video camera outside the door. It was a security measure that Wellman had insisted upon. Standing patiently on the other side of the entrance was the young man

Mary had met the night before. She opened the door. He was holding a book in his hand.

"Mr. York. It is York, right?"

"Yes, but we agreed last night that you'd call me Thomas." He
smiled. "Can Toby come out and play?"

"What?"

"I'm joking," Thomas said. "I promised Toby that I would
teach him some Greek, and I was hoping that this was a good time.
I hope I'm not interrupting anything."

"Oh, well, Toby and I were just . . . talking."

"It's okay, Mom," Toby said from the doorway between the
foyer and the recreation room. "I'd like to learn that language. If
it's okay."

"Are you sure?" Mary said with a questioning look.

"Yes. Please."

Mary smiled reluctantly. "Okay, I guess we can finish our talk
later, but only if you're sure."

"I'm sure," Toby said. He seemed excited to see Thomas, and
Mary was glad to see a positive emotion from her boy. "Come in,
Thomas."

Walking in, Thomas followed Toby into the adjoining room
where he and Mary had been playing chess a few minutes before.
Mary followed behind.

"Wow," Thomas said. "Cool. You have all kinds of stuff in here.
Look at these books. There must be two hundred of them."

"Five hundred and twelve," Toby said nonchalantly.

"Five hundred and twelve," Thomas repeated seriously. "Are
you sure? Maybe it's five hundred and eleven."

"Nope. Five hundred and twelve. They average 314 pages per
book, which means there are—"

"One hundred and sixty thousand, seven hundred and sixty-
eight pages," Thomas interjected.

For the first time since Toby had been born, Mary saw surprise
on his face. He narrowed his eyebrows, then laughed out loud.
"How did you know that?"

Thomas shrugged. "Numbers come easy to me. I don't know why. Math has always been a cakewalk."

"Cakewalk?" Toby said.

"Yeah, sure. It means easy. You know: cakewalk, piece o' cake, can o' corn, a walk in the park, easy as pie, like falling off a log ..."

A burst of giggling erupted from Toby. Mary found herself laughing with him. "Can o' corn?"

"Well, I can see that you are slang impaired," Thomas said. "Maybe we should put aside the Greek and learn the important stuff first. Please repeat after me." Thomas pulled his posture fully upright and spoke in a professorial tone. "Way ... cool."

"Way cool," Toby repeated. "I know that one."

"Very good. Now let's use it in a sentence. Thomas York is way cool."

Toby laughed.

"This is serious, young man," Thomas deadpanned. "Please do not make a mockery of my teaching."

"Toby Matthews is way cool," Toby said.

"Close enough. Now another. This is the proper way to answer a question posed by a friend. Your friend says, 'Would you like a can of Dr. Pepper?' You say, 'Yeah, baby!'"

"Yeah, baby," Toby parroted.

"More excitement please."

"Yeah, baby!"

"Much better."

"One more," Thomas said. "Please repeat: Cowabunga!"

Toby exploded into laughter. "Cow-a-bung-a."

"Pretty good for the first time. It's a term from an ancient California people known as 'surfers,' who it is said would ride the ocean waves while standing on specially designed boards."

"I know what a surfer is," Toby said with a mirthful smile. "What's in your hand?"

"This, young man, is called a book." Thomas stopped and looked back to the long bookshelves. "But we've already established that you know something about books. This is a Greek primer."

He held out the thin volume. "It was my first book on Greek. I want you to have it. It only has one hundred and ninety-eight pages which brings your total pages up to—"

"One hundred sixty thousand, nine hundred sixty-six."

"Wrong," Thomas said with an artifice of gravity. "You missed it by one page."

Toby furrowed his brow. "No, I didn't."

"Okay, so I lied. You're right." A second later, Thomas guffawed. Toby joined him.

Mary watched with grateful amusement. The two could not be more different physically. Thomas was just over six feet tall with thick muscular shoulders. Toby was small for his age and thin as a sapling. Yet she could sense a connection that went beyond the age and size difference. Thomas didn't talk to Toby as man would a child. Instead he spoke like one unique person to another.

"Would you two clowns like something to drink?" Mary asked.

Toby and Thomas exchanged glances, then replied in unison, "Yeah, baby!"

chapter 16

It's a little early for that, isn't it?" Burdick asked, pointing to the tumbler in Wellman's hand as he entered Wellman's massive office.

Wellman looked at the glass of scotch he held, then to Rudy, who stood beside him at his large teak desk. "I'm celebrating," he replied.

Burdick raised an eyebrow. "If you're celebrating, then it must have something to do with money."

"Very astute. Unneeded sarcasm, but nonetheless true."

"So I've been summoned to hear your good news." Burdick crossed the room and took a seat in a leather chair across from the desk without Wellman having offered it. Wellman started to make a point of it, but let it go. Burdick was a man who was used to getting his way. He had all the money a man could want or spend. Now that he was healthy, he was a man to be reckoned with.

"We're going global."

Burdick raised an eyebrow. "Really? How so?"

"I got a phone call," Wellman said. "An unusual but not unexpected phone call. I knew something like this would happen sooner or later. It was just a matter of time and publicity."

"You're being cryptic, Richard. Cut to the chase."

Instead of answering, Wellman nodded at Rudy, who took over the conversation while his boss leaned back in his leather office chair, a near-Cheshire grin pasted on his face. "One hour ago, we took a call from overseas—P'yongyang, to be exact."

"North Korea," Burdick said with great surprise. "You got a call from the capital of North Korea?"

"I'm impressed," Wellman said. "Not many people would know that."

"Agriculture is an international business, Richard. It pays to know which countries will have food shortages and which ones the government lets us trade with. During the last Korean famine, we sold to a dozen relief groups. Made for a good year."

"Our involvement will be a little more direct," Wellman said. "And we'll be dealing with only one person in need. Carry on, Rudy."

"A staff member working for Chi Choon Lee has asked for our help and has made a generous offer. It appears he has a need that no one in his country can meet."

"Let me guess. He's sick." Burdick shifted in the chair.

"Correct," Wellman said. "You understand his position, don't you?"

"I haven't forgotten how bad I was," Burdick said. "There isn't an hour that goes by that I don't think about it."

"Then you can sympathize," Wellman said. "He wants to meet with Toby."

"Do you know who that man is?" Burdick's words were cold. "Chi Choon Lee is the Minister of Defense and an outspoken critic of the United States. He lobbied against Western food being used to feed the starving people of his country. By his own testimony, he is the sworn enemy of the United States."

"Ironic, isn't it?" Wellman said. "He hates everything our country stands for, and now he needs us."

"You're not seriously thinking of taking the boy to North Korea," Burdick objected.

"And why not? Maybe we can further world peace," Wellman said with a slight smile.

"You'll be empowering Lee to continue his tirades against the U.S. You are aware that he could become the head of that country."

"I'm not an expert in world politics, but I am an expert on what we do here, and this could be a big break for us. The money alone makes the request irresistible." Wellman stood and then downed the remains of the scotch.

"It always comes back to the money," Burdick said.

"Look who's talking," Wellman countered. "You've been rolling in money all your life. You wouldn't know how to get by on a normal salary if you had to."

"I make no apologies for my wealth," Burdick snapped, leaping to his feet and pointing a finger at Wellman. "But I earned every dollar. I made no deals with the devil."

"Oh, please," Wellman said. "Spare me your noble rise to prominence. I do my research. Harrison Donald Burdick III made his money like his father and grandfather before him, on the backs of underpaid migrant workers."

"Now you've gone too far!" Burdick shouted. "How dare you impugn my family's name."

"That's enough, gentlemen," Rudy commanded. Both men turned to face him. "We're here to make plans about putting Toby and Lee together, not to chew each other up. I suggest we return to the business at hand."

"This is not good business. This is not right." Burdick was inconsolable. "As far as I'm concerned, we're aiding the enemy."

"With all due respect, Mr. Burdick," Rudy said, "we're not at war with North Korea. It is true that our country has no diplomatic relations with them, but that's no reason to turn our back on another man's need."

"Hypocrisy," Burdick snapped. "Every meeting, your boss there turns his back on people in need. Only those who are major contributors get up on stage. The rest are out of luck."

Wellman spun on his heels. "I have worked with the public for twenty-two years, Burdick. I know what I'm doing."

"This isn't a radio show where you can make up conspiracies and talk about amorphous lights in the sky. People come here desperate for help."

"When did you get a conscience?" Wellman shouted back. "I know as much about you as you know about me. We're much more alike than you like to admit."

"Except I came close to losing my life to cancer. My money was no help. My social standing was useless. That makes a man think, Wellman. That makes a man reconsider his life and his achievements."

"I notice you still take your cut of the gate," Wellman said.

"Listen to you. You speak like this is all some kind of rock performance." Burdick shook his head. "Cut of the gate, indeed. At worst, I'm merely recouping my investment."

"Toby is going to Korea and there's nothing you can do about it."

"You don't control Toby," Burdick objected. "He doesn't belong to you."

"No, he belongs to his mother, and I control her." Wellman was surprised by his own words. He fell silent, as did Burdick.

Rudy spoke, "The last eighteen months have been stressful for everyone. Things have moved quickly, maybe too quickly. But here we are. We can't unwind the clock. We can only move forward. This kind of fighting between the principals can only destroy what has been built. Mr. Burdick, you have invested heavily in the Church of New Jerusalem. Do you want to see it all go down the drain because of infighting?"

"No, of course not."

"How about you, Rich?" Rudy asked. "You've poured twelve to eighteen hours a day into this effort. Certainly you don't want to see it dissolve in front of your eyes?"

"No, but I will not take a backseat to anyone. I call the shots."

Rudy held up his hands. "Everyone knows that. That was the original agreement, and it was a good one. We just need to let our brains make the decision and not our emotions."

"Okay, okay," Wellman uttered. "You're right. But we must

agree on this: Toby meets with Lee. The global implications are enormous. Other world leaders will turn to us. It will make us a global organization. The opportunity is too good to pass up. Can you see that, Burdick?"

Burdick stroked his chin, and Wellman knew that he was weighing the situation. There was nothing to do but wait for the millionaire to finish his pondering. Wellman crossed to the wet bar at the side of his office. He poured three glasses of scotch without asking if the others were interested, then handed the tumblers to Burdick and Rudy.

Taking the glass, Burdick said, "I want to be brought in earlier on the major decisions. No more ambushing me as I walk into the office."

"You agree then that Toby should go see Lee?"

"I'd rather Lee came here."

"There's no chance he'll do that," Rudy said. "As you said, he hates America."

"Then a neutral country. Something that is safer and easier to get into and out of." Burdick took a drink of the golden liquid. "Lee can't be trusted, nor can his government."

"I'll make sure Toby is safe," Wellman said. "I won't let anything happen to that boy."

Setting the glass down on Wellman's desk, Burdick said, "You know my concerns and convictions. See that you don't violate them."

Wellman fought down the urge to walk over to the elderly man and bury a fist in the man's face. "We're partners, Burdick. I understand that. The question is, do you?"

"I understand," Burdick answered. "I understand a great deal." He turned and walked from the office.

"He's a pompous clown," Wellman said. "I'm the one who has made all this work. Burdick is an albatross around our neck. Somehow we have to get out from under his thumb. He's a bump in every road we try to go down. Not only that, he's undermining my position with Toby. I can't allow that."

"What do you want to do?" Rudy asked.

"I'm not sure . . . yet. Something will come to mind." He gulped down the remaining alcohol in his glass. "Let's step up our surveillance of him. I want him watched all the time. I also want his communications monitored. The old bird has something up his sleeve. He backed off too quickly at the end."

"I thought it was my persuasive argument."

"Nonsense," Wellman said. "You did very well, but Burdick does what he wants, when he wants. He's not used to having someone like me in the captain's chair."

"You think he's planning to unseat you?"

"Not yet. It's too soon, but he'll try, all right. He needs me for the moment, but he'll make that change."

"You don't trust him, do you?"

"No, and you'd be wise not to trust him, either." Wellman sat down again. "Enough of Burdick. We have plans to make. Pull up a chair; it's time to get to work."

Melvin Torr opened the rear door of the limo and Burdick slipped in. Torr joined him. "Take us on a drive," Burdick ordered the chauffeur.

"Any place in particular?" the driver asked.

"Just around the island," Burdick said bluntly, pushing a button that raised a dark privacy glass that separated the front seat from the spacious back area. "How much did you get?" he asked Torr.

"Every word," Torr said, holding up a small cassette recorder. "The transmitter worked perfectly."

"So the bug is working?"

"Flawlessly. The private detective we hired has placed a man on the janitorial staff. He's been able to make entry into Wellman's office and place the bugs."

"Good," Burdick said. "Wellman will tip his hand and when he does, we'll have his own testimony to sink him."

"To whom will you give the information?"

"Whoever benefits us the most: the police, the FBI, Mary, or maybe just Wellman himself. Where reason doesn't work, blackmail does. All we need to do is wait. Guys like Wellman always make the big mistake. When he does, I'll be there to bring the world crashing down on his shoulders."

chapter 17

I t's vitally important," Pratt said to the thickly built guard. The guard was dressed in a flat gray uniform and a billed hat that read SECURITY. His arms were massive, stretching the hem of his short-sleeve shirt to the breaking point. He eyed Pratt and Edison carefully, as if he could judge their intent at a glance.

"I can't let you in, sir," the guard said. He wore a name tag that read D. NETTLES. "I have standing orders. The compound is off-limits to everyone except on service nights."

"But this isn't a normal situation," Pratt objected. "We're not here for a service. I need to speak to one of your employees. There's a family emergency."

"I can take a message and try to get it to him as soon as I can." The guard was resolute and unflappable. "That's the best I can do."

"I don't understand why you're turning a deaf ear to us," Pratt said in frustration. "I'm not asking for a special favor. I just need to talk to Thomas York. Am I asking so much?"

"Look, Mister," Nettles said. "I stand out here every day, eight hours a day, five days a week. In every one of those hours, someone comes up to me with a special request. Their need is more important than anyone else's. Their disease is the worst, their problem, whatever it may be, is greater. I don't doubt their sincerity, but I do know that we can't let in everyone who wants to wander around the compound. My job is to make sure things are safe and secure. I follow my orders, which are to keep everyone out until service days, and then make sure everyone behaves. Look behind you."

Pratt turned and saw a sinuous line of people bordering a tall wrought-iron fence. Each upright of the fence ended in a pointed, spearlike head. Climbing over it was possible, but risky. The people, who patiently waited on a grass strip that bordered the fence, were a mix of able-bodied and lame. Some sat in wheelchairs, others rested on pallets, and each was staring at them, watching closely. Pratt suddenly understood what Jesus saw at the Pool of Bethesda. Scores of people in dire need with nothing left but hope. Unlike Jesus, Pratt had nothing to offer them. It was a pathetic sight and tugged at Pratt's heart. The guard's point was clear: If he let Pratt in, then he would have to explain himself to everyone in that line.

"They've started calling themselves pilgrims," the guard explained, "since so many of them have traveled great distances to be here. In that line are people from India, Europe, and most states in the Union. That group was unable to get into Sunday night's service, so they've camped out right where they were, waiting for the next service on Wednesday."

"I can understand your problem," Pratt said, "and surely you can understand ours. We need to speak to Thomas York."

"As I said, you can write him a note, and if there really is a Thomas York, I'll see that he gets the message."

"Of course there's a Thomas York," Edison interjected. "We're not making this up."

"I can't know every employee or volunteer that works here, sir."

Pratt lowered his head in frustration. "What if I told you we weren't leaving until we see York."

"Then I call the sheriff's department and they come and cart you off. They're getting used to it now. Our police force isn't big, but it is efficient."

"Leave a note," Edison said tersely. "It's the best we can do right now."

"I don't suppose you have any paper, do you?" Pratt asked the guard.

"That I can help you with." Pulling a piece of notebook paper from a pad, he handed it to Pratt, who scribbled down a quick message, then stopped suddenly.

"What is it?" Edison asked.

"I was hoping to talk to him personally," Pratt replied. "How is he going to get hold of us while we're on the island?"

Edison grunted. "Makes me wish I carried a cell phone."

"Me too," Pratt said. He turned to the guard and asked, "Can you recommend a hotel?"

The guard chuckled. "Man, you are having a hard day. The hotels are filled up and have been that way for months. If you haven't already made arrangements, then you're probably out of luck."

"I don't believe in luck," Pratt said. He wrote a few more words on the paper and handed it back to the security man. "This isn't some ruse," Pratt told the man. "Thomas York needs to receive this note as soon as possible. Can I count on you to get it to him?"

"I'll do what I can. That's the only promise I'll make."

Pratt turned and walked away from the entrance gate, strolling down a winding concrete path that led to the street. "What did you write?"

"I told Thomas to call his mother as soon as possible."

"So our job is done, then."

"I don't think so," Pratt said solemnly. "I don't want to leave until I know that Thomas received the message."

"You doubt the guard?"

"Did you look in the guard shack? There must be one hundred notes in there. I have doubts that Thomas will see the message."

"What are the other notes?" Edison asked.

"I assume they're notes to Toby Matthews. You saw the people in the line. Some of them are desperate for help."

"What now?"

"I'm going to stay and see if I can't get a room somewhere."

"If you're staying, then I'm staying, too. Although I don't relish the idea of spending the night on someone's front lawn."

"Lord willing, we won't have to."

The carpet in the hall outside Toby's bedroom was a checkerboard of jade green and pastel yellow. Toby stood on one green square with his feet close together. He bent his knees, gripped the Greek primer tightly in his hand, and leaped forward, landing with both feet on another green square nearly three feet in front of him. Once again, he set himself and did another broad jump, landing just inside the target square. He almost lost his balance but regained it with a wild waving of his arms.

"Whew!" Toby said. The game continued for five minutes as he methodically worked his way from one green square to another.

"Hurry up, Toby," his mother called from the living room on the first floor. "We're wasting sunlight."

"Okay," Toby shouted back as he took the last leap that landed him at the top of the stairs. "I'm coming." Being careful not to step on a yellow square, Toby continued his game, stretching forward to reach the polished oak banister that ran along the stairs. He threw one leg over the edge. To Toby's right were the stairs, to his left, a fifteen-foot drop to the living room floor. Once situated, his legs straddling the slippery banister and his book tucked under one arm, Toby began his descent, sliding quickly down the rail.

"And don't slide down the banister ... Toby!"

The banister ended in a curlicue just above the first step, and Toby managed to stop abruptly before sliding off the end onto the floor.

"Toby Matthews, what were you thinking?" Mary scolded.

"That it was fun." Toby's lips parted in a sincere smile that always melted his mother's heart.

"You're going to make me old before my time," Mary complained. She was wearing a solid blue, two-piece bathing suit and a light white terrycloth robe.

The doorbell rang. Toby stiffened and Mary straightened. Apart from Thomas's earlier visit, no one came to the house except Wellman. Toby looked at his mom; she seemed at once nervous and excited. "I meant to tell you," Mary said. "We're going to have company at the beach."

"You said it was just going to be us," Toby said.

"I know, but Mr. Wellman called, and I mentioned that we were going out to get some sun. Asking him to join us was the polite thing to do."

"I didn't hear the phone ring," Toby said, frowning.

The doorbell chimed again. Mary opened the door. "Good afternoon," Wellman said. He was dressed in a pair of red and green swim trunks from which his thin white legs emerged, ending in a pair of blue sandals. Toby found the image comical. He also wore a plain white T-shirt. "Ready to take the beach by storm?"

"Hi, Richard," Mary said. It sounded to Toby like she had choked down a giggle. "Come in. I just have to grab a towel."

"There's the man of the hour," Wellman said to Toby. "That tan makes you look like a true California boy."

Toby felt the room grow cold. He shivered.

"Say hello to Mr. Wellman, Toby," his mother admonished him. "Don't forget your manners."

"Hello, Mr. Wellman," Toby uttered softly, looking at the carpet.

"You know," Wellman said, entering the house and closing the door behind him. "We've known each other for a long time, Toby. I think you can call me Richard or Rich."

Toby looked at his mother. He wanted her to make the man go away, to push him out the front door. Something about him was wrong. He was a friend of the Shadow Man. But instead of seeing his discomfort, Mary just stared at Wellman and smiled. Toby felt ill.

"Well," Mary said, "I'll just run upstairs and get a towel. I better get some sun block, too. I may be a minute or two."

"Take your time," Wellman said. "I'll visit with Toby."

"Make yourself comfortable," Mary said. "Then we'll go soak up more sun."

Mary walked up the stairs slowly. Toby noticed that Wellman's eyes were fixed on her. He turned to see the thin white terrycloth robe swaying with each step. Wellman was smiling.

Toby walked over to the brown leather sofa and plopped down. The leather felt warm on his bare legs. Wellman took a place on the matching loveseat. "Well, Toby, how are you today?"

"Okay, I guess."

"You did a great job Sunday night. The way you identified that reporter, I mean."

Toby shrugged. A subtle movement to his left caught Toby's eye. He turned but saw nothing. "He was lying. There are lots of liars."

"I'm sorry to say that you are right. We must always be careful who we trust."

Toby didn't respond.

Wellman leaned forward. "Can you always tell when someone is lying?" He rubbed his hands together.

"No," Toby answered. "Only if they know they're lying. Sometimes people believe their own lies. That confuses me."

"I see," Wellman said. He leaned back again and laid one arm across the back of the loveseat. "You don't like me, do you, Toby?"

Quickly, Toby cut his eyes away. Another movement, this time to his right, caught his attention. Turning again, he saw nothing. The room grew a few degrees colder.

"You can be honest with me, Toby. I promise not to bite your head off."

Toby shrugged. "I dunno."

"I think you're uncomfortable with me because I'm interested in your mother and she's interested in me. Is that it?"

"I dunno," Toby repeated.

"You love your mother, don't you, son?"

"I'm not your son," Toby snapped.

Wellman's eyes narrowed and his mouth tightened. Fear twisted in Toby. Again, Wellman leaned forward. He spoke softly, but his words were hard like granite and his gaze was hot, melting Toby's brief bravado like a candle. "You don't have to like me, boy. You just have to do as I say. You owe me an awful lot. This house, every toy you play with, every book you read, every bite of food you take, you owe to me. I rescued you out of a foster home and put you back with your mother. You will show me the respect I'm due. Is that clear?"

Toby nodded. Another movement crossed his peripheral vision. This time Toby didn't bother looking. He knew what it was ... who it was.

"Your mother has turned into a beautiful woman," Wellman continued. "She's been very helpful to me ... and to you, of course. I'm sure you love her very much. Is that true, Toby? Do you love your mother very much?"

"Yes," Toby whispered.

"I'm sorry. I didn't hear you."

Toby raised his head and said, "Yes."

"I'm sure you'd be sad if anything happened to her. Yes, that would be very sad indeed, wouldn't it?"

Toby waited. The Shadow Man would appear. He always did. Any moment, he would see the thing standing behind Wellman, peering over his shoulder as he did every service, as he did nearly every time he saw Wellman. He would be there, his eyes empty sockets, his featureless face staring down at him, intimidating him, gazing into his soul. The air would grow colder, the light darker, and the Shadow Man would grow more and more real. Toby felt like a condemned man waiting for the hangman to release the trapdoor beneath him.

"I'm ready now," Mary called as she came down the stairs. "Sorry to keep you waiting, but that's what a woman is supposed to do, isn't it?"

"I wouldn't have it any other way," Wellman said cheerfully. "However, I don't believe I was properly greeted when I came in."

"Really?" Mary said with surprise.

Wellman grinned and held out his arms. "Where's my hug?"

"Oh," Mary said. "Where are my manners?" She stepped forward and let Wellman take her in his arms.

Wellman turned so that Toby could see his smiling face. Except it wasn't his face that he saw—it was the Shadow Man who held his mother. The sharp appearance of Wellman's face had merged with the dark, abysmally black countenance of the Thing. Toby felt his stomach turn. Not only did the temperature in the room drop to that of a deep freezer, but Toby noticed something else—something new: a putrid, acrid, nauseating smell that reminded him of a long dead animal. He could do more than smell it; he could see it roll off Wellman in yellow-brown sheets and adhere to his mother.

"Don't you want to join in this hug, Toby?" Wellman asked. "It's not a group hug unless you join in."

Toby fought the urge to vomit. Slowly he walked into the rotting yellowish aura that surrounded the two and lifted his arms.

"That's better," Wellman said. "See, it's not that hard, is it?"

Care for a beer?" Rudy asked.

"No thanks," Thomas replied as he took a seat in a booth of the Aviary, one of Avalon's premier restaurants. Pictures and artwork of birds from around the world decorated the open eating area. It was Thomas's first time in the restaurant, although he had heard others speak of it. "I don't drink."

"Really," Rudy said. "I don't think I've met anyone your age who doesn't drink beer."

"It's a personal decision," Thomas explained as he took his seat. "This is quite a place."

Rudy agreed. "It's one of my favorite hangouts. Not much else to do on the island if you're not a tourist. There are only so many times a man can go swimming or boating."

"I think they call it 'island fever.' Living on an island makes it hard to take a road trip without first crossing over twenty miles of ocean. Still, it beats living in downtown L.A."

"I don't know," Rudy said. "I liked Phoenix. This is quite a change for me. But I didn't invite you to lunch so that you could hear me whine about island life. Let's order, then we can talk. I recommend the sea bass. It's to die for. You do eat fish, don't you?"

"That's one thing I do very well."

The waitress took their order, brought warm sourdough bread to their table, a second beer for Rudy, and a diet cola for Thomas.

"I understand you met with Toby at his home yesterday," Rudy said.

"Yes. We had a good time."

"Explain," Rudy pressed.

"Explain what?"

"I want to know how Toby reacted to you. Tell me everything."

Thomas was nonplussed. "There's not that much to tell. I visited with him, told jokes, played chess, and taught him the Greek alphabet."

"You told jokes?"

"Sure. Kids love jokes."

"And he laughed?" Rudy sucked down a mouthful of beer. "You know, I've never seen the kid smile, let alone laugh."

"He's a unique child in an unusual situation," Thomas said. "I was considered a prodigy when I was his age. Nothing like Toby, of course, but everything came easy to me. It's a hard title to bear. Especially in his case."

"What do you mean, 'in his case'?"

"When was the last time you saw a child's face on *Time* magazine? Adults look at him as a wonder, but he sees himself as a freak."

"He told you that?"

"He didn't have to," Thomas said. "You can read it in his eyes and in his behavior."

"I was afraid of that," Rudy admitted. "How do we make him happy? I mean, he's a kid, he must have some kind of happy switch. What's he want? More toys? Computer games?"

Thomas forced himself to pause before speaking. The man across the table from him was one of his employers, and he needed to choose his words carefully. "Toby has no happy switch. People are complex, children even more so. Prodigies are fragile, easily bruised and broken. Almost every child who has been properly classified a genius has social difficulties. They live maladjusted lives, misunderstood by everyone around them, unable to fit in. Toby is no different than the other prodigies that have gone before him."

"How many child prodigies do you know that can heal a person?" asked Rudy.

"None," Thomas admitted, "but I think we're on different pages here. I'm not so sure that Toby heals anyone because he is a prodigy. I think those are miracles and only God can work a miracle. The fact that Toby is mentally gifted may not be related at all."

"All my life," Rudy said as he turned to face the ocean, "I've denied miracles and anything supernatural. I tend toward the technical in my thinking. That's one reason I went into radio production. I used to listen to all those people who called Rich each night and laugh to myself. 'What morons,' I used to say. But here I am, an executive in the Church of New Jerusalem, and twice a week I watch a little boy do things that cannot be explained."

"He does boggle the mind."

"So you and he hit it off. Is that right?"

"I think so. I'm supposed to see him tonight. He asked me to come over, so I take that as a good sign."

"That's good, real good." The waitress brought two plates of blackened sea bass, garlic mashed potatoes, and glazed carrots. The conversation lulled while the plates were set before them. After the waitress left, Rudy continued. "I wanted to make sure you understand the important position you're in. As you may have noticed, CNJ is unlike any other organization in the world. We're not a church in the truest sense of the word, nor are we a business. We defy description. Every day thousands—and I mean this literally—thousands of people call us from all over the world. Everyone has some need. Everyone insists on meeting Toby. Some offer us bribes, some threaten our lives, and those are the ones that believe that Toby is for real. There are others out there that see the boy like he's some kind of demon out to destroy Christianity, Islam, Buddhism, and every other group you can think of. Did you know that we average two bomb threats a week?"

Thomas was surprised. He had been working at the compound for months and had never heard a word about bomb threats or experienced an evacuation. "I had no idea. Shouldn't the buildings be cleared when such threats come in?"

"No. Absolutely not." Rudy poked at the air with his fork. "That kind of publicity would ruin us. We're safe. Our security is the best possible. No one gets on the grounds without our guards knowing of it. They're just threats, that's all. That's the beauty of a bomb threat. You can disrupt everything and not ever touch an explosive. We're careful. Especially when it comes to Toby."

"Still . . . bomb threats."

"I mention that to bring up this point: You will be working closely with Toby. If he likes you as much as you say he does and as much as his mother says—"

"You spoke to his mother about me?"

"Of course I did. Her opinion about you matters a great deal. It's important that she be comfortable with you, too. That doesn't surprise you, does it?"

"No, I guess not. You're thorough, I'll say that."

"We have to be. It didn't take us long to learn that there are too many crazies out there and too few rational people. As someone who will be close to Toby, you will become a target. Not just for the wackos, but for everyone who wants attention from Toby. That means outsiders and even employees. I don't know how cynical you are, but it's not enough. In this setting being paranoid is an advantage. More than that, it's a requirement."

Thomas smiled.

"Don't think I'm kidding, Thomas. Love can kill as quickly as hatred. There's a reason Elvis and the Beatles had the deep security they did, and that was to protect them from fans. We're dealing daily with people who have no hope in life, and that desperation can lead to some pretty bizarre behavior."

"What do you mean bizarre?" Thomas's curiosity was growing.

"I've been propositioned by teenagers and grandmothers. I've had executives offer me houses, boats, and even airplanes. My life has been threatened so many times that I can't keep count. And here's the kicker—I'm just an office jockey. I don't appear on stage. I have nothing to do with the public. All I do is serve as an aide to Rich Wellman and oversee the production values of the services. I've been in a few pictures with Rich and Toby, and that made me fair game. The same is going to happen to you."

"Are you trying to frighten me off?" Thomas asked.

"Not at all. Quite the contrary. I pushed for you. I wanted someone like you who could connect with Toby. You seem to have achieved that."

"I'm one of the few people in the world who doesn't want anything from him," Thomas confessed. "I'm happy just watching him do what he does. It's amazing."

"There's something else you should know," Rudy said as he buttered another piece of warm sourdough bread. "I've hidden your existence here."

"Hidden my existence?"

"I've made you disappear as far as the database, employee records, and the like are concerned. It's going to be impossible for anyone to get hold of you. I've done that to keep people from pestering you about Toby. It's amazing how many friends you'll have and how many cousins, nephews, nieces, and aunts who will come out of the woodwork once they know who you are working for. It's best that you not have contact with anyone outside the compound. It's asking a lot, I know, but it's the best thing for Toby, and he's my primary concern. Can you live with that?"

Thomas didn't hesitate. "Yes."

"There's one more thing," Rudy said. "Rich, Toby, and Mary will be leaving the country in a few days. Arrangements are still being made. Rich wants you to go with them to keep the boy company."

"Out of the country?" Thomas was surprised. "I don't have a passport."

"I'll take care of that. I'll make the arrangements. You'll have to sign a document or two and have your picture taken. You don't mind flying, do you?"

"Not at all. I enjoy it. Where are we going?"

"Asia. That's all I can tell you now."

Thomas nodded. "Just let me know what I need to do and when we're leaving. I'll be there with bells on."

"Just bring your enthusiasm. Leave the bells home."

chapter 18

I t's a fair price, considering."

"Considering what?" Pratt asked as he stood on the shiny wood deck of the thirty-four-foot Chris Craft Sedan. The boat was moored in the portion of Avalon Harbor reserved for the yacht club. It bobbed on gentle swells thirty yards from the club dock. Standing next to him was a short man with black and gray hair pulled back into a ponytail and two days' growth of beard on his chin. He chewed a toothpick as if it provided nourishment. The man, who had identified himself as Norm, wore jeans, a T-shirt with a picture of a giant golf ball on it, and sneakers without socks.

The boat looked old, but well taken care of. "The *Becky J* is a classic," Norm said proudly. "I've done all the interior restoration myself. They don't build them like this anymore."

"It looks old," Edison said.

The toothpick in Norm's mouth began to move excitedly, slipping along his down-turned mouth. "Not a yachtsman, are you? She was built in 1963, back when craftsmanship still existed and boats were made of more than fiberglass."

"My friend meant no insult," Pratt interjected.

"People can't find a place to stay on the island anymore. Every hotel, bed and breakfast, and campsite is booked for months in advance. What you're looking at is the only available place to sleep tonight. Five hundred a night isn't all that bad in light of the situation."

Dr. Edison groaned, echoing everything Pratt felt.

"Don't blame me," Norm said. "It's supply and demand. You seem like smart men; you can understand that."

Pratt rubbed his eyes. "It's been a long day," Pratt said. "We've been going from hotel to hotel and getting nowhere. That's when someone told us about you."

"The Colonnade?" Norm asked.

"Yes. How did you know?" asked Edison with surprise. "We didn't mention that on the phone."

"You spoke to a lady with red hair and looks to be in her fifties?" Norm added.

"Right again," Pratt said.

"My sister-in-law. Her husband left her last year. Made working on her almost impossible—the boat, I mean. That's not to say that my sister-in-law couldn't use a little work herself. She used to live on the boat until just a few days ago. Moved the last of her stuff off yesterday. Got too lonely, she said, so my wife let her move in with us. The husband was a nice guy until he reached fifty—he turned into an idiot. Started chasing women. Me? I'd rather chase a golf ball around a nice green course. Anyway, my wife says she would rent the boat out and make some money while the making is good. I don't much like the idea, but I gave in. This is the first day it's been open."

"We're only going to be here for a day or two," Pratt said. "We're just a couple of graduate school professors. Can't you give us a break?"

"If you're planning to be in one of those church services you'll be here a lot longer than a couple of days."

"What do you mean?" Pratt asked.

"That Jerusalem church thing, you're here for that, aren't you? The island used to attract tourists by the hundreds; now everything is overrun by people who want to see the kid."

"Actually, we're not here to see . . . the kid. We're here on other business."

"You sure? I don't mean to insult you, but I've run out of patience with those folks. This used to be a nice place to live, but now everything has changed. Toby-ites we call them. It's Toby this, Toby that. The roads are clogged with those people. It's getting to where you can't spit without hitting one of them."

"I don't suppose you know anyone who works inside, do you?" Edison asked. "We're trying to reach one of the employees."

"Nope. Don't care to know any of them. I know plenty who have tried to get in, but have been turned away because they couldn't afford the entrance fee."

"It was worth asking," Edison said.

"You want to rent the boat or not?" Norm asked bluntly. "It's in great shape. I've owned her since I was twenty-five. I lived on it until I married. Too dangerous to bring up rug rats around the water, so we bought a house. We kept it for vacations and for when company came."

"It's beautiful," Pratt said, taking in the long curved lines. A highly polished redwood deck circled the boat's superstructure. Everything else was covered in thick white paint. "But the price is too high. I'm sure four or five Toby-ites could pool their resources and pay what you're asking."

Norm's face soured as if he had just eaten a bad prune.

"That's true," Edison said, picking up on Pratt's tactic. "How many people can this boat sleep?"

"A few," Norm admitted. Pratt watched him work the tooth-pick more.

"Five or six Toby-ites," Pratt continued. "Well, at least you'd get your five hundred dollars a night."

Norm sighed dramatically and cut his eyes to Pratt. "You aren't trying to take advantage of me, are you?"

"Look," Pratt said. "We just want the place for a couple of nights, that's all, and we can't afford a thousand dollars."

"How about five hundred dollars for two nights?"

"Agreed," Pratt said quickly, squelching the sting of the expense.

"I can't take credit cards," the man said. "This isn't a regular business for me—yet."

"No problem," Edison said. "I saw an ATM not far from here. I'll get some cash. Will that work?"

"Cash works great," Norm said. "I'll show you around the boat."

It took another half hour for the tour to be given and the rules recited. Once done, the three piled into the tiny dinghy that had initially brought them to the boat, and Norm directed the craft back to the small dock from which they had departed. Edison found an ATM next to the local bank and withdrew five hundred dollars from his personal account. Norm had taken the money eagerly and watched as Pratt and Edison motored back to the *Becky J.*

The sun was setting and the evening sky was filling with the darkness of a new night. The breeze of the ocean was sweet and mixed with the aroma of juniper and sage that covered the island. Voices echoed off the low hills and rolled across the water. Any other time and the setting would be salubrious, but Pratt's mind would not settle. Frustration stewed in him, and the taxing events of the day had left him as weary as if he had spent the time in physical labor. Unlike Edison, he could not sleep. The night was still young, but Edison had lain down on the bed for a nap and was soon snoring loud enough to rattle the windows. Pratt had started to wake him, then thought better of it. Instead he climbed to the upper deck, found a chaise lounge, and settled in to watch the ocean darken as the sun set over the hills in the west. Gazing east, Pratt could see the lights of the Los Angeles basin. From better than twenty miles away, they looked lovely, but no matter how hard he tried, he could not lose himself in the beauty that surrounded him. While his body lay still, his mind churned like water around a propeller.

As he gazed at the distant lights that brightened as the darkness increased, Pratt wondered if he had made a mistake. Was he meddling? Was he poking his nose in where it didn't belong and where it could be cut off? The aching voice of Thomas's mother played back in his ears. There was a desperation in her words, fear saturated in every syllable. And he had made a promise. He would not go back on that.

Still, the road ahead was blocked by an obstacle that Pratt had no idea how to overcome. Before he and Edison had settled into the boat for a little rest, he had tried to call the CNJ again, but was told that no Thomas York worked there. That had surprised him, because he had called several times before deciding to travel to Catalina, and each time the operator had taken a message for Thomas. Now they denied he had ever worked there. Had he quit or been fired? He had no way of knowing. Pratt was as much in the dark as the ocean before him would be in another hour.

Closing his eyes, he lay his head back and inhaled the briny ocean air. As his body relaxed, his soul became active. A prayer, soft as foam, rose in his mind. There was no formality to it, no carefully crafted prose, just the percolation of concern that he directed heavenward. Few words were used, but the emotions were clear. Apprehension adorned with uncertainty and confusion took wings in silent prayer. What few words were murmured were requests for guidance and direction. Then Pratt did what was so hard for him to do. Born with a keen mind, his thoughts were seldom still or silent, but Pratt waited. He listened for the response of God. He had no expectation of words written in the sky, or an audible whisper in his ears. He did expect that direction would be laid upon his heart and he would gain a peace about that which lay ahead.

He asked God point-blank questions: Do I belong here? Have I misjudged your leading? In less than five minutes, Pratt knew that the journey he started was the right one, and he chastised himself for expecting it to be easy. Thomas was worth redeeming, his mother worth assisting.

"Hungry?" a voice said behind him. It was Edison.

"I haven't given it any thought, but I could eat."

"I have thought about it and now that my nap is over, I'm ready to go to that little seafood place we saw."

Pratt rose. "Fine with me. Then we can make another stop."

"Oh? Where?"

"The sheriff's office. It's time to recruit some help."

You're doing it all wrong," Thomas said seriously.

Toby studied him for a moment and said, "What?"

"You're doing it wrong," Thomas repeated. "How someone who can learn the Greek alphabet in ten minutes can mess up so badly on the techniques of taco construction is beyond me." Thomas waited for Toby's response.

Toby looked down at the taco he held in his hand. On the dining room table before him were bowls of chopped lettuce, shredded beef, grated cheese, onions, tomatoes, and salsa. "You can't mess up a taco," Toby protested. "You just put all the stuff in the tortilla and eat it."

"Well, that's the way an amateur does things, but some of us know that there is only one way to prepare a taco correctly." Thomas straightened in his chair and with a stiff formality said, "Please observe and learn."

Mary, who had prepared the meal, chuckled. Toby's face was a mask of suspicion.

"First," Thomas continued, "one opens the fried tortilla—and it must be fried, just as your mother has done with these. With the tortilla now flat upon your plate, you add the first ingredient, which is ... ?"

"The meat," Toby answered.

"Wrong. That's the big mistake. The meat is always second. First comes the cheese. Why, you ask? Because when the cheese hits the hot tortilla, it melts. Then comes the meat, which further melts the cheese. If you put the cheese on last like the rest of the world does, your taco will look pretty, but it will not be constructed for the best possible flavor. Now we add the onions on top of the meat—lots of onions. Next a little tomato and lettuce, then a nice salsa and a dollop of sour cream." Thomas performed each step like a television chef. "If done properly, you'll have the best-tasting taco possible and one . . ." He took a big bite. Contents plopped out the back of the taco, landing in the middle of his plate. ". . . that is properly messy." He took a napkin and wiped his mouth.

Toby laughed loudly. "You're nuts," he said.

"Don't knock it until you try it."

After Toby had finished his first taco, he prepared another the "Thomas way" and took a big bite.

"Well," Thomas said. "Am I right, or am I right?"

"It tastes the same," Toby said.

"Hmm," Thomas said. "And to think I spent all that money getting that process patented."

"Do they have tacos in Asia?" Toby asked, his smile melting away.

"I don't think so, honey," Mary said as she rose and began clearing the table.

"So you know about the trip," Thomas said. "Sounds exciting."

"Mr. Wellman told me when we were at the beach today." Toby played with his fork.

"You don't seem very happy about it," Thomas observed. "Don't you want to see another country?"

Toby shrugged.

"I think he's nervous about going to a strange place," Mary said. She rose from the table and went into the kitchen.

"No, I'm not," Toby shot back.

"Easy, buddy," Thomas said. "Did Mr. Wellman tell you that I was going, too?"

"No. Really? You're really going with us?" Excitement poured from Toby.

"They asked me today. I said yes. I think it could be fun. I might even learn something."

"Cool!" Toby enthused. "You can teach me more Greek."

"That's the plan." Thomas turned to Mary when she returned to the table. She carried three bowls of chocolate chip ice cream. "Did they tell you where in Asia we were going?"

"No," Mary answered. "I didn't ask."

"I did," Toby interjected. "But Mr. Wellman wouldn't tell me. He keeps lots of secrets."

"I imagine he has to," Thomas said. "He has a lot to deal with every day."

"He's an important man," Mary added. "He's been a big help to us."

Toby poked at his ice cream, meticulously carving out the tiny bits of chocolate. Thomas watched him for a few moments. It was easy to see that he was upset, even fearful.

"You okay, pal?"

"Yeah," Toby said without enthusiasm. He continued digging at the ice cream.

Thomas looked to Mary, who shrugged.

"May I be excused?" Toby asked.

"You don't want to eat your ice cream?" Mary asked.

"No."

"What say we hit the Greek, Toby," Thomas suggested, hoping to brighten the boy's mood. "You did say that you memorized the alphabet."

"In ten minutes," Toby reminded him.

"So you keep saying. Now it's time to show me."

"You boys go on," Mary said. "I'll clean up."

In the rec room Thomas lowered his large frame to the thickly carpeted floor. Toby plopped down next to him. Both were propped up on their elbows. Before them was a pad of lined paper, the Greek primer Thomas had given Toby, and an open book written in Greek. Toby was scribbling down characters on the pad.

"Outstanding," Thomas said. "You got every one right and in the correct order, both capitals and small letters."

"Thanks," Toby said, clearly pleased.

"Greek is different than English in many ways," Thomas explained. "For example, sentences begin with small letters, not capitals like we're used to. Only proper nouns begin with capital letters. Do you know what a proper noun is?"

"Names and places," Toby answered.

"Right. Now sometimes two vowels are put together and form a diphthong."

"Dif-thong," Toby repeated.

"Exactly. A diphthong is composed of two vowels that make one sound. Our word *oil* has a diphthong. The 'o' and 'i' make a single, smooth sound. So ..." Thomas took the pad, leaned on one arm, and wrote two Greek letters: an alpha and an iota. "This diphthong sounds like the letter 'i.' In fact, our English word *aisle* does the same thing. Got it?"

"Got it," Toby said.

"There are seven proper diphthongs—"

"Why Greek?" Toby asked suddenly.

"Why diphthongs in Greek?" Thomas was confused by the sudden question.

"No," Toby said. "There are lots of languages in the world. Why did you choose Greek to study?"

"Ah," Thomas said. "I was a student at a special graduate school in Riverside. I studied Greek and Hebrew there as part of my training."

"Training for what?"

"I was a theology and Bible student. The New Testament is written in Greek, and most of the Old Testament is written in Hebrew. Some passages are written in Aramaic."

"I don't understand. New Testament and Old Testament?"

Thomas pushed himself up into a sitting position, crossing his legs in front of him. Toby did the same. Reaching to the book that lay open on the floor, Thomas held it out to Toby. "This is a Greek New Testament. It's part of the Bible. Anyone can get a Bible in their own language. You've seen a Bible before, right?"

"No," Toby said. "I know all the books we have. We don't have a Bible."

Thomas suddenly felt foolish. Why had he assumed that Toby would know these things? "Have you ever been to church, Toby?"

"No. Never."

The meaning of that revelation rebounded in Thomas's mind. "You've never been to church on a Sunday?"

"Just the services we do here. Do you go to church a lot?"

"I used to," Thomas replied. "A few years ago. I stopped completely a few months before I came here."

"How come?"

"I'm not sure," Thomas admitted. "I was looking for something I couldn't find in church."

"Like what?"

"The miraculous," Thomas said. "That's why I'm here on the compound. I first heard about you on Mr. Wellman's radio show and I became interested. After you settled here and the Church of New Jerusalem was founded, I left school and applied for a job."

"You left school to come here and meet me?"

"That's it in a nutshell."

Toby lowered his head in thought. "But you haven't asked me for anything. Everyone asks me for things."

"I didn't come here so you could do something for me; I came here so I could do something for you. At first, I just thought I'd do office work, but this is better."

"The church you went to before you came here, was it the same as our church?"

"No, not really. There are some differences."

"Like what?"

"Well, they sing, like we do here, and then the pastor stands up and preaches a message out of the Bible."

"Does he preach out of any other books?" Toby inquired.

"No, just the Bible. You see, most churches believe the Bible is the Word of God."

"But it's not."

"I didn't say that," Thomas added quickly.

"Then it is," Toby pressed.

"Yes, I believe it to be."

"Word of God," Toby repeated as if he were tasting the words. "Word of God? Does that mean the Bible has God's words in it?"

"It's a little more complex than that, but yes."

"If the Bible is from God, then why don't we use it here?"

"I don't know, Toby," Thomas admitted. "I don't think Mr. Wellman knows much about the Bible. He just knows about you."

A puzzled look crossed Toby's face, and he tilted his head to one side. "Can I read the Bible?" he finally asked.

"I don't see why not. I'll bring one to you tomorrow."

Toby reached over and took the Greek New Testament from Thomas. "God's Word," he said softly. He fanned the pages looking at the strange characters that made up stranger-looking words. He could now recognize the letters, but he had no vocabulary to go with it. "What does this say?" he asked, pointing at a line of text.

"Let's see," Thomas replied, taking the book back. He ran his finger along the line of text, soaking in the words. "It says—" He stopped. "How ironic. It's from the gospel of Mark, and it says, 'People were bringing small children unto Jesus to have him touch them, but the disciples scolded them. When Jesus saw it, he was angry. He said to them, 'Let the little children come to me, and do not hinder them, for the kingdom of God belongs to such as these. I tell you the truth, anyone who will not receive the kingdom of God like a little child will never enter it.'"

"God loves children," Toby said reflectively. "I'm ... I'm a child. Does that mean me?"

"Yes," Thomas answered. "I believe with all my heart that it does."

"It said that Jesus blessed the children?"

Thomas smiled. "Yes, it did. The Bible shows that Jesus loved children."

"I don't know any of this," Toby admitted. "But it must be important." He paused in thought. "Tell me more about Jesus and the Bible."

Thomas took a deep breath and let it out slowly. There were more layers to Toby than Thomas had imagined, maybe more than he could fathom. Not only was he a genius, but he was incredibly insightful. "Okay," Thomas said. "Let's start at the beginning."

Toby laid on his back and closed his eyes. "I'm ready."

I don't understand why you won't help," Pratt complained to the officer who stood behind a wide counter at the Sumner Avenue sheriff's substation.

"Because you're asking us to do something that goes beyond our duties as deputy sheriffs." The man was of average height with rough skin and a thick middle, and he wore a khaki shirt to which was affixed a six-pointed star. "We have no legal reason to enter the church's compound. If a crime was being committed, then that would be a different matter, but I can't send an officer out there and say, 'You had better let these guys come in and find their friend.' If your student wants to disappear behind those walls and fences, then that's his choice."

"But what if he were abducted?" Edison asked.

"That would be different. Forcibly abducting someone is certainly a crime." The officer studied them for a moment. "Are you telling me that someone has kidnapped your friend?"

"No," Pratt said. "His father is sick and he needs to call home, but no one can contact him. As isolated as he is, he might as well be abducted."

"I'm sorry to hear about his old man, but that doesn't change the situation."

"What can we do?" Pratt asked in frustration. "When we call they tell us that he doesn't work there, but every time I called before, they took a message. That doesn't sound right."

"Maybe he quit," the officer suggested.

"It doesn't strike you as odd that the Church of New Jerusalem is being so secretive?" Pratt leaned his elbows on the counter. "How many churches do you know that have that kind of security?"

"How many churches have Toby?" the officer rejoined. "Every day, we have someone in a holding cell, someone who thought they could sneak in and see the boy. Some of them are downright loony. The church has a right to secrecy. They have to protect the boy somehow."

Pratt suddenly understood: The deputy saw them as possible troublemakers, trying to worm their way in. "Have you been to one of the services?" Pratt asked, suppressing any hint of accusation or innuendo.

"Not that that has anything to do with your problem, but yes. The church held a special service for sheriff's personnel. But don't read anything into that. They did the same for fire crews and business owners."

Pratt could only nod. What better way to secure support and aide than to include those who might later be a problem? "Is it everything they say it is?"

"More," the deputy said in softer tones. "They were a big help to me."

"Family member?" Pratt guessed.

"My wife. Cervical cancer. It's all gone now. Baffled the doctors. Baffled me, but I'm grateful."

"I understand," Pratt said and shook the officer's hand. "I'm happy for you and your wife."

"I hope things work out for you," the deputy replied. "Sorry I can't be of more help."

Pratt and Edison exited the small sheriff's station. As the glass doors closed behind them, Pratt turned in time to see the deputy pick up the phone. The sight made him uneasy.

chapter 19

"Sit down, Thomas," Wellman said, firmly motioning to a chair.

Thomas entered the cavernous office and took a seat in a chair opposite Wellman's desk. He was uncertain why, but he felt like he had just been called to the principal's office.

"You seem to have become very popular in the last twenty-four hours," Wellman said without preamble. "Have you told anyone of your new relationship to Toby?"

"No," Thomas replied. "The only people I've spoken to in the last two days have been you, Rudy, Mary, and Toby."

"You've made no phone calls?"

"I haven't touched a phone in a month." Thomas crossed his legs and folded his hands. He was not one to get excited, and few things intimidated him. "What is all this about?"

"I received a report from one of our members in the sheriff's department stating that two men came looking for you. They were complaining that they couldn't get past the front gate. I called security and sure enough, one of our men filed a report which said that two men came to the main gate of the compound asking to see you. They were sent packing, of course. Anyone can claim that they know someone in the compound."

"Two men?"

"I'm not finished," Wellman said raising a hand. "It turns out that the switchboard has recorded no less than a dozen calls asking for you. Some from right here on the island."

"I haven't heard anything about the calls. Why wasn't I told?"

Wellman waved off the question. "I was led to believe that you understood the need for privacy and security when it came to Toby."

"I have spoken to no one," Thomas said firmly. "Who are the two men?"

"We've been able to determine the name of one of them: Aaron Pratt. I don't know the name of the other. Here's a still captured from the security camera at the front gate. Recognize them?"

Thomas took the glossy printout and studied the grainy image. "That's Dr. Pratt all right," he said. "The other man is Dr. Morris Edison."

"Should I know those names?" Wellman leaned back in his chair and steepled his fingers.

"I don't see why," Thomas answered. "Dr. Pratt was one of my professors at grad school. He was also my curriculum advisor. Dr. Edison is the president of the school. I don't know why they're here. At least I don't think I do."

"Guess," Wellman prompted sternly.

Thomas shrugged. "CNJ is about as far from the mainstream of contemporary church life as one can get. Not to put too fine a point on it, most evangelical churches consider you a cult."

"That's not surprising. You think they're here to rescue you?"

"Maybe," Thomas admitted. "But why now? I've been out of school for close to a year. Why show up now?"

"I couldn't begin to guess," Wellman said. "I want you to avoid them at all costs. They pose a threat to our work."

"These men are the least threatening guys you'll ever meet. They're spiritual men with nothing but pure motives."

"Wars have been started by spiritual men, Thomas. Don't forget that. You said it yourself, we are not in the mainstream. For all I know, these two could be cranks."

"They could also be looking for something more spiritual. Maybe they need to see Toby."

"They can't know that you're Toby's companion. I want that understood. The more who know about that connection, the more danger there is to you and to Toby's privacy. I say it again: Stay away from them. If you can't do that, I'll have you replaced. Is that clear?"

Thomas rose and set the printout on the table. "It is."

"Don't fail me, Thomas."

Thomas studied Wellman for a moment. There was something about him that didn't sit well, something out of place, something that didn't belong. Whatever it was, it unsettled Thomas, who walked from the room with no further comment.

Once again, Toby was on the floor. Sofas and chairs were fine, but he preferred the thickly-carpeted floor where he could lay everything out in front of him. To Toby, it was like sitting on a giant table. This morning the only thing before him was the Bible that Thomas had dropped off that morning. Toby wanted him to stay, but Thomas had said that he had a meeting with Wellman.

The image of Wellman and the Shadow Man made Toby shudder. He had tried to tell his mother about the Shadow Man, about the evil darkness that followed him and now followed Wellman, but they had been interrupted. His mother had brought it up at the beach, but he didn't want to talk about it around Wellman. The subject seemed forgotten—but not to him.

Pushing the image out of his mind, Toby opened the Bible. It was old and tattered around the edges. The leather cover was scarred. He fanned the pages and saw notes written in the margins and sentences underlined. Turning to the front of the book, Toby found what he was looking for: a table of contents.

Immediately he noticed the phrases "Old Testament" and "New Testament." Just like Thomas had said. Under each heading were names and titles. Toby quickly discerned that these were the names of smaller books within the greater book. He counted them. Thirty-nine in the Old Testament; twenty-seven in the New Testament. Sixty-six books total.

Where to start? Toby wondered. There were over two thousand pages in the Bible. Even though he read two or three times faster than most people, it would take him a long time to read it all. There were parts in the back of the Bible that seemed different than the rest. There was something called a "concordance" which Toby quickly gleaned would lead him to certain passages based on particular words. He thought that interesting. There were colorful maps too, which he studied closely.

Thirty minutes later, Toby had read the articles in the front of the Bible, learning that what Thomas had given him was called a study Bible. There were notes at the bottom helping the reader understand some of the passages. Still there was so much to read.

Turning the pages, Toby found the beginning of the New Testament. When he had glanced through the pages earlier, he had taken notice of Thomas's notes in the margins. There were many more notes in the New Testament than the old. *That must be his favorite,* Toby reasoned. It had been a New Testament passage that Thomas had read—the passage about Jesus and the children. The night before, prompted by Toby, Thomas had described the Bible and Jesus. He had said that the subject for the entire Bible was Jesus, even though most of it had been written centuries before Jesus was born. This had puzzled Toby, but he remained quiet while Thomas gave a casual and personal lecture. Toby had quickly grasped the history and importance of the Bible, but many of the things Thomas spoke of mystified him. Thomas had spoken of Jesus' life and death and resurrection; he used terms like salvation, faith, and grace. While Toby understood the definitions, he somehow felt that he was missing something. It was an unusual sensation.

Sensation was a good term, Toby decided. Unlike other topics he studied, the talk of Jesus touched him inside in a way he could not describe. He was confused.

Of one thing he was certain: He had to know more. Turning to Matthew, Toby began to read.

He had read ten chapters of the gospel when he first noticed the chill.

He had read another chapter when he noticed the acrid smell. With it came a memory—a terrifying recollection of the day before.

Toby shuddered but kept his eyes glued to the page. He was no longer reading, but he could not look up. He knew, not just in his mind, but in the deep part of his heart, that he was no longer alone.

The light in the room changed. The warm ivory glow of the sun shifted to a yellow brown. The lights seemed to dim as if some object were sucking out the radiance like soda through a straw.

Mustering all his discipline, Toby kept his gaze fixed on the Bible. An iceberg cold ran through him in prickly waves, one surge following another. Toby's heart no longer pounded rhythmically; it stuttered, skipped, and rattled in the cage of his chest. His mouth went dry like sand as the putrid odor surrounded him. It felt thick and viscous like oil. It covered him, clung to him, oozing along his face and bare arms. He could feel it work its way between his fingers and creep along the edges of his ears and nose. A gag lodged in Toby's throat.

Toby snapped his head up and looked at what he already knew was there. And it *was* there. Ten feet away. Then nine. Then eight. It didn't walk. Its legs didn't move. The black shape that he had always seen as a shadow slowly solidified. The creature's hollow eyes stared at him as a wild animal might stare at its prey. Eight feet, seven feet.

The odor that filled the room thickened as though it might coagulate, coalescing into a gel that would soon be impossible to breathe. Toby was sure he would suffocate in the rancid air.

Six feet, five feet. Closer, darker, more fetid. Unable to move, Toby, who had faced down a tornado, talked face-to-face with an insane gunman, was terror stricken. The Shadow Man wanted him. The Shadow Man had come for him. Toby didn't fear impending death. He was sure the Shadow Man had something worse in mind.

Four feet.

The Shadow Man rippled, and his formless, featureless countenance changed as if it were seeking just the right face for the moment. Toby thought he saw a man's face, his father's face, then he saw the gunman's face from the grocery store, then he saw his mother's face, then Wellman's.

Three feet.

Toby pushed himself back. A smile—toothless, lipless, but somehow still a smile—parted the roiling, featureless face of the Shadow Man. Toby felt ill. His limbs began to shake and his lip quivered involuntarily.

Two feet.

Shadow Man reached forward with an arm that seemed to bubble like boiling tar. The creature was no longer a shadow. It was solidifying, coagulating into something terrible.

"No," Toby said just above a whisper.

The creature nodded and extended its reach until it nearly touched Toby's face. Toby recoiled, instinctively putting the only shield in reach between him and it. Only the worn Bible separated Toby's face from the touch of the black shadow.

Toby curled into a ball and screamed. And screamed. And screamed. The shrill of it pierced the air and walls. His own voice deafened him, and he wished it would blind him.

The door to the rec room exploded open. Something grabbed Toby. A sound filled the room. Toby screamed again.

The touch was warm and soft, but most of all, it was familiar.

"Toby! What is it, Toby?" It was his mother's voice. "Talk to me, Toby."

Slowly, Toby lowered the Bible and peeked over its edge. The thing was gone. "It was here." Toby quivered. "It was coming after me. Me. It hates me. It wants me."

"What was coming after you?" Mary sat on the floor, wrapping Toby in her arms and gently rocking side to side.

"The Shadow Man," Toby answered. "The Shadow Man."

"I don't see anyone," Mary said. "It's okay. You're safe now.

I won't let anything happen to you. Maybe you just fell asleep and had a bad dream."

"But he was here," Toby insisted. "I saw him."

"Well, he's not here now," Mary said. She paused, then asked, "What is that smell?"

BOOK III

dance of shadow

For certain men whose condemnation was written about long ago have secretly slipped in among you. They are godless men, who change the grace of our God into a license for immorality and deny Jesus Christ our only Sovereign and Lord.

JUDE 1:4

"Are not my few days almost over?
Turn away from me so I can have a
*   moment's joy*
before I go to the place of no return,
to the land of gloom and deep shadow,
to the land of deepest night,
of deep shadow and disorder,
where even the light is like darkness."

JOB 10:20–22

chapter 20

W hat does he want?" Toby asked.

"I'm not sure," Thomas said as he led the way from Toby's home to the Gull Auditorium, where Wellman had said they were to meet. Above them white gulls flew in lazy circles through a crisp blue sky, and the disk of the morning sun still shone through the still air. It was a short walk and they strolled leisurely. "I think he wants you to meet some people. Maybe he wants to talk about our trip. He just said to be there at 10:30."

"I don't want to go on the trip," Toby said.

"I think it could be interesting, buddy. You, me, and your mother seeing the world. Not many kids can say they've gone overseas."

"I won't see anything," Toby said. "Mr. Wellman won't let me. He doesn't let me go anywhere off the compound."

"He's concerned about your security. He just wants to protect you from people who want to hurt you."

"He can't protect me from ..." Toby trailed off.

"Your mother told me about what happened yesterday. She said you were pretty scared. Do you want to talk about it?"

"No," Toby replied. "Talking won't help."

"It might. Sometimes just talking about things makes people feel better."

Toby shook his head. "It won't help me."

Thomas sighed and put his hand on Toby's shoulder. "I'm not going to pry, buddy, but I want you to know that you can talk to me anytime. I don't care what it is or when it is. We're friends, and friends listen to one another."

"Do you have lots of friends, Thomas?" Toby asked.

Thomas thought before answering. "Not many," he admitted. "I'm pretty much a loner, have been all my life."

"But you had some? Right?"

"I guess."

"Were any of them older than you?"

"I had a professor who was older than me. I liked him a lot. Best teacher I ever had. I can't say that we were really friends, because we didn't hang out together."

"Like we hang out?"

"Exactly," Thomas responded. "I like to hang out with you."

"But now you're here," Toby said cryptically.

"What do you mean?"

"You don't see your friends anymore. You left them behind to come here."

"I suppose I did," Thomas confessed. "I left a great many things behind to be here. But I think you're worth it." Toby lowered his head, and Thomas saw his shoulders droop. "Hey, what's the matter?"

"You'll leave this place sometime, too. Just like you left the place you were before. You left your friends to come here. You'll leave me to go someplace else."

"No, I won't."

"You did before."

"That was different," Thomas argued.

"How?"

Thomas's thoughts stumbled. With any other child, he could offer some simple assurance and be believed. Not so with Toby. The boy was more than a prodigy; he possessed an insight that went beyond anything he had ever encountered. "I don't know, it just is."

"You'll leave someday and I'll be alone. I'll be alone all my life."

Thomas stopped abruptly and turned Toby to face him. "Look at me, Toby. Look into my eyes. Read my thoughts or whatever it is you do, but listen carefully. I will be your friend forever. Nothing will ever change that. Friends stick together."

Toby gazed through crystal blue eyes. "You have a friend who will need you. And you need him."

"What are you talking about?" Thomas pressed.

"He will need you soon. Be ready."

Toby had fallen into his cryptic speech pattern. Mary had described it to Thomas, and he had seen it before when Toby was on stage. At first Thomas had assumed that he was purposefully being vague like unscrupulous televangelists, but he soon dismissed the idea. Being close to Toby over the last few days had confirmed what Thomas had previously suspected: Toby, while being a genius, was still a little boy who lacked the ability to describe difficult situations. Mary had told him how he had described a waitress's breast cancer as "lumps and bumps." He was older now and he had learned many medical conditions from his encounters with the infirm who flocked to the services, but some adult concepts were still beyond the reach of his communication skills.

"Who, Toby? Who will need my help?"

Toby shrugged. "Your friend, that's all I know."

"Okay, Toby," Thomas said, puzzled. "Cheer up, will you? People are going to think I stole your smile."

Toby started forward. "Let's get this over with."

Ten minutes later, Thomas and Toby walked into the Gull House theater where the twice-weekly services were held. Another service would be held tonight, but that was four hours away. At the moment, the theater-style seats were empty, the yawning room dark and foreboding. It seemed strange to be in such a large room void of the natural noises of people. The thick carpet that ran the length of the aisle muted every step. The only sounds emanated from the stage area, where a small group had gathered. Although a ring of chairs had been set up on the wood platform, the people stood in a tight group.

"Wonderful," came the booming voice of Wellman. "Ladies and gentlemen, here is Toby Matthews." The small group broke into enthusiastic applause, and all eyes turned to them. "Come on up here, son. There are some people I want you to meet."

Thomas placed his hand on Toby's shoulder and was surprised to feel how tense his muscles were. "You okay?" he asked just above a whisper.

Toby didn't answer; he just marched forward.

"Toby," Wellman said. "Some very special people have come to meet you." To the group he said, "Folks, this is Toby and his mentor, Thomas."

Several people tried to speak at the same time, and a few reached for Toby. Toby took a step back, evading their grasp.

"Why don't we all have a seat," Wellman said with a laugh. "We don't want to gang up on the boy." There was an excited cacophony of agreement, words smashing into each other destroying any sense they carried. "Come here, son," Wellman said, motioning Toby to stand in the middle of the chair circle. Toby looked smaller, younger, and more vulnerable.

Wellman hunkered down in front of Toby. "These are some very special people, Toby. They've come from all over the country to meet you and to help us. You see, they believe in you just like I believe in you, and they want to make our church bigger and better so that more people can be helped. So they come from New York, Chicago, Miami, Detroit, Fort Worth, and other important cities to see what we do and how we do it."

Toby looked into Wellman's eyes and uttered a single word so softly that no one more than two feet away could have heard it. "Money."

From where Thomas stood just outside the ring, he could see Wellman's eyes turn cold. "I would like you to meet each one. I'm sure you'll like them."

Toby turned to the closest member of the group, a dark man with an ill-fitting toupee, dark blue suit, and thick glasses. Tilting his head to the side, Toby stared at the man for a few seconds, then said, "Eyes peeling." He then turned to the next person, but before he could take the two steps necessary, the man raised shaking hands to his face.

"Everything is blurry. I can't see! What has he done to me? What has he done?"

"Toby?" Wellman asked harshly.

"Glasses," was all that Toby said.

Wellman stepped forward and removed the man's glasses. "How's that?" he asked.

The man's mouth moved, but no words came out. Wellman chuckled. "I take it that you can see better."

"Per . . . perfectly."

"You don't need these anymore," Wellman said, handing the thick lenses back to the man. "Tell the others why you're here."

"My eyes," he said. "I have an incurable retinal degenerative disease. I just wanted the disease to stop, but now I see better than when I was a kid."

"Toby doesn't do anything halfway," Wellman said.

"Me next," someone said loudly.

"Be patient, madam," Wellman said. "Toby is not a vending machine. He's gifted. Let's give him time to let the gift work."

The next person in the circle was a husky older woman with thick eyebrows. Hope draped her face like a mask. "Sweet blood," Toby said and walked on.

"That's it," the woman said. "I've offered half a million dollars, and that's all I get?"

"What is your condition, madam?" Wellman asked.

"Diabetes. I've been on dialysis for years, and I need help. My kidneys are failing."

"How do you feel?" Wellman inquired.

"Well, a little warm inside . . . lots of energy."

"How did you feel when you came in?" Wellman pressed.

"Tired. Very tired." She stopped. "You mean . . . you mean I'm healed?"

"Healed," Toby said and moved on to the next. Thomas watched in amazement as Toby looked at each person, then pronounced the problem and moved on. Each was healed. Stomach cancer, emphysema, tumors, and more. The degree or intensity of the disease mattered nothing to Toby; he just gazed, spoke, and moved on. It took less than twelve minutes for him to make the circuit of the twelve people. Each gushed with gratitude. Some wept; others jumped for joy. The only one who appeared unhappy was Toby, who stood next to Wellman, his eyes cast down as those around him sang his praises and wrote checks.

It was the saddest thing Thomas had ever seen.

Wellman's cell phone had rung just as the last of his wealthy guests had left the theater for their hotel rooms. Impatient with the interruption, he snapped the phone from his belt, said, "What?" and then listened for thirty seconds. Pushing the END button, he hastily left the converted theater and jogged up the stairs to the security center. The center was a large office down the hall from his own. It was manned twenty-four hours a day by well-paid employees who watched scores of video monitors.

Wellman wasted no words, pushing his way through the small lobby and into the surveillance room. "Where?" he demanded.

The room was darker than the lobby. It was warm, and the acrid smell of electronics hung in the air. Four rows of monitors, one stacked upon another, covered one wall. A young man no older than twenty-five sat in a secretary's chair that allowed him to scoot along the floor. "Here," he said crisply, pointing at a monitor in the second row. "This is the front entrance. They've been there about ten minutes."

"Do you have audio?" Wellman asked as he studied the color image of two men arguing with the uniformed guard.

"Yes, sir," the security man said.

"Let's hear it," Wellman commanded.

The fuzzy voices of the three men played from an overhead speaker.

"I can't make it any clearer, sir," the guard was saying. "I have no record of a Thomas York working here."

"That's not what you said yesterday," one of the men said. He was taller than his companion. Both men were dressed casually.

"I was wrong. Sue me." It was clear that the guard's patience was wearing thin.

"I demand you call your supervisor," the taller man said.

"The next call I make, buddy, will be to the police," the guard snapped back.

"Call the police," Wellman heard Pratt say. "Maybe they can get you to see reason."

"Get your supervisor in here," Wellman demanded of his employee.

"Yes, sir," the man replied. He disappeared from the room.

"So you're Professor Pratt," Wellman said to himself. "You're persistent, I'll give you that." A sudden chill ran through him, and the dim lights darkened slightly. Wellman raised a hand to his head and closed his eyes. His mind was spinning; his skin crawled as if alive and possessing an intelligence of its own. He swore to the empty room. This had happened before, and it was happening with greater frequency. The chill grew icier but his blood seemed hot, ready to boil. He shuddered and tried to will away the sensations, but a part of him hesitated. The initial feeling was uncomfortable, but within seconds he would feel more alive than ever before. His heart would pound with new energy; his blood would race through his veins, searing and forceful, like magma deep within the earth.

The confusion would pass, and when it did, his mind would be awash with new thoughts. He would feel smarter, cleverer— more devious. For a moment, a tiny passing of a second, Wellman felt guilt for the thoughts he had, but that remorse was pressed down, crushed beneath a force he didn't understand and could not bring himself to believe. *It's stress,* he told himself as he had so many times before. *Mere stress, that's all.* But he didn't believe his lie. Nor did he want to.

At first he was ashamed to admit it, but he enjoyed the thrill of the episodes. At first he fought the feelings, but not hard. There was power in these events, and he had come to love the power.

In the beginning he found his thoughts unsettling. He had always been an angry man, a self-serving man, but not one prone to violence, yet imagined scenes of brutality played in his mind more and more, and he had no control over them. When they came, they seemed right and proper. Who in the world had the right to doubt him, to challenge him? If others found his attitude, his efforts unpleasant, then too bad, he no longer cared. They could be ignored. And those that opposed him, well, they could be handled.

The room darkened.

The chill grew cold as an iceberg.

His blood boiled.

And a new idea came to Wellman—an idea in which he found a perverse pleasure. A warmth bathed his brain.

The door to the surveillance room opened with a snap. "Mr. Wellman." Jim Kline, the director of security, entered. Behind him followed the security guard.

"Jimmy, I want you to see something," Wellman said without preamble. Then he turned to the surveillance guard. "I need a few minutes alone with your boss." The guard nodded and left the room, closing the door behind him.

"What's up?" Kline asked. Unlike the guard, who wore a white shirt and blue pants uniform, Kline wore a gray suit. He stood just under six feet tall and had a round face and stark hazel eyes.

Wellman tapped the screen. "These two men pose a threat to Toby. I want you to get rid of them."

"I'll handle it. They'll be gone in five minutes."

"I don't want them back—ever," Wellman said, an edge to his voice. "Do you understand?"

Kline looked puzzled, cocking his head to the side. Wellman waited for the response. "I've read the report from my guard, and I'll admit the two men are annoying, but no more than others," Kline said.

"They're connected to someone who is close to Toby," Wellman snapped. "That makes them different than everyone else. I want a permanent solution." Wellman paused, then added, "It's not like it's your first time. You know that. I know that. Hopefully no one else will know it."

The subtle threat did not escape the chief of security. Kline paused, squinting in the dark room. "I understand," he finally said.

"You'll be well compensated for your extra effort."

Kline nodded silently.

Wellman stared at the monitor for a moment, then said softly, "Good-bye, Dr. Pratt."

chapter 21

I now know what the term 'bum's rush' means," Pratt complained as he and Edison stepped aboard their rented boat. The early afternoon sun pushed through the craft's small windows. "I don't think I've ever been shown the door so quickly before."

"It was a new experience for me, too," Edison said from the tiny galley, where he retrieved two sodas. They had stopped at a small store, picking up toothpaste, snacks, and other odds and ends. "We should have expected it. Our first meeting with the police didn't go any better." He offered one of the bottles to Pratt.

"I know. Still, we had to try."

"I don't think we're getting on that compound anytime soon. Do you think that they will pursue a restraining order?"

"Probably," Pratt grumbled. "The police sure gave us the third degree. They asked about everything but who we voted for in the last presidential election. I'm not comfortable with them having all that information about us."

"The police?" Edison asked. "It was pretty routine. Name, rank, and where we're staying on the island. The officer almost seemed sympathetic."

"I don't think so," Pratt said. "He and the guard seemed to know each other."

"You'd expect that, wouldn't you?" Edison asked, seating himself on the bench inside the cabin. "I bet they get called out there all the time. We know they have their share of crazies try-ing to get in."

"Like us?"

Edison chuckled. "We knew we wouldn't get past the gate when we went out there."

"I had to try again," Pratt said. "I want to be able to tell Thomas's mother that I did everything possible. Besides, there was still some hope that Thomas would come to the gate."

"You've done everything you can, Aaron. You've besieged them with calls, made personal visits, and left notes."

"Notes that aren't sent on to Thomas, messages that he never receives."

"We don't know that," Edison countered. "Maybe Thomas has just written us off."

"I don't think he would do that. I never saw that weakness in his personality."

Edison leaned over the table and spoke softly. "I'm not trying to be the devil's advocate here, Aaron, but we need to face a few facts."

"Such as?"

"Thomas might want nothing to do with us. It appears he's written off his parents and his past. What makes us so special that he would feel compelled to respond to anything we say?"

"I don't think he's truly written his parents off. The relation-ship was strained before all of this happened. His mother admit-ted as much to me on the phone. I don't think he'd turn his back on his father, not as ill as he is. His Christian character won't let him do it."

"Maybe you're right. I guess I'm feeling a little helpless and—"

The sound of a small gasoline engine caught their attention. A dinghy was pulling alongside the *Becky J.*

"The landlord?" Pratt asked. Edison shrugged.

"Dr. Pratt?" a voice called out.

Pratt got up and walked out of the cabin and onto the deck. "Yes, who is—" He stopped suddenly when he saw the director of security that had ordered them away from the front gate. He wore the same gray suit he had been wearing then. A suited man in a boat struck Pratt as odd. "Oh, it's you."

"I didn't think you'd be happy to see me," Kline said smoothly, standing.

"You thought right."

Edison stepped out and stood next to Pratt. "We gave at the office," he said.

"I didn't come to make your lives any more miserable; I came to give you something."

Pratt cut his eyes to Edison and saw the same suspicion on his face that he himself felt. "I believe your last words to us were, 'Don't let me see your face again.'"

Kline lowered his head. "That's pretty much what I said. I came to apologize."

"Apologize?"

"Yes," Kline said. "This is a little embarrassing, but when I went back to my office after our ... meeting, I was called in to see my employer."

"Who precisely is your employer?" Edison asked.

"Mr. Richard Wellman," Kline replied. "He's the head of the Church of New—"

"I know who he is," Pratt interjected.

"He just became aware of your requests. He also saw how you were treated at the front gate and ... well, he thought I was way out of line, and he has sent me to apologize for my actions."

"You were out of line," Pratt said. "We're not asking to be treated like royalty. We just want to speak to Thomas York."

"I understand," Kline said. "You have to understand that we have had some security issues to deal with lately. There have been threats against Toby and against the church. I tend to err on the side of caution. I apologize for the way you've been treated."

"I appreciate the effort, Mr. Kline ... It is Kline, isn't it? That's the name you gave the police officer."

"Yes, James Kline."

"I appreciate your apology, Mr. Kline, but it doesn't really help us, does it?"

"That's the second reason I'm here," Kline said. "I've been asked to take you to meet Mr. York."

"This is quite a change from an hour ago," Edison remarked.

"We've been told that he doesn't work at the compound," Pratt said.

"Yes, I know. It was by his request that we shield him from the outside. He's become very important at the church, and we were just trying to protect him."

"Where is he?" Pratt demanded.

"Not far, actually. He's on a boat that is owned by one of our supporters. They've been on an all-night fishing trip. They got back a couple of hours ago. The boat is on the other side of the marina. We can be there in a few minutes."

Pratt and Edison exchanged glances.

"Come on, gentlemen," Kline offered. "Let me make it up to you. You do want to see Thomas York, don't you? We can take my dinghy and cruise straight there. You'll be talking to Thomas in less than five minutes. That's our boat moored out there." He pointed across the crescent-shaped bay.

Pratt searched the harbor and saw a large cabin cruiser bobbing lightly in the blue harbor. Even at a distance, Pratt could see the yacht dwarfed the *Becky J*.

The dinghy was a white and gray rigid inflatable boat with a ten-horsepower outboard motor. Kline waited in the craft while Pratt and Edison lowered themselves from the *Becky J* and into the tender.

"It looks pretty small," Edison said.

"There's plenty of room in the boat for the three of us," Kline said. "It's not that far to the Tiara."

"The what?" Pratt asked.

"I'm sorry," Kline answered as he removed the rope from the bollard. "The yacht is a Tiara 5000. I think you'll like it. It's impressive."

Pratt strained his eyes in the direction of the large craft, hoping to catch a glimpse of Thomas, but he saw no one. "Are you sure Thomas is on the boat?"

"Positive," Kline replied. "Toby is there too. It was his first real fishing trip. Thomas said he loved it."

"We're going to meet Toby?" Edison asked.

"That's why we're doing it this way. I could have had Thomas and Toby meet us somewhere, but Toby tends to draw a crowd. Mr. Wellman thought meeting Toby might be interesting for you. It's all part of our apology."

"I would have settled for a phone call from Thomas," Pratt said. Despite the serene setting, Pratt felt ill at ease. Turning to Edison, he asked, "What do you think?"

Edison shrugged. "It's what we came here to do. I say we do it."

Pratt turned his attention back to Kline. "Very well, Mr. Kline, apology accepted."

The boat was small, able to seat four men but no more. Pratt and Edison sat on a simple wood seat that spanned the distance from one side of the rigid inflatable frame to the other. Kline remained at the stern of the boat and started the outboard motor. It roared to life, belching blue smoke into the air for a few seconds, then settling into an easy thrum.

Slowly the small craft moved from the Chris Craft, and then with a flip of a switch, Kline powered the boat forward. As the boat lurched, Pratt felt himself slipping backward. He grabbed the seat to steady himself, then caught the startled expression on Edison's face. Twisting in his seat, Pratt turned to see Kline smiling.

"There's something invigorating about the ocean," Kline shouted over the noise of the motor and wind. "Don't you agree, gentlemen?"

"As long as we don't end up in it," Pratt shouted back.

"Can't swim?"

"I can swim just fine, but I'm not dressed for it," Pratt said.

The trip to the Tiara, which was anchored less than one hundred yards from the shore, took less than four minutes. Kline expertly guided the little Zodiac to the stern of the power yacht. As he pulled the craft within four feet of the transom, a thick, deeply tanned man appeared on the deck, stepped through a small door at the gunwale, and dropped down onto a fiberglass swimmer's platform that protruded from the back of the yacht. "Toss me that line," he shouted. Pratt took the thin white nylon rope that was attached to the bow of the Zodiac and threw it toward the man. The throw was weak and Pratt, who had stood to make the toss, thought he might fall. The man on the Tiara stretched forward just in time to snatch the line from the air. He pulled the boat close as Kline cut the power.

"Welcome aboard, gentlemen," the crewman said. His face was deeply lined by the sun. "Watch your step. The water is wet."

Pratt let the wisecrack slip without comment. He was glad to be out of the tiny Zodiac and onto something more substantial. Moments later he, Edison, and Kline were standing on the main deck.

"She's beautiful, isn't she?" Kline said.

"Gorgeous," Edison said. "I often thought it would be great to have a boat like this."

"What's stopping you?" Kline asked.

"Fear and money," Edison answered glibly. "Unlike my friend, I can't swim. I'm not rich, either."

"Where's Thomas?" Pratt asked bluntly.

"In the shower," the crewman answered as he finished securing the Zodiac. "He said you should wait for him below deck. There are drinks in the fridge. Sandwich makings too, if you're hungry."

"I'll show you where you can wait," Kline offered.

"This thing has a shower?" Edison asked.

"Sure," Kline explained. "It sleeps four, has a master berth, and boasts all the comforts of home—except home doesn't have twin diesel engines that can move you over 30 knots an hour. I think you'll find it has a few more amenities than that tub you've been on."

Kline led them down a short-stepped ladder into the interior of the boat. The area below was striking in its beauty. Nearly every vertical surface bore a honey ash veneer. The deck was an artwork of highly polished wood. All the appointments bore the unmistakable mark of wealth.

"Have a seat, gentlemen," Kline said as he closed the door behind him. "Can I get you something to drink? Beer? Soda?"

"Nothing for me," Pratt said, sitting on a cobalt blue bench sofa. Edison declined also. The sense of discomfort Pratt had felt earlier rose like a siren. He could not define it, but something was wrong. Then it struck him. He should be able to hear a shower running, especially on a boat like this. Instead he heard another sound—the powerful rumble of large diesel engines and the sound of a wench pulling up an anchor.

"What's going on?" Edison asked, alarmed.

Kline said nothing. He stood in the small galley, his gaze directed down to a drawer he had just opened.

Pratt rose and took one step toward Kline.

"Sit down!" Kline demanded. He removed something from the drawer—a large black handgun. He pointed the gun at Pratt's forehead. "Sit down or I'll put a bullet in your forehead."

Pratt complied.

"What is this?" Pratt asked.

"The end of your meddling," Kline said.

One of the things to remember about Greek is that word order is not as important as word endings." As had become their custom, Thomas and Toby lay on the thick carpet of the recreation room, books strewn in front of them. Thomas was lecturing. "The endings of Greek words can tell you a lot about them, such as the tense and the . . . You're not listening, are you?"

Toby didn't respond.

"Earth to Toby. Earth to Toby. Come in, Toby."

"What?" Toby said, snapping his head in the direction of Thomas.

"Where were you?" Thomas asked. Toby's face was dark, troubled. "Something is bothering you, isn't it?"

"Something's wrong."

"What?" Thomas asked with concern.

"Your friends. They need you." Toby sat up, then pulled his knees to his chest and wrapped his thin arms around them. He began to rock. "It's starting. I told you that they would need you, and now they do. It's starting."

"What's starting?"

Toby rocked faster, his eyes fixed on the wall in front of him.

"Need you. They need you. Need you."

"Come on, Toby, you're scaring me," Thomas said. "Do you feel all right?"

"It's the Shadow Man's fault," Toby said. "It's all his fault. Shadow Man. Shadow Man. Shadow Man."

"There is no Shadow Man, Toby. That's just your imagination."

"Shadow Man's fault. He's real. I've seen him. He hates me."

Thomas sat up and called, "Mary! Mary, I need you." He then took Toby in his arms. "It's all right, buddy. I'm here."

Mary burst into the room on a run. "What? What's the matter?"

"Toby's upset."

Mary crouched down next to her son. "What's he looking at?"

"It's the Shadow Man's fault," Toby repeated. He continued rocking in Thomas's arms.

"Who is the Shadow Man?" Thomas asked.

"Let me have him," Mary said.

"Your friends need you, Thomas. The Shadow Man is going to get them. Hurry. Need you."

"I don't understand," Thomas said.

"Hurry, hurry," Toby pleaded. "The water. The ocean."

"He mentioned the Shadow Man to me before," Mary said. "But he never talked about it again. I thought it was just his imagination. You know how children are."

"He's real!" Toby shouted. "Why won't you believe me? The water. The ocean. Shadow Man."

"It's okay, son," Mary cooed.

"No, it's not!" Toby yelled. "It's not okay. Not okay. Not okay."

"Toby," Thomas said. "Look at me." Toby continued to stare unblinkingly ahead. "Toby, look at me! Tell me what you see."

Toby turned his head in Thomas's direction. "Water. Ocean. Head thing. Jewel thing. Princess thing."

"Come on, buddy, don't go cryptic on me now," Thomas pleaded. "What princess thing?"

"Head thing. Princess thing."

Thomas looked at Mary questioningly. "Do you understand?"

She shook her head. "I've never seen him act this way."

Thomas turned back to Toby. "Head thing? Princess thing? I don't—Wait. Do you mean a crown?"

"Not crown."

"Not a crown, but like a crown?" Thomas pressed.

"Head thing."

"A tiara," Mary suggested.

"Maybe," Thomas said. "But what does it mean?"

"I don't know," Mary admitted, then stopped abruptly. "Richard showed me a boat in the harbor," she said. "You can see it from his office window. He called it a Tiara. I thought that was an odd name, but he said it was the manufacturer's name, not the name of the boat."

"In the harbor? Avalon Bay?"

"Yes."

"That would fit with Toby's fixation on water and ocean."

"Go," Toby said. "Your friends need you. Go. Shadow Man is evil."

"I can't leave you like this, buddy."

"You had better go," Mary said. "It might calm him down."

"Okay. I'll check in later. Maybe I should call for an ambulance first—"

"No," Toby said. "No, no, no. Go, go, go."

Thomas rose, his heart ricocheting in his chest. A second later, he bolted from the room.

I've put up with an awful lot of nonsense in this job," Kline said, the gun in his hand aimed at his two prisoners. He spoke loud enough to be heard over the drone of engine noise. They had cruised slowly until they were out of the harbor and well into open water. Now the boat bounced its way through the small swells of unsheltered ocean. "I've had people disguise themselves as delivery people, postal workers, and even cops to get on the compound. I've watched the Toby-haters march outside our fence. Bomb threats have become routine. By the same token, I've had to send away mothers pleading for the health of their children, men in tears about their dying wives. It never ends. Then, there are you two."

"We just wanted to speak to Thomas," Pratt protested.

"Maybe," Kline admitted. "Then again, maybe not. Someone thinks you two pose a threat to Toby. Such threats will not be tolerated."

"What someone?" Pratt asked. He stole a look at Edison. The older man was pale and sweating. "Richard Wellman?"

"Doesn't matter," Kline said. "You're a real nuisance."

"This goes a little beyond security concerns, don't you think?" Pratt was surprised by his own calm. He thought it odd that he felt concern and worry, but not fear. "Surely there have been those who have been bigger nuisances than we have."

"True, but you present a different kind of threat. You have connections to Thomas, and he has connections to Toby. You influence Thomas, Thomas influences Toby, and things change. We like things the way they are."

"How does a man sink as low as you?" Pratt asked.

"Sink? I've risen higher than I've ever been before." Kline leaned over the small counter, his gun still held steady on Pratt and Edison. "Let me tell you something, *Dr*. Pratt. I used to be a pretty straight-up kind of guy. Police officer in Miami, doing my job, paying my bills best I could, but then I learned a few things, and I learned them on the street. The good guys lose more often than the bad guys. I watched the crooks—the smart ones, not the street punks, but the big guys—get away with murder. Literally. Why?

Because they had money. Lots of money. Me? I worked myself to the bone only to be spit upon by the very people I protected. Low pay and even lower appreciation, that's what police work got me. So I found a new line of work. I set up a security company and protected those who had what others never would. I asked no questions. I kept my mouth shut, and I did what I had to do to keep my clients happy."

"Like abducting people," Pratt spat.

"That and more," Kline said. "As you are about to find out."

"So this is a one-way trip for us," Pratt remarked as casually as he could.

"Yeah, that's pretty much it."

"You have no conscience," Pratt said.

"You say that like it's a bad thing." Kline grinned.

"It is. It means your soul has become callused."

"I was wondering when this would come up, Dr. Pratt. I did a little research on you and know all about your and Dr. Edison's religious backgrounds. Actually, I thought you would have burst into prayer by now."

"It was a good guess," Edison remarked weakly. Pratt noticed that he was perspiring more and his skin looked like chalk. He was rubbing his left arm—all the signs of a heart attack.

"You look a little seasick," Kline said to Edison.

"Thanks for the . . . concern." Edison grimaced.

"I think it may be his heart." Pratt leaned toward his mentor. "He needs a doctor. Turn the boat around."

"No need." Kline looked at his watch. "His heart won't be bothering him much longer."

chapter 22

The phone was ringing when Mary closed the door behind Thomas. Toby stood by her side, nearly catatonic with fear. Picking up the phone, she said hello.

"Good afternoon, Mary," came the voice of the caller.

"Hi, Richard," Mary said softly. Toby stepped away from the phone.

"You sound different. Is everything all right?"

"It's Toby. He's upset. Real upset."

"What happened? Is he okay now?"

"I don't know. Thomas was over teaching Toby Greek when Toby got upset and started talking funny. He kept talking about Thomas's friends and the ocean."

"Let me talk to Thomas," Wellman demanded.

"He's not here."

"Where did he go?"

"To find his friends. Richard, I'm scared. I've never seen Toby like this. What should I do?"

Wellman hung up.

The quickest way around the compound and around the tiny city of Avalon was by golf cart. The locals called them autos; the tourists recognized them as gas-powered vehicles that scooted around the perimeter of fairways. Scores of the little cars lined the streets, out-numbering sedans and trucks by a huge margin. Thomas raced from Toby's home and to the street having no intention of spending any more time on foot than was necessary. The cart he had used to cover the distance between his apartment and Mary's home was parked at the curb. Its small gas engine whined in protest as Thomas pressed the accelerator to the floor. Against the slow, pedestrian lifestyle of the city, Thomas's rushed and erratic driving was certain to stand out, but he didn't care. If Toby was right—and he had never known him to be otherwise—then Pratt and Edison were in danger. He had to help them, but how? All he had to go on were the obscure remarks of the terrified boy.

Thomas repeated Toby's enigmatic comments over and over in his mind but was left with only two clues: "ocean" and "tiara." The latter had been an insight from Mary. It was the only thing that made sense. There was a boat manufactured by Tiara in the harbor, and it was owned by CNJ. He had no idea what that had to do with his former professor.

Wellman slammed the receiver down with such force that the phone tipped over. He swore, then took a deep breath to calm himself. It didn't work. He swore again. Picking the receiver up again he punched in a number.

"Front gate," a voice said.

"This is Richard Wellman. Has Thomas York passed through yet?"

"No, sir. No one has left the compound in the last half hour."

"Good," Wellman said, slightly relieved. "No one is to leave the compound until I say so. I mean no one. I want the place locked down."

"I understand. Has there been a threat I should know about?" the guard asked.

"Just make sure no one leaves the grounds. If York shows up, hold him there and contact my office. Got it?"

"Yes, sir. I've got it."

Wellman hung up and placed another call, this time to security. He issued a single command: "Find Thomas York and bring him to me."

The cart carried Thomas through the macadam streets of the compound and to the large front gate. In the distance he could see the crystalline blue water of Avalon Bay. He brought the cart to an abrupt stop at the gate.

"Can I help you?" the guard asked. He was a powerfully built man, with calculating eyes and a sour expression.

"You can open the gate," Thomas said.

"And you are ... ?"

"None of your business," Thomas shot back. "Just open the gate."

"I can't do that."

"Look, I don't have time for you to play policeman. Just open the gate, and I'll be on my way."

"The compound has been locked down by order of Richard Wellman. No one is going through my gate."

Thomas switched off the cart and exited. "There is an emergency. I'm an employee here, and I have a right to leave the compound."

"That gate is going to stay closed until I receive orders to the contrary." The man stepped into the guard shack and picked up the phone. "Connect me to Mr. Wellman's office."

Thomas stepped into the shack and snatched the handset from the man's grasp. "Which button opens the gate?" he asked, hanging the phone up.

"You can't come in here."

"I just did. Answer the question."

"That's it!" The man shouted. "Outside. Put your hands on the cart." He reached for a pair of handcuffs, removing them from the black leather pouch on his Sam Browne belt.

Thomas backed out of the shack onto the asphalt drive. "I don't have time for this."

"I said, put your hands on the cart," the guard ordered. Then he pushed Thomas with one hand, holding the cuffs in the other.

"Don't do this," Thomas warned.

The guard, who was as tall and looked to be as strong as Thomas, smiled. "Really?" He raised his free hand again and placed it on Thomas's chest. "I think I know what I'm doing—"

In a single fluid motion, Thomas seized the man's extended right hand and twisted. The guard folded over, his face directed to the ground. Thomas placed his left hand on the man's shoulder blade and drove him face first to the asphalt.

"Hey!"

"I told you that I don't have time for this. Release the hand-cuffs."

"No." Thomas twisted the guard's wrist until the tendons reached the breaking point. "Okay, okay. Just don't break my arm." He let the metal cuffs loose.

"I take it you weren't a wrestler in school," Thomas said calmly as he picked up the cuffs. One minute later the security officer was seated on the floor of his guard shack, his hands secured behind him.

"Let me go."

"All you had to do was open the gate," Thomas said.

"Wellman would have had my head."

Thomas looked down at the man and felt sorry for him. "He may have it yet." Turning his attention back to the control panel before him, Thomas activated the switch that sent the gate sliding back. Without another word, he entered the cart, switched it on, and slammed the pedal to the floor.

Five minutes after he had pulled through the gate, Thomas stood on the frontage road of the bay. Boats of all sorts bobbed leisurely in the water, dotting the surface like tiny houses. Sailboats, power boats, cabin cruisers, and more made the scene the favorite of photographers. Thomas cared nothing for the beauty. He was looking for one particular boat.

Having never been on the Tiara, he had to rely on Mary's description, and she had only seen the boat at a distance. Unfortunately the description she gave was vague, and as he studied the boats before him he saw several that fit the portrayal given him. He needed more information. The street upon which he stood was bordered on one side by a narrow sandy beach and on the other by tourist-oriented businesses. Over the door of one business was a sign that read BOAT RENTALS. He walked in.

The small room had a counter that separated patrons from the office area in back. Behind the counter was a man Thomas judged to be in his fifties. His skin was dark with tan, and deep creases lined his face. His eyes were blue and reflected intelligence. There was a day's growth of stubble on his chin. "Yes, sir, can I help you?"

"I'm looking for a boat," Thomas said, trying not to sound anxious. "A particular boat called Tiara."

"Is Tiara the name of the boat, or are you referring to the manufacturer?"

"I'm not sure," Thomas admitted. "Manufacturer, I think." That was what Mary had said.

"I can't say that I know the name of every boat in the harbor, son. Too many tourists even this time of year. However, there is a Tiara 5000 that moors out here all the time. Belongs to that church that came to the island a year and half or so ago."

"That's it," Thomas said.

"You with the church?" The man studied Thomas.

Thomas wasn't sure how to answer. It was well known that some of the locals despised the influence the CNJ had had on the economy and lifestyle of the island. Others, however, had benefited from Toby's unique gifts. To which group did this man belong? Thomas decided that honesty was the best strategy. "Yes."

The man grunted, shook his head, then said, "I know the boat. It went out about half an hour ago. I was working on one of our rentals and saw it leave myself. She's a beauty, all right."

"Did you see who got on the boat?"

"Yup. Three men went out on a tender. The boat left a short time after that. That's all I know."

"Tender?" Thomas asked.

"A tender is a small boat that is associated with a larger boat. It's how people get back and forth from anchorage in the bay. Can't walk out there, you know."

"Half an hour ago," Thomas repeated. "How far could a boat like that go in thirty minutes?"

"All depends on how fast they move, doesn't it?"

"Of course. Let me ask it this way: What's the farthest it could go in thirty minutes?"

The man thought for a second and answered, "Well, a boat like that can make maybe thirty or thirty-two knots, so if they opened her up she might make twelve or even fifteen miles. Nautical miles, that is."

"Did you see which direction they went?" Thomas pressed.

The man looked puzzled.

"I need to find someone on the boat," Thomas explained.

"They headed north once they were out of the harbor."

Without hesitation, Thomas said, "I need a boat."

Mary sat on the sofa next to Toby and watched him closely. He was rocking back and forth again, still peering off in the distance. He was no longer folded into a fetal position as he had been in the rec room, but his posture was not normal. At times he would lift his face toward the ceiling and then gulp for air. Mary noticed that he held his hands funny, too, pressing the heels of his hands together as if he were bound by rope.

"It's going to be all right, honey. Mommy is here with you."

Toby gulped for more air.

Mary was moving from fear to terror. "Are you having trouble breathing, Toby?"

"Water. Ocean."

Mary scooped him up on her lap and held him tightly. Softly she began to sing a lullaby. Gently she pressed his head against her breasts and ran her fingers through his hair. Tears began to run down her cheeks.

A loud bang came from the front door. A second later Wellman charged in, startling Mary. Toby jumped in her lap. Wellman's face was tinged red, and anger flashed in his eyes.

"Richard," Mary gasped.

"Where is . . ." Seeing Toby, Richard marched straight to him.

"I think we should take him to the hospital," Mary said. "I'm scared. Real scared."

Wellman picked Toby up from Mary's lap. "What's wrong with you, boy?" His tone was harsh. Toby recoiled at Wellman's touch and tried to wriggle from his grip, but Wellman held tightly to his thin arms.

Mary stood. "What are you doing?"

"I asked you a question, boy. What are you up to?"

"Stop it, you're going to hurt him." Mary reached for her son.

"He doesn't look like he's in a trance now, does he?"

"Why are you so angry? Put Toby down."

Wellman set Toby on the sofa roughly. "Where is Thomas, Toby? I need to know. Where is Thomas?"

Toby pushed himself back into the cushions as far as he could, then pointed at Wellman. "The Shadow Man is in you. The Shadow Man is in you."

"What is all this about?" Mary pleaded.

"I got a call just before I came over. Thomas attacked one of our guards."

"I don't believe it," Mary responded. "Thomas wouldn't do that."

"How do you know?" Wellman retorted. "You've only known him for a few days. You know nothing about the man."

"Toby knows these things," Mary said. "Toby trusts him, and that makes me trust him."

"You think he's that insightful, do you? Then what's all this nonsense about a Shadow Man?"

"I don't know, but this isn't the first time he's brought it up."

Wellman turned back to Toby. "Where is Thomas?" he demanded.

"Don't you yell at him. He's my son." She reached for Toby.

"Shut up, woman," Wellman spat and backhanded her. The sound of his hand against her face reverberated through the living room.

"No!" Toby shouted. "You leave her alone!"

"Stop wasting my time," Wellman shouted. "If he says anything about Thomas, you call me on the cell phone. You got the number, use it." He then leaned forward, placing his face a mere inch away from hers. "This is serious. I'm serious. I want to know every word that comes out of his mouth."

Mary refused to touch the place where he had struck her; she wouldn't give him the satisfaction of knowing that she was hurt. Tobias had hit her a lot harder. She would hold in the pain as she used to do back home. What wounded her most could not be touched. No medicine or painkillers could reach it. She stared at the man she had thought she might love and for the first time realized what an animal he was. Toby had been right about him, and she had been foolish not to listen.

Wellman marched to the door and exited, slamming it loudly behind him. Quickly Mary was on her feet and looking out the front window. Two uniformed security guards were waiting on the front lawn. Through the glass she could hear Wellman's loud voice, "One of you cover the back, the other stay here. No one goes in or comes out."

She returned to Toby and again took him in her arms. This time she began to rock. Toby was mumbling, "Shadow Man. Shadow Man."

chapter 23

The cold water swirled around Pratt's head and the ocean salt stung his eyes. He thrashed about in the water as a fish might on the deck of a boat. Pungent sea water rushed up his nose, and he coughed involuntarily. His cough was muted by the same kind of duct tape that bound his wrists behind his back. Commanding himself to be calm, he allowed his natural buoyancy to bring him back to the surface. His back broke the surface and immediately, he rolled over and took in the sweet air through his nose. He was afloat long enough to hear another splash. Edison! He would be dead in minutes unless Pratt could figure something out quickly.

He heard another sound—the diesel engines of the big cabin cruiser. Pratt saw the white froth kicked up by the propellers. As he sank beneath the water again, he saw the boat pull away, and with it their last hope for survival. Pratt was tempted to surrender to death, to accept this as his fate, but something inside him urged him on. If he was going to die, it was going to be while he fought for life.

Pratt kicked as hard as he could with feet that were as tightly bound as his wrists, exhaling through his nose as he did. His head broke the surface, and he inhaled as much air as he could, filling his lungs until they could hold no more. With his lungs full, Pratt floated on the surface. Forcing panic from his mind, he focused on what he must do. A short distance away, he could hear Edison shouting through the tape and struggling to keep his head above the water.

Thankful that he was still trim, Pratt lay facedown in the water and drew his legs up to his chest and stretched his arms down. He had to get his hands in front of him as soon as possible, but he was as good as handcuffed. Still he tried stretching his arms until it felt like every tendon would give way. He felt his sneakers rub against his wrists. *A little more,* he told himself. He rolled in the water, but he didn't care. All that mattered now was getting his arms in front. He didn't care if he was upside down when it happened as long as it happened.

His lungs were on fire, his shoulders were a scorching, piercing pain as they came close to dislocating from their sockets. Pratt stretched more and moaned with the agony of it. He wished that his shoes were off, but with his ankles taped, they were impossible to remove.

A searing pain streaked from his left shoulder and down his back. Something had given way, but it didn't matter. In a few minutes he would be dead, drowned in the cold waters of the Pacific, his body left to the elements and the creatures of the sea. He began to wish they had just shot him, but Kline was too sharp for that. "Blood," he had told the other crewman. "If I shoot them, blood will splatter, and no matter how thoroughly we clean up, the police or the FBI could find traces. It's better if we do it this way. They won't be able to stay afloat for more than five minutes and since, according to our radar, there are no boats within two miles of us, they'll be dead long before anyone finds them."

"Won't their bodies wash ashore?" his partner had asked.

"Doubtful. The current should carry them out to sea."

Pratt's vision was dimming; the effort to pull his arms under his feet and in front of him was quickly using up the oxygen in his lungs. Soon, his body would take over, forcing him to inhale the water that surrounded him, and there would be nothing he could do about it.

A new panic set in. Pratt realized he was stuck. His feet were now tangled with his arms, and he was slowly spinning underwater. "Help me, God," he prayed in his mind. "Just a little more. Please God, let me stretch a little more."

With an effort borne of desperation, Pratt pulled his legs to his chest tighter and forced his wrists down. He exhaled a cascade of bubbles, shrinking his chest a few crucial inches.

Free.

His hands slipped past his feet and were now in front of him. He kicked hard until his head breached the surface once again. Air flooded his lungs. Sweet air. Cool air.

Quickly, he reached up and pulled the tape from his mouth. "Morris! Morris!" he called. He saw no sign of his friend. He had to be near, Pratt reasoned. It had only been a few moments. He scanned the sea around him and saw nothing except the stern of the Tiara pulling away. Pratt's arms hurt from the painful gymnastics he had done to bring his hands forward, and his back and legs were aching as he tried to tread water with his hands and feet bound. A shadow just under the surface caught his eye. It was five feet to his right and just below the water. Pratt dove. Through the green murk of seawater he saw a familiar shape. It was Edison, and he was struggling to get his head above the surface. He had his back turned to Pratt.

Mustering what little strength remained in his overly taxed muscles, Pratt swam toward his friend, his arms in front of him, his body undulating up and down as he propelled his body through the water. He made the distance, but slowly. Edison was struggling less and less, giving in to fate. Pratt didn't believe in fate. He kicked three more times, and felt his hands touch Edison's back. He clutched the man's shirt in his fingers, then began kicking toward the surface. They broke into the air fifteen seconds later, a fifteen seconds that passed like hours.

Pratt rolled onto his back and sucked in air by the bushel. Edison coughed into the tape that sealed his mouth and inhaled loudly through his nostrils. Pratt could hear the air racing in and out of Edison's nose. He began to thrash about again.

"Easy, Morris. Easy," Pratt said breathlessly. "Just take a few deep breaths."

Edison calmed down and breathed in short, ragged inhalations. "Good," Pratt said. "Now relax as much as you can and you'll float." Since Pratt was close to vertical in the water, he kept sinking, forcing himself to kick to keep his head up.

Once Edison's breathing had slowed, Pratt said, "Listen. I can't go ... on like this. I don't have enough strength to swim with my hands and feet tied up." Again Pratt sank beneath the water but brought his head up a second later. His breathing was labored. Water trickled down his trachea, gagging him. He coughed convulsively. When he could speak again, he said, "I have my hands in front of me. I'm going to pull the tape from ... your wrists and feet. We're going to sink. Stay calm. Okay?"

Edison nodded his head unconvincingly.

"Go limp. Let me do the work. Once your hands are free—" Pratt sank again. The muscles of his legs, unaccustomed to kicking in such an awkward fashion, ached feverishly, and Pratt began to fear cramps. Once again he forced his way to the top, coughed twice, and continued on as if nothing had happened. "Once your hands are free, I'll do your feet, then you can float easily. Then you'll have to do my hands. Okay?"

Again, Edison nodded slightly. Pratt wondered if his boss's heart could hold out under the strain. He had, however, no options.

"Jesus," Pratt prayed softly, "help us." Pratt heard Edison mumble something through the tape. He recognized the single word: "Amen." Pratt inhaled deeply, held it, and then released the air. This he did several times before counting down from five. When he said, "One," he ceased his kicking, pushed against Edison's shoulders, lifting him a few inches higher, and forced himself under the water. He felt along Edison's body until he found his bound hands. Then, with his exhausted lungs demanding more air, he carefully ran his fingers along the tape binding until he felt the rough edge where their captors had cut the tape. He picked at the edge until a small corner of it came up, allowing him to take hold of it between his index finger and thumb. Pratt hoped that his friend was ready, because the next part was certain to pull them both under. Taking hold of the tape's edge, Pratt began pulling, but as he did, Edison's body turned in the water. He was certain that Morris's head was beneath the swells. Still, Pratt pulled and pulled and with each jerk, more of the tape came free. To Edison's credit, he did not resist. Instead, he pushed his arms back so that Pratt would have more room to work.

The duct tape had been wrapped around Edison's wrist four times, but it finally came free. When it did, Edison began to flail wildly, reaching for the surface. Pratt kicked and clawed at the water to raise himself. When his head broke the surface, he saw the terrified face of his mentor. He was struggling to stay afloat. One of his thrashing arms caught Pratt on the bridge of the nose. Blood gushed.

"Easy," Pratt said loudly, raising his still-bound hands. "Relax. Don't fight the water." He ducked under the water, kicked, and came up behind Edison. He grabbed his shirt again. "Lean back." Edison did. "Good. Extend your arms."

Edison was obedient to every word and moments later, he was floating on his back, his feet a few inches below the water but his head just above the surface. They bobbed in the swells. Pratt let go and rolled over on his back, breathing raggedly. Since he could not put his arms out to the side, he tended to roll over, facedown in the water. "Great," Pratt said. "Here's what's next. First . . . get that tape off your mouth. If you slip under, that's okay. Take a deep breath first . . . and you can't sink very far. Can you do that?"

Edison didn't answer, he just reached up with his right hand and removed the tape. He did better than Pratt could have hoped. "This . . . is . . . another fine mess . . . you've gotten us into, Ollie."

Pratt chuckled despite himself. "Stranded in the middle of the ocean. No help. You're quoting Laurel and Hardy movies."

"I'm desperate," Edison gasped. "I always turn to old movies when I'm desperate." He paused then asked, "What now?"

"I have to release your feet; you'll be able to float better then."

"What about your hands and feet?"

"You are going to have to do those. I'm almost spent."

"I can do it."

"I know."

Edison fell silent for a few moments, still gathering his breath. "I thought I was going to die. Thanks, Aaron."

"Just as man is destined to die once . . ." Pratt began.

"And after that to face judgment."

"If this is God's appointed time, then so be it, but I think we should let him make that decision."

"Agreed."

"How's the heart?" Pratt asked.

"Not so bad, not so good."

"I'm sorry I got you into this," Pratt said softly.

"It was my choice," Edison replied. He took another deep breath. "Let's get to work. I'm starting to get cold."

That was another concern that had crossed Pratt's mind. Temperatures in the Pacific were mild compared to some oceans, but the water was still no more than the mid-fifties. They both were losing body heat. Floating on the surface they could warm themselves in the sun, but if they had to stay adrift through the night . . . Pratt tried not to think about it. "You're right," he said. "Let's get this over with. Ready?"

"No, but let's do it anyway."

Pratt lowered his feet in the water and began working on Edison's taped feet. His hands were shaking from the stress, the physical effort, and the cold water, but after five minutes of effort, he had freed Edison's feet.

"Okay, now the hard part," Pratt said. "If you can get my hands free, I can take care of my feet."

"Okay."

"You're going to have to straighten up to free me. That means that . . ."

"I'm going to sink."

"We both are, but only for a few moments. Your legs are free now, so you can kick your way to the surface. If you kick evenly, you can keep your head above water."

Edison bent his knees and immediately came upright. He began kicking, wincing as he did. Pratt knew if he was truly having a heart attack, this effort could kill him, yet he did it anyway. His friend was willing to sacrifice himself to free Pratt.

Pratt held out his hands and kicked against the water the best he could. He slipped under but his hands remained high over his head. He could feel Edison clawing at the tape. An eternity of moments later his hands were free. Pratt pushed down with his arms, and he surfaced once again. "You did it," Pratt said, treading water with his arms.

"I thought I was going to drown you."

"Not a chance," Pratt said, wondering how many moments he had had left before blacking out. "Start floating. I'll take care of the rest." Saturating his blood with oxygen, Pratt bent over and went to work on his feet. The effort was difficult and he had to make several attempts at it, but he prevailed. With his feet free, he could kick his shoes off. He could now swim and tread water. Pratt wiped the blood from his face. His nose had stopped bleeding.

His breathing was labored and his body ached. Every movement of his arms sent ripping pain through his shoulders and back. He had hurt himself and he knew it, but there was nothing to be done about it. Survival was the key. Once again he scanned the sea. He had no idea how far from shore they were. He could see the island, which looked relatively close, but he knew that was deceptive. His best guess was that they were at least fifteen miles north-northeast of Catalina. The mainland shore was further away. Their captors had been certain to take them off the well-traveled boat and ferry routes and drop them in the drink an equidistance from any shore. Pratt rolled onto his back and gazed at the blue sky. Fifteen miles might be possible for a trained athlete, but not for him and certainly not for Edison. Rescue was their only hope.

"Any ideas?" Edison asked. Pratt glanced his way, he was getting better at floating. Fortunately, the sea was calm. One- to two-foot swells passed under them. In that sense they were blessed.

"I'm . . . thinking," Pratt said.

"That's good," Edison offered. "You think, I'll pray."

The despair that covered Thomas was as wide as the azure sea that loomed before him. He might be able to find the Tiara, but then what? There was no way he could board the vessel like a one-man raiding party, especially from the seventeen-foot Alcar Fisherman he was steering. He needed help. Reaching for the microphone of the onboard radio, Thomas raised it to his lips, then stopped. Something caught his eye. A boat, a large cruiser that fit the description Mary had given, was coming back from the direction the boat rental manager had said the Tiara had gone.

What now? Were Drs. Pratt and Edison onboard?

Thomas turned the wheel and guided the Fisherman on a course away from the large craft. He didn't want to be recognized. The Tiara was returning at a leisurely pace. Two men were on the bridge. Neither looked like Pratt or Edison. Of course, they could be below, but Thomas doubted it. Toby was beside himself with fear, and Thomas had to believe Toby.

Once Thomas was sure he was far enough away from the Tiara to avoid being recognized, he again raised the microphone to his lips and said, "Mayday, mayday, mayday." He then steered his small craft in the direction from which the Tiara had come.

chapter 24

Thirteen. Fourteen. Fifteen.

"Aaron?"

Pratt gulped another lungful of air. He estimated that they had been afloat for thirty minutes. His eyes burned from the glare of the sun and the salt that caked around his lids and lashes. His right shoulder ached with the heat of a blowtorch, his left only slightly less. He tried to ignore the pain, ignore the cold water, and ignore the fact that the sun would be down long before they got near shore and they would be enveloped in a Stygian gloom. Focus and denial were the two elements of his strategy. Focus on the distant island, deny his pain, his fatigue, and the hopelessness of the situation. Instead, he continued his silent counting. *Sixteen. Seventeen. Eighteen.* Each number represented a stroke of his right arm in the water, and the thrust of his legs. At twenty-five he would roll to his other side and begin stroking with his left arm, holding onto Edison's shirt with his right hand. Every one hundred strokes he would rest, floating on his back for a few moments, then begin the process again.

"Aaron?" Edison repeated.

"Yes?" Pratt croaked.

"You know that you would do better if you let go of me." Edison's words were matter-of-fact, as if he were discussing an interesting article in some theological journal.

"Yeah, I know," Pratt said. *Nineteen. Twenty. Twenty-one.*

"If you released me, you could swim for help, then come back for me."

Edison was showing a deep courage, the kind that only surfaced in a man when he was faced with the impossible. "You're stuck with me." *Twenty-two. Twenty-three. Twenty-four.*

"I'm serious. If I could swim, it'd be different."

"I'm serious, too." Pratt had played with the idea of teaching Edison to swim. The breast stroke was the easiest to learn, but Edison was still having chest pain. It had diminished, but the effort needed to swim even a dozen yards could kill him. *Twenty-four. Twenty-five. Switch.*

"I'm your boss. I could order it."

"So fire me," Pratt said. "But I demand two weeks' notice." *One. Two. Three.*

Edison fell silent for a moment then recited: "'You hurled me into the deep, into the very heart of the seas, and the currents swirled about me; all your waves and breakers swept over me.'"

"Jonah," Pratt said. Edison was famous around campus for his ability to recite biblical prayers. "'And the LORD commanded the fish, and it vomited Jonah onto dry land.'"

"Until now, that never sounded good."

Pratt grunted with each stroke.

"You really should leave me," Edison said again, his voice thick with seriousness.

"I got you into this mess. With God's help . . . I plan on getting you out."

"I chose to join you. It's not your fault. Life finds its completion in sacrifice."

Pratt stopped swimming suddenly. "Listen."

Edison rocked in the water, almost tipping over. A drone, deep and resonant, skipped along the water.

"It sounds . . . it sounds like a boat," Edison said with excitement.

"Watch," Pratt said. "Do you have a watch?"

Pratt moved to Edison's side and looked at his right wrist, searching for a watch.

"Other hand," Edison said. Pratt stayed where he was and gently spun Edison around until he could reach his left wrist and saw Edison's dress watch. It was silver with a matching metal band. Pratt, whose fingers were swollen from the water, fumbled over the latch. He made three attempts before unlatching it and slipping it from Edison's wrist. "What are you planning?"

The watch slipped from Pratt's stiff fingers and disappeared beneath the surface. Without taking time to inhale, Pratt dove after it. He had only moments before it would be too deep to retrieve. The water was murky and green. Kicking his weary legs harder than he thought possible, he pursued the watch. He could see it glitter in the diminishing sunlight. It was just out of reach. He stretched arms that refused to stretch. His middle finger touched it, but it was still just out of reach. Down it traveled, twisting and turning. He kicked again and again and again. His lungs were ablaze; the pressure of the water pushed against his eardrums, sending ice-pick pain through his head.

With an excruciating lunge, he shot out his right arm again, clutching the watch in his hand. He felt his right shoulder slip out of joint.

Under the Pacific surface, Aaron Pratt screamed, the sound of it muffled by the thick water. Bubbles erupted from his mouth and nose and rose to the surface.

Blackness began to consume him.

What's up, Rich?" Rudy said as he entered Wellman's office. "You sounded agitated on the phone."

"We're moving the trip up," Wellman snapped. "I want everything moved up."

"To when?"

"The sooner the better. Today. Make it today."

"What's going on?" Rudy asked. "I've never seen you like this."

Wellman was pacing the room, his hands clasped behind his back. "I'm not entirely sure, but I think Toby may be in trouble. He's acting frightened. He may be in danger."

"Have you told security?"

"Rudy, I don't want to play twenty questions," Wellman snapped. "If this is too difficult for you, then I'll find someone who can do the work."

"All right, all right," Rudy said. "Settle down. You don't have to bite my head off. I'll have the plane fueled and alert the pilots. It's going to take a few hours. I'll let the rest of the team know."

"Forget them. It's just going to be me, Toby, Mary, and you."

"What about Thomas, Burdick, and the others?"

Wellman crossed the room and placed his face a few inches from Rudy's. "I told you to forget them. They can catch up with us later. Now get out. Let me know when things are ready to go."

"Shall I make sure Toby and Mary are ready?"

"No—you stay away from them. I'll see to that. Now go."

Rudy spun on his heels, his face clouded with anger, and marched from the room. Wellman turned to the large glass window that overlooked the sea. He wondered if Kline had been successful. Something to his left moved. He snapped his head around but saw nothing. He returned his gaze to the window, but before he focused his vision on the distant ocean he saw himself in the window's reflection. He saw another face just over his left shoulder. A dark face.

A face with empty eye sockets.

A featureless face.

A shadow.

It took a moment for Pratt's eyes to clear and several moments longer for his thoughts to do the same. He was coughing hard and felt that a lung might come up. Then it hit him. Edison! Where was Edison? More coughing, but this time it was his. Turning, he saw Edison struggling to tread water. Pratt grabbed his collar, lifted, and pulled back until Edison was once again floating on his back.

Both men cleared their throats, and when Pratt could speak he asked, "What happened?"

"You didn't come back."

"You came after me?" Pratt was amazed at the sacrificial gesture.

"I . . . I don't want to teach your classes next year."

"You're amazing."

"No, just tired. Did you get the watch?"

"Yes." Pratt held up a hand. The watch was intertwined in his fingers. Straining his ears, he listened for the sound of a boat motor. To his relief, he could still hear it. Scanning the surface again he saw a small white boat skipping along the surface. Next, he glanced at the sun, taking note of its position.

"A signal?" Edison's voice betrayed his desperation. He seemed to be in more pain. "Do you think it will work?"

"I don't know." Pratt began to move the watch, first trying to get the reflection to shine on the water in front of him. Then he panned the watch face up to the sky, then back down again. He repeated the process time and time again, but the boat kept on its course. "Come on, come on," Pratt wished aloud. "Look this way."

As long as he could remember, Thomas had wanted to see a miracle. He had wished for it, prayed for it, studied about it, but until he first saw Toby, he had been disappointed. All of those hours of thought and study and searching were nothing compared to his desire to have one more miracle—the one that would save his friends.

Thomas was also filled with doubt. He had no way of knowing if Pratt and Edison were out here. They very well could have been on the Tiara, but Toby's words and reaction made him believe that they were in life-threatening trouble. He also felt it in his gut. There was no logic to that, but he believed it nonetheless.

What had he gotten himself into? he wondered as he guided the Fisherman through the water. Worse, what had he gotten Pratt and Edison into?

A spot of light caught his attention. It came from his left. He looked again and saw the dim glint of something reflecting the sunlight. A bottle or beer can, he supposed. He started to turn from it but saw it again. There was a rhythm to it. But then a floating bottle would rise and fall with the swells. No, he told himself, he needed to look for people, not flashes of light.

It happened again.

Against logic, Thomas turned the wheel and made for the flash.

He's ... he's turning our way," Pratt shouted.

"Praise God," Edison uttered just above a whisper. "Praise God."

Pratt continued flashing the watch.

chapter 25

You're certain of this?" The sheriff's deputy who asked the question stood next to Pratt's bed at the Catalina Community Hospital. He held a black notebook in his hand. He was a portly man with receding brown hair and dark eyes. On the other side of the bed stood a petite woman doctor with raven black hair who looked to Pratt as if she had just graduated from high school. Next to her was Thomas, his shoulders slumped and his face a mask of deep concern.

"It's not something I could make a mistake about," Pratt answered. "There were two men involved. One identified himself as Kline; the other didn't introduce himself."

"And these two men tied you up and tossed you overboard?"

"Taped us up," Pratt answered.

The officer shook his head. "While you were in radiology, I called the personnel office of the CNJ, and they said that no one named Kline worked in security or any other department."

"They told me the same thing about Thomas, and he has told you that he worked there," Pratt countered.

"I asked about Mr. York, too. They denied that he has ever worked there."

"What about the boat?" Thomas interjected. "You can trace the registration on it and you'll see that it belongs to the church."

"So what?" the sheriff said. "There's no crime in owning a boat. If it were, ninety percent of our residents would be in jail."

"Even if it's used in a crime?" Pratt asked.

"How do we prove that?" the deputy countered.

"Maybe you could find the duct tape they used on us."

The officer shook his head. "Duct tape is everywhere. I bet you could find a roll or two of it in the hospital. That wouldn't prove that the doctor here bound you up with it."

"So our word means nothing? We didn't swim out there."

"Your word means a great deal. I don't doubt that what you said happened, but I can't arrest someone who doesn't exist. Maybe the men who attacked you stole the church's boat. The church could be a victim, too."

"I don't believe this," Pratt said with exasperation. "Thomas, did you meet a Kline at the CNJ?"

"I wish I could say that I had, Dr. Pratt, but a lot of people work there, and I didn't meet them all. Unless he was in public relations, I wouldn't know."

"Whom did you talk to at the CNJ?" Pratt asked the sheriff.

"I started with marketing and they transferred me to Mr. Wellman himself. I have to admit, that was a surprise."

"So you're going to do nothing?" Pratt asked the deputy, concealing none of his frustration.

"I'll turn my report in to my superiors and do a little more investigating. I've also put out a description of the two men you gave me. Something may turn up yet. Of course, we have another problem."

"Oh?"

The deputy turned to Thomas. "My next stop is the CNJ compound. There's a guard there that says you assaulted and handcuffed him. You can bet the farm he's going to press charges."

Thomas lowered his head.

"He saved our lives, Officer," protested Pratt. "If he hadn't seen my signal and come along, Dr. Edison and I would be facedown in the deep. He had the foresight to call for help and directed your patrol boat to our location."

"I know. That's why he's not under arrest right now."

Thomas raised his head and spoke. "He assaulted me. I just defended myself."

"He has the right to restrain you in the course of his duty," the officer said solemnly.

"That might be true if I were attempting to break into the compound. I was trying to leave, but he refused to let me go. That's some kind of false imprisonment, isn't it?"

"I'll sort it out," the deputy said, scratching his head with the capped end of his pen. "You can count on that."

The doctor spoke up. "If you're finished now, Officer, I'd like to talk to my patient."

"Yeah, I'm done for now. You two try to stay out of trouble." The deputy closed his notebook and exited the room.

"Unbelievable," Pratt said to no one in particular.

"Dr. Pratt, I've examined your Xrays and have good news. I found no serious damage. My exam suggests that you have strained several muscles in your arms as well as some of the tendons. That, of course, would explain your dislocated shoulder. You say it slipped back into place while you were still afloat?"

"Yes. I'd rather not experience that again."

"I imagine not. You're going to be fine, but you're also going to be sore for quite a while. You need to see your own doctor who will, I'm sure, prescribe some physical therapy. If problems persist, there may be a need for surgery on one or both of your shoulders."

"How's Dr. Edison?"

She offered a small, understanding smile. "He's been stabilized and is being airlifted to a hospital in Long Beach. He'll probably stay one or two days for observation. His EKG looked normal. Personally, I think he was having an anxiety attack instead of a cardiac episode. Considering the tale you told me, an anxiety attack would make sense."

"Good, that's very good," Pratt said. "He really had me scared."

The doctor nodded. "I'll prescribe some pain relievers for you. You can leave anytime you wish, but go easy on the arms. You have a lot of healing to do."

"Thank you, Doctor."

She flashed another smile and left.

Pratt closed his eyes and tried to push down the frustration that was threatening to erupt with volcanic force. His shoulders ached, dulled only slightly by the painkillers he had taken less than an hour ago. The small of his back was tightening like a watch spring, and his legs were stiffening, erupting occasionally in tiny spasms. His eyes and throat were raw from the salt water, his face and neck burned by the sun.

"I'm terribly sorry, Dr. Pratt," Thomas said, almost in tears. "I wish I could unwind all this. You went through all this torture for me."

"Actually, my plan was just to deliver your mother's message, then talk to you about some spiritual matters. I hadn't considered taking a long swim."

"I feel horrible."

"Don't," Pratt said with a father's tone. "It's not your fault. Have you spoken to your mother?"

Thomas nodded. "While you were having X rays taken and Dr. Edison was being examined."

"I hope the doctors are right about him. He's a great man and a good friend."

"As are you," Thomas said.

Pratt looked up into the face of Thomas and saw concern, confusion, and disappointment. "How is your father?"

Thomas shrugged. "Mom says he's the same, still unresponsive. It doesn't look good."

"I'm sorry, Thomas. I'll continue to pray for him."

"Thank you." Thomas paused. "I'm concerned about Toby."

"How so?"

"The deputy said that he spoke to Wellman. That means Wellman knows you're alive and I'm with you. He's not going to be happy."

"Wellman never gave you an indication of the kind of person he was?"

"I've only spent a few minutes with him. I suppose I should have known."

"Not really," Pratt said. "We all get fooled by those around us. The more trusting you are, the more likely you are to be fooled."

The words came out in a rush, Thomas unable to hold himself back any longer. "Toby is real, Dr. Pratt. Wellman may be a crook, but Toby is as real as they come. I've spent hours with him and he's a true genius—a prodigy in every sense, but he goes beyond that. Miracles happen around him."

"I'm sure it might seem that way—"

"It's true, Dr. Pratt. I've seen it with my own eyes. It was because of him that I went in search of you. He saved your life. Haven't you wondered why I was out there in a boat?"

Pratt thought for a moment, then replied, "Not really. I was just so glad to see you. I had assumed God had sent you our way."

"I'm sure he did," Thomas said, "but he used Toby. That boy is unique. He has a power that I can't describe or explain. And it's not just me who thinks this about him. His mother believes in the miracles, and she knows him better than anyone."

"Are you saying he's a new messiah or apostle?" Pratt asked seriously. "Surely you can see the heresy in that."

"I'm not saying he can supplant Jesus," Thomas said. "I'll confess that I was leaning that direction when I first came to the CNJ. Everyone there thinks that way. It's encouraged, and at first it made sense. I've seen him work. Amazing doesn't even come close to describing it. I've studied miracles and the modern church. You know of my obsession with that."

"Obsession is a good word, Thomas."

"I've gone to countless healing services and watched them closely. Toby is different. I've seen cataracts disappear, skin lesions dissolve, deformities made right. Once I saw a child with a twisted spine stand upright. I'm not gullible, Dr. Pratt. I'm neither naive nor stupid."

Thomas pulled a chair near the bed and continued, "But here's what puzzles me. He's not a spiritual leader. In fact, he's spiritually ignorant. He has never read or owned a Bible. He's never been in a church. He is just what he is and things happen around him—remarkable, unbelievable, inexplicable things."

"How does that fit into what you know of God?" Pratt asked. "What do you do with someone like Toby?"

"I was hoping you could tell me."

Wellman sprang at Kline the moment the man entered his office, grabbing him by the throat with his right hand and squeezing. Pushing as hard as he could, Wellman drove Kline back into a wall, while the surprised security officer clutched at Wellman's wrist. "They lived!" Wellman growled. "You idiot. You imbecile. You failed me. Now everything is in danger."

Kline croaked as he struggled to breathe. In desperation he clenched his hands together and brought them up in a hard sweeping motion, trying to dislodge his boss's grip. Wellman's arm didn't budge. Wellman could see the surprise on the bigger man's face. Wellman felt a new and strange strength.

"What do you think will happen now?" Wellman screamed. "Do you think I can buy off the entire sheriff's department? Not likely." Wellman let go, and Kline slumped to the floor, gasping.

"They can't be alive," Kline said harshly, rubbing his throat.

"I just got a phone call from some deputy sheriff who wants to come over and interview me. He called earlier to see if you worked here. I denied it, of course, but if they dig very deep they'll know that I've been lying. Everything could come tumbling down, thanks to you."

Kline stood and brushed himself off. Wellman could see that anger had replaced the surprise that had draped his face seconds ago. He didn't care. Wellman was changing, and he didn't know why. He didn't care about that either. Protecting what he had built up was all that mattered; keeping control of Toby, that was the only goal worthy of his attention.

"How could they have survived? It's simply not possible."

"Thomas York found out. He rescued them."

"How could he find them? I took them fifteen miles out, bound them, and dropped them over. No one could survive that."

"Don't be stupid. I just told you that they did and that the sheriff's department is asking questions."

"Can't you call them off? We have friends in the department."

"I can ask many favors, but covering up a murder attempt is asking too much." Wellman began to pace the room. "We're leaving in one hour. The plane will be ready then. It's going to be your job to make sure that we get on board that plane before the police arrive."

"Leaving?"

"I've moved up our trip to North Korea. We have to get off this island and take Toby with us. Rudy has made all the other arrangements. All we have to do is pick up Toby, board the plane, and be off. You make sure we can get to the island's airport without being stopped."

"You said a deputy is going to come over and speak to you."

"I set an appointment. He should be here in ninety minutes. By that time we'll be in the air. Make sure he gets in without any trouble. One of my secretaries will show him into my office, where he'll wait. It should take him at least twenty minutes to figure out that I'm not going to show."

"Why not just talk to him? They can't link anything to you."

"Are you sure? Are you willing to risk losing Toby to some social service employee? I'm not. We'll start over. That's all there is to it. A new work—a new country. Maybe somewhere in South America. Who knows, maybe we'll like Korea and stay. Now get out of here. And this time, don't let me down."

We should do something about Toby," Pratt said. Thomas was helping him lower himself into the front seat of a rental car he had acquired. No true rental agency existed on the island. Some residents had autos, but the number of cars and trucks was small.

Tourists rented golf carts or got around on foot. Thomas had rented the car from the same man from whom he had rented the boat. The businessman kept three cars for the occasional V.I.P. The Ford Focus sedan seemed unusually cramped, but Pratt knew that the fault lay with his stiff and aching body, not the automotive designers. Pratt, who was situated on the front passenger seat, pulled his legs up and swung them into the car. As he did, his lower back cramped, his leg muscles protested, and his shoulders sent razor-like pain coursing through his body. It would be weeks before he was close to normal.

"I agree," Thomas admitted. "I'll bet we're worried about the same thing."

Pratt wiped his hands on the new jogging pants he wore. The clothes he had worn to the island were ruined by the sea water. Thomas had purchased the jogging suit, new underwear, socks, and sneakers immediately after renting the car and had done so in less than an hour. He had been in the hospital a mere ninety minutes, but it seemed far longer. "What do you suppose the CNJ people will do if they find out Dr. Edison and I are still alive?"

"I'm sure they already know," Thomas said as he shut the passenger door. A moment later he had rounded the car and took his place behind the wheel. "Like you, I'm growing suspicious of the police."

"I doubt they're all tied to the CNJ, but some certainly are. I learned that when I first tried to elicit their help. Word is bound to get around to those who feel connected to the church."

"You're thinking that we now present a threat to the leaders," Thomas said as he switched on the car. The engine came to life.

"Exactly," Pratt answered. "You know them better than I do. What do you think they will do next?"

"I don't know the leaders that well. But I can say that they're not stupid. The organization has grown faster than anything the world has seen. That took planning and great effort." Thomas pulled away. "But I plan to find out as soon as I drop you off."

"Drop me off where?" Pratt asked quickly.

"I'm going to take you to one of the helicopter shuttles," Thomas said as if he were stating the obvious. "You've had enough excitement for a lifetime. You deserve to recoup at home."

"Why don't you come with me?" Pratt suggested. "You can make plans to see your parents from there."

"Not yet," Thomas said quickly. "I've got to check on Toby."

"From what you told me happened at the gate, I don't think they'll be all that happy to see you."

"True enough, but I still have to do what I can."

"What can you do?" Pratt asked pragmatically. "You can't just walk in, pick up the boy, and walk out. You could be arrested for kidnapping. It wouldn't do you, your parents, or anyone else any good for you to spend the next ten years in jail."

"I've thought about that. The key is Mary. If Mary believes that she and her son are in danger—and from the way Toby was act-ing, she might already know that—then she can walk out with Toby. If they insist that they stay, they could be charged with false imprisonment."

Pratt thought for a moment, then said, "It can't be that simple. They have already gone to great extremes to protect you from me. Attempted murder is the act of desperate or crazy men."

"That's another reason I need to get back to Toby," Thomas said. "There's no telling what they're going to do next. The police will want to talk to them. You're still alive to testify against Well-man's thugs. Toby is acting in new and unstable ways. The whole situation is volatile."

"You still can't just stroll onto the compound. Security is bound to be on the alert."

"I have to try."

Pratt rubbed his chin, then said, "I'll bet they're not going to stay on the compound. Didn't you say that an overseas trip was planned?"

"Yes, they were to start their trip after the Sunday night ser-vice." The car slowed. Thomas's eyes narrowed in thought. "Do you think they'll try to flee?'"

"It's very possible. They can't have the entire sheriff's department in their pocket. I don't think the officer who interrogated us was part of their following. In fact, he seemed to sour each time the CNJ was mentioned. If they did want to make a quick move, what would they do?"

Thomas shrugged, but Pratt could tell his brain was running full tilt. "Asia." The word erupted from his lips. "They could leave early for Asia. All they would have to do is get to the airport and fly off. Once airborne they could fly to any number of airports until they made their way to whatever country they choose. Once out of the United States they could start over. Funds could be transferred, new people hired. And if the authorities can't link the murder attempt to them, they could always come back to what they have."

"So we could wait at the airport," Pratt said. "When they show up, we somehow detain them—cause a scene or something—then when the police arrive, Mary can ask for help. She would ask for help, wouldn't she?"

"I don't know," Thomas said. "But it's worth a try."

"I could be way off base," Pratt admitted.

"You are. You said 'we,' and it's only going to be me after I get you on the helicopter. You'll land fifteen minutes later."

"I can't let you go alone," Pratt said.

"You don't have any choice."

Pratt turned and smiled. "So where is the helicopter that's supposed to ferry me back to Long Beach?"

"It's on the other side of Avalon Bay."

"Where's the airport?"

"The other direction," Thomas replied.

"So they could be flying off while we're driving the other direction," Pratt stated.

Thomas frowned. "You're working me here, aren't you?"

"I promise to be good."

"You're in no condition to be anything else," Thomas said.

chapter 26

"We're going," Wellman commanded as he stormed into Mary's house. "Grab whatever personal things you need. We leave in ten minutes."

"I don't understand," Mary said. Her heart jackhammered in her chest. Wellman had arrived with Rudy. The two uniformed guards that had been posted at the house joined them.

"You don't have to," Wellman snapped. "This is an emergency. I'm doing this for Toby's benefit."

Toby stepped from the rec room and stared at Wellman. He held the Bible that Thomas had given him. Mary could see a new expression on Toby's face, one she had never seen before: anger.

"What kind of emergency?" Mary asked.

"Someone has threatened Toby's life and we think it's for real," Wellman answered. His words shot from his mouth like bullets from a machine gun. "That's all I can tell you now. Get your stuff."

"You're a liar," Toby said so easily that he might have been commenting on something he had seen through his telescope.

"Toby!" Mary exclaimed.

"He's lying, Mom."

Mary watched a brilliant flash of anger cross Wellman's face, then disappear. He spoke softly, but his voice was tight like a spring. "Listen, son, I know this is hard for you to understand, but I think it's best that we get moving. I don't want anything to happen to you. You're my only concern."

"You are the danger," Toby countered. "You and the Shadow Man."

"The what?" Wellman started to speak again when his cell phone rang. He answered, listened, swore, and then hung up. Turning to Rudy he said, "That was one of our men. I sent him to the hospital to check on . . . our friend. He's gone. He checked himself out thirty minutes ago."

"You're talking about Thomas's teacher," Toby said.

Wellman raised a finger and pointed it at Toby like it was a knife. "I told you to get your things."

"I don't want to go," Toby said.

"We've made promises, Toby," Wellman thundered, his façade cracking.

"This isn't about promises. You're scared. You want to run away with me."

"Come here, Toby," Mary said. Fear sparked through her like electricity. Wellman was acting stranger than she had ever seen him behave. His eyes were dark and stormy, his lips pulled tight against his teeth. This wasn't the man she knew. That man could be firm, even hard, but this was so much worse.

"You're crazy, kid," Wellman bellowed. "I don't have time for this."

"Don't let him take me, Mom. The Shadow Man has got him. I can see him. He's inside Mr. Wellman."

"I've had enough of this nonsense," Wellman shouted. He turned on his heels and stepped to Rudy. "Get on the phone. Call the police. Tell them Thomas has just phoned in a threat . . . No, tell them that he's attacked one of our guards and has threatened to kill Toby."

Rudy removed his cell phone from his belt, stepped between the guards, and walked outside.

Wellman turned back to Mary, his eyes darker than when he arrived. All about him appeared different, but in ways she was unable to define. It was more than his eyes, more than his anger, and more than words. At a visceral level, he was both alien and familiar. He was the one who had rescued Toby and her. He had gone out of his way to take them and give them a new life. They had money, a home, and even prestige. Toby was famous and had been the catalyst in the lives of so many people. She was a changed woman. Everything about her was new: her clothes, her speech, her health, everything. But now Wellman was different. There was nothing chivalrous about him. His words were hard and hot, pointed like darts. Those darts were aimed at her son. He had become violent. She touched the cheek he had struck. The change had come so quickly, the violence so unexpectedly.

Toby was a mystery, too. He remained the sweet boy, full of innocence and hope, but he was changing. The episode earlier that day had frightened not only her, but Thomas also. Now he stood before the man who had been their benefactor and called him a liar—right to his face. Toby had never confronted anyone before, certainly not Wellman. Despite his newly displayed bravado, Mary could tell her son was terrified. He stood more behind her than next to her, one furtive, uncertain hand touching her leg, the other clutching the Bible.

"No more stalling," Wellman snapped. He took two quick steps toward them, spun Mary around by the shoulders, and placed a hand on the back of her neck. He squeezed, pinching the nerves under her tender skin. She let slip a tiny cry of pain.

"Rich, please stop."

"There's no stopping now. You and Toby are going to do exactly what I tell you to do. Do you understand that? You will obey every word and do it without question. Now let's get those things."

You okay?" Thomas asked. "You've been pretty quiet." Once again, Thomas pressed the brake to avoid hitting a pedestrian that stepped from one of the local shops.

"I was thinking about Toby," Pratt said.

"Trying to fit him into the scheme of things?"

"Exactly." Pratt rubbed his wrists. The duct tape that had bound him so securely a few hours before was long gone, but he could still feel it. The skin where it had been was red and inflamed. "There's no chance that the miracles you saw were contrived?"

"It's no magic act, I can tell you that," Thomas said. "As much as I've longed to see a miracle, I've always been skeptical of what I see. I want to see the real thing."

"And Toby is it?"

"The best I can tell, he is. But I can't make it work in my theology. Maybe my theology has been wrong all along."

Pratt shook his head. "You don't believe that."

Thomas sighed. "That's the hard part. I don't believe that. Everything I've learned about Jesus, everything I learned about our Creator, I believe. But where does someone like Toby fit? I don't buy into all the psychic phenomena nonsense. I can't bring myself to see him as some evolutionary advancement. But he is as real as the car we're riding in."

"And you say that he has no spiritual elements to him?"

"No, what I said was that he had no knowledge of the Bible or anything of a Christian nature. Totally naive. But I do know that he has a right to a safe and happy life. I no longer believe that CNJ can provide that." He ran a hand through his hair and spoke with shallow, sad words. "I should have seen it coming, should have recognized the signs."

"The problem with lies, Thomas, is that they sound so much like the truth."

"There was no meat to the services. Just fluff and music, then Toby. Toby was always there, always helping, always doing what he was asked to do." Thomas turned the car north, climbing the narrow road, moving closer to the airport.

"He could have said, 'Your friend is in trouble. He's afloat in the ocean.'"

"He frequently talks that way. Mostly when he's doing something special ... something miraculous."

"How do you mean?" Pratt prodded.

"He has trouble with things he has yet to experience. Say during a service, someone with a tumor comes on stage. Toby has no medical experience. He learns quickly. He's a true genius. I have no doubt that he could consume medical books in a year or two, but right now he sees things he can't explain. So the tumor becomes a 'bump' or a 'lump,' or even a 'sharp marble.'"

"A sharp marble? Isn't that an oxymoron?"

"Yes, but that doesn't matter. He means a painful growth. It could be a bundle of nerve endings, a cancerous cell, or a tumor. But to Toby, it's something else."

"So he describes things the best he can within his limited experience," Pratt offered.

"That's my take on it."

"So the problem isn't that Toby doesn't fit," Pratt said, "it's that he doesn't know how to fit."

"I don't understand," Thomas said.

"You told me that you gave him a Bible and that you told him about our Lord. How did he respond to that?"

Thomas thought for a moment. "He asked a lot of questions. Simple ones at first, then deep inquiries. He was overjoyed when I brought him the Bible."

"And that was just this week?"

"Just a couple of days ago."

"I've always assumed that someone with God-given miraculous powers would be intimate with the basic truths of God's Word and work. But that isn't always the case, is it? I mean, think of the people God has called in the past. Not all of them were brilliant or even spiritual; some seemed the worst possible choice."

"Like Paul the apostle," Thomas remarked. "He admitted to persecuting the church to the death. He had the intelligence, the training, and the zeal to do something great for God, but it took a dramatic intervention on God's part to turn him around."

"Exactly—the road to Damascus experience in which Jesus himself appears to Paul and blinds him. But it goes beyond that. In the Old Testament God called Amos who was a farmer, David who was a shepherd boy, and Jonah who was as disobedient as they come. Yet he used each one in a particular setting. God even used a donkey to speak to Balaam the prophet."

"So it isn't that Toby lacks a spiritual dimension, just that God's call on his life is not yet complete."

"That would explain many things," Pratt said. "The real question, assuming we're correct, is, what does God have planned for young Toby?"

Mary's fear and confusion was compounded by the scene that played before her eyes. She and Toby had been led out of the house and were halfway down the walk headed for one of two silver Mercedes SUVs that were parked curbside when the sudden appearance of Harrison Burdick threw fuel on the fire that raged in Wellman.

"What do you want, Burdick?" Wellman's voice was controlled but carried an unmistakable heat. "Time is crucial."

"You're going to have to make time for me." Standing next to Burdick was his constant aide, Melvin Torr, dressed as always in a gray three-piece suit. The expression on his face was one of calm determination.

"What are you doing here, Burdick?" Wellman snapped. "I thought you were back in Fresno looking after farms."

"I was, but word of your trip got to me anyway. We're not supposed to leave until Sunday night."

"Change of plans," Wellman said as he started to push past his partner.

Torr stepped in front of him and placed a hand on Wellman's chest.

"Unless you want to pull back a stump, Torr, you had better remove that hand."

Torr didn't budge. Wellman looked at his two guards and nodded. One stepped forward and took Torr's outstretched hand by the wrist. He pulled the hand away from Wellman's chest. Wellman smiled, but the smile died when he saw Torr reach across his body, seize the guard's hand, and pull, bringing a right elbow to the side of the man's head in a smooth but brutal blow. The guard crumpled like a rag doll. Blood pooled in the ear closest to the spot where the blow landed.

Torr said nothing.

The other guard started forward, but Torr withered him with a stare that could freeze water.

For several moments, Mary watched Burdick and Wellman stand in silence, each waiting for the other to speak. Then something happened, something Mary couldn't believe. The sneer that crossed Wellman's face dissolved into a grin—a humorless, evil, malevolent parting of the lips. The smile was chilling, but the expression that followed it was terrifying. It seemed to Mary that Wellman was changing right before her eyes. His skin seemed to darken, his shoulders seemed to broaden, and his eyes turned the color of coal. For a moment, it seemed as if Wellman had no eyes at all, just empty, gaping sockets.

"What the—" Torr began but cut himself short as Wellman took a step forward.

"Out of my way," Wellman growled. His voice was sandpaper rough and dripped with threat.

"I'm not finished with you," Burdick said.

"Put them in the car," Wellman ordered the other guard. The man sprung into action, clearly glad to be away from the confrontation. Mary picked Toby up before the guard reached them. She didn't want anyone touching him.

"I don't think so," Burdick said. "I'm as much a part of this organization as you, Wellman. You'd still be hocking someone else's wares on late-night radio if it weren't for me and my money."

"I don't need you anymore."

"Too bad, Wellman. You're stuck with me. No one is leaving here until I know exactly what is going on."

Wellman started forward. Again Torr blocked his way. Wellman stopped and looked up at the taller man. What happened next,

Mary could not fully comprehend. An appendage, dark as tar, shot out of Wellman's chest. One moment, Torr stood like a granite statue; the next he was cut and bloodied as if a whirlwind of razor blades had engulfed him. Torr dropped as if he had been shot in the heart. Mary screamed. Wellman ignored her. He took one step toward Burdick, who began to backpedal. He wasn't fast enough. Wellman had him by the throat. He pulled him forward, then pushed him back in a single violent move. There was a loud snap, like the breaking of a branch from an aged oak tree. Burdick dropped to the concrete walk in convulsive spasms.

Mary covered Toby's eyes.

"I said get them in the car." Wellman's voice boomed as if it had been electronically amplified. Waves of revulsion and terror raced through Mary. She wanted to run, to flee, but she knew that she wouldn't make ten yards before being caught. He would take Toby from her. She knew it. Obediently she placed Toby in the backseat and then joined him in the vehicle.

Wellman started for the car, and as he did, Mary thought that she saw a sulfur-yellow haze around him. She felt sick to her stomach.

chapter 27

Burdick was dead. Toby had not seen Wellman's violence, but he knew the truth of it, nonetheless. He was as certain of it as if he had witnessed the brutality with his own eyes. There were other ways of seeing things, Toby had learned. Most people just saw with their eyes, but he could sense the death, as if he could feel Burdick's soul evacuate his body.

He had never seen death, never known anyone who had died. The thought frightened Toby greatly. His small heart chattered in his chest, pounding out an impossible rhythm. His mother was frightened, too. She was trying to act calm, but she was doing it for his sake. She pulled him closer, and although he found her ever-tightening embrace uncomfortable, he didn't resist.

There were other emotions flying around the car. Rudy, who was behind the wheel, was awash in fear and confusion. Toby could sense his concern for Burdick, his fear that he had just witnessed a murder, maybe two, and his sudden apprehension about Wellman.

Wellman was talking on his cell phone. He hung up. "The plane is ready," he said. "Kline is there and he said everything looks perfect. I think you're safe now, Toby."

Toby kept his silence.

Wellman's voice was normal now, but Toby could see what the others could not. The Shadow Man was with them in the car. More accurately, in Wellman himself.

"You shouldn't have left Burdick and that guard on the ground," Rudy said.

"Just drive the car, Rudy, and leave the thinking to me." Wellman looked in the side mirror. "Make sure you don't lose the follow-up car. We're down to the one guard and Kline at the plane."

"I think we should call the police," Rudy said. "At the very least we should call an ambulance. You may have hurt Burdick."

"He killed him," Toby said. "Mr. Burdick is dead."

"He's all right, Toby," Wellman said with mock sincerity.

"No, he's not. You killed him, and you killed Mr. Torr. And the guard is hurt real bad."

"I didn't hurt the guard, Toby. Torr did. The guard was making sure that you could get away safely. We'll be in the air in twenty minutes, and then we can call the police."

"Twenty minutes might be too late," Rudy said.

"Toby is wrong," Wellman said to Rudy. "Burdick will be fine."

"Toby is never wrong," Rudy snapped. "You know that. You killed Burdick, and I'm helping you escape. That makes me an accessory. How did I get into this?"

Once again, Wellman darkened as if he were somehow sucking in the light around him. The strange, putrid mist that Toby had seen before emanated off him like steam.

"You are not you," Toby said firmly.

"Hush, son," Mary said. There was a tremor in her voice.

"Listen to your mother, boy," Wellman said.

"You're not you," Toby repeated. "You're like them."

"Them? Them who?"

"The people in the Bible," Toby said with authority. "The people with the creatures living in them—the demons."

Wellman laughed loudly. "You think I'm demon possessed? That's a good one, Toby. Kids your age don't usually have a sense of humor like that."

"The Shadow Man is in you. He's inside you right now."

Cold ran down Toby's spine like an icy waterfall. Wellman turned his head to the side. He paused, then his head continued to turn until he was staring straight back at Toby, except it wasn't the head of Wellman that turned, nor his face that glowered at him. It was the eyeless gaze of the Shadow Man.

Toby pressed himself back in the seat. How the creature could see without eyes was a mystery he didn't care to fathom. He just wanted it to go away, go away forever. Raising the Bible to his chest, Toby attempted to seal himself behind it. Was this thing what he had read about in the Bible? Thomas had said that the Bible was the Word of God, that it told the truth about all things. Toby shuddered.

Wellman snapped his head forward again. "Why are we slowing?"

"There's a car in front of us," Rudy said.

"Go around. I don't want to waste a minute."

Rudy frowned deeply, pursed his lips, and pressed the accelerator, shooting around the Ford sedan in front of them.

Toby sat up straight, straining to look past his mother. He whispered a single word, "Thomas."

The Mercedes SUV appeared suddenly next to Thomas who jerked involuntarily, pulling the car as far to the right as he could without hitting parked cars and carts. "What's his problem?" He turned, looking for the driver. Instead, he saw the terror-stricken face of Mary. "That's ... that's them." Another Mercedes passed them, staying close to the first car. Pratt saw a single occupant.

"Are you sure?"

"Positive." Thomas sped the car.

Pratt watched the autos pull away. "They're in a hurry."

"I saw Mary and I'm pretty sure I saw Wellman." Pratt took hold of the armrest as Thomas accelerated, keeping the two vehicles in sight.

"It will only take a minute before they realize you're following them. The cat will be out of the bag then." Pratt was surprised how calm his words sounded. Calm was far from what he felt.

"I'm not sure what else to do," Thomas said. "They must be headed to the airport just as we guessed they might. If that's the case, they can be on a private plane in a few minutes. We can't let that happen."

Thomas was right. What he didn't know was what to do next. They could follow the two SUVs, but then what? "Maybe we can attract the attention of the police," Pratt said.

"I'll take all the help we can get."

We're being followed," Rudy said. "I think I may have ticked off the driver."

"Too bad. He'll have to get over it." Wellman turned to look behind them.

"I don't think he forgets very easily," Rudy replied. "He's coming up on us."

Toby's heart had skipped a beat when he saw Thomas behind the wheel, but things were still wrong. His eyes were fixed on Wellman, and fearfully he watched him change. The yellow aura separated from Wellman's body and rose through the roof of the car. For a moment Wellman's shoulder seemed to soften, his head lower, and his tension evaporate. Seconds later the yellow haze was back. Wellman stiffened. "It's them," he growled.

"Who?" Rudy asked.

"Thomas York and his nosy professor."

Mary gasped and covered her mouth.

Wellman ignored her, removed his cell phone, and placed a hasty call. He then turned his attention to the mirror on his passenger door. He saw exactly what he had hoped.

Watch it!" Pratt shouted, extending a hand toward the dashboard. The car in front them had slammed on its brakes. The tires complained in loud, piercing squeals. Smoke erupted from beneath the wheels.

Instinctively, Thomas hit the brake pedal and steered to the left, narrowly missing an oncoming cart. Both cars came to a complete stop. Thomas attempted to press forward, but the Mercedes pulled in front of them, blocking his way. Putting the car in reverse, Thomas backed up quickly.

"He's going to ram us," Pratt shouted.

Smoke from the Mercedes' overheated, spinning tires billowed in the air. Like a guided missile, the driver directed the car at them, aiming the rear end of his vehicle at the front of the Ford. The impact was bone jarring, and Pratt's already aching body exploded in pain. The car's airbags deployed.

"You all right?" Thomas asked, pushing aside the now flaccid bag.

"I'll live."

Steam rose from the crumpled hood of the rental car.

The Mercedes pulled forward again, stopped, and paused long enough for the driver to shift the car back into reverse. The backup lights came on.

"He's going to do it again," Pratt said.

"Brace yourself," Thomas cried. The Ford rocked with the impact. The sound of tortured metal reverberated through the vehicle. There was a new noise. The tires of the Mercedes were screeching again, but this time for a different reason. The car was stuck, attached to the Ford at the bumpers. The driver was trying to pull forward but moved slowly, dragging Thomas and Pratt's car with it. Thomas slammed the gearshift into park, locking the transmission, and then tried to open his door, but it moved only a foot. The bent frame was pinching the sheet metal, preventing the door from opening any further. Releasing his safety belt, Thomas struggled to lay on his back. It was a tight fit, but he managed it by wedging one shoulder under the dash. His head lay on Pratt's lap. Pulling his knees up, Thomas kicked the door, grunting with the effort. It moved another foot. Thomas kicked again, and the door sprang open.

Without a word, Thomas slipped out of the car and jogged toward the Mercedes. The tires continued to squeal. Pratt popped his seat belt and moved painfully across the seats and exited the car on the driver's side. He got out in time to see Thomas open the driver's door. The guard was ready for him and came out spoiling for a fight. Before Pratt had crossed half the distance he needed to reach Thomas's side, he saw the guard bring a powerful right hand to the bridge of Thomas's nose. Blood gushed down his face, and he staggered back. The blow had caught him off guard. The guard exited the vehicle spewing a steady stream of vile epithets. Thomas had his hands raised to his face.

The guard wasted no time in attacking. He threw a body punch to Thomas's middle, then followed with a roundhouse left. The attack was so smooth and so brutal that the man must have spent most of his life in the boxing ring.

Pratt was running before he knew it. The pain that had been haunting him the last few hours slipped from his thoughts. He lowered a shoulder and plowed into the guard's side, sending both of them tumbling to the warm asphalt, Pratt landing face first, skinning his chin and right check. Rolling to his side, Pratt started to get up, but the guard was younger and not hindered by injuries. He bared his teeth and took a step back, ready to deliver a rib-breaking kick. Pratt saw the foot start forward, and he braced himself for the blow he could not avoid.

The kick never landed. The guard was snatched backward. Thomas had grabbed him by the collar just in time. The guard suddenly spun, and Pratt thought he was setting up to throw another haymaker, but Thomas was ready for him. Before the guard could throw a punch, Thomas slapped his large hand on the attacker's face, tilting his head backwards. Then in a single, fluid movement, he grabbed the man's belt, lifted, and drove the man to the ground hard. He landed on his back. Even ten feet away, Pratt could hear the air leave the guard's lungs. Thomas stood and stared at the writhing man.

"How badly is he hurt?" Pratt asked a moment, wincing as he touched the abrasion on his chin.

"Not bad," Thomas said. He was breathing hard and blood trickled from his nose and mouth. "He's just lost his wind. It's happened to me several times. He'll come out of in a few minutes."

"Then let's not waste any time," Pratt said. "I'll check him for a cell phone. See if you can't get the cars unhooked." Leaning over the squirming man, Pratt quickly patted his pockets and checked his belt for a phone, finding nothing. He then moved to the Mercedes and checked inside. A small gray phone lay on the passenger seat. Pratt grabbed it. As he was reaching for the device, the car began to bounce. Thomas was standing between the vehicles jumping on the entangled bumpers.

"We're loose," Thomas shouted.

"You guys need help?"

Pratt turned to see a man in a red pickup truck. "Do you have a cell phone?"

"No," the man said. "What happened?"

"Here," Pratt said, moving to the man. "Take this one. Call the police and tell them there's been an accident. Also tell them there's an emergency at the airport and not to let any planes take off."

"What kind of emergency?"

"Just tell them," Pratt insisted. He limped back to the car. Thomas had already seated himself behind the wheel. Pratt got in the Mercedes. "Do you think this thing will still run?"

"It has a better chance than our rental," Thomas said. He pressed the accelerator. The man in the truck shouted something, but Pratt couldn't hear what he said.

"Good thinking having that guy call the police."

"Thinking I'm good at. It's my tackling that needs improvement."

Thomas threw a quick glance at Pratt. "As far as I'm concerned, you did a great job. Good timing, too. I was stupid to approach him that way."

"Hopefully you'll never have to do it again."

"I don't know," Thomas said somberly. "I've got a feeling that it's about to get worse."

Let's go." Wellman exited the car and opened the back door.

Mary remained seated, holding Toby tightly under one arm. Toby still clutched the Bible to his chest.

"I said, let's go."

"This is all wrong," Mary said. "Toby is right. You are not you."

"Nonsense," Wellman barked. "Get out of the car."

"No," Mary said. "We're not getting on that plane." She looked at the sleek white Gulfstream V business jet that waited for them just fifteen yards away. She could hear the whine of the jet engines crescendo. A door was open and a set of metal stairs descended from the front of the craft to the tarmac. At the top of the stairs was a man Mary didn't recognize. Behind the aircraft she could see the airport's single runway.

"I'm doing this for Toby's good," Wellman said. "Don't make me pull you from the car."

Rudy opened the other passenger door. He held out his arms and said in a calm voice, "Come on, Toby. I think we better get on the plane." Toby pressed closer to Mary. "I'm not going to hurt you, Toby."

"You stay here with me, Toby. You hear?" Mary commanded. Her voice was shaky and uncertain.

"Mary, I'm only going to ask one more time—" Wellman began.

"You're not asking, you're ordering," Mary snapped, surprised at her own words. She had so seldom stood up for herself that she couldn't believe she was doing so now. Fear for Toby's well-being had compelled her to leave Tobias. Now she was forced to assert herself again. She cut her eyes away to avoid looking into the fierce face of the man she had once thought her hero.

Pain shot through her scalp. Wellman had grabbed her by the hair and was pulling her from the car. "Get the kid," he shouted to Rudy.

"Leave her alone!" Toby screamed. "You leave my mom alone—" His words were cut off.

Mary grabbed Wellman's wrists and tried to pull his hand free, but he was far stronger than she expected. "Let go of me," Mary cried. "You're hurting me."

"Get him on the plane," Wellman ordered Rudy. "She won't stay back with him onboard."

"Gotcha."

Pain rippled down her neck as Wellman snapped her head up. "Stop making a scene. I have enough problems as it is."

"Let us go," Mary pleaded. Burning tears welled up in her eyes.

"Look," Wellman snapped, drops of spittle flying onto her face. "Look at where your son is, Mary. He's on the plane. Can you see that? Can you?"

Mary saw Toby held in the tight grip of Rudy. Toby was reaching for her, calling her name. "I want my boy."

"I can leave you here, woman. Him I need, you I don't. Now you can go with us, or you can watch your son fly off. What's it going to be?"

"I'll go." She had no other choice. The thought of being without Toby was crushing. "Just let go of my hair."

"Don't do anything stupid," Wellman said. "Now let's walk calmly over to the plane and board. In a few minutes all this will be behind us. Nothing but fame and fortune ahead."

"I was happier poor," Mary snapped. She walked to the plane, Wellman by her side, his hand on her arm.

Once at the steps, Wellman gave Mary a shove and said, "Up the steps. Kline will make sure you're seat-belted in."

Mary stumbled on the first step and had to catch herself by placing both hands on the treads in front of her. Looking behind her, she saw Wellman remove his cell phone and dial. She rose slowly and looked at the man at the top of the stairs. He wore an expensive suit, and his expression said he was not a patient man. As Mary straightened herself she heard Wellman say, "Who is this? How did you get this phone? How long ago?" A barrage of swearing followed.

"Kline," he called. "Get the pilot moving. We have to get out of here *now*."

Pratt gritted his teeth and fought back the urge to groan aloud. His body was once again a throbbing bundle of pain, and Thomas's rapid driving and tight turns were making things worse. If lives of innocents had not hung in the balance, he would complain loudly. For now, he just tightened his jaw and prayed silently.

"There!" Thomas said loudly as he pulled through the parking lot of the small airport. "There's their car—and there's Mary."

Pratt was pressed back in the seat as Thomas turned the car tightly and headed for an open gate. Tires skidded noisily on the pavement. Pratt saw Wellman turn and face them. A second later he was pushing Mary up the short set of stairs.

The two jet engines at the rear of the Gulfstream sang noisily. The pilot began to taxi, the aircraft slowly moving away as the stairs began to rise.

"We can't wait for the police," Pratt said. "We have to stop the plane."

"How? I can't ram it. Crack a fuel tank and we could burn Mary and Toby to death."

"What about cutting the jet off. You know, pull in front of it."

"No. We can't take the risk that the pilot couldn't stop in time," Thomas said.

"We're going to have to do this the hard way."

"Right." Thomas pressed the pedal to the floor, and Pratt's stomach dropped. He brought the Mercedes to a halt just a yard away from the wing tip. Thomas was out of the car before Pratt could release his seat belt, but he hadn't made three steps before Pratt was on his heels. They raced forward just as the stairs continued to rise from their down position. Pratt saw Wellman push Mary further up the stairs where another man grabbed her—a man he recognized: the man who threw him overboard and left Edison and him to drown.

Without hesitation, Thomas stepped on the rising stairs and started up. Pratt had to jump, grabbing the handrail that was folding into the hatch where it would be secure during flight. Pratt and Thomas's weight slowed the hydraulic steps, but did not stop them.

The jet began to move faster. Pratt scrambled to a crawling position and saw that Thomas had done the same thing. Inexorably the stairs rose past the halfway mark of their journey, and Pratt realized that he was now looking down into the hatch rather than up at it. Thomas continued forward until he disappeared into the maw of the jet. Pratt continued onward, but could not keep his footing and fell into the interior of the craft, arms and legs flailing. As he hit the interior deck his only thought was, *Now what?*

He didn't have to wait for an answer. Scrambling to his feet, he quickly took in the situation. The Gulfstream had seats for eight. Mary and Toby were in the beige leather chairs at the rear of the aircraft. A narrow aisle ran between the seats. That aisle was filled with Thomas, who faced the back of the jet, and another man who faced forward. Thomas was standing as if he were made of stone. Pratt could see the terror-laced faces of Toby and Mary, and realized the source of the terror. The man facing Thomas was Kline, and he had a gun pressed against Thomas's forehead. Another man stood to the side of Kline holding onto the back of one of the seats.

"You must be the problem that Mr. Wellman spoke of," Kline said to Thomas. "I don't believe you have a ticket for this flight."

The boarding ramp closed behind Thomas. Pratt heard it seal.

"Several of us would be happy to leave," Thomas said.

"You and your friend back there are the gate crashers. Everyone else has an invitation."

The business jet rumbled slowly down the tarmac, then lurched to a stop. "What's the problem?" Pratt heard from behind him. The voice came from the pilot's cabin.

"We don't have clearance," a man Pratt took to be the pilot said.

"Get it and get us in the air before something else goes wrong."

"Yes, sir."

Wellman stepped from the pilot area through the small galley and faced Pratt. "The man with nine lives," Wellman said. "It looks like your luck has run out." He pressed his hand into Pratt's chest and pushed him to the side. "Sit down, Dr. Pratt. You have annoyed me enough for a lifetime."

Pratt staggered back and crumpled into one of the empty leather seats. He then watched Wellman take the three steps necessary to reach Thomas, who still stared unshakably at Kline.

"I see you've met my chief of security," Wellman said to Thomas. "Or have you had the pleasure before?"

"No, and this is no pleasure," Thomas retorted.

"What do we do with them now?" Kline asked.

"Not much we can do right now," Wellman said. "We can't drop them out without delaying our takeoff."

"It would take less than five minutes," Kline said.

"We don't have five minutes," Rudy broke in. He pointed out one of the oval windows. "Cops."

"They can't be here for us," Wellman intoned.

"Yes, they can," Pratt said. "They know there's a problem."

"Mr. Wellman," the pilot called. "I'm getting word that we should hold our takeoff and return to the terminal."

"Don't do it," Wellman commanded. "Take off."

"Sir, that's against every FAA regulation there is. They'll have my license."

"I'll have more than that if you don't get this jet in the air."

"I'm sorry, sir. I can't do that."

Wellman changed before Pratt's eyes. A dark fierceness that went beyond anything that Pratt had ever seen enveloped the man. Fear washed over him like a tsunami. It was not the fear a man felt in the presence of another man. Pratt was repulsed by the evil he saw in Wellman's eyes—eyes that had turned black from lid to lid, from corner to corner. The sclera, the white of the eye, was gone. His blue irises were afloat in a sea of inky black. With an unexpected swiftness, Wellman spun back to Thomas, grabbed his collar, and delivered a crushing blow to his right kidney. Wellman struck vicious blow after vicious blow. Thomas went limp. Pratt felt sick. A moment later he realized that he had been holding his breath. Pratt rose and started for the aisle. Wellman spun, striking Pratt with a backhand. Pain shot through his jaw and head. So unexpected was the blow that Pratt stumbled back again, his hands raised to his face.

"Give me the gun," Wellman demanded. Kline hesitated, taken aback by what he had just seen. "Give me the gun!" The words were little more than an animal growl. Kline complied. Wellman took long strides back into the pilot's cabin. From his position Pratt could see Wellman walk to the cockpit and point the gun at the pilot. "Get this plane in the air and do it ... *now!*"

Again Pratt struggled to his feet and moved toward his fallen friend. "Unless you want some more," Kline said, "I suggest you stay right where you are." Despite the fiery pain in his head, Pratt moved forward, simultaneously filled with anger and terror. He feared for Thomas, for Toby and Mary, and for his own life. His heart rattled in his chest and his legs felt weak. He took another step. "I should have shot you on the boat." Kline took a step forward, his fists clinched into tight fleshy hammers. He lifted one leg to step over Thomas's unconscious body. To Pratt's surprise, Kline suddenly fell forward, facedown on the carpeted deck. At first he thought Thomas had tripped the security man, but then he saw it: Mary was on Kline's back, her fingers full of the man's hair. Kline screamed furiously. Pratt turned to Rudy, whom he expected to enter the fray, but the man stood still, as if in shock at what he was seeing. Wellman's aide would be no problem, but Wellman would.

"Enough!" The words rolled down the plane like thunder. Pratt thought the words had made the jet itself tremble. "No ... more ... interference ... from ... you."

Pratt stood to face the man ... the black-eyed thing marching toward them. As he had done before, Pratt lowered his head and charged, attempting to knock Wellman from his feet. He failed. A knee came up and caught Pratt in the face.

"Stop it!" a young voice shouted.

Pratt felt a hand grab his hair and snap his head up. Before he could raise his hands, Wellmans pistol-whipped him across the forehead. Lights flashed in his mind, darkness washed in, and Pratt felt his knees weaken as Wellman threw him onto a seat as if he were a sweater.

"Stop it. Stop it!" Toby demanded.

There was a scream.

Unconsciousness beckoned Pratt with a near-irresistible siren's call. The blackness would mean no more pain. The darkness would mean no more fear. But Pratt refused the call. Thomas was hurt. He had heard Mary cry out. The task before him was impossible, but he had to try. He didn't feel brave; he had no sense of courage. All he knew was that lives were in danger, and he had to do whatever he could. The rest was left up to God. He forced himself to his feet, his knees wobbling beneath him.

There was another motion and another sound. The aircraft was moving again. Pratt felt the plane turn. They were pulling onto the runway.

Mary had pushed herself off Kline, her hands to her mouth. Blood ran between her fingers. Kline had caught her with an elbow or forearm. Kline was on his feet in a second and facing Mary. Blood trickled from his scalp.

"Stop it, stop it, stop it," Toby pleaded.

Kline raised a fist, ready to send it plummeting to Mary's face.

"No." Toby was on his feet, his head tilted down. *"No . . . more."*

Kline stopped abruptly and lowered his hand. He flexed his fingers and stared at them with a puzzled expression. The arm went limp. He turned to face Wellman. "Help . . . me." His speech was slurred and one eyelid drooped. He tried to speak again, but no words came from his lips. His left arm useless, Kline raised his right hand to his head. His face twisted in pain, then his left leg gave way. Kline closed both eyes and fell limp across a row of seats.

Pratt started for Wellman, but stopped when Wellman raised the gun, letting it hover an inch away from his nose.

"What happens to the plane if a bullet punctures the hull of the jet?" Pratt asked with false bravado. His mouth was dry and his palms wet, but he was determined not to back down. It was the eyes that frightened him most. They were more than just ugly, they were vile, and reflected a wicked, hellish evil. Pratt felt as if he were looking into the face of Satan himself.

"I'll risk it." Wellman's voice sounded hollow, resonant, multivocal.

Pratt knew nothing about guns, but he knew that he was an inch from death.

The plane picked up speed. Pratt could hear the rubber wheels thumping down the runway. In mere seconds, they would be airborne.

The engines went silent. The jet slowed.

"What are you doing?" Wellman called forward to the pilots. "I ordered you to take off."

"Power failure, sir," the senior pilot shouted back.

"Well, fix it. Fix it now."

Pratt looked down the muzzle of the gun. He thought of death. "To live is Christ, to die is gain," he muttered. Most of his life he had placed his trust in Christ. Throughout his professional life, he had taught that Christians need not fear death, for death was a positive experience. Now, facing down the barrel of a gun, he felt a sense of peace. How bad could death be if one saw Christ?

"You can't win," Pratt said.

"I think I already have."

"No, you've lost everything, including control of your life."

"Religious talk. You sound like the kid. He thinks I'm possessed."

Pratt nodded. "I think he's right."

"Really? I gave him everything. Can you understand that? I gave him a home and food and books and everything else he could want. He's famous and lacks for nothing. He owes me his very life."

"His life belongs to another," Pratt said.

"What? He belongs to God? Is that your point?" Wellman laughed deeply. "He belongs to me."

"Not now," Pratt answered. "Not ever."

Wellman pulled the hammer back on the gun, smiled, and winked one shiny black eye.

Then he disappeared.

At first Pratt didn't know what to think. One second Wellman stood before him, the next second he was gone. A thud to Pratt's left turned his head. Wellman was flat on his back at the front of the craft. Somehow the man had flown fifteen feet and impacted the galley cabinet, and Pratt had seen nothing of it. Amazing as that was, Pratt was more surprised to see Wellman immediately rise.

"Toooobyyyy!" Wellman screamed. "I warned you." He raised the gun and aimed it at Toby, then at Mary. "You I need, her I don't." Wellman pulled the trigger.

Instinctively Pratt leapt forward, interposing his body between the gun's muzzle and Mary. He steeled himself for the slug's impact. It never came. Had Wellman missed? There had been no sound, no report from the gun. Wellman looked at the gun quizzically, then lowered his arm. "Why are you doing this to me, Toby? I'm your friend."

"No you're not," Toby said boldly. The boy started forward, pushing by his stunned mother and stepping over the unconscious Thomas.

"Stay back, son," Pratt said, reaching for the boy's shoulder. Toby shook it off.

"You have the Shadow Man." Toby took another step forward. "You hurt my friends. You hurt my mother."

"Let's put an end to this, Wellman," Pratt said.

"Let's not." Wellman smiled, then sneered.

Pratt had not thought it possible, but Wellman's eyes grew blacker, then receded into his head. There was a slight sucking sound. A second later, Wellman crumbled in a heap, but someone, something, remained standing. Pratt wanted to say something, to utter some words of shock and fright, but no words came to mind. He was too stunned to think. Before him was a translucent, ebony figure, a shadow with substance, a black specter whose "skin" roiled in constant motion. It had no features except two holes where eyes should have been. Around it emanated a yellow-brown aura, visible but less substantial than mist.

"What is going on back there?" the pilot called through the opening between cabins. The door that sealed the cockpit from the cabin closed with a bang. Pratt could hear the pilot pounding on the door.

"Toby," Pratt whispered. "Come back here, son. Move back to me slowly."

Toby walked forward.

"Toby, come back," Mary called. There were tears in her voice.

Toby continued on until he was within arm's reach of the creature. Mary tried to push on, but Pratt caught her by the arm. "Wait," he said. "Look."

The putrid yellow haze began to engulf Toby, and just as Pratt thought that the noxious vapor would enfold the boy completely a new light appeared. It was warm and golden. Each second the light grew brighter, effusing the cabin with a gold tint. Toby opened the Bible.

"I know the truth now," he said to the malevolence before him. "Thomas showed me the truth in this book." It seemed to Pratt that the creature moved back a few inches. Toby recited, "'In him was life, and that life was the light of men. The light shines in the darkness, but the darkness has not understood it.'"

The golden glow intensified, and the Shadow Man retreated another foot.

"I'm not afraid of you anymore," Toby said heroically. "You're just shadow, he is light." Toby began to quote again, "'Even though I walk through the valley of the shadow of death, I will fear no evil, for you are with me; your rod and your staff, they comfort me.'"

The golden effulgence intensified and as it did, the Shadow Man diminished. His blackness became gray like spent charcoal. "Go away, Shadow Man. You can't hurt us anymore. We're not afraid of the Shadow of Death. We're not afraid of you. Jesus is the light of the world. He's our light. He's my light."

The air in the cabin began to move, first like a spring breeze then faster, harder. Loose papers danced around on eddies of invisible current. Pratt felt his hair and clothing flap in the tiny storm. He raised a protective hand to his eyes, squinting into a wind that threatened to topple him from his feet. The airstream spun in powerful currents, mini-twisters.

"To ... by!" Mary cried out. She shook loose from Pratt and raced forward, the currents knocking her from side to side, her hair streaming, twisting, tangling in the wind.

Pratt forced himself to stare into the unnatural storm and saw Toby facing down the hideous thing. He seemed unperturbed by the wind. The light grew as the wind did, becoming so much like gold that it sparkled.

There was a growl, a snarl like that of a threatened, cornered animal. The growl grew into a howl, then a banshee-like scream that rebounded off the cabin walls with ear-piercing severity. Instinctively, Pratt raised his hands to his ears.

Then there was nothing.

The wind ceased.

The noise disappeared.

The golden glow was gone.

Wiping away tears from eyes that had been assaulted by the wind, Pratt looked down the narrow aisle and saw Mary holding Toby in her arms. She was weeping.

The Shadow Man was gone.

"What ... what just happened?" the man Wellman had called Rudy asked.

"A miracle," Pratt said.

In the aisle lay three men: Wellman near the front of the craft, Kline in the middle, and Thomas just a step away from Pratt's feet. Pratt dropped to his knees and placed two fingers to the side of Thomas's neck. There was a pulse.

The door that had locked the pilots in the flight arena swung open. Pratt watched as the two puzzled men took in the scene. "What happened?"

"We need an ambulance right now," Pratt shouted forward.

"The police are right outside," the pilot said. "I'll open the door."

"No," Toby said, wriggling from his mother's arms. "Not yet." As soon as his feet touched the deck, he walked back to Thomas, stepping over Kline's body. He looked at Thomas for a moment and said, "Bloody inside."

"Internal bleeding?" Pratt said.

Toby nodded. "Here," he said, pointing at Thomas's lower back.

"His kidneys," Pratt uttered. "Can you help him, Toby?"

Toby smiled. "I just did."

Thomas moaned, rolled on his back, and twisted his face into a tight grimace. He opened his eyes and stared first into Pratt's face, then Toby's. "I feel strange."

"You look stranger." Toby giggled.

"Very funny," Thomas rejoined. "Come here so I can hit you."

Pratt helped Thomas to his feet. His student looked around the cabin for a moment then said, "It appears I missed something."

"You have no idea," Pratt said. "Toby just fixed you up."

Thomas kneeled so that his eyes were level with the boy. "Are you okay, buddy?"

"Yeah."

Thomas took him in his arms and held him for a long moment. Looking up he saw Mary, tears running down her face. Standing again, he motioned for her to join them. The three embraced.

"What about them?" Rudy asked.

Pratt started to speak, but Toby separated from Thomas and his mother and walked to Kline's unmoving body. "Bleeding inside," he said, echoing his earlier words. "Here." He pointed to the man's head. "Bloody brain."

"A stroke," Pratt said.

Toby then worked his way over to Wellman and gazed at him. "Nothing. He's asleep. He'll wake up soon."

"Toby," Pratt asked. "Did you do all this? Did you cause Kline to have a stroke? Did you stop the plane, did you make it so the gun wouldn't fire?"

Toby shook his head. "I didn't do anything."

epilogue

Y our father looks well," Pratt said, nodding in the direction of
a white-haired man who stood at a barbecue. A few feet away,
Toby swung on an old swing set. Mary sat in the swing next to him,
but was swinging much lower.

"He does, doesn't he?" Thomas replied. He was seated at a redwood picnic table in his parents' backyard. Pratt sat across from
him, drinking lemonade. The early spring sun bathed them in
warm light. "I'm so thankful that God sent Toby our way. I'm also
thankful that you came looking for me. There's no telling what
would have happened if you hadn't."

"I should have started earlier," Pratt confessed. "I let way too
much time pass."

"Not really," Thomas countered. "I wouldn't have listened
then. I wasn't close to Toby or Wellman. I needed to make my own
mistakes and see things for myself."

Pratt laughed and pointed at the barbecue. "It looks like Dr.
Edison is giving your father a lecture on the proper way to barbecue pork ribs."

"Dr. Edison is a brilliant man, but he's outgunned on the barbecue front. My dad takes a backseat to no man when it comes to
burning burgers, hot dogs, and ribs."

"How's your relationship with your family?" Pratt asked. "If
I'm not being too nosy."

"It's been four weeks since we left Catalina and things have done nothing but get better. I think the more time that passes since my father's healing, the closer we become. My parents are good people; I don't know how I could have turned my back on them the way I did."

"Sometimes separation can draw us closer."

"Perhaps, but I was in sin. I know it. I should have been a better witness to my parents than I was. They go to church regularly now."

"And you?"

"Me too. You know, there's an old country-western song that talks about looking for love in all the wrong places. Well, I was looking for faith in all the wrong places. I was seeking signs and wonders when I should have been seeking fellowship with God through Christ. I may have been a child prodigy, but I sure can be dense."

"Can't we all."

"I assume the DA has sent you papers calling you as a witness against Wellman, Kline, and the Church of New Jerusalem," Thomas said.

"Oh, yes. We're going to be in and out of court for weeks, maybe months."

"The authorities have brought every imaginable charge against Wellman and his lackeys. Embezzlement, abduction, false imprisonment, attempted murder, assault with a deadly weapon, and a dozen more."

"And when that's all over, the IRS has a case against them for misusing church funds and other irregularities. Wellman will be off the streets for quite a while."

"I've been meaning to ask you something," Thomas said, brushing a fly from the table. "Do you really think Wellman was possessed?"

"Yes," Pratt said. "I saw something I can't define, the thing Toby called the Shadow Man. Exactly what it was I don't know, but it was pure evil."

"A demon?"

"It fits with Scripture. I've never seen a demon before, so I can't say for certain. Whatever it was, it sure scared me."

"But not Toby," Thomas said. "What you told me about how he marched up to that thing ... well, it amazes me."

"As it should. I know I'll never forget it." Pratt took a sip from his iced tea. "Has Mary decided what she will do next?"

"She has to stay in California for the trials," Thomas explained. "My parents have said that they can stay here as long as they want. They're comfortable and feel safe."

"And they get to see you every day."

"I suppose."

"Come on, you can't fool your old professor. Even a middle-aged bachelor can see that she's interested in you. She's not much older than you."

Thomas smiled. "Just a year, actually. She was just a teenager when she gave birth to Toby."

"Go slowly, Thomas. Let the Lord work in his time."

"It's Toby I worry about," Thomas admitted. "He's much happier now, but what does the future hold? His spirituality is amazing. Over the last few weeks he has read the Bible through and retains almost all of it. How should his powers be used? Many people were helped by him, but he had to live a carnival life. Always on stage like some kind of sideshow attraction."

"I think it's best if he stays out of the limelight until the time is right," Pratt advised. "God has gifted him in a unique way. Remember that Jesus waited thirty years before he started his ministry. We have no record of his life from the age of twelve until he was an adult. Toby's time will come."

Thomas sighed. "I know. Just keeping the media away is a full-time job."

"No time for school?"

"I'll be back next quarter, if that grant is still available."

"It is," Pratt assured him. "And no one deserves it more than you."

"I'll be there."

"Good. And bring Toby from time to time. I think he'll enjoy it."

"I know he will."

"Hey, Thomas," Toby called across the yard. "Mom needs your help. She can't get any altitude."

"I don't want more altitude," Mary retorted.

Pratt saw a glint in Thomas's eyes and watched as his student rose from the table, walked to the swing set, put his hands on Mary's waist, and gave a gentle shove.

"Higher," Toby shouted. "Like me."

Thomas gave another shove, and Mary kicked her feet. Her laugher sweetened the air.

Pratt looked into the azure sky. "You are amazing," he said to heaven.

J.D. STANTON MYSTERIES

A SHIP POSSESSED

Alton Gansky

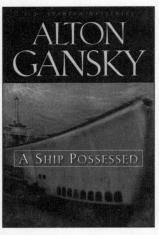

It arrived fifty years late and without its crew—but it didn't arrive alone.

The USS *Triggerfish*—an American World War II submarine—has come home over fifty years after she was presumed lost in the Atlantic. Now her dark gray hulk lies embedded in the sand of a San Diego beach. The submarine is in the wrong ocean, her crew is missing . . . and her half-century absence is a mystery that's about to deepen.

To J. D. Stanton, retired Navy captain and historian, falls the task of solving the mystery surrounding a ship possessed. What he is about to encounter will challenge his training, his wits, and his faith.

Softcover 0-310-21944-2

Pick up a copy today at your favorite bookstore!

ZondervanPublishingHouse
Grand Rapids, Michigan 49530
http://www.zondervan.com
A Division of HarperCollinsPublishers